SANDRA CISNEROS

BESTSELLING AUTHOR OF THE HOUSE ON MANGO STREET

CARAMELO

A NOVEL

Tria Hufnagel
303-838-4878

SANDRA CISNEROS

Caramelo

Sandra Cisneros was born in Chicago in 1954. Internationally acclaimed for her poetry and fiction, she has been the recipient of numerous awards, including the Lannan Literary Award and the American Book Award, and of fellowships from the National Endowment for the Arts and the MacArthur Foundation. Cisneros is the author of numerous books, including a children's book, *Hairs/Pelitos*. She lives in the Southwest.

Caramelo

or

Puro Cuento

A NOVEL

SANDRA CISNEROS

VINTAGE CONTEMPORARIES
VINTAGE BOOKS
A DIVISION OF RANDOM HOUSE, INC.
NEW YORK

FIRST VINTAGE CONTEMPORARIES EDITION, SEPTEMBER 2003

Some of the chapters have been previously published in the following: "The Detour That Turns Out to Be One's Destiny" in *El Andar*. "Dirt" in *Grand Street*. "Esa Tal Por Cual" in *Poet's & Writers*. "A Man, Ugly, Strong & Proper" in *Bomb*. "Mexico Next Right" in *Conjunctions*. "Que Elegante" in *Latina*. "Spic Spanish" in *Si Magazine*. Excerpts from the chapters "When an Elephant Sits on Your Roof," "A Godless Woman, My Mother," and "Everything a Niña Could Want" in *San Antonio Express News*.

Permissions acknowledgments can be found at the end of the book.

The Library of Congress has cataloged the Knopf edition as follows:
Cisneros, Sandra.
Caramelo / Sandra Cisneros.—1ˢᵗ ed.
p. cm.
ISBN 0-679-43554-9
1. Mexican American families—Fiction. 2. Grandparent and child—Fiction. 3. Women—Mexico—Fiction. 4. Chicago (Ill.)—Fiction. 5. Grandmothers—Fiction. 6. Mexico—Fiction. 7. Girls—Fiction.
I. Title
PS3553.I78 C37 2002
813'.54—dc21   2002025488

Vintage ISBN: 0-679-74258-1

Book design by Iris Weinstein

www.vintagebooks.com

Printed in the United States of America
10 9 8 7 6 5 4 3

Para ti, Papá

Contents

PART 1

Recuerdo de Acapulco

1   Verde, Blanco, y Colorado   5
2   Chillante   6
3   Qué Elegante   10
4   Mexico Next Right   16
5   Mexico, Our Nearest Neighbor to the South   19
6   Querétaro   22
7   La Capirucha   25
8   Tarzan   27
9   Aunty Light-Skin   31
10 The Girl Candelaria   34
11 A Silk Shawl, a Key, a Spiraling Coin   38
12 The Little Mornings   46
13 Niños y Borrachos   50
14 Fotonovelas   63
15 Cinderella   64
16 El Destino Es el Destino   67
17 Green Rice   71
18 La Casita de Catita   73
19 Un Recuerdo   76
20 Echando Palabras   79

PART 2

When I Was Dirt

21 So Here My History Begins for Your Good Understanding
    and My Poor Telling   91
22 Sin Madre, Sin Padre, Sin Perro Que Me Ladre   97
23 A Man Ugly, Strong, and Proper *or* Narciso Reyes,
    You Are My Destiny   103
24 Leandro Valle Street, Corner of Misericordia,
    Over by Santo Domingo   111
25 God Squeezes   118
26 Some Order, Some Progress, But Not Enough of Either   124
27 How Narciso Loses Three of His Ribs
    During the Ten Tragic Days   127
28 Nothing But Story   133
29 Trochemoche   137
30 A Poco—You're Kidding   143
31 The Feet of Narciso Reyes   145
32 The World Does Not Understand Eleuterio Reyes   148
33 Cuídate   153
34 How Narciso Falls into Disrepute Due to Sins of the Dangler   155
35 The Detour That Turns Out to Be One's Destiny   160
36 We Are Not Dogs   164
37 Esa Tal por Cual   168
38 ¡Pobre de Mí!   174
39 Tanta Miseria   182
40 I Ask la Virgen to Guide Me Because
    I Don't Know What to Do   188
41 The Shameless Shamaness, the Wise Witch Woman
    María Sabina   192
42 Born Under a Star   196
43 El Sufrido   198
44 Chuchuluco de Mis Amores   201
45 'Orita Vuelvo   205
46 Spic Spanish?   208
47 He Who is Destined to Be a Tamale   210

48 Cada Quien en Su Oficio Es Rey   212
49 Piensa en Mí   214
50 Neither with You Nor Without You   222
51 All Parts from Mexico, Assembled in the U.S.A. *or* I Am Born   231

PART 3

The Eagle and the Serpent, or My Mother and My Father

52 Cielito Lindo   237
53 El Otro Lado   249
54 Exquisite Tamales   255
55 The Man Whose Name No One Is Allowed to Mention   264
56 The Man from Mars   276
57 Birds Without a Nest   282
58 My Kind of Town   286
59 Dirt   294
60 When an Elephant Sits on Your Roof   299
61 Very Nice and Kind, Just Like You   308
62 A Godless Woman, My Mother   311
63 God Gives Almonds   318
64 Sister Oh   324
65 Body Like a Raisinette   326
66 Nobody but Us Chickens   331
67 The Vogue   336
68 My Cross   341
69 Zorro Strikes Again   344
70 Becoming Invisible   347
71 The Great Divide *or* This Side and That   349
72 Mexican on Both Sides *or* Metiche, Mirona, Mitotera, Hocicona—en Otras Palabras, Cuentista—Busybody, Ogler, Liar/Gossip/Troublemaker, Big-Mouth—in Other Words, Storyteller   351
73 Saint Anthony   358
74 Everything a Niña Could Want   359
75 The Rapture   361
76 Parece Mentira   365

77 On the Verge of Laughable   368
78 Someday My Prince Popocatépetl Will Come   372
79 Halfway Between Here and There,
        in the Middle of Nowhere   379
80 Zócalo   381
81 My Disgrace   391
82 The King of Plastic Covers   396
83 A Scene in a Hospital That Resembles a Telenovela
        When in Actuality It's the Telenovelas That Resemble
        This Scene   402
84 No Worth the Money, but They Help a Lot   410
85 Mi Aniversario   413
86 The Children and Grandchildren of Zoila and Inocencio Reyes
        Cordially Invite You to Celebrate
        Thirty Years of Marriage   417

    Pilón   433

    Chronology   435

    Acknowledgments   443

Cuéntame algo, aunque sea una mentira.

Tell me a story, even if it's a lie.

DISCLAIMER, OR I DON'T WANT HER, YOU CAN HAVE HER, SHE'S TOO *HOCICONA* FOR ME

The truth, these stories are nothing but story, bits of string, odds and ends found here and there, embroidered together to make something new. I have invented what I do not know and exaggerated what I do to continue the family tradition of telling healthy lies. If, in the course of my inventing, I have inadvertently stumbled on the truth, *perdónenme*.

To write is to ask questions. It doesn't matter if the answers are true or *puro cuento*. After all and everything only the story is remembered, and the truth fades away like the pale blue ink on a cheap embroidery pattern: *Eres Mi Vida, Sueño Contigo Mi Amor, Suspiro Por Ti, Sólo Tú.*

PART ONE

Recuerdo de Acapulco

•

We're all little in the photograph above Father's bed. We were little in Acapulco. We will always be little. For him we are just as we were then.

Here are the Acapulco waters lapping just behind us, and here we are sitting on the lip of land and water. The little kids, Lolo and Memo, making devil horns behind each other's heads; the Awful Grandmother holding them even though she never held them in real life. Mother seated as far from her as politely possible; Toto slouched beside her. The big boys, Rafa, Ito, and Tikis, stand under the roof of Father's skinny arms. Aunty Light-Skin hugging Antonieta Araceli to her belly. Aunty shutting her eyes when the shutter clicks, as if she chooses not to remember the future, the house on Destiny Street sold, the move north to Monterrey.

Here is Father squinting that same squint I always make when I'm photographed. He isn't *acabado* yet. He isn't *finished*, worn from working, from worrying, from smoking too many packs of cigarettes. There isn't anything on his face but his face, and a tidy, thin mustache, like Pedro Infante, like Clark Gable. Father's skin pulpy and soft, pale as the belly side of a shark.

The Awful Grandmother has the same light skin as Father, but in ele-

3

phant folds, stuffed into a bathing suit the color of an old umbrella with an amber handle.

I'm not here. They've forgotten about me when the photographer walking along the beach proposes a portrait, *un recuerdo,* a remembrance literally. No one notices I'm off by myself building sand houses. They won't realize I'm missing until the photographer delivers the portrait to Catita's house, and I look at it for the first time and ask, —When was this taken? Where?

Then everyone realizes the portrait is incomplete. It's as if I didn't exist. It's as if I'm the photographer walking along the beach with the tripod camera on my shoulder asking, —¿*Un recuerdo?* A souvenir? A memory?

Verde, Blanco, y Colorado

Uncle Fat-Face's brand-new used white Cadillac, Uncle Baby's green Impala, Father's red Chevrolet station wagon bought that summer on credit are racing to the Little Grandfather's and Awful Grandmother's house in Mexico City. Chicago, Route 66—Ogden Avenue past the giant Turtle Wax turtle—all the way to Saint Louis, Missouri, which Father calls by its Spanish name, San Luis. San Luis to Tulsa, Oklahoma. Tulsa, Oklahoma, to Dallas. Dallas to San Antonio to Laredo on 81 till we are on the other side. Monterrey. Saltillo. Matehuala. San Luis Potosí. Querétaro. Mexico City.

Every time Uncle Fat-Face's white Cadillac passes our red station wagon, the cousins—Elvis, Aristotle, and Byron—stick their tongues out at us and wave.

—Hurry, we tell Father. —Go faster!

When we pass the green Impala, Amor and Paz tug Uncle Baby's shoulder. —Daddy, please!

My brothers and I send them raspberries, we wag our tongues and make faces, we spit and point and laugh. The three cars—green Impala, white Cadillac, red station wagon—racing, passing each other sometimes on the shoulder of the road. Wives yelling, —Slower! Children yelling, —Faster!

What a disgrace when one of us gets carsick and we have to stop the car. The green Impala, the white Caddy whooshing past noisy and happy as a thousand flags. Uncle Fat-Face *toot-tooting* that horn like crazy.

Chillante

— If we make it to Toluca, I'm walking to church on my knees.

Aunty Licha, Elvis, Aristotle, and Byron are hauling things out to the curb. Blenders. Transistor radios. Barbie dolls. Swiss Army Knives. Plastic crystal chandeliers. Model airplanes. Men's button-down dress shirts. Lace push-up bras. Socks. Cut-glass necklaces with matching earrings. Hair clippers. Mirror sunglasses. Panty girdles. Ballpoint pens. Eye shadow kits. Scissors. Toasters. Acrylic pullovers. Satin quilted bedspreads. Towel sets. All this besides the boxes of used clothing.

Outside, roaring like the ocean, Chicago traffic from the Northwest and Congress Expressways. Inside, another roar; in Spanish from the kitchen radio, in English from TV cartoons, and in a mix of the two from her boys begging for, —*Un nikle* for Italian lemonade. But Aunty Licha doesn't hear anything. Under her breath Aunty is bargaining, —*Virgen Purísima*, if we even make it to Laredo, even that, I'll say three rosaries . . .

—*Cállate, vieja*, you make me nervous. Uncle Fat-Face is fiddling with the luggage rack on top of the roof. It has taken him two days to get everything to fit inside the car. The white Cadillac's trunk is filled to capacity. The tires sag. The back half of the car dips down low. There isn't room for anything else except the passengers, and even so, the cousins have to sit on top of suitcases.

—Daddy, my legs hurt already.

—You. Shut your snout or you ride in the trunk.

—But there isn't any room in the trunk.

—I said shut your snout!

To pay for the vacation, Uncle Fat-Face and Aunty Licha always bring along items to sell. After visiting the Little Grandfather and Awful Grandmother in the city, they take a side trip to Aunty Licha's hometown of Toluca. All year their apartment looks like a store. A year's worth of weekends spent at Maxwell Street flea market* collecting merchandise for the trip south. Uncle says what sells is *lo chillante*, literally the screaming. —The gaudier the better, says the Awful Grandmother. —No use taking anything of value to that town of Indians.

Each summer it's something unbelievable that sells like *hot queques*. Topo Gigio key rings. Eyelash curlers. Wind Song perfume sets. Plastic rain bonnets. This year Uncle is betting on glow-in-the-dark yo-yos.

Boxes. On top of the kitchen cabinets and the refrigerator, along the hallway walls, behind the three-piece sectional couch, from floor to ceiling, on top or under things. Even the bathroom has a special storage shelf high above so no one can touch.

In the boys' room, floating near the ceiling just out of reach, toys nailed to the walls with upholstery tacks. Tonka trucks, model airplanes, Erector sets still in their original cardboard boxes with the cellophane window. They're not to play with, they're to look at. —This one I got last Christmas, and that one was a present for my seventh birthday . . . Like displays at a museum.

We've been waiting all morning for Uncle Fat-Face to telephone and say, —*Quihubo*, brother, *vámonos*, so that Father can call Uncle Baby and say the same thing. Every year the three Reyes sons and their families drive south to the Awful Grandmother's house on Destiny Street, Mexico City, one family at the beginning of the summer, one in the middle, and one at the summer's end.

—But what if something happens? the Awful Grandmother asks her husband.

—Why ask me, I'm already dead, the Little Grandfather says, retreating to his bedroom with his newspaper and his cigar. —You'll do what you want to do, same as always.

—What if someone falls asleep at the wheel like the time Concha Chacón became a widow and lost half her family near Dallas. What a barbarity! And did you hear that sad story about Blanca's cousins, eight people killed just as they were returning from Michoacán, right outside the Chicago city limits, a patch of ice and a light pole in some place called Aurora, *pobrecitos*. Or what about that station wagon full of gringa nuns that fell off the mountainside near Saltillo. But that was the old highway through the Sierra Madre before they built the new interstate.

All the same, we are too familiar with the roadside crosses and the stories they stand for. The Awful Grandmother complains so much, her sons finally give in. That's why this year Uncle Fat-Face, Uncle Baby, and Father—el Tarzán—finally agree to drive down together, although they never agree on anything.

—If you ask me, the whole idea stinks, Mother says, mopping the kitchen linoleum. She shouts from the kitchen to the bathroom, where Father is trimming his mustache over the sink.

—Zoila, why do you insist on being so stubborn? Father shouts into the mirror clouding the glass. —*Ya verás*. You'll see, *vieja*, it'll be fun.

—And stop calling me *vieja*, Mother shouts back. —I hate that word! I'm not old, your mother's old.

We're going to spend the entire summer in Mexico. We won't leave until school ends, and we won't come back until after it's started. Father, Uncle Fat-Face, and Uncle Baby don't have to report to the L. L. Fish Furniture Company on South Ashland until September.

—Because we're such good workers our boss gave us the whole summer off, imagine that.

But that's nothing but story. The three Reyes brothers have quit their jobs. When they don't like a job, they quit. They pick up their hammers and say, —Hell you . . . Get outta . . . Full of *sheet*. They are craftsmen. They don't use a staple gun and cardboard like the upholsterers in the U.S. They make sofas and chairs *by hand*. Quality work. And when they don't like their boss, they pick up their hammers and their time cards and walk out cursing in two languages, with tacks in the soles of their shoes and lint in their beard stubble and hair, and bits of string dangling from the hem of their sweaters.

But they didn't quit this time, did they? No, no. The real story is this. The bosses at the L. L. Fish Furniture Company on South Ashland have begun to dock the three because they arrive sixteen minutes after the hour, forty-three minutes, fifty-two, instead of on time. According to Uncle Fat-Face, —We *are* on time. It depends on which time you are on, Western time or the calendar of the sun. The L. L. Fish Furniture Company on South Ashland Avenue has decided they don't have time for the brothers Reyes anymore. —Go hell . . . What's a matter . . . Same to you mother!

It's the Awful Grandmother's idea that her *mijos* drive down to Mexico together. But years afterward everyone will forget and blame each other.

The original Maxwell Street, a Chicago flea market for more than 120 years, spread itself around the intersections of Maxwell and Halsted Streets. It was a filthy, pungent, wonderful place filled with astonishing people, good music, and goods from don't-ask-where. Devoured by the growth of the University of Illinois, it was relocated, though the new Maxwell Street market is no longer on Maxwell Street and exists as a shadow of its former grime and glory. Only Jim's Original Hot Dogs, founded in 1939, stands where it always has, a memorial to Maxwell Street's funky past.[†]

[†]*Alas! While busy writing this book, Jim's Original Hot Dogs was gobbled up by the University of Illinois and Mayor Daley's gentrification; tidy parks and tidy houses for the very very wealthy, while the poor, as always, get swept under the rug, out of sight and out of mind.*

3.

Qué Elegante

Pouring out from the windows, "Por un amor" from the hi-fi, the version by
Lola Beltrán, that queen of Mexican country, with tears in the throat and
a group of mariachis *cooing, —But don't cry, Lolita, and Lola replying,*
—I'm not crying, it's just . . . that I remember.

A wooden house that looks like an elephant sat on the roof. An apartment so close to the ground people knock on the window instead of the door. Just off Taylor Street. Not far from Saint Francis church of the Mexicans. A stone's throw from Maxwell Street flea market. The old Italian section of Chicago in the shadow of the downtown Loop. This is where Uncle Fat-Face, Aunty Licha, Elvis, Aristotle, and Byron live, on a block where everyone knows Uncle Fat-Face by his Italian nickname, Rico, instead of Fat-Face or Federico, even though *"rico"* means "rich" in Spanish, and Uncle is always complaining he is *pobre, pobre.* —It is no disgrace to be poor, Uncle says, citing the Mexican saying, —but it's very inconvenient.

—What have I got to show for my life? Uncle thinks. —Beautiful women I've had. Lots. And beautiful cars.

Every year Uncle trades his old Cadillac for a brand-new used one. On the 16th of September, Uncle waits until the tail of the Mexican parade. When the last float is rolling toward the Loop, Uncle tags along in his big Caddy, thrilled to be driving down State Street, the top rolled down, the kids sitting in the back dressed in *charro* suits and waving.

And as for beautiful women, Aunty Licha must be afraid he is thinking of trading her, too, and sending her back to Mexico, even though she is as beautiful as a Mexican Elizabeth Taylor. Aunty is jealous of every woman, old or young, who comes near Uncle Fat-Face, though Uncle is almost bald and as small and brown as a peanut. Mother says, —If a woman's crazy jealous like Licha you can bet it's because someone's giving her reason to be, know what I mean? It's that she's from over there, Mother continues, meaning from the Mexican side, and not this side. —Mexican women are just like the Mexican songs, *locas* for love.

Once Aunty almost tried to kill herself because of Uncle Fat-Face. —My own husband! What a barbarity! A prostitute's disease from my own husband. Imagine! *Ay*, get him out of here! I don't ever want to see you again. *¡Lárgate!* You disgust me, *me das asco*, you *cochino*! You're not fit to be the father of my children. I'm going to kill myself! Kill myself!!! Which sounds much more dramatic in Spanish. —*¡Me mato! ¡¡¡Me maaaaaaaatoooooo!!!* The big kitchen knife, the one Aunty dips in a glass of water to cut the boys' birthday cakes, pointed toward her own sad heart.

Too terrible to watch. Elvis, Aristotle, and Byron had to run for the neighbors, but by the time the neighbors arrived it was too late. Uncle Fat-Face sobbing, collapsed in a heap on the floor like a broken lawn chair, Aunty Licha cradling him like the Virgin Mary cradling Jesus after he was brought down from the cross, hugging that hiccuping head to her chest, murmuring in his ear over and over, —*Ya, ya. Ya pasó.* It's all over. There, there, there.

When Aunty's not angry she calls Uncle *payaso*, clown. —Don't be a *payaso*, she scolds gently, laughing at Uncle's silly stories, combing the few strands of hair left on his head with her fingers. But this only encourages Uncle to be even more of a *payaso*.

—So I said to the boss, I quit. This job is like *el calzón de una puta*. A prostitute's underwear. You heard me! All day long it's nothing but up and down, up and down, up and down . . .

CARAMELO

—Don't tell stories like that in front of the children, Aunty scolds, though she says this while she is laughing, dabbing her Cleopatra eyes with the tip of a twisted paper napkin.

But it's our Uncle Baby and Aunty Ninfa who live like movie stars. Their apartment smells of cigarettes and air-conditioning; ours of fried tortillas. For a long time I think of air-conditioning and cigarettes as the smell of elegance. From her hi-fi Aunty's favorite records are playing: "Exodus," "Never on Sunday," Andy Williams singing "Moon River." Everything smells like cigarettes in Aunty's house, curtains, rugs, furniture, the poodle with the pink-painted toenails, her teased beehive, even her kids. Except for the girls' bedroom with the princess beds, which smells like pee because Amor and Paz still wet the bed.

—Shut up, stupid.

—I'm telling. Ma, Amor told me "shut up, stupid."

—Jesus! Will you girls shut up and let me hear my music or do I have to make you shut up!

Though their apartment itself is little, the furniture is big. Iron kitchen chairs with high backs like thrones. Bedroom sets that poke out beyond the door frames and keep the doors from shutting completely. A thick wedge of clothes on hangers behind every door. It's hard to walk. Whenever someone wants to pass, someone else has to sit down; when someone wants to open a door, someone else has to stand up. In the kitchen a life-size portrait of an Italian street beggar bending over to take a drink from a fountain. —We bought it because she looks just like our little Paz. Wall-to-wall shag carpeting covered with plastic floor runners and area rugs. A marble coffee table like a coffin lid. Speckled Venetian blown-glass knickknacks—a rooster, a tropical fish, a swan. Onyx ashtrays. My favorite is a gold swag lamp of the Three Graces laced with strings of real water like a fountain. Even our Carmen Miranda lamp with the night-light, maraca hiss, and rotating stand can't compete.

In our own flat, things of beauty are not forever. The little birds perched around the birdbath candy dish fly away and disappear. The porcelain twin boxer puppies attached by a gold chain to the mama boxer somehow escape and can't be found. The Japanese geishas in the shadow box are missing their paper parasols even though the shadow box is high and hard to reach. Who knows where they've gone? Once the marble coffee table at Uncle Baby and Aunty Ninfa's was ours, till too many of us cracked our heads on it. That's how it is with beauty.

It's because Aunty Ninfa is from Italy, that's why she's used to fancy things. Uncle Baby met her in a Laundromat on Taylor Street and fell in love with her voice, sexy and sad as a trombone in a smoky cafe.

—My family didn't want me to marry Baby because he ain't Italian, but I married him anyways . . . maybe because they said don't.

Is she ever homesick for Italy?

—I don't know, honey, I've never been there.

Everything in Aunty's home is white or gold and looks like a wedding cake, like Marie Antoinette. A couch with lots of buttons. Brocade bucket chairs that swivel with tufted backs and fringed bottoms. Footstools shaped like cupcakes. Uncle Baby made them. He made the plastic covers, too. And the draperies and quilted cornices are Uncle Baby's work. Above the dining room table, a porcelain chandelier with porcelain roses and porcelain vines brought back one summer from Guadalajara. Their dining room table isn't Formica, but a thick sheet of glass held in an iron frame with curly white iron rosettes climbing up the legs and chairs. Every room has several ashtrays, even the kitchen and the bathroom—a pair of white women's hands cupped palms up; a crystal basket; a naughty lady lying on her back, her legs up in the air swaying back and forth, a fan in her hand fluttering. There are huge mirrors in lumpy gold frames. There are lamps with giant silk shades, still wrapped in cellophane, shaped like a lady's corset. The living room carpet a champagne color covered with plastic floor runners. Mirrors, and glass, and figurines. Things that are a lot of work to keep clean.

That's why you have to make sure you wear your good socks when you visit. And have washed your feet. Because you must take your shoes off and leave them in the hall. Everyone walks about in their socks, except the yellow poodle with the rusty eyes.

Aunty Ninfa's apartment is so clean we don't like to visit. —Don't touch anything. Watch you don't run, you might break something. Be careful not to touch the mirrors when you switch on the bathroom light. Honey, that chair's not to sit on. Never sit on Aunty's bed, sweetie, or it might bring on one of her asthma attacks. Put all the throw pillows back exactly like you found them when you leave, okay? Baby, would you like some candy? —No, thank you, while at home we would've sat there eating and eating, even picking up the crumbs.

Our own home is made up of furniture on loan, mismatched Duncan Phyfes and Queen Annes, Victorian horsehair settees, leather wing chairs with shoulders like Al Capone. Anything left over, abandoned, or sitting in storage at the shop winds up at our house until reupholstered and reclaimed. Could Father's customers ever imagine us sitting on their fancy furniture while drinking strawberry Nestlé's Quik and watching the Three Stooges? Once Father found a real pearl in the folds of one of these couches, a silver-blue pearl that he had made into a tie pin because the color matched his favorite suit. We wedge our hands into the cracks between the cushions searching for buried treasure better than Father's blue pearl, but only come up with a leather button, two pennies and a Canadian dime, a handful of dog hair, the yellow moon of a fingernail.

Sometimes if we're lucky, a customer will forget a piece of furniture, and then we get to keep it, which is how we got the orange Naugahyde La-Z-Boy, Father's favorite and my bed at nighttime. Once it belonged to a dentist, but he never came back for it. Would he pull someone's tooth and suddenly remember? Too terrible to think about. Father loves his La-Z-Boy. Whenever he suffers one of his famous migraines, he asks for one of Mother's nylon stockings and ties it around his forehead Apache style. Mother serves him his dinner in the living room on a metal TV tray while he sits on his La-Z-Boy watching the Mexican *telenovelas.* —*¿Qué intentas ocultar, Juan Sebastián? ¿Qué intentas ocultar?** We pull up the footrest, and Father falls asleep like a W for a while, his mouth open, before rolling to his side and curling into a question mark and calling out, —*Tápame.* We bring a blanket and cover him, even his head because that's the way he likes to sleep.

All the rooms in our house fill up with too many things. Things Father buys at Maxwell Street, things Mother buys at the secondhand stores when Father isn't looking, things bought here to take to the other side and things bought on the other side to bring here, so that it always feels as if our house is a storage room. Gold cherub lamps with teardrop crystals, fine antiques and Aunt Jemima dolls on top of a stack of photo albums, souvenir Mexican dolls, an oversized table lamp bought when a hotel went bankrupt and liquidated all its furnishings, a pink plastic tree in a plastic pot, a beautiful down-filled chaise lounge covered with a Mexican *poncho,* a tiger-skin love seat covered in a floral sheet, Bugs Bunny, five mismatched dining room chairs, a huge 50's stereo, a broken drapery rod, and everywhere, halls, walls, sheets, chairs—florals, florals, florals at war with each other.

---

*—¿Qué intentas ocultar?
—¿Por qué eres tan cruel conmigo?
—Te encanta hacerme sufrir.
—¿Por qué me mortificas?
    Say any of the above, or say anything twice, slower and more dramatic the second time 'round, and it will sound like the dialogue of any telenovela.

Mexico Next Right

Not like on the Triple A atlas from orange to pink, but at a stoplight in a rippled heat and a dizzy gasoline stink, the United States ends all at once, a tangled shove of red lights from cars and trucks waiting their turn to get past the bridge. Miles and miles.

—Oh, my Got, Father says in his gothic English. —Holy cripes! says Mother, fanning herself with a Texaco road map.

I forgot the light, white and stinging like an onion. I remembered the bugs, a windshield spotted with yellow. I remembered the heat, a sun that melts into the bones like Bengay. I remembered how big Texas is. —Are we in Mexico yet? —No, not yet. [Sleep, wake up.] —Are we in Mexico yet? —Still Texas. [Sleep, wake up.] —Are we . . . —Christ Almighty!!!

But the light. That I don't remember forgetting until I remember it.

We've crossed Illinois, Missouri, Oklahoma, and Texas singing all the songs we know. "The Moon Men Mambo" from our favorite Rocky and Bullwinkle album. *Ah, ah, aaaah! Scrooch, doobie-doobie, doobie-do. Swing your partner from planet to planet when you dooooo the moon man mamboooo!* The *Yogi Bear* song. *He will sleep till noon, but before it's dark he'll have ev'ry picnic basket that's in Jellystone Park . . .* We sing TV commercials. *Get the blanket with the A, you can trust the big red A. Get the blanket made with ACRYLAN today . . . Knock on any Norge, knock on any Norge, hear the secret sound of quality, knock on any Norge! Years from now you'll be glad you chose Norge. CoCo Wheats, CoCo Wheats can't be beat. It's the creamy hot cereal with the cocoa treat . . .* Until Mother yells, —Will you shut your *hocicos* or do I have to shut them for you?!!!

But crossing the border, nobody feels like singing. Everyone hot and sticky and in a bad mood, hair stiff from riding with the windows open, the backs of the knees sweaty, a little circle of spit next to where my head fell asleep; "good lucky" Father thought to sew beach towel slipcovers for our new car.

No more billboards announcing the next Stuckey's candy store, no more truck-stop donuts or roadside picnics with bologna-and-cheese sandwiches and cold bottles of 7-Up. Now we'll drink fruit-flavored sodas, tamarind, apple, pineapple; Pato Pascual with Donald Duck on the bottle, or Lulú, Betty Boop soda, or the one we hear on the radio, the happy song for Jarritos soda.

As soon as we cross the bridge everything switches to another language. *Toc*, says the light switch in this country, at home it says *click*. *Honk*, say the cars at home, here they say *tán-tán-tán*. The *scrip-scrape-scrip* of high heels across *saltillo* floor tiles. The angry lion growl of the corrugated curtains when the shopkeepers roll them open each morning and the lazy lion roar at night when they pull them shut. The *pic, pic, pic* of somebody's faraway hammer. Church bells over and over, all day, even when it's not o'clock. Roosters. The hollow echo of a dog barking. Bells from skinny horses pulling tourists in a carriage, *clip-clop* on cobblestones and big chunks of horse *caquita* tumbling out of them like shredded wheat.

Sweets sweeter, colors brighter, the bitter more bitter. A cage of parrots all the rainbow colors of Lulú sodas. Pushing a window out to open it instead of pulling it up. A cold slash of door latch in your hand instead of the dull round doorknob. Tin sugar spoon and how surprised the hand feels because it's so light. Children walking to school in the morning with their hair still wet from the morning bath.

Mopping with a stick and a purple rag called *la jerga* instead of a mop. The fat lip of a soda pop bottle when you tilt your head back and drink. Birthday cakes walking out of a bakery without a box, just like that, on a wooden plate. And the metal tongs and tray when you buy Mexican sweet bread, help yourself. Cornflakes served with *hot* milk! A balloon painted with wavy pink stripes wearing a paper hat. A milk gelatin with a fly like a little black raisin rubbing its hands. Light and heavy, loud and soft, *thud* and *ting* and *ping*.

Churches the color of *flan*. Vendors selling slices of *jícama* with *chile*, lime juice, and salt. Balloon vendors. The vendor of flags. The corn-on-the-cob vendor. The pork rind vendor. The fried-banana vendor. The pancake vendor. The vendor of strawberries in cream. The vendor of rainbow *pirulís*, of apple bars, of *tejocotes* bathed in caramel. The meringue man. The ice cream vendor, —A very good ice cream at two *pesos*. The coffee man with the coffeemaker on his back and a paper cup dispenser, the cream-and-sugar boy scuttling alongside him.

Little girls in Sunday dresses like lace bells, like umbrellas, like parachutes, the more lace and froufrou the better. Houses painted purple, electric blue, tiger orange, aquamarine, a yellow like a taxicab, hibiscus red with a yellow-and-green fence. Above doorways, faded wreaths from an anniversary or a death till the wind and rain erase them. A woman in an apron scrubbing the sidewalk in front of her house with a pink plastic broom and a bright green bucket filled with suds. A workman carrying a long metal pipe on his shoulder, whistling *ffffttt-ffffttt* to warn people— Watch out!—the pipe longer than he is tall, almost putting out someone's eye, *ya mero*—but he doesn't, does he? *Ya mero, pero no.* Almost, but not quite. *Sí, pero no.* Yes, but no.

Fireworks displays, *piñata* makers, palm weavers. Pens, —Five different styles, they cost us a lot! A restaurant called —His Majesty, the Taco. The napkins, little triangles of hard paper with the name printed on one side. Breakfast: a basket of *pan dulce,* Mexican sweet bread; hotcakes with honey; or steak; *frijoles* with fresh *cilantro; molletes;* or scrambled eggs with *chorizo;* eggs *a la mexicana* with tomato, onion, and *chile;* or *huevos rancheros.* Lunch: lentil soup; fresh-baked crusty *bolillos;* carrots with lime juice; *carne asada;* abalone; *tortillas.* Because we are sitting outdoors, Mexican dogs under the Mexican tables. —I can't stand dogs under the table when I'm eating, Mother complains, but as soon as we shoo two away, four others trot over.

The smell of diesel exhaust, the smell of somebody roasting coffee, the smell of hot corn *tortillas* along with the *pat-pat* of the women's hands making them, the sting of roasting *chiles* in your throat and in your eyes. Sometimes a smell in the morning, very cool and clean that makes you sad. And a night smell when the stars open white and soft like fresh *bolillo* bread.

Every year I cross the border, it's the same—my mind forgets. But my body always remembers.

Mexico, Our Nearest Neighbor to the South

*B*lacktop. If you stare at the center stripe ahead, a patch of water rises and disappears before you catch up to it, like a ghost going to heaven. The car swallowing the road, and the white stripes coming and coming, quickly quickly quickly, like the stitches on Father's sewing machine, and the road making you sleepy.

It's Memo's turn to sit up front, between Mother and Father. Every once in a while Memo leans over and Father lets him help with the steering wheel, and every once in a while, just for a few seconds, Father lets go of the wheel and Memo's driving! Until Mother yells, —Inocencio!

—Just playing, Father says, chuckling, his hands on the wheel again. —Excellent road, he says, trying to change the subject. —Look how pretty this road is, Zoila. Almost as good as the ones in Texas, right?

—A hell of a lot better than the old Pan American Highway, Mother adds. —Remember when we had to drive through the Sierra Madre? What a headache!

—I remember, I say.

—How could you remember? You weren't even born yet! Rafa says.

—Yeah, Lala, Tikis adds. —You were still dirt! Ha, ha!

—I do so remember. Honest!

—You mean you remember the stories somebody told you, says Mother.

One time on the old highway through the Sierra Madre, Rafa and Ito threw half the clothes from our suitcases out the window just to see them whoosh out of their hands. T-shirts flagged on the spikes of the *magueys,* socks tangled in the dusty scrub brush, underwear worn like party hats on the flowering *nopalitos,* all the while Mother and Father were looking straight ahead, worried about what was in front and not behind them.

Sometimes the mountain roads are so narrow the truck drivers have to open their doors to see how close they are to the edge. Once a truck fell off and rolled down the canyon in slow motion. Did I dream it or did someone tell me the story? I can't remember where the truth ends and the talk begins.

The towns with their central plazas, always with a bandstand and iron benches. The smell of the countryside like the top of your head on a sunny day. Houses now and then painted the colors of flowers, and now and then sprouting on the shoulder of the road, roadside crosses to mark where someone's ghost walked away from his body.

—Don't look, says Mother when we drive past, but that only makes us want to look even more.

In the middle of nowhere, we have to stop the car to let Lolo out to pee. Father lights a cigarette and checks the tires. We all tumble out to stretch our legs. There isn't anything in sight, only hills of cacti, *mesquite,* sage, that tree with white flowers like little hats. The heat rippling the blue-purple mountains in the distance.

When I turn around three barefoot kids are staring at us, a girl sucking the hem of her faded dress and two dusty boys.

Father talks to them while he checks the tires. —Is that your sister? Remember to take good care of her. Where do you all live? Where over there?

Talking and talking like this for what seems a long time.

Just as we are about to leave, Father takes my rubber doll from the car and says, —I'll buy you another one.

Before I can say anything, my baby is in the arms of that girl! How can I explain, this one is my Bobby doll, two fingers missing on his left hand because I chewed them off when I was teething. There isn't another Bobby doll like it in the world! But I can't say this fast enough when Father hands the girl my Bobby.

Lolo's and Memo's Christmas Tonka trucks disappear too.

The three kids clamber off into the hills of dust and loose gravel with our toys. We can't take our eyes off them, our mouths open wide, the backseat filled with our howls.

—You kids are too spoiled, Father scolds when we drive away.

Over the shoulder of the running girl do I imagine or do I really see the rubber arm of my Bobby doll, the one with three fingers, raised in the air waving good-bye?

Querétaro

ecause we're kids, things happen and someone forgets to tell us, or they tell us and we forget. I don't know which. When I hear the word "Querétaro," I start to shudder, hope everyone won't remember.

—Cut it.

—All of it? Father asks.

—All, the Grandmother says. —It will grow back thicker, you'll see.

Father nods and the beautician obeys. Father always does whatever the Grandmother orders, and in two surprised snips I am turned into a *pelona*.

Snip. Snip.

The twin braids I've had since as far back as I can remember, the ones so long I can sit on them, now lie like dead snakes on the floor. Father wraps them in his handkerchief and tucks them in his pocket.

Snip, snip, snip. The scissors whisper mean things in my ears.

In the mirror an ugly wolf-girl is howling.

All the kilometers to Mexico City.

Especially because the brothers laugh and point and call me a boy.

—Oh, brother! What a *chillona* you turned out to be. Now what? Mother asks.

—What could be worse than being a boy?

—Being a girl! Rafa shouts. And everyone in the car laughs even harder.

At least I'm not the oldest like Rafa, who one day doesn't come home with us on one of our trips from Mexico.

—We've forgotten Rafa, stop the car!

—It's okay, Father says. —Rafa is staying with your grandmother. You'll see him next year.

That's true. It is a year before we see him. And when he comes back to us in a clean white shirt and with hair shorter than we've ever remembered it, his Spanish is as curly and correct as Father's. They made him go to a military school just like the one the Little Grandfather had to go to when he was a boy. When Rafa comes back with a class photograph of himself in his military school uniform, when he comes back to us taller and quieter and strange, it's as if our other brother Rafa was kidnapped and this one sent back in exchange. He tries talking to us in Spanish, but we don't use that language with kids, we only use it with grown-ups. We ignore him and keep watching our television cartoons.

Later when he feels like it and can talk about it, he'll explain what it's like to be abandoned by your parents and left in a country where you don't have enough words to speak the things inside you.

—Why did you leave me?

—It was for your own good, so that you'd speak better Spanish. Your grandmother thought it for the best . . .

It was the Awful Grandmother's idea. *That* explains it.

The Awful Grandmother is like the witch in that story of Hansel and Gretel. She likes to eat boys and girls. She'll swallow us whole, if you let her. Father has let her swallow Rafa.

We'd been to Querétaro for the day. For lunch and walking around looking at old buildings and, at the very last minute, the Grandmother suggests she have her hair done, because it's cheaper in small towns than it is in the capital. A sign says so as we are walking off our lunch, and that's how it is that Father, the Grandmother, Mother, and me find ourselves in the beauty parlor, the boys bored and waiting outside in the *plaza*.

Because I don't understand, they cut my braids off before I can say anything. Or maybe they don't even ask me. Or maybe I'm daydreaming when they tell me. I only know when the braids let themselves go and fall on the tiles, it takes my breath away.

—As if they'd cut off your arms! the Grandmother scolds. —It's just hair. You should've seen the terrible things that happened to me as a girl, but did I cry? Not even if God commanded it.

—We'll have them woven into a hairpiece for when you grow up, Father says when we're in the car. —You'll like that, won't you, my queen? I'm going to throw a big party with everyone in gowns and tuxedos, and I'll buy a big, big cake, bigger than you are tall, and a band will play a waltz when I take you out to dance. Right, my heaven? Don't cry, my pretty girl. Please.

—Quit babying her, Mother says, annoyed. —She'll never grow up.

Querétaro 33 kilometers. As soon as the word is said, I hope everyone won't remember, but they never forget, my brothers.

—Querétaro. Hey, remember that time they cut off Lala's hair!

Then they're on me again with their laughter like sharp teeth.

Querétaro. A chill like scissors against the neck. Querétaro. Querétaro. The sound of scissors talking.

7.

La Capirucha

—We're almost there, he keeps saying. *Ya mero.* Almost. *Ya mero.*

—But I have to make *pipí*, Lolo says. —How much longer is almost?

—*Ya mero, ya mero.*

Even though we still have hours to go.

Father is already ignoring the rest of the scenery, watching the road side signs that tell us how many kilometers more. How many? How many? Imagining driving through the green iron gates of the house on Destiny Street, the hot supper and the bed. The sleep that will come when the road ends and his right leg stops throbbing.

Green Impala, white Caddy, red station wagon. We hobble forward, each car filthier than the next—inside and out—dust and dead bugs and vomit. The road crowded with buses and big trucks lit like Christmas trees as we get closer. No one even tries to pass each other. Kilometers, kilometers . . .

Then, all at once, after we've forgotten *ya mero* . . .

—¡*Ay, ay, ay, ay, ay!* There it is!

A silence in the car. A silence in the world. And then . . . The rising in the chest, in the heart, finally. The road suddenly dipping and surprising us as always. There it is!

Mexico City! *La capital. El* D.F. *La capirucha.* The center of the universe! The valley like a big bowl of hot beef soup before you taste it. And a laughter in your chest when the car descends.

A laughter like ticker tape. Like a parade. People in the streets shouting hurray. Or do I just imagine they are shouting hurray? Hurray when the giant Corona beer billboard appears with its silver spangles. Hurray when the highways turn into avenues and boulevards. Hurray when the Mexico City buses and taxis glide alongside us like dolphins. *Ya mero, ya mero*. The shops with open doorways brightly lit. Hurray the twilight sky filling with stars like twists of silver paper. Hurray the rooftop dogs that welcome us. Hurray the smell of supper frying in the streets. Hurray *la colonia* Industrial, hurray Tepeyac, hurray La Villa. Hurray when the green iron gates of the house on Destiny Street, number 12, open, abracadabra.

In the belly button of the house, the Awful Grandmother tossing her black *rebozo de bolita* crisscross across her breasts, like a *soldadera*'s bandoleers. The big black X at the map's end.

Tarzan

We come in all sizes, from little to big, like a xylophone. Rafa, Ito, Tikis, Toto, Lolo, Memo, and Lala. Rafael, Refugio, Gustavo, Alberto, Lorenzo, Guillermo, and Celaya. Rafa, Ito, Tikis, Toto, Lolo, Memo, *y* Lala. The younger ones couldn't say the older ones' names, and that's how Refugito became Ito, or Gustavito became Tikis, Alberto—Toto, Lorenzo—Lolo, Guillermo—Memo, and me, Celaya—Lala. Rafa, Ito, Tikis, Toto, Lolo, Memo, *y* Lala. When the Grandmother calls us she says, —*Tú*. Or sometimes, —*Oyes, tú*.

Elvis, Aristotle, and Byron are Uncle Fat-Face and Aunty Licha's. The Grandmother says to Uncle Fat-Face, —How backwards that Licha naming those poor babies after anyone she finds in her horoscopes. Thank God Shakespeare was stillborn. Can you imagine answering to "Shakespeare Reyes"? What a beating life would've given him. Too sad to think your father lost three of his ribs in the war so that his grandchild could be named Elvis . . . Don't pretend you don't know! . . . Elvis Presley is a national enemy . . . He is . . . Why would I make it up? When he was making that movie in Acapulco he said, "The last thing I want to do in my life is kiss a Mexican." That's what he said, I swear it. Kiss a Mexican. It was in all the papers. What was Licha thinking!

—But our Elvis was born seven years ago, Mother. How was Licha to know Elvis Presley would come to Mexico and say such things?

—Well, someone should've thought about the future, eh? And now look. The whole republic is boycotting that pig, and my grandchild is named Elvis! What a barbarity!

Amor and Paz are Uncle Baby and Aunty Ninfa's, named "Love" and "Peace" because, —We were happy God sent us such pretty little girls.

They're so evil they stick their tongues out at us while their father is saying this.

Like always, when we first arrive at the Grandparents' house, my brothers and I are shy and speak only to one another, in English, which is rude. But by the second day we upset our cousin Antonieta Araceli, who is not used to the company of kids. We break her old Cri-Crí* records. We lose the pieces to her Turista game. We use too much toilet paper, or at other times too little. We stick our dirty fingers in the bowl of beans soaking for the midday meal. We run up and down the stairs and across the courtyard chasing each other through the back apartments where the Grandparents, Aunty Light-Skin, and Antonieta Araceli live, and through the front apartments where we stay.

We like being seen on the roof, like house servants, without so much as thinking what passersby might mistake us for. We try sneaking into the Grandparents' bedroom when no one is looking, which the Awful Grandmother strictly forbids. All this we do and more. Antonieta Araceli faithfully reports as much to the Awful Grandmother, and the Awful Grandmother herself has seen how these children raised on the other side don't know enough to answer, —¿Mande usted? to their elders. —What? we say in the horrible language, which the Awful Grandmother hears as ¿Guat? —What? we repeat to each other and to her. The Awful Grandmother shakes her head and mutters, —My daughters-in-law have given birth to a generation of monkeys.

Mi gorda, my chubby, is what Aunty Light-Skin calls her daughter, Antonieta Araceli. It was her baby name and cute when she was little, but not cute now because Antonieta Araceli is as thin as a shadow. —¡Mi gorda!

—Mama, please! When are you going to stop calling me that in front of everybody?

She means in front of us. Antonieta Araceli has decided she's a grown-up this summer and spends all day in front of the mirror plucking her eyebrows and mustache, but she's no grown-up. She's only two months younger than Rafa—thirteen. When the adults aren't around we shout, —¡Mi gorda! ¡Mi gorda! until she throws something at us.

—How did you get named Antonieta Araceli, what a funny name?

—It's not a funny name. I was named after a Cuban dancer who dances in the movies wearing beautiful outfits. Didn't you ever hear of

María Antonieta Pons? She's famous and everything. Blond-blond-blond and white-white-white. Very pretty, not like you.

The Awful Grandmother calls Father *mijo. Mijo.* My son. —*Mijo, mijo.* She doesn't call Uncle Fat-Face or Uncle Baby *mijo,* even though they're her sons too. She calls them by their real names, —Federico. Or, —Armando—when she is angry, or their nicknames when she is not. —Fat-Face, Baby! —It's that when I was a baby I had a fat face, explains Uncle Fat-Face. —It's that I'm the youngest, says Uncle Baby. As if the Awful Grandmother doesn't notice Uncle Fat-Face isn't fat anymore and Uncle Baby isn't a baby. —It doesn't matter, says the Awful Grandmother. —All my sons are my sons. They're just as they were when they were little. I love them all the same, just enough but not too much. She uses the Spanish word *hijos,* which means sons and children all at once. —And your daughter? I ask. —What about her? The Awful Grandmother gives me that look, as if I'm a pebble in her shoe.

Aunty Light-Skin's real name is Norma, but who would think to call her that? She's always been known as la Güera even when she was a teeny tiny baby because, Well, just look at her.

The Awful Grandmother is the one whose name ought to be the Parrot because she talks too much and too loudly, who squawks from the courtyard up to the second-story bedrooms, from the bedrooms down to the kitchen, from the rooftop all through the neighborhood of La Villa, the hills of Tepeyac, the bell tower of la Basílica de la Virgen de Guadalupe, the twin volcanoes—the warrior prince Popocatépetl, the sleeping princess Iztaccíhuatl.

Father's name is el Tarzán, Tío Tarzan to my cousins, Uncle Tarzan, even though he doesn't look like Tarzan at all. In his bathing suit he looks like an Errol Flynn washed up on the beach, pale and skinny as a fish. But when Father was a little boy in Mexico he saw a Johnny Weissmuller movie at the neighborhood movie theater, The Flea. From that moment on, Father's life was changed. He jumped from a tree holding a branch, only the branch didn't hold. When his two broken arms were set and his mother cured from the fright she asked, —*¡Válgame Dios!* What got into you? Were you trying to kill yourself, or kill me? Answer!

How could Father answer? His heart was filled with so many wonders there were no words for. He wished to fly, he wanted to shout with the voice of the wind, he wanted to live in the sea of trees with the monkeys, satisfied picking each other's lice, glad to be shitting on people below. But how can one say this to one's mother?

Forever after Father was nicknamed el Tarzán by his *cuates*. Inocencio took his nickname in stride. El Tarzán was not so bad. Inocencio's best friend since the first grade was el Reloj, the Clock, because he was born with his left arm shorter than his right. At least Inocencio was not as unlucky as the neighbor who lost an ear in a knife fight and was, from that day till his death, called la Taza, the Cup. And what about the *pobre infeliz* who survived polio with a gimp foot, only to be named la Polka. *Pobrecito* el Moco, the Snot. El Pedo, the Fart. El Mojón, the Turd. Life was cruel. And hilarious all at once.

Juan el Chango. Beto la Guagua because he could not say *"agua"* when he was little. Meme el King Kong. Chale la Zorra. Balde la Mancha. El Vampiro. El Tlacuache. El Gallo. El Borrego. El Zorrillo. El Gato. El Mosco. El Conejo. La Rana. El Pato. El Oso. La Ardilla. El Cuervo. El Pingüino. La Chicharra. El Tecolote. A whole menagerie of friends. When they saw each other at a soccer match, they'd shout, —There goes el Gallo over there. And instead of shouting, —Hey, Gallo!—they'd let loose a rooster crow—*kiki-riki-kiiiiiii*—which would be answered by a Tarzan yell, or a bleat, or a bark, or a quack, or a hoot, or a shriek, or a buzz, or a caw.

Before Jiminy Cricket, there was Cri-Crí, the Singing Cricket, the alter ego of that brilliant children's composer Francisco Gabilondo Soler, who created countless songs, influencing generations of children and would-be poets across América Latina.

Aunty Light-Skin

Aunty Light-Skin sleeps like a drowned lady, so far away from the living. A tiny speck in the horizon. Her limbs heavy and soaked with salt water. A terrible effort to raise that waterlogged body from the bed. The Awful Grandmother must help her up each morning, button Aunty into her pink-quilt robe, lead her by the hand up the stairs and past the dining room where we are cracking little eggshell hats on our soft-boiled eggs.

—How did you sleep, Aunty?

—Like the dead, Aunty says. The Awful Grandmother leading the way to the bathroom, Aunty Light-Skin with her eyes closed letting herself be led.

Aunty Light-Skin wears metallic thread cocktail dresses to work, tight skirts with a kick pleat in the back and matching *bolero* jackets with cloth buttons. Beaded sweaters, grasshopper-green silk blouses with mandarin collars, or sleeveless crepe de chine. Crocodile-skin stilettos and crocodile handbag. Brown suede with leopard collar and leopard gloves. Pillbox hats with rhinestones on the veil. Aunty always looks elegant. Because she doesn't shop at El Palacio de Hierro or Liverpool like the other office girls. Her clothes are from Carson Pirie Scott and Marshall Field's.

—*Ay,* so much for just a little office job! Aunty Licha sniffs when the Grandmother and Aunty Light-Skin have left the room.

—How the hell does she afford such fancy duds? Aunty Ninfa adds.

—I mean, Jesus Christ, with just a secretary's salary? Nice work if you can get it.

Mother says, —Well, if you ask me she must be very, very good at what she does.

The daughters-in-law burst out laughing.

Aunty Light-Skin has to dress up because she works for a very important man. Señor Vidaurri.

Señor Vidaurri of the pearl-gray suits and pearl-gray hair. Señor Vidaurri of the handsome fedoras. Señor Vidaurri of the big black car. Señor Vidaurri who drives our pretty Aunty Light-Skin to his construction company every day and delivers her home each evening. Señor Vidaurri whose skin is as dark as my mother's. *That* Señor Vidaurri gives our cousin Antonieta Araceli her *domingo,* her Sunday allowance each week, he never forgets, even though he is not her grandfather. It's because he's Aunty's boss and has too much money.

When Mother and the Aunties are not discussing Aunty Light-Skin, or Señor Vidaurri, or the Awful Grandmother, they like to talk about Aunty's husband, the one she divorced so long ago Antonieta Araceli doesn't even remember him, whose name no one is supposed to mention because Aunty will have fits.

—Yeah, well, if you want my two cents there wasn't a divorce, because there wasn't a marriage, Mother says. —Know what I mean?

—How could there be a marriage? He was still legally married to two others, Aunty Ninfa whispers too loudly.

—*¡No me digas!* Aunty Licha says.

—One in Durango and one in Tampico. That's why she had to leave him, Ninfa continues. —That's the way I heard it.

—*¡A poco!* What a barbarity! says Licha.

—I'm just telling you what I heard.

We are already finished with breakfast, wiping away the milk mustaches with our napkins when Aunty Light-Skin reemerges from the bathroom, her little eyes bright apostrophes, her mouth a tangerine heart, hair finger-combed into wet waves. She is rushing about asking someone to zipper her into an aqua dress with spaghetti straps and pink sequins, she is stumbling into black patent leather stilettos that crisscross at the ankle, tossing things hurriedly from last night's silver sequin clutch to this morning's black envelope bag, her high heels grating along the corridor tiles.

From the courtyard Aunty's voice sounds almost like the parrot voice of the Awful Grandmother.

—Oralia, move the rubber tree into the sun, and make sure you water it thoroughly. Mamá, ask for three tanks of gas this time from the gas man, don't forget. Antonieta Araceli, *mija*, the money for the flowers for the dead nun, look on my dresser, I left it knotted in a handkerchief. Oralia, have Amparo iron my silk blouse, the one with the embroidered flowers, not the white one, the other one. And have her take care not to scorch it. Mamá, can you have my things picked up from the cleaners? Don't wait to have supper with me, I'm eating out tonight. Antonieta Araceli, stop chewing your fingernails. You'll only make them worse. Use a nail file. . . . Ask your *abuela* to find you one. ¡Antonieta Araceli! ¡Oralia! ¡Mamá! ¡Oralia!

She doesn't stop yelling until the *tán, tán, tán* of Señor Vidaurri's car horn. The green iron gate slamming shut with a reverberating *clang*.

The Girl Candelaria

The first time I see anyone with skin the color of a *caramelo* I am walking behind the Grandmother and step on the Grandmother's heel.

—Clumsy! Look where you're going!

Where I am looking is the rooftop laundry room where the girl Candelaria is feeding clothes through a wringer washer. Her mother, the washerwoman Amparo, comes every week on Monday, a woman like a knot of twisted laundry, hard and dry and squeezed of all water. At first I think Amparo is her grandmother, not her mama.

—But how could a girl with skin like a *caramelo* have such a dusty old mother?

—*¡Hocicona!* the Awful Grandmother says, calling me a big-mouth. —Come here. And when I am within reach, *thwacks* me on the head.

The girl Candelaria has skin bright as a copper *veinte centavos* coin after you've sucked it. Not transparent as an ear like Aunty Light-Skin's. Not shark-belly pale like Father and the Grandmother. Not the red river-clay color of Mother and her family. Not the coffee-with-too-much-milk color like me, nor the fried-*tortilla* color of the washerwoman Amparo, her mother. Not like anybody. Smooth as peanut butter, deep as burnt-milk candy.

—How did you get like that?

—Like what?

But I don't know what I mean, so I don't say anything.

Until I meet Candelaria I think beautiful is Aunty Light-Skin, or the dolls with lavender hair I get at Christmas, or the women on the beauty contests we watch on television. Not this girl with too many teeth like white corn and black hair, black-black like rooster feathers that gleam green in the sun.

The girl Candelaria with long bird legs and skinny arms is still a girl, even though she is older than any of us. She likes to carry me and pretend she is my mama. Or I can say, —*Caw, caw, caw*—and she will drop a little piece of Chiclets gum in my mouth as if I was her little bird. I say, —Candelaria, swing me in a circle again, and she will swing me. Or, —Be my horsie, and she tugs me on her back and gallops across the courtyard. When I want, she lets me sit on her lap.

—And what do you want to be when you grow up, Lalita?

—Me? I want to be . . . a queen. And you?

Candelaria says, —I want to be an actress, like the ones that cry on the *tele*. Watch how I can make myself cry. And we practice trying to make ourselves cry. Until we start laughing.

Or she takes me with her down the street when she is sent to run an errand. On the way there and back, we say, —Let's play the blind game, and take turns walking down the street with our eyes shut, one leading, the other being led. —Don't open your eyes until I say. And when I do, I am standing in front of the gate of a strange house, the girl Candelaria laughing and laughing.

> *¿Qué quiere usted?*
> *Mata rile rile ron.*
>
> *Yo quiero una niña.*
> *Mata rile rile ron.*
>
> *Escoja usted.*
> *Mata rile rile ron.*
>
> *Escojo a Candelaria.*
> *Mata rile rile ron.*

When we play *mata rile rile ron* I want to hold hands with you, Candelaria, if your mother will let you, just for a little, before you go back to the job of the laundry, please. Because did I tell you? The girl Candelaria is a girl who likes to play even though she wakes up with the rooster and rides to work asleep on the hard shoulder of her mother, the old washerwoman, the long ride into the city, three buses to the Grandmother's house on Destiny Street each Monday, to wash our dirty clothes.

—How can you let that Indian play with you? my cousin Antonieta Araceli complains. —If she comes near me, I'm leaving.

—Why?

—Because she's dirty. She doesn't even wear underwear.

—Liar! How do you know?

—It's true. Once I saw her squat down behind the laundry room and pee. Just like a dog. I told the Grandmother, and the Grandmother made her scrub all of the roof with a bucket of soap and the broom.

Who can say if the cousin Antonieta Araceli is telling the truth or telling a story? To see if it's true that Candelaria doesn't wear underwear, my brother Rafa makes up this game.

—We're going to play "It" except you can't be tagged "It" if you squat down like this, understand? Now I'm "It." Run!

Everyone, brothers and cousins, scatters across the courtyard. When Rafa tries to tag Candelaria, she hunkers like a frog, and the rest of us squat down too and look. Candelaria smiling her big corn teeth smile, skinny legs drawn beneath her.

Not underpants. Not exactly. Not little flowers and elastic, not lace and smooth cotton, but a coarse pleat of cloth between her legs, home-made shorts wrinkled and dim as dish towels.

—I don't want to play this game anymore, Rafa says.

—Me neither.

The game ends as suddenly as it began. Everyone disappears. Everyone is gone. Candelaria squatting in the courtyard, grinning her big teeth grin like kernels of white corn. When she gets up finally and comes toward me, I don't know why, I run.

—Stop that! Stop it, Mother scolds. —What's wrong with you?
—It's that my hair is laughing, I say.

Mother makes me sit on her lap. She tugs and parts my hair in every direction.

I'm rushed to the outdoor sink, my scalp scrubbed raw with black soap till my crying makes Mother stop. Then I'm not allowed to play with Candelaria. Or to even talk to her. And I'm not to let her hug me, or chew the little cloud of gum she passes from her mouth to her fingers to my mouth, still warm with her saliva, and never let her carry me on her lap again as if I was her baby. —Never, understand?

—Why?

—Because.

—Because what?

—Because they won't let me, I shout from the courtyard balcony, but before I can add anything else they bring me inside.

Candelaria in the courtyard leaning against the wall, biting a thumbnail, or standing on one stork leg, or slipping off her dusty shoes with the backs squashed like house slippers, making a circle with her big toe on the courtyard tiles, or folding sheets, or hauling a tin basin of wet laundry to the rooftop clothesline, or hunkered in a game we made up, the dingy cloth of her underpants like the wrinkled diaper Jesus wears on the cross. Her skin a *caramelo*. A color so sweet, it hurts to even look at her.

11.

A Silk Shawl, a Key, a Spiraling Coin

—A silk *rebozo*? From Santa María? For what? So that Celaya can mop the floor with it? Really, Inocencio, where's your head? What does a little girl need a silk shawl for?

—It's that I promised Lalita we'd find her one one day. Isn't that right, Lala? Father says, tapping his cigarette into his coffee cup, the ash dropping with a sizzle. Then he breaks into a Cri-Crí song about a duck that wears a *rebozo*.

—But silk, Inocencio! How exaggerated! the Grandmother says, plucking the cup off the table and replacing it with a "souvenir" ashtray stamped "Aeromexico." —You're talking about shawls that cost a fortune. They don't make them anymore. Good luck trying to find one.

—Not even here in the capital?

—They're disappearing. If you want an authentic one, you'll have to find a family that's willing to part with it. Some old lady who needs the *centavos*, somebody going through hard times. No, the famous *rebozos* from my village you can't find anymore. Go look here in the capital. Look in the countryside. Ask and see if I'm lying. All you'll come back with are the ones they sell in the market. Factory made. *Rebozos* that look as if somebody made them with their feet. And not even artificial silk! Of that, you can be sure. Look, the more work is put into the fringe, the higher the price. Like this one I'm wearing, count how many rows of braiding . . . Just count. This one?!!! I already told you. Not for sale. Not even if God commanded it. Not while I'm alive. Don't even ask.

—What, what, what? What's not for sale? the Little Grandfather says, coming back to the table for his second cup of coffee and another *pan dulce.*

—We were talking about silk *rebozos,* Papá, Father says. —I wanted to find one for Lalita.

—I was saying you can't find them anymore, Narciso. You tell him. Better he buy Celaya one of the cotton ones in the market, am I right? No use spending on something she can't even wear till she grows up. And what if she grows up and doesn't even *want* to wear it. Then what, eh? So that she can save it for her funeral? Over there on the other side do they even wear them? I don't think so. They're too modern. Why, my own daughter doesn't even want to be seen wearing a *rebozo.* In another generation they'll look on them as rags, barbarities, something to spread on a table or, God forbid, a bed. If you find a real silk one, better buy it for your mother. I'm the only one who knows the true worth of a *rebozo* around here.

—Listen to your mother, Inocencio. The Devil knows more from experience . . .

—Than from being the Devil. I know, I know.

After coffee and a sugared *cuernito,* the Little Grandfather is satisfied and makes the same joke he always makes after each meal:

—I sleep. And it makes me so huuuun-gry. Then I eat. And it makes me so sleeeee-py!

—Out, out, all of you! the Grandmother scolds, shooing us out of the dining room with her shawl as if we are flies. —How are we ever going to get this table clean with everyone dawdling about after every meal?

It's the hour of the nap. The house is finally quiet, all the apartments are still, front and back, up and down, even the courtyard. The world is napping. As soon as Oralia has cleared off the lunch dishes, the Grandmother retreats to her room. Bedroom door shut, key *click-clicking* twice behind her. Everyone knows better than to knock.

—Never bother your grandmother when she's napping, understand? Never!

From our side of the door we can hear the Little Grandfather snoring, the Grandmother's nervous shuffling about in her *chanclas* with the squashed heels. They used to be the Grandfather's slippers. The Grandfather says she never throws any of his things away even though he hasn't worn them since . . . since when I was dirt.

Tikis, who is always complaining about how much work he has to do, who never sits down and eats with the rest of us, because he's too busy washing Father's new station wagon for extra money, or polishing Father's shoes the way only Tikis can polish them, or making a chart with how many *pesos* there are to dollars, and finds an excuse to run off and eat somewhere alone, comes back from wherever he's been hiding with his empty glass and plate. Everyone else has gone to their rooms to sleep after eating. Except for me and Tikis.

—How come the Grandmother always locks the door when she goes in there? I ask, pointing to the Grandmother and Little Grandfather's room.

—Beats me.

I lie on my belly and peek under the door.

—Get up, Lala, before someone sees you!

But when I don't get up, Tikis lies down on his belly and peeks too. The Grandmother's *chanclas* stop in front of the windows, the metal venetian blinds shutting their metal eyes, and then the curtains screeching shut, *chanclas slap-slapping* over to the walnut-wood armoire, a key turning, the armoire doors creaking open, drawers opening and closing. The feet of the Grandmother, fat little *tamales* shuffling over to the overstuffed velvet chair and the chair's springs groaning under her weight. The legs crossing themselves at the thick ankles. Then the best part; the Grandmother who cannot sing, singing! It's hard not to laugh. Singing in a high parrot voice and humming.

—What she got locked in the *ropero*? I ask, —Money? A treasure? Maybe a skeleton even?

—Who knows? But I betcha anything I'm gonna find out.

—Honest?

—When Grandfather goes to his shop and the Grandmother runs to church. Watch. *I'm* going in there.

—Nuh-uh!

—Yup! You want to help? Maybe if you're nice, I'll let you.

—Really? Please, Tikis. Please, please, pleeeease!

—But you gotta promise not to tell, big-mouth. Promise? Honest, hope to God you don't lie, step on your mother's eye?

—I promise, honest-honest!

*I*t's true. I can't keep a secret. Before the end of the day all the brothers find out and want to help us too. It's Rafa, same as always, who takes over. It's because of that year he went to Mexican military school. That's why Rafa likes ordering us about. He studied ordering.

—Toto, to the kitchen. Ask Oralia to make you something to eat. Lolo, you stay on the balcony and watch over the courtyard. Memo, your job is to keep the cousins busy, start a game of Turista. Tikis, your post is the rooftop, keep an eye down the street. If anyone comes to the gate, just start whistling. And make sure you whistle good and loud!

Tikis whines, —I always get stuck doing the dirty work. Why do I have to stay up on the roof when this was my idea?

—Because I'm in command, Captain Tikis. That's why. And that's an order. Ito comes with me. No one is to leave their position until I say. Any more questions, men? You stay here, Lala . . . naw, on second thought, you're better off with us. If we leave you alone, you're liable to squeal.

The Little Grandfather has already gone back to his *tlapalería* for the afternoon. Finally, the Grandmother leaves the house with her purse full of coins for the candles she is going to light at *la basílica*, her good silk *rebozo* looped around her shoulders and her fancy crystal rosary in her pocket. She shouts commands to everyone she sees even as she crosses the threshold, the door-within-the-gate clanging behind her. Rafa, Ito, and me move into our positions.

Ito swings me up on his back and carries me piggyback. I must be holding on to his neck too tight. —Hey, what's the matter, you turning chicken, Lala?

—Uh-uh. I like this a whole lot better than playing *mata rile rile ron*, don't you?

—Shh! You guys keep quiet unless I say you can talk, Rafa says. —Is that clear, donkey-private Lala?

—Yes, sir! I say. I've already been demoted twice this summer, from a skunky-private to a monkey-private, and then to a donkey-private. So far there is nothing lower than a donkey-private.

We have to be extra careful Oralia doesn't see us. The Grandparents' bedroom is across the breakfast room, just beyond the kitchen. When Oralia goes up the back staircase to the roof, her footsteps *clink-clanging* on the metal spiral stairs, it's our chance. Rafa leads, then Ito gallops off with me bouncing on his back like a sack of rice. As soon as we get inside, Rafa shuts the bedroom door behind us, and Ito slides me off his back. On a hook behind the door, the Grandfather's tired pajamas smelling of cough medicine and cigars.

I've only seen the Grandmother and Grandfather's room from the doorway. The Grandmother always chases us out. She says we break things, she says things are always missing when we come to visit. Even here, inside the bedroom, you can smell the smell of the house on Destiny Street, a smell like meat frying. Rafa won't let us switch on the light, and with the venetian blinds closed it's spooky, the air heavy and full of ghosts.

The bed high and fat like a big loaf of bread, so white and clean I'm afraid to touch it. Nubby bedspread, white pillowcases and sheets starched and ironed and edged with crocheted lace. On top of the pillows, more pillows, the Mexican kind with doves and flowers and sayings embroidered on them.

—What do they say? I whisper.

—*Amor de mi vida,* Ito whispers. —*Sólo tú. Eres mi destino. Amor eterno*—Narciso *y* Soledad.*

The room full of things that make you itch, that make you want to sneeze from just looking at them. On top of the bedside tables, wobbly lamps in ivory silk shades ribboned and scalloped with lace like a girl's underwear. Tortoiseshell hair combs and hairpins, hairbrush with a nest of the Grandmother's curly gray hairs.

—Don't touch *any*-thing! Rafa says, touching everything.

All the furniture in the room dark and gloomy. Up on the tall dresser, a Santo Niño de Atocha is staring at me, his scary eyes following me around the room. *Don't touch,* he seems to say. Under a glass bell, a pretty gold clock with pink roses *tick-tick-ticking.* Above the bed a Palm Sunday cross, la Virgen de Guadalupe, and a rosary on the wall. Crocheted doilies everywhere, even on the big television set with the cabinet doors. A music box that plays a sad waltz when I open it—*plunk, plunk, plunk.*

—I said don't touch anything!

An ashtray with a scorpion frozen in the glass. A jar filled with buttons. A brown photograph of the Little Grandfather when he was young, wearing a striped suit, sitting on a bench, leaning on someone who's been cut out. A framed paper with curly handwriting and gold seals.

—What's it say, what's it say? Read it, Rafa.

—*En la facultad que me concede . . . el Presidente de la República confiere a Narciso Reyes . . . En testimonio de lo cual se le . . . Dado en la Ciudad de México . . . en el año de nuestro Señor . . .* A whole lot of fancy words just to say Grandfather was loyal to the Mexican government during the war.

Holy Communion photo of Aunty Light-Skin when she was a little girl, her mouth a heart, her hands clasped like Saint Theresa, the brothers standing next to her holding long candles with ribbons. An oval baby photo of Father, his eyes like little houses even then, sausage legs stuffed into old-fashioned leather boots, on his head a big fluted sunflower hat. The Grandfather's newspapers folded neatly on his nightstand. A clay bowl full of coins. A teacup where the Grandfather sleeps his teeth. Inside the bedside drawers, the Grandfather's tubes of cigars. On the Grandmother's side, a thick pile of *fotonovelas* and a box of chocolates with all the candies half-bitten.

—Want one? Ito says laughing.

—Never!

We look everywhere, even under the cushions of the overstuffed chair, but can't find a key to the walnut-wood armoire. Are we hot or are we cold?

—Look what I found, Ito says, crawling out from under the bed with pieces from our Lego blocks, our best double-issue Archie comic book, and my missing jump rope.

—Holy cow! How'd this stuff get here?

—Bet I know! Ito says, slapping the dust from his hair. —That big snitch Antonieta Araceli. Who else?

Before we can find the key, Tikis starts whistling his alarm whistle. We run around like the Three Blind Mice, until Rafa calms down and orders us to be still.

I try to jerk the door open, but Rafa holds it shut. He opens the door a crack, then pushes us all back in.

—Oralia's at the sink. Hold on, he says. Tikis' whistles sounding more and more urgent. We can hear the green iron gate downstairs creaking open and clanging shut. Pretty soon the Grandfather's footsteps will be climbing up the stairs and crossing over the balcony on the other side of the venetian blinds. I feel like crying, but if I say this, Rafa for sure will make up something worse than a donkey-private.

Again Rafa opens the door.

—We can't wait anymore, he whispers. —Men, we're going to have to make a run for it.

When Oralia turns to the stove he shoves Ito out first, then me, and then slinks out, shutting the door quietly behind him. The Little Grandfather is just lifting his foot onto the first step when we come colliding downstairs into the courtyard.

—*Mi general,* Rafa says, saluting.

—*Coronel* Rafael, are my troops ready for inspection? the Grandfather asks.

—*Sí, mi general.*

—Well, then, *coronel,* call in my troops.

From a fuzzy string around his neck, Rafa pulls out a metal whistle and lets out a screech loud enough to call in the whole neighborhood. From all corners of the house, rooftop, courtyard, bedrooms and stairs, from nooks under stairwells, from the apartments in front and the apartments in back, from hiding places in pantry and closets, thirteen kids come pouring out into the courtyard and form a straight line from short to tall. We stand as stiff as possible, our eyes straight ahead, and salute.

The Grandfather struts up and down.

—Captain Elvis, where are your shoes?

—I didn't have time to put them on, *mi general.*

—Next time, you *make* time to put them on. And you there, Lieutenant Toto, quit scratching like a dog. Be dignified. We are not dogs! Remember, you're a Reyes and a soldier. *Coronela* Antonieta Araceli, there will be no slouching in my army, do you hear! Private Lala, what are you smirking about? We can't have you grinning like a clown, this isn't the circus, is it? Corporal Aristotle, you will not kick your fellow soldiers when in formation, understood? *Coronel* Rafael, are these all my troops?

—They are, *mi general.*

—And how have they behaved?

—Like true soldiers, *mi general.* You'd be proud.

—Well done, well done, the Little Grandfather says. —That's what I like to hear. And now . . . He starts fishing in his pockets. —And now . . . the Little Grandfather says, tossing heavy Mexican coins in the air, —Who loves Grandfather?

And with that, everyone who has been standing like a statue suddenly is leaping and scrambling, coins dancing on the tiles, shouting under the rain of copper and silver, yelling, —Me! Me! Me!

Mexican pillows embroidered with Mexican piropos, sugary as any chuchu-luco. Siempre Te Amaré, I'll Always Love You. Qué Bonito Amor, What a Pretty Love. Suspiro Por Ti, I Sigh For You. Mi Vida Eres Tú, My Life Is You. Or the ever popular Mi Vida, My Life.

12

The Little Mornings

—Don't laugh so hard, the Grandmother scolds. —You'll swallow your tongue. Watch, see if I'm wrong. Don't you know whenever you laugh this hard, you'll also cry as hard later the same day?

—Does that mean if we cry hard first thing in the morning, we'll laugh just as hard before we go to sleep?

I ask and ask, but the Grandmother won't answer.

The Grandmother is too busy supervising the tables and chairs being carried out to the courtyard. She's ordered the hi-fi placed on the other side of the living room and turned around to face the courtyard windows. The entire dining room has been replastered and repainted for the occasion. For weeks workmen have trooped in and out, leaving a trail of white footprints from the dining room, across the covered balcony, down the stairs, and over the courtyard tiles to the green iron gates. The Grandmother has scolded them daily; first for being such *cochinos,* and finally for being lazy and slow. Only yesterday, wearing newspaper hats and speckled work clothes, did they finish their work, just in time for tonight's party.

But now that they're gone, it's the grandchildren she shouts at for being everywhere they're not supposed to be; playing army hospital in her larder, spitting at passersby from the rooftop, running outside the gates and into the street.

—Barbarians! Never, never-never-never step outside the courtyard gates! You could be stolen and have your ear cut off by kidnappers. How would you like that? Don't laugh, it happens every day. You could be hit by a car and worn on the bumper like a necktie! Someone could put out your eye, and then what, eh? Answer!

—*Sí.*

—Yes, what?

—*¿Gracias?*

—How many times do I have to tell you? You're to say, "*Sí*, Abuela."

It's Father's birthday. All week the Grandmother has been marketing for everything herself because she can't trust the servant girl Oralia to buy the freshest ingredients for Father's favorite meal—turkey in the Grandmother's *mole* sauce.

When the Grandmother goes to the market, she samples from each vendor, pinching, and poking, and pocketing their wares. She makes believe she doesn't hear them cursing when she walks away without buying anything. The Grandmother couldn't care less. It's *mijo*'s birthday.

This year, because there are already so many people in the house, only a few guests have been invited, some of Father's boyhood friends— his *compadre* from Juchitán they call Juchiteco, or Hoo-chi, only I hear it as Coo-chi, like the word in Spanish for "knife" almost.

Throughout the house, the Grandmother shouts her orders from the balcony overlooking the courtyard, above the laundry fluttering on the rooftop, from the apartment upstairs rear where she and the Little Grandfather sleep, from Aunty Light-Skin and Antonieta Araceli's rooms below, to the two front apartments facing the street where both tenants have been let go this summer so that her three sons and their families can visit all at once. Imagine the sacrifice. The Grandparents aren't rich after all. —There's just the rents, and Narciso's pension, and the little earnings from his *tlapalería*, which is hardly anything, to tell the truth. But what's money compared to family? the Grandmother insists. —Renters come and go, but my sons are my sons.

Every year Father's birthday is celebrated in Mexico City and never in Chicago, because Father's birthday falls in the summer. That's why on the mornings of Father's birth we wake to "The Little Mornings," and not "Happy Birthday to You." The Awful Grandmother makes sure to personally shake everyone awake and assemble them to serenade Father while he is still in bed. Every year a record of Pedro Infante singing "Las Mañanitas" booms throughout the house, across the courtyard, through the front and back apartments, upstairs and down, beyond the roof where

Oralia lives, to the grimy mechanic's pit next door, above the high walls capped with broken glass, over to the neighbor's rooftop chickens, across the street to la Muñeca's house and the Doctor Arteaga's office three houses over, and down Misterios to the Grandfather's *tlapalería* shop, beyond the sooty walls of *la basílica,* to the dusty little derby of a hill behind it called Tepeyac. Everyone, everyone in La Villa, even the rooster, wakes to Pedro Infante's dark and velvety voice serenading the little morning of Father's birth. *Estas son las mañanitas que cantaba el rey David, a las muchachas bonitas, se las cantamos aquí . . .*

Because he was made to wake up early every day of his childhood, Father is terribly sleepy. There is nothing he likes better than to sleep late. Especially on his birthday.

And so, everyone else is already dressed and ready to greet the morning of his birth with a song. —*Despierta, mi bien, despierta . . .* But this means everyone. The Awful Grandmother, the Little Grandfather, Aunty Light-Skin and cousin Antonieta Araceli, the girl Oralia, exhausted from having to cook and clean for eighteen more people than usual, and even Amparo the washerwoman and her beautiful daughter, Candelaria.

Everyone else who can be forced to pay their respects—the cousins, the aunts and uncles, my six brothers—all parade into our bedroom while we are still asleep under the sheets, our crusty eyes blinking, our breath sour, our hair crooked as brooms—my mama, my father, and me, because I forgot to tell you, I sleep in their room too when we are in Mexico, sometimes on the rollaway cot across from them and sometimes in the same bed.

—You all behave like ranch people, the Grandmother scolds after the birthday singing is done with. —Shame on you, she says to me. —Don't you think you're big enough to sleep alone now?

But who would want to sleep alone? Who on earth would ever want to sleep alone unless they had to, little or big?

It's embarrassing to be sung to and then yelled at all before breakfast while you are still in your scalloped T-shirt and flowered underwear. Is Mother embarrassed too? We're pinned to the bed, unable to get up until everyone has congratulated Father on his birthday.

—*¡Felicidades!* Happinesses!

—Yes, thank you, says Father, blinking. *His chin is gray with stubble, his T-shirt not quite white enough,* Mother thinks, *and why did he have to wear* that *one with the hole?*

—Guess what I've saved just for you, *mijo!* The *nata* from today's milk! Would you rather get dressed and come and have breakfast, or shall I bring you a tray?

—Thank you, Mamá. I'll get dressed. Thank you all. Thank you, many thanks.

Then, after what seems like a very long while of the Grandmother nodding and supervising everyone's well wishes, they all file out.

Mother leaps up and looks at herself in the dresser mirror.

—I look awful, she says, brushing her hair furiously.

She *does* look terrible, her hair sticking up like it's on fire, but no one says, —Oh, no, you don't look terrible at all, and this only makes her feel worse.

—Hurry up and get dressed, she says to me in that way that makes me do what I'm told without asking why.

—Your mother! I bet she thinks she's pretty funny barging in every year without even knocking. She gets the whole neighborhood up earlier and earlier. If she thinks I don't know what's going on she's got another "thing" coming . . .

Father pays no attention to Mother's complaints. Father laughs that laugh he always laughs when he finds the world amusing. That laugh like *las chicharras*, a laugh like the letter "k."

13.

Niños y Borrachos

La Petenera

Vi a mi madre llorar un día,
cuando supo que yo amaba.
Vi a mi madre llorar un día,
cuando supo que yo amaba.

Quién sabe quién le diría
que eras tú a quién yo adoraba.
Quién sabe quién le diría
que eras tú a quién yo adoraba.
Después que lo supo todo
la vi llorar de alegría.

Petenera, Petenera.
Petenera, desde mi cuna,
mi madre me dijo a solas
que amara nomás a una.

Una vela se consume
a fuerza de tanto arder,
una vela se consume
a fuerza de tanto arder.

Así se consume mi alma
por una ingrata mujer.
Así se consume mi alma
por una ingrata mujer.

The Woman from Peten

I saw my mother cry one day
when she realized I loved someone.
I saw my mother cry one day
when she realized I loved someone.

Who knows who it was who told her
that it's you whom I adore.
Who knows who it was who told her
that it's you whom I adore.
After she knew it all
I saw her weep from joy.

Petenera, Petenera.
Petenera, since I was a child in my crib,
my mother told me
I'd love only one.

A candle consumes itself
from so much burning,
a candle consumes itself
from so much burning.

My soul consumes itself like that
for an ungrateful woman.
My soul consumes itself like that
for an ungrateful woman.

Petenera, Petenera.	Petenera, Petenera.
Petenera, desde mi cuna;	Petenera, since I was a child in my crib;
¿por qué no sales a verme	why don't you come out to see me
en esta noche de luna?	on this night of moon?
Ay, soledad, soledad,	Oh, solitude, solitude,
qué soledad y qué pena;	what solitude and pain;
aquí termino cantando	here I finish singing
versos de la Petenera.	the Petenera's verses.

—Go on, say hello. Don't make me ashamed, Father whispers. —Be polite and greet all the guests.

The living room crowded with people drinking highballs before dinner. I don't like going into the living room, but Father insists. The men under a tent of cigarette smoke, their amber drinks clinking in their hands, their breath a sweet stinky when they talk into your face. How can I tell Father they frighten me? They always talk too loud, as if everything they say is funny, especially if they're talking about you.

Father's *compadre* Señor Coochi is playing his guitar. The sound of Señor Coochi's voice trembling like tears, like water falling clear and cold. Señor Coochi's fingernails long like a girl's, and his eyes a green-green that jumps out and surprises you when he closes and then opens them as he sings. It's funny to have someone singing to you like in the movies. When he starts singing to me, I can't help myself and start laughing. Then the guitar music suddenly stops.

—And you?

When Señor Coochi talks, the whole room becomes quiet as if everything he says is pearls and diamonds.

—And you, what are you?

—I'm a little girl.

The room laughs as if it's one person laughing.

—Ah, a little girl, is it? Well, what luck. It just so happens I'm looking for a little girl. I need one, in fact. Would you like to come home with me and be my little girl?

—Nooooo!

Again a huge laugh I don't understand.

—But I've got to have a little girl of my own. What if I told you I have a garden with a swing and a very nice little dog. And you wouldn't have to do a thing but play all day. What do you say to that? Now will you come and be my *niña*?

—No, never!

—But what if I gave you a room full of dolls . . .

—No!

—And wonderful toys . . .

—Nope!

—And a windup monkey that does somersaults . . .

—Oh, no!

—And! How do you like this? . . . A blue bicycle. And your own lit-tle guitar. And a box of chocolates.

—I already told you. No and no and no.

—But how about if I give you your very own room. I'll buy you a bed fit for a princess. With a canopy with lace curtains white-white like the veils for Holy Communion. Now, will you come with me?

—Well . . . O-kay!

The room roars into a laughter that terrifies me.

—Women! That's how they all are. You just need to find their price, Coochi says, strumming his guitar.

—Just like the saying goes, Aunty Light-Skin adds, winking, —chil-dren and drunks always tell the truth. Isn't that so, Juchi?

But Señor Coochi just throws his head back and laughs. Then he begins singing "La Petenera" without bothering to look at me again, as if I'm not even here.

At the Grandmother's, I sleep on the rollaway cot in Mother and Father's room when I'm not sleeping in their bed. And back home in Chicago, my bed is the orange Naugahyde La-Z-Boy in the living room. I've never had a room of my own. Every night the blankets and pillows are brought out from the closet and my bed made. Father's glow-in-the-dark travel alarm clock watches over me from its crocodile box. Before I close my eyes, Father winds it and places it nearby so I won't be afraid.

Father makes the same joke he always makes at bedtime. —*¿Qué tienes? ¿Sueño o sleepy?*

—*Es que tengo sleepy.* I have sleepy, Father.

—And who loves you, my heaven?

—You do.

—That's right, my life. Your father loves you. Never forget it. And who do you love more—me or your mama?

—Inocencio! Mother shouts angrily from out of nowhere.

—I'm only playing, Father says. —Right, Lalita? I was only playing. *Ahora,* time to *mimi. Que duermas con los angelitos panzones,* sleep with the fat little angels, my heart, he adds before putting out the light.

If I wake in the middle of the night or if sleep won't come, I can hold the clock up to my ear and listen to its heart *tick-ticking,* sniff the leather and imagine this is what crocodiles smell like. The green numbers floating in the dark. I would like a room all for myself someday, white and lacy like the princess bedrooms in the Sears Roebuck catalog. Señor Coochi knows what girls like.

Memo, Elvis, Aristotle, and Byron are following the trays of *antojitos.* Just as soon as Oralia sets them down, they start eating, quickly-quickly, and don't leave until the plates are empty. I'm helping them finish the *chile* peanuts when the Grandmother comes over and shoos us away with her *rebozo. ¡Changos!* But if she doesn't want us to eat, why is there food set out everywhere?

The smell of fresh plaster and paint mixed with the smell of the Grandmother's *mancha manteles mole.* The grown-ups seated at the big blond table, and the table covered with a lace tablecloth, and the lace tablecloth covered with clear plastic, even tonight on Father's birthday.

—I don't care, the Grandmother says. —Why do you think they call this dish *mancha manteles?* It really does stain tablecloths, and you can't ever wash it out, ever!

Then she adds in a loud whisper, —It's worse than women's blood.

They put us in the breakfast room at the "baby table," even though we're not babies—Tikis, Toto, Lolo, Memo, me, Elvis, Aristotle, Byron, Amor, and Paz. Rafa and Ito get to sit at the big table with the grown-ups, because the Grandmother says they're *hombrecitos.* Antonieta Araceli isn't a grown-up either, but she's too stuck up to sit with us. Still, we can hear everything they say in the big dining room next door as if we were there ourselves instead of at the baby table.

—Delicious *mole,* Mamá! Uncle Baby says.

—Delicious? says Fat-Face. —Mamá, it's rich!

—Are you crazy? Father says, wiping the *mole* from his mustache with his napkin. —Don't even listen to them! It's exquisite, Mamá. The best. You've outdone yourself as always. This *mole* is excellent. I always say, there's no food like the one made by Mamá.

—*Ay*, it's no trouble at all, even though I made it from scratch! I'm not like these new modern women. Oh, no! I don't believe in cooking shortcuts! the Grandmother says, not looking at her daughters-in-law. —To make food taste really well, you've got to labor a little, use the *molcajete* and grind till your arm hurts, that's the secret.

—But, Mamá, why didn't you use the new blender I brought you last summer? Did it break already?

—The blender! Forget it! Not even if God willed it! It never tastes the same. The ingredients have to be ground *by hand*, or it never comes out tasting authentic. These modern kitchen gadgets, really! What do you men know? Why, your own father's never even entered in my kitchen. Isn't that so, Narciso?

—I don't even know what colors the walls are, the Grandfather says, chuckling.

—And now everyone, when you're all done, please come downstairs to the courtyard for the cake and punch!

There is a loud scraping of chairs and a lot of hurrays from the baby table at this news. Then from the big dining room a horrible scream. We run over to the doorway of the big dining room and peer in.

—My dress! Antonieta Araceli is howling. —Somebody spilled *mole* on my chair! My dress is ruined!

It's true. There's an ugly chocolate stain on her bottom that makes us all laugh.

—Don't worry, *mi gordita*, I'm sure the dry cleaners can fix it.

—But it's *mole*! It'll never wash out. And this dress was my favorite-favorite!

—Sweetheart, don't cry. Go downstairs and get into another dress, okay? You have lots of pretty dresses. Rafa and Ito will help you downstairs, right, boys? One walk in front and one behind.

—Are you sure it's *mole*? Rafa asks. —Maybe it's diarrhea.

—Are you trying to be funny?

—Well, how did it happen? Pretty strange, huh? Rafa continues. —Ito, tell me the truth. Did you see *mole* on that chair when you sat down?

—No, I didn't.

—Me neither, says Rafa. —Sure is a mystery.

—Sure is, Ito says.

—Whose plate is this? The Grandmother says, inspecting the baby table.

—Mine, I say.

—Celaya, you didn't even touch your *mole*.

—I can't eat it, Grandmother. *Pica*. It makes little needles on my tongue.

—What do you mean? You like chocolate, don't you? It's practically all chocolate, with just a teeny bit of *chile*, a recipe as old as the Aztecs. Don't pretend you're not Mexican!

—Leave her, Mamá, she's just a little girl.

—Inocencio, have you forgotten in this country we don't throw food away! Why, I remember during the war we were happy if we even found a bit of dog meat. Young lady, don't you dare leave the table till you've finished your *mole*, do you hear me? No birthday cake for you until you've finished that entire plate.

—But it's cold.

And whose fault is that? You're under my roof now!

—And what am I, painted? the Grandfather asks, pointing at himself with his cigar. —Don't I have a say around here anymore?

—You? You're almost dead, you don't count.

—I'm already dead, don't ask me, the Little Grandfather says, shrugging and shuffling off to his room in a trail of sweet tobacco.

The girl Oralia is busy shuttling dishes back and forth, from upstairs to down, from the dining room to the kitchen. She doesn't pay any attention to me sitting there in front of an ugly plate of cold *mole*. She couldn't care less. I shake one foot and watch my shoe wobble off my white-socked foot. I shake the other foot and watch the other tumble off. I hum a little song I make up. I pull the sheer overlay of my favorite dress over my eyes and look at the world through the sprigs of lilacs, but it's no use. Downstairs they start to sing "The Little Mornings." *Estas son las mañanitas que cantaba el rey David, a las muchachas boni-tas* . . . I bunch my hands into fists, bunch my fists into my eyes, and start to cry.

—What's this? What's this?

It's the Little Grandfather in the doorway. He's taken off his party shirt and jacket, but still looks all dressed up because he's wearing his Sunday trousers with the suspenders. In his sleeveless undershirt his arms are fleshy and white as pizza dough. A thick cigar glows in one hand, and in the other he holds a crumpled newspaper.

—What a silly you are, Private Lala! No need to cry because of a plate of *mole*. Come now, *niña*.

—But the Grandmother said . . .

—Never mind what she said. Do you think she's the boss around here? Watch what I'm going to do. Oralia!

—*Sí, señor.*

—Give this to the neighbor's dog. And if my wife asks, say the child ate it.

—*Sí, señor.*

—You see how easy that was?

—But it's a lie.

—Not a lie! A healthy lie. Which sometimes we have to tell so that there won't be trouble. There, there, stop crying. Would you like to watch television with me in my room? You would! Well, then first you have to stop crying. I can't have you crying all over my room, that's for sure! Put on your shoes. That's a good girl.

The Little Grandfather grunts as he walks like a Pekingese.

—Don't tell the others, because they'll get jealous, but you're my favorite, the Grandfather says, winking.

—Really?

—Truly. *Eres mi cielo.* You are my sky, the Little Grandfather says, showing off his English. —Did you know I used to live in Chicago once? A long time ago, before you were even born, when I was a young man I lived with my Uncle Old in Chicago. I bet you don't know the capital of Illinois. What's the capital of Illinois? What's the capital of California? What's the capital of Alaska? Don't they teach you anything in school?

—I don't go to school yet.

—That's no excuse. Why, when I was your age I knew the names of all the states in the republic and their capitals, as well as the capitals of all . . . What are you looking at?

—Abuelito, how did your hair get like fur?

The Little Grandfather laughs like the letter "k," exactly the way Father laughs.

—It used to be like yours. For many years. Then, when I retired, it started growing white. I dyed it at first—I was very vain once. Then one day I just let it go, just like that, and it went from shoe-polish black to white-white-white in a matter of days. Like the snowy peaks of the twin volcanoes Popocatépetl and Iztaccíhuatl, he says, laughing. —Do you know the story of the twin volcanoes? . . . You don't?!!!

—Nobody tells me anything. They say I talk too much and can't keep a secret. That's why they say they can't tell me things.

—Is that right? Well, let me tell you. Izta and Popo, Izta and Popo, the Grandfather says, adjusting his cigar and looking up at the ceiling. —A Mexican love story. He clears his throat. He puts his cigar down and then picks it back up. He scratches his head.

—Once, under the sky and on the earth there was a prince and a princess. The prince's name was Popocatépetl. You can imagine how difficult it was for his mother to shout, "Popocatéptl, Popocatéptl." So she called him Popo for short.

There is a pause. The Grandfather stares at a spot on the rug. —Now, the princess's name was Iztaccíhuatl and she was in love with this Prince Popo. But because the families of Izta and Popo hated each other, they had to keep their love a secret. But then something happened, I forget what, except I know he killed her. And then as he watched her die, he was so overcome with her beauty he knelt down and wept. And then they both turned into volcanoes. And there they are, the Grandfather says, raising the venetian blinds and pointing to the volcanoes in the distance. —See? One lying down, and one hunched over watching her. There. That's how you know it's true.

—But if he loved her so much, Abuelito, why did he kill her?

—Well, I don't know. I don't know. That's a good question. I don't know. I suppose that's how Mexicans love, I suppose.

—Abuelito, what's in there?

—Where?

—In there. Inside that.

—¿El ropero? Oh, lots of things. Lots. Would you like to see?

The Grandfather walks over to the walnut-wood armoire, runs his hand along the top, and brings down a small key with a faded pink tassel at the end. This he turns twice and the tumblers give their familiar click, then the doors open with a sigh that smells of things old, like a shirt ironed till it's brown.

In one drawer the Little Grandfather shows me his cadet uniform, and in another a red bundle.

—This handkerchief used to belong to my mother. During the revolution she made a promise to la Virgencita to keep me safe. They had to saw three ribs out of me. And here are the three ribs, he says, undoing the cloth and placing them in my hand.

They're as light as old wood and yellow like dog teeth.

—Grandfather, is it true you lost them in a terrible battle?

—Oh, yes! Terrible, terrible.

—But don't you miss your three ribs?

—Well. Not very. He picks up an old sepia photo of himself. Seated on a cane bench, a young man with the surprised eyes of someone who knows nothing of the world. The person he is leaning on has been cut out of the picture. —You can get used to anything, I've learned, he adds, looking at the photograph and sighing. —Well, almost.

—And what's this? I say, tugging an embroidered pillowcase.

—This? the Grandfather says, pulling out of the pillowcase a cloth of caramel, licorice, and vanilla stripes. —This was your grandmother's *rebozo* when she was a girl. That's the only *recuerdo* she has from those times, from when she was little. It's a *caramelo rebozo*. That's what they call them.

—Why?

—Well, I don't know. I suppose because it looks like candy, don't you think?

I nod. And in that instant I can't think of anything I want more than this cloth the golden color of burnt-milk candy.

—Can I have it, Grandfather?

—No, *mi cielo*. I'm afraid it's not mine to give, but you can touch it. It's very soft, like corn silk.

But when I touch the *caramelo rebozo* a shriek rises from the court-yard, and I jump back as if the *rebozo* is made of fire.

—¡¡¡Celayaaaaaaaaaaaaaaaaaaaaaaaaaaaaaaaaaaaaaa!!!

It's the Awful Grandmother yelling as if she's cut off a finger. I leave the Grandfather and the *caramelo rebozo*, and run slamming doors behind me, jumping down stairs two at a time. When I get to the courtyard, I remember to answer the way the Grandmother instructed.

—¿Mande usted? At your orders?

—Ah, there she is. Celaya, sweetness, come here. Don't be fright-ened, my child. Remember how she used to sing when she was just a baby? *¡Qué maravilla!* She was the same as Shirley Temple. I-den-ti-cal, I swear to you. Still in diapers but there she was singing her heart out, remember?

We should have put her on the *Chocolate Express Show,* but no, no one listens to me. Think of the money she could've brought home by now. Come, Celaya, dearest. Get up on this chair and let's see if you can still sing like you used to. Let's see. *Ándale,* sing for your granny. Watch.

—I . . . don't know.

—What do you mean you don't know?

—I don't know if I can remember. That was when I was little.

—Nonsense! The body always remembers. Get up here!

The relatives begin chanting, —*Que cante la niña Lalita, que cante la niña Lalita.*

—Stand up straight, the Grandmother orders. —Throw your shoulders back, Celaya. Swallow. A big gulp of air. That's it. Now, sing.

—Pretty baby, pretty baby, *tan tarrán-tara taran-ta, tara-ranta-rantarán* . . .

My voice tiny in the beginning, but then I puff up like a canary and sing as loud as I can.

—PRETTY BABY OF MINE, OF MINE. PRETTY BABY OF . . . MIIIIIIIIIIIIIINE!

A small silence.

—No, the Grandmother announces matter-of-factly. —She can't sing. Juchi, play that song I like, the one from my times, "Júrame." Come on, don't be bad, play it for me. *Todos dicen que es mentira que te quiero* . . .

For the rest of the evening I hide upstairs and watch the party from the covered balcony where no one can watch me watching, my face pressed against the rails, the rails cool against my hot skin. Once I got my head stuck between the space between an "s" and a flower. They had to use the brown bar of laundry soap to set me free, and afterward my head hurt . . . from the iron bars and from the scolding. And my heart hurt from the brothers laughing, but I don't like to think about that.

The music and the spirals of cigarette smoke rising up like genies. The other kids already asleep wherever they fell. Draped on a chair. Or on a volcano of coats. Or under a table. Everywhere except in their beds. But no one notices.

The bodies below moving and twirling like bits of colored glass in a kaleidoscope. Tables and chairs pushed to the edges to make room for dancing. "Vereda tropical" playing from the hi-fi. Aunties in silk dresses so tight they seem to explode like orchids, aunties laughing with their big flower mouths, and the air sweet-sweet with their ladies' perfume, and sweeter still the men's cologne, the kind men wear here in Mexico, sweeter than flowers, like the sugary words whispered in the women's ears—*mi vida, mi cielo, muñeca, mi niña bonita.*

The men in their shark suits, gray with a little lightning bolt of blue, or olive with a gleam of gold when they move. A stiff white handkerchief in the pocket. The man's hand leading a woman when they dance, just a little tug, just a little like when you yank a kite to remind it—Don't go too far. And the woman's hand nesting inside the man's big heart-shaped hand, and his other hand on her big heart-shaped hips. A beautiful woman with black-black eyes and dark skin, who is our mother in her good fuchsia satin dress bought at the Three Sisters on Madison and Pulaski, and her matching fuchsia cut-glass earrings. Swish of stockings against the cream-colored nylon slip with its twin shells of lace on top and an accordion pleat at the hem, and one strap, always one, lazy and loose asking to be put back. My father with a curl of lavender cigarette smoke, his mouth hot next to my mother's ear when he whispers, his mustache tickling, the roughness of his cheek, and my mother throwing her head back and laughing.

I'm so sleepy, except I don't want to go to bed, I might miss something. I lean my head against the balcony rails and shut my eyes, and jump when the guests start roaring. It's only Uncle Fat-Face dancing with a broom as if it was a lady. Uncle likes to make everyone laugh. When I've had enough of the broom dance, I get up to look for the Grandfather. The dining room door is heavy, I have to pull it open with both hands.

But when I step inside I don't move.

I scramble downstairs to tell everyone, only I don't have the words for what I want to say. Not in English. Not in Spanish.

—The wall has fallen, I keep saying in English.

—What?

—Upstairs. In the big dining room. The wall fell. Come and see.

—What does this kid want? Go see your mother.

—It's that the wall has fallen.

—Later, sweetie, not now, I'm busy.

—The wall in the dining room, it came down like snow.

—How this child loves to be a pest!

—What is it, my queen? Tell me, my heaven.

—*La pared arriba, es que se cayó. Ven, Papá, ven.*

—You go, Zoila. You're the mother.

—*¡Ay!* Always, always I'm the mother when you can't be bothered.

All right, all right already. Quit pulling at me, Lala, you're going to rip my dress.

I tug Mother upstairs, but it's like tugging a punching clown. She tips and wobbles and laughs. Finally, we make it all the way up the stairs.

—Now, this better be good! . . . Holy Toledo!!!

The dining room is powdered with a layer of white plaster like sugar. White plaster over everything, rug, tables, chairs, lamps. Big chunks of plaster here and there, too, like pieces of birthday cake.

Mother shouts downstairs. —Everybody, quick! The ceiling's fallen!

¡Se cayó el cielo raso! Father says.

And then it is I learn the words for what I want to say. "Ceiling" and "*cielo.*" *Cielo*—the word Father uses when he calls me "my heaven." The same word the Little Grandfather reaches for when he wants to say the same thing. Only he says it in English. —My sky.

—You know I don't like to say, and I tell you this in confidence, but it's that Memo who is responsible. I found him hiding on the roof just this morning.

—You don't say! That monkey! Leave it to me. I'll take care of it.

—Poor thing. He's so much slower than our Elvis. After all, they're only a month apart in age. Have you ever considered that maybe he's retarded?

—Like hell! It's the cheap contract work, for crying out loud!

—Aunty, this is the truth! Antonieta Araceli hid some of our toys under the Grandfather's bed. I saw.

—*¡Mentirosa!* It wasn't me! You just like to invent stories, *mocosa.* You believe me, don't you, Mami?

—*Ya mero.* Almost! Did you see that? He almost put out her eye!

—Who did this to you, my heaven?

—It was . . . cousin Toto.

—You know my *gorda* has never lied to me. Never. If she says she didn't do it, she didn't do it. I know my own daughter!

—*¡Chango!* If I catch you touching my kids again I'll take off my belt . . .

—Take your hands off my boy, or I'll beat the crap out of you myself.

—*Estás loca*, I wasn't going to . . .

—You can't address my wife like that, *tarugo!*

—Who are YOU to call me an idiot? You're the one who organized this picnic.

—*¡Ay, caray!* Don't start, brother. Don't even begin. Don't YOU blame me for your bright ideas.

—You know I usually keep out of the affairs of my daughters-in-law, but are you aware Zoila is calling your child a liar?

—*Válgame Dios.* It never fails—a hair in the soup!

—My life, I told you this was going to happen. First you loan your brother money, and now look. This is how he pays you back.

—That's it. I've had it. Licha, start packing. Tomorrow we leave for Toluca. It's settled.

All of a sudden the Grandmother's children are planning to leave. Uncle Baby and family to Veracruz. Uncle Fat-Face and Aunty Licha to her relatives in Toluca. But tonight there is a great slamming of doors and crying as the children are led whimpering off to bed and the guests accompanied to the courtyard gates.

—Thank you. Happinesses. Good night, good night, some of the guests say, while others say only "good, good," too tired to say the "night" part.

The girl Oralia unlocks the gates and yawns. The gates on their squeaky hinges yawn too. Señor Coochi leaves without even looking at me. Then the gates shut with a terrible *clang* like in prison movies.

Maybe he forgot. Maybe he has to get my princess room ready. Maybe he meant tomorrow. The next night after our hot milk with a little drizzle of coffee, I go down to the courtyard, wedge the tips of my black patent leather shoes onto the bottom lip of the gate, pull myself up to the open square where the mailman drops the letters, and into this frame squeeze my face. The hiss of car wheels on wet streets after it rains, and the car lights coming toward our house that make me think maybe it's him, but each time it's not.

—Lalaaaa!!! Are you coming up, or do I have to come down and get you?

—Coming!

But he doesn't come for me.

Not the next night. Nor the next. Nor the next next next.

14.

Fotonovelas

Now that the others are rid of, the Awful Grandmother can unlock the walnut-wood armoire and indulge her favorite son. She brings out of hiding what she has been saving since his last visit. Lopsided stacks of *fotonovelas** and comic books. *El libro secreto. Lágrimas, risas y amor. La familia Burrón.* Father reads these and his *ESTO* sports newspaper printed with an ink the color of chocolate milk. Father spends whole days indoors in bed, smoking cigarettes and reading. He doesn't leave the room. The Awful Grandmother brings him his meals on a tray. From outside the door there is nothing but the sound of pages turning and Father laughing like the letter "k."

---

*The Grandmother saved him her favorite fotonovelas:
    "Wives There Are Plenty, But Mothers—Only One"
    "Virgen Santísima, You Killed Her!"
    "The So-and-So"
    "Women—They're All Alike!"
    "I Killed the Love of My Life"
    "Don't Make Me Commit a Craziness"
    "He Doesn't Give a Damn What You Feel"
    "The Story without End"
    "The Unhappiest Woman of All"
    "I Married a Worker without Culture (But with Me He Became Refined)"
    "The Glories of His Love"
    "I Was His Queen . . . Why Did He Change?"
    "The Woman with Whom He Had Relations"
    "Should I Leave, or What?"
    "I Ask God to Guide Me Because I Don't Know What to Do"

15.

Cinderella

—Whenever I enter a room, your Aunty Light-Skin and your Grandmother stop talking.

That's what Mother says to me when she's scrubbing our clothes in the rooftop sink. The washerwoman Amparo washes on Mondays, but Mother begins washing our clothes herself, because the Grandmother has been complaining about the high water bills, and the high electric bills, and the servants, and the food bills, and this and this and this. That's what Mother tells me, spitting it out under her breath when she sprinkles our clothes with the detergent and pours cold water from a coffee can, and washes my brothers' pants in the stone sink with the ridged bottom, or scrubs a shirt collar with the little straw broom shaped like a dancer's dress. The coffee can scraping against the ridged bottom, and Mother muttering and spitting and grunting things I can't quite hear under her breath.

Every afternoon, Mother gets dressed and takes me with her on her walks.

—Lalita, let's go.

—Where?

—I don't care.

And every day we walk a little farther. First only to the kiosks at the corner for magazines and Chiclets gum. And later down the boulevard *la calzada de* Guadalupe or Misterios. And sometimes toward downtown. On the shady part of the sidewalk, the sweet smell of oranges. The orange lady on a towel stacking oranges into pretty orange mountains, her baby asleep on a lumpy sack. In another doorway, spread over a speckled *rebozo*, a pumpkin seed mountain, the pumpkin seeds sold in newspaper cones. A very old man with one eye shut and the other milky holds out his hand and whispers, —Blessed charity, and then roars, —God will pay you back, when we give him two coins.

Other times we walk toward La Villa, the air foggy with the rumble and wheeze and hum of buses and taxis and cars, the yelp and bark and bellow of vendors selling balloons and souvenir photographs and candles and holy cards, and the women slapping sweet *gordita* cookies on the griddle, frying plate lunches, pouring fruit drinks. The burnt smell of *gorditas* and roasted corn.

But we never go inside *la basílica*. We sit in the sun on the plaza steps till our bones warm up and our behinds get tired, eating hot *gorditas* and drinking pineapple sodas, watching a drunk man dancing backward with a dog, a girl crocheting doilies with pink string, a widow under a black umbrella wobbling to church on her knees slowly slowly, like a circus lady on a high wire.

Or sometimes we go toward the stink of the butchers' market where the heads of the dead bulls—from the bullfight?—slouch in a big sticky pool, their fat ugly tongues drooping, and their eyes full of buzzing flies. —Don't look!

And one day we even walk into a restaurant on a corner boulevard with shiny green and black tiles on the walls like a checkerboard, inside and out, and metal curtains that open wide onto both boulevards so that when you look in you can see clear to the other street, cars and buses and people coming home from work hurrying past, and a truck with a chain rattling from its bumper sending sparks and dust. And we sit down at a nice table covered in clean brown paper with a salt shaker with grains of uncooked rice mixed in with the salt, and a salt shaker with toothpicks inside, and a drinking glass stuffed with triangle napkins, and the table dances until the waiter wedges a folded match cover under one leg. And we order the lunch special that comes with *fideo* soup and limes, and hot *bolillo* bread and little balls of butter, and a breaded steak, which Mother cuts for me.

On the radio Jorge Negrete is singing a sad song about a flower the river carries away. Mother with those cat-eyed sunglasses, looking out at the street, out at nowhere, out at nothing at all, sighing. A long time. In a new white dress she bought especially for this trip. A sleeveless dress she ironed herself, that makes her dark skin look darker, like clay bricks when it rains. And I think to myself how beautiful my mother is, looking like a movie star right now, and not our mother who has to scrub our laundry.

Mother breaking toothpicks into a little mountain, until there aren't any more toothpicks left. When she finally remembers I'm sitting next to her, touches my cheek and asks, —Is there anything else you want, Cinderella? Which means she is in a good mood, because she only calls me that when she isn't angry and buys me things, Lulú sodas, milk gelatins, cucumber spears, corn on the cob, a mango on a stick.

—Is there anything else you want, Cinderella?

And I'm so happy to have my mother all to myself buying good things to eat, and talking, just to me, without my brothers bothering us.

When we return to the house on Destiny Street, I can't help it. The happiness bubbles out of my mouth like the fizz from a soda when you shake and shake it. The first thing I say when I run into the courtyard is, —Guess what! We went to a restaurant! And it's as if we were in a magic spell, my mother and I, but with those words I've broken the spell.

The Grandmother makes a face, and Aunty Light-Skin makes a face, and Father makes faces too, and later Mother scolds me and says, —Bigmouth, why did you have to go and tell? But if I wasn't supposed to tell, why wasn't I supposed to? And why didn't Mother tell me not to tell *before* and not after? And now why is everyone angry just because we ate in a restaurant? I don't know anything, except I know this. I am the reason why Mother is screaming:

—I can't stand it anymore, I'm getting the hell out of here. I can't even open the refrigerator and eat an apple if I feel like it. *¡Me voy a largar, me oyes!*

And Father saying, —Zoila! Be quiet, they'll hear you!

And Mother yelling even louder, —I don't give a good goddamn who hears me!

And then I don't know why, but I'm crying, and the thing I can't forget, Mother taking off one of her shoes and tossing it across the room, and later when I think about it, how I'll remember it different, outdoors, against the night sky, even though it didn't happen like that. A Mexico City twilight full of stars like the broken glass on top of the garden walls, and a jaguar moon looking down on me, and my mother's glass shoe flying flying flying across the broken-glass sky.

16

El Destino Es el Destino

—What do you take me for, a machine? Cleaning up last week's dining room disaster alone was a huge task. Enormous. Monumental. You have no idea of the labor. I'm only flesh and bone, God help me, and what with that lazy Oralia, how am I supposed to handle so much for so many, tell me? And did I mention the expenses? We're not rich, you know. Thank God for your father's pension and *tlapalería,* and your sister's handsome salary. But remember, we've lost the income from the two apartments this summer; because I asked the tenants to vacate and leave the rooms for you all. No, I'm not complaining. Of course, I'd rather have my family near. What's money compared to the joy of having one's family close by? You have to make sacrifices. Family always comes first. Remember that. Inocencio, haven't I taught you anything?

The Awful Grandmother complains daily even with the two younger sons and their families gone. To make matters worse, because of the Grandmother's rages, Oralia has threatened to quit.

—If you don't like my services, *señora,* you can go ahead and fire me.

—So that you can run off while you still owe me for the cash advances I gave you? Not even if God commanded it! Don't make faces. Look at me, Oralia, I said look, don't interrupt, look at me. I'll find another girl to help you, *te lo juro.* Listen, do you know anyone we can trust? Ask around. See if you can't find some poor thing from the country. The ones from the country are always more decent and hardworking. I don't like the idea of people I can't trust sleeping under my own roof.

But in the end it's just Candelaria who is finally sent for and delivered washed, scrubbed, and scoured the following week. A cot is set up in the same rooftop room as Oralia's, so that she doesn't have to travel the hours back and forth to her mother's, except on her one day off. The girl Candelaria is to live in the house of the Grandmother!

—Not for always, don't you get any illusions, missy, but for now. And you're to bathe every day and keep your hair very clean, understand? This isn't the ranch.

So that she might rest a little, so that the dining room repairs can take place without the children running underfoot, the Grandmother insists Father take his family to Acapulco for eight days. It won't cost much. We can stay at Señor Vidaurri's sister's house. Acapulco is only a few hours away. We can drive.

Mother, who never agrees with the Grandmother, begs Father this time:

—Every time we come to Mexico it's the same old crap. Nothing but living rooms, living rooms, living rooms. We never go anywhere. I'm sick and tired, do you hear? Disgusted!

Finally, Father gives in.

At first the trip to Acapulco is only to include Father and Mother, the six brothers, and me. But the Grandmother sighs so much Father has to ask her to come along.

—Why the hell did you *insist* on bringing her? Mother hisses while she's packing.

—How could I say no to my own mother? Especially after she was kind enough to loan us the money for this trip.

—Oh, yeah, well, I've had it with her damn kindnesses.

—Shhh. The kids.

—Let the kids hear! Better they should find out sooner than later who their grandmother is.

On the morning we are to leave, Aunty Light-Skin and Antonieta Araceli are packed and coming too. The Grandmother has gone herself to the *secundaria* to inform the Mother Superior about my cousin falling ill with *la gripa*.

Even Candelaria is coming along!

Because just as the final suitcase is being lifted to the luggage rack, the Grandmother whines to Father, —Bring her, poor thing. She can help with the babies.

So at the last minute, Candelaria is sent to her rooftop room to fetch a plastic shopping bag filled with a few raggedy clothes. But Candelaria's village is in Nayarit. She's never seen the ocean. Before the eight days are up, she will be sent back on the next Tres Estrellas de Oro bus to Mexico City with the Awful Grandmother's address pinned to her underslip to prevent her from becoming one of the countless unfortunates seen hic-cuping terrible tears on the television's public announcements . . . *If you recognize this young lady, please call* . . . since she is new to the city and can neither read nor write, because a huge Acapulco wave will knock her over, and the ocean will come out of her mouth and eyes and nose for days when it is discovered Candelaria can't take care of the babies with-out someone first taking care of her.

It's no use. *El destino es el destino.* A person's destiny is her destiny. The little note pinned to her slip with the house address is lost. Who can say where it went? And Candelaria *does* appear on television crying and crying *telenovela* tears. Who would've thought! Salty water like the ocean running out of her eyes, the servant Oralia shouting for the Little Grand-father to come see, and the Grandfather having to send Oralia downtown to fetch her, and her mother Amparo the washerwoman will beat Cande-laria badly for giving her a fright, and then come and ask permission to have her removed from her job at the Grandmother's because her daugh-ter is already of an age, and a mother can't be too careful, can she? And the Grandfather will say, —Well, yes, I suppose, I imagine so. And both Amparo and the girl Candelaria will disappear back to their village some-where in Nayarit, because by the time the Grandmother returns, it will be as if the earth swallowed them up, the washerwoman and the washer-woman's daughter both gone, and who knows where, and nothing to be done about it.

But this is before Candelaria swallows the Pacific and is sent back to Mexico City on the next Tres Estrellas de Oro. We are on our way to Aca-pulco in Father's red station wagon, all of us. Father at the wheel. The Awful Grandmother sitting where Mother usually sits, because her feel-ings get hurt if she isn't given this seat of honor. Antonieta Araceli seated between them on the bump because, —I always get carsick when I sit in the back. Mother and Aunty Light-Skin and Candelaria take the middle each with a "baby" on their lap—Lolo, Memo, me. Rafa, Ito, Tikis, and Toto claim the best seat, the one that faces backward.

—Why do they get to sit in the back and not us?

—Because they're a bunch of *malcriados*, the Grandmother says.
—That's why. She means "badly raised," though it's only Mother who notices when she says this.

We wave good-bye to the Little Grandfather, to Oralia, and Amparo standing at the courtyard gates.

—Good-bye! Good-bye!

—If we don't stop, maybe we can get there in seven hours, Father says.

—Seven hours! Not even if God willed it! We just want to get there alive. Don't you worry who's honking, Inocencio. You just take your time, *mijo*. Take your time . . .

Pulling shut the green iron gates with a *clang*, the washerwoman Amparo in the trembling circle of side-view mirror.

17

Green Rice

    —And then what happened?
        —I don't remember.
    —Try, Father.
    —It happened a long time ago.
    —Were you in school, or were you sitting in a tree? What did you say when they first shouted, "Tarzán, Tarzán!" Did it make you cry?
    —What questions you ask me, Lalita. How am I supposed to remember things like that?
    —Are we almost there? Tikis asks from the seat that faces backward. —It's taking too long.
    —Too long! the Grandmother says. —These nice roads are here thanks to your grandfather's hard labor. Before the highway commission built this very highway, it used to take three weeks to travel what we cross in only a few hours now. Imagine what it must've been like for us with the heat and the bugs and the being bumped about on *burro*. We suffered, believe me.
    —I thought Grandfather was just a bookkeeper, Tikis says. Ito shoots him a dirty look, and Rafa sends him an elbow.
    —He may have been a bookkeeper, the Grandmother says, —but he had to fight the dust and jungles and mosquitoes and dynamite blasts just as much as anyone who picked up a shovel. This was nothing but wilderness before the highway commission. People had to travel by boat, and by rail, and horse, and when the rains arrived, by *burro* or on the backs of Indians. They say the emperor of China once sent a gift to Hernán Cortés that was supposed to travel over this route. Two beautiful Chinese vases big enough for a man to hide inside. But the way they tell it, the

Spanish viceroy had to send them back, all the way to the Chinese emperor across the sea, imagine. Because the mountain trails were so bad he couldn't be sure the vases would survive the trip.

　—Why didn't he just say they broke, Grandmother, and keep them for himself instead of sending them back to China and hurting the emperor's feelings?

　—What nonsense you talk, child! How am I supposed to know?

On the side of the road, a dog making *caca*.

　—Don't look! the Grandmother shouts. —You'll get a sty on your eyelid.

We pass towns with big mudholes in the streets and runaway pigs, and mountains a green-green-green that makes you want to cry. Everything smells like silver. As if it just rained. As if it wanted to.

In Taxco we have lunch in a restaurant open to the street. A dead man passes on the shoulders of a funeral procession just as we are shoveling big spoonfuls of green rice into our mouths.

The road to Acapulco is so winding, it's better to look where you've been instead of where you are going. The hot wind smelly like an aquarium. We have to stop for Antonieta Araceli to drink Tehuacán mineral water because of a queasy stomach. Then we have to stop further on because all of us kids need to pee from drinking too many bottles of Lulú and Pato Pascual. Before we get to Acapulco we're throwing up in several flavors. *Tamarindo,* tutti-frutti, lime, orange, strawberry.

18.

La Casita de Catita

Acapulco. In a house shaped like a boat. Everything curled like the fronds of a fern. The ocean. Our hair. Our sandals drying in the sun. The paint on the boat-shaped house.

The woman Catita is Señor Vidaurri's ugly twin, but how could a twin of Señor Vidaurri live in a rusty boat of a house that smells of over-ripe mangos and moldy jasmine? Señor Vidaurri's face is not ugly on a man, but it's not pretty on a woman. Señor Vidaurri has a big burnt face like the sun in the Lotería cards. *La cobija de los pobres, el sol.* Catita has had to make do with this borrowed man's face. It frightens me to look at her and see Señor Vidaurri.

Except this Señor Vidaurri has two long gray braids on either side of his big burnt face. This Señor Vidaurri is dressed in a pinafore apron, the kind the house servants wear, plaid so it won't show the dirt, with flowers embroidered on each pocket—a daisy, a carnation, a rose.

The first time I meet Catita I don't want to kiss her, even though Father insists.

—Leave her, Catita says. —It's that she has shame.

Is Señor Vidaurri also frightened when he looks into his sister's face and sees himself?

The driveway of Catita's house is very steep. That's what makes our feet walk as if we're in a hurry, so that we all come waddling down like pull toys. We wear ugly rubber sandals Father buys us the first day and silly straw hats. When I take mine off, the Awful Grandmother squawks:

—*¡Necia!* Put that back on, or I'll put it back for you!

Except for Candelaria, who the Grandmother says is already more burnt than *chicharrón*, everyone gets a silly hat. Mother and Father. All six brothers. The Grandmother, Aunty Light-Skin, and Antonieta Araceli. Straw hats with ACAPULCO stitched in orange yarn, two palm trees on either side, or a maguey stitched in green on one side and on the other, a Mexican man asleep under a *sombrero*.

Catita and her daughter sleep in the stern, a room with round windows like portholes. In the room above them sleep the Grandmother, Aunty, and Antonieta Araceli. Under a mosquito net in a courtyard cot, the girl Candelaria. We sleep above the kitchen, beyond a balcony with wet towels and bathing suits drying on the rail. Green suction-cupped toes of a tree frog. Fuchsia flowers with furry tongues. Lizards frozen into "s"s on the ceiling until the flick of a tail sends them scurrying.

We sleep with the sheets pulled over our heads because of the lizards, even though it is very hot. We insist on sleeping like this. With nothing showing but our noses. Under the sheets, the sour smell of skin.

Here is Catita and here is her fat daughter who smells of *chocolate*. Maybe it's only her skin that is the *color* of *chocolate*, and I'm confused. That could be. I won't remember the daughter's name. Only her fat arms and fat *tetas*. And what she said once about the townspeople never swimming in the ocean.

—Why not?

—Because we never think of it.

—But how could anyone who lives in Acapulco forget the ocean?

When she does come with us finally to la Caleta beach one morning, she swims so far away she is a little brown donut in the distance, waving and bobbing in the harsh waves.

—Come back or the sharks will eat you!

But that's how the people who live here swim when they remember to swim, forgetting sharks.

All the smells swirl together. The old woman smell of Catita the same smell as the steamy dishcloth that holds the hot corn *tortillas*. The sleepy land breeze of rotten bananas and rotten flowers. The curly wind from the ocean that smells of tears. The yeast smell of our bodies asleep under the sheets. The daughter without a name and the lazy, sweet tang of *chocolate*.

19

Un Recuerdo

—Say "whiskey," the Indian in a straw cowboy hat commands.

—Whiskeeeeeeey!

Click, says the camera. When the camera finishes winking, Rafa, Ito, Tikis, and Toto sprint down the beach to watch the next parachute rider float across the sky. Aunty wipes a grain of sand out of Antonieta Araceli's eye with a flowered hankie and spit. Lolo and Memo tug Mother by the hand to the lip of the water to jump over waves. And the Grandmother whispers too loudly into Father's ear, —Don't pay that peon one *centavo* in advance, or we'll never see him again.

The Indian cowboy adds Catita's address to his notebook, folds the tripod, and hitches it on his shoulder shouting in a nasally voice, —*Fotos, un bonito recuerdo, fotos.* Very pretty and very cheap!

Beyond la Caleta bay, the ring of green mountains dipping and rising like the ocean. And beyond that, sky bluer than water. Tourists yelling in Spanish, and yelling in English, and yelling in languages I don't understand. And the ocean yelling back in another language I don't know.

I don't like the ocean. The water frightens me, and the waves are rude. Back home, Lake Michigan is so cold it makes my ankles hurt, even in summer. Here the water's warm, but the waves wash sand inside my bathing suit and scratch my bottom raw. La Caleta is supposed to be the good beach, but I stay out of the water after the ocean tries to take me.

The froth of the waves churning and rolling and dragging everything in sight. I make sand houses where the sand is muddy and sucks at my feet, because the dry sand is so hot it burns. The ocean foam like the *babas* of a monkey, little bubbles that turn from green, to pink, and snap to nothing.

Candelaria, wearing a shell necklace, weaves a rose for me out of strips of braided palm fronds.

—Where did you learn how to do that?

—This? I don't know. My hands taught me.

She puts the rose in my hat and runs into the ocean. When she moves into the deep water her skirt billows out around her like a lily pad. She doesn't wear a bathing suit. She wears her street clothes, an old blouse and a skirt gathered up and tucked in her waistband, but even like this, bobbing in the water, she looks pretty. Three tourists drinking coconut drinks in the shade of the palm-leaf *palapas* sing a loud Beatles song, — "I Saw Her Standing There." Their laughter all across the beach like seagulls.

—Cande, watch for sharks!

The ocean bottom is ridged like the roof of a mouth and disappears beneath your feet sometimes when you least expect it. That's why I have to shout to Candelaria to be careful when she wades out in the deeper water. The Acapulco water, salty and hot as soup, stings when it gets in your eyes.

—Lalita! Come on in.

—No, the water's mean.

—Don't be a silly-silly. Come on. Her voice against the roar of ocean, a small chirping.

—Noooo!

—And if I throw you in, then what?

We've been to la Roqueta island across the bay on a glass-bottom boat, and on the way there we've seen the underwater statue of la Virgen de Guadalupe all made of gold. We saw the donkey that drinks beer on la Roqueta beach. And we've seen the cliff divers at la Quebrada and the sunset at los Hornos where the ocean is out to get you and comes down slamming hard, like a fist in a game of arm wrestling. And we've had a fish dinner outdoors at a lopsided table set in the sand, and afterward swung in a hammock. Father, in a good mood, bought us all shell necklaces, Mother and me, Aunty and Antonieta Araceli, the Grandmother, and even Candelaria.

Candelaria wearing her shell necklace and jumping with each wave, as brown as anybody born here, bobbing in the water. Sunlight spangling the skin of water and the drops she splashes. The water shimmering, making everything lighter. You could float away, like sea foam. Over there, just a little beyond reach. Candelaria sparkling like a shiny water bird. The sun so bright it makes her even darker. When she turns her head squinting that squint, it's then I know. Without knowing I know.

This all in one second.

Before the ocean opens its big mouth and swallows.

20

Echando Palabras

I'm looking for Candelaria's face in the dirty windows of dirty buses lined up and roaring hot air. Father has picked me up and put me on his shoulders, but the Grandmother has marched Cande off in a hurry, and I don't know which bus is hers. Finally, I see the Grandmother making her way back to us rolling and pushing her way through the sea of people. The Grandmother swats at anyone who gets in her way, a handkerchief held to her mouth as if she isn't feeling well.

—*¡Ay, ay, qué horror!* she keeps muttering when she finally returns to Father and me. — Get me out of this inferno of Indians, it smells worse than a pigsty.

—But aren't we going to wait for Candelaria's bus to leave? I ask.

—I said let's get out of here before we catch fleas!

There is nothing else to be said. We are moving away from that heat of bus belches and song of vendors balancing trays of ham *tortas* on their heads, away from the people traveling with bulging shopping bags and cardboard boxes tied in hairy string.

We've left everyone waiting in the car, and now they're camped about in whatever patch of shade they could find, eating ice cream cones, their faces shiny, their voices whiny and impatient. —What took you so long?

Every door of our car is yawning open. Antonieta Araceli, looking miserable, is lying down in the back with a wet handkerchief on her head, because, as Aunty explains it, —*Pobrecita*. La Gorda practically fainted from the heat.

It's already the hottest part of the afternoon. To save the day from being ruined, the Grandmother suggests we drive to the port and catch a boat ride.

—I remember there are some nice inexpensive excursions. So refreshing. That way we can at least enjoy the sea breezes. You'll all thank me in the end.

But at the port, the price of the tickets is not as inexpensive as the Grandmother remembers.

—All the soft drinks you can drink! Absolutely free! the ticket seller says.

We climb on board while Father and the Grandmother haggle over a group rate with the ticket seller. —I have *siete hijos,* Father begins, bragging about his seven "sons."

At the boat's rail, we watch a bunch of noisy neighborhood boys dive for coins. Rafa is whispering orders, pinching and pulling at us. —And Lala, don't you start whining about wanting anything extra. Papa doesn't have any money.

—I wasn't going to . . .

—*Seño, seño,* the divers shout, not saying *señora* nor *señorita* but something halfway, their bodies shiny and dark as sea lions. They leap and disappear in the oily waters, followed by a trail of bubbles, and come back with the coins in their mouths. Didn't their mothers tell them never put money in your mouth? They swim as if it isn't any trouble at all, laughing and calling out to us. I'm afraid of water. The boys of Acapulco are not afraid.

Horns blast, the wooden plank is pulled up, the motor starts roaring, and we start to move away from the shore, flags fluttering in the wind, water churning about us. The Acapulco boys bobbing in the water wave to us. I take off my sun hat and wave back.

As if it has moth wings, the rose Candelaria made for me flutters away from my hat. I watch helplessly as it swirls in the air, lifts for a moment, then drops into the water, bobbing and laughing before it's swallowed by foam.

But everyone's gone. My cousin and brothers have all disappeared. Only the grown-ups are within sight, climbing the stairs to the top deck, the wind whipping their hair like flames. It's too late. By the time I catch up with them, the shore is getting smaller and smaller.

—Now what? Mother asks, because she sees I'm crying.

—My flower, it fell in the water.

—Big deal.

—Don't cry, Lalita, Father says. —I'll buy you another one.

—¿Qué, qué, qué? the Grandmother asks. —What are we going to waste money on?

—She's crying over some flower she says she lost.

—Crying over a flower! Why, I lost both my parents when I was your age, but do you see me crying?

—But it was the flower Cande made for me! Do you think those boys could dive and find it maybe, Father? When we get back, I mean?

—Of course, my heaven. And if they don't, I'll jump in and find it myself. Don't you cry, corazón.

—Yeah, Mother adds. —Now run along and leave us alone.

I walk up and down the length of the boat, twice to the bathroom, drink three Cokes on the top deck, two on the bottom, wedge myself under stairways, lie down on benches, pick the cork out of sixteen bottle caps, but I can't forget. Maybe the ocean will wash my flower up on the beach maybe. Just as I'm making another trip to the bar for another Coke, a thick hairy arm grabs me by the shoulders and holds a plastic sword to my throat. It's a pirate with a mustache and eyebrows like Groucho Marx!

—Say whiskey.

A flashbulb flashes.

—Un recuerdo, the photographer says. —A lovely souvenir ready for you before we return to dock, very inexpensive. Go tell your parents, kid.

But I've already remembered what Rafa told me about how there isn't any money for any extras. It's too bad no one has told the Groucho Marx pirate and the photographer. Too late; they're already busy taking pictures of my brothers.

Father and Aunty Light-Skin have had it with the wind on the top deck and are busy telling stories to Rafa and Antonieta Araceli at the bar. Only the Grandmother and Mother are still up there when I get back. I can see the Grandmother's mouth opening and closing but can't hear what she's saying over the roar of wind and motor. Mother is sitting looking straight ahead saying nothing. Behind them, the town of Acapulco with its fancy hotels where the rich people stay—Reforma, Casablanca, Las Américas, El Mirador, La Bahía, Los Flamingos, Papagayo, La Riviera, Las Anclas, Las Palmas, Mozimba.

Before the sun even sets, the sea turns wild on us. We're all sick from the free Cokes, and can't wait to get back to land. It seems like forever before we pull into port and pile into the station wagon, the big boys climbing in the back, Antonieta Araceli in front between Father and the Grandmother, the little kids in the middle row on laps. Mother takes her place behind Father.

The Grandmother in a good mood insists on telling funny stories about her sons when they were little. Everyone's jabbering like monkeys, glad to be on shore, anxious to get back to Catita's and have a nice supper after having our stomachs cleaned out with Cokes.

I must look messy because Aunty sits me on her lap, takes my hair out from its rubber band, and combs it with her fingers. Then I remember:

—My flower! Stop the car. We forgot to go look for it!

—What flower, my heaven?

—The one I lost in the water, the one Candelaria made for me!

Mother starts laughing. Hysterically. Wildly. Like a witch who has swallowed a baby. At first we laugh too. But when she won't stop, it scares us. Like when Antonieta Araceli gets one of her seizures, or Toto suffers his famous nosebleeds. We don't know if we should hold her arms up, raise her feet, force her to lie down, press down on her tongue with a spoon, or what. Then, just as suddenly as she started, she stops, aims her eyes ahead toward the rearview mirror, locks eyes with Father's, and says one word:

—How?

Father's eyebrows crumple.

—How . . . could . . . you . . . think? What do you take me for? A fool? An imbecile? A complete *alcahueta?* Do you enjoy making me look stupid in front of your family?

—*Estás histérica,* Father says. —*Domínate.* Control yourself. You don't know what you're talking about.

—That's right. I don't. That's the big joke around here, isn't it? Everyone knows but the wife.

—Zoila! For the love of God! *No seas escandalosa.*

—Your mother had the kindness to finally tell me. Now . . . you who like stories so much, tell me this story, or should I tell it for you?

Aunty tries to hug me and cover my ears, but I've never seen Mother like this, and I squirm free. The whole car is quiet, as if the world has dissolved and no one else exists except Father and Mother.

Father is silent.

Mother says, —It *is* . . . It *is* true, isn't it? Everything your mother told me. She didn't make it up this time. She didn't have to, did she? Did she? Inocencio, I'm talking to you! Answer me.

Father looks straight ahead and keeps driving as if we aren't here.

—¡Canalla! You lie more by what you *don't* say, than what you do. You're nothing but a goddamn, shitty, liar! Liar! Liar!! Liar!!! And then she starts hammering Father's neck and shoulders with her fists.

Father swerves the car, almost hitting a man on a bicycle with a basket of sweet bread on his head, and screeches to a stop. The Grandmother opens her macaw wings and tries to shield Father from Mother's *trancazos,* crushing a yelping Antonieta Araceli. Aunty tries to straitjacket Mother with her arms, only this makes Mother even more furious.

—Let go of me, you floozy!

—Drive, drive! the Grandmother orders, because by now a small crowd has gathered at the curb, enjoying our grief. Father floors the station wagon, but it's hopeless.

—Let me out. Let me out of this car, or I'll jump, I swear! Mother starts to shriek. She opens the door as the car is moving, and forces Father to lurch to a halt again. Before anyone can stop her, Mother springs out like a *loca,* darting across busy traffic and disappearing into a scruffy neighborhood plaza. But where can Mother go? She doesn't have any money. All she's got is her husband and kids, and now she doesn't even want us.

Father jerks the car to a stop, and we all pile out.

—Zoila! Father shouts, but Mother runs as if the Devil is chasing her.

It's the hour everyone in Mexico parades out into the streets, just as dark comes down and the night air is damp and sticky with the smell of supper frying. Men, women, children, the plaza is bubbling over with people, roiling with the scents of roasted corn, raw sewage, flowers, rotten fruit, popcorn, gasoline, the fish soup of the Pacific, sweet talc, roasted meat, and horse shit. Across the square, a scratchy big-band version of "María bonita" blasts from plaza speakers. Streetlights stutter on just as Mother bumps into a vendor sprinkling lime juice and chile powder over a huge pork rind as large as a sun hat, almost knocking it out of his hands. —¡Ey, cuidado!

Mother stumbles over shoeshine boys and shoves her way through a knot of young men as lean and dark as beef jerky, standing idly about the newspaper kiosks.

—*Chulita,* am I the one you're looking for?

She scurries beyond the sad horse carriages with sad horses and sad drivers.

—Where can I take you, ma'am, where?

Mother runs on hysterically.

Children with seashell necklaces draped over both arms lap at her elbows. —*Seño, seño.* Mother doesn't see them.

She zigzags past idling buses, freezes in the middle of the street, then darts back toward the nearest park bench, where we find her settled calm as could be next to an innocent; a little girl with a dark, square face and braids looped on her head like a tiara.

Rafa and Ito are the first to catch up with Mother, but they stop short of getting too near her. Mother ignores everyone and everything and only comes back to life when Father appears.

—Zoila! Father says, out of breath. —For the love of God! Get back in the car!

—I'm never going anywhere with you again, you big fat liar! Never! What do you take me for?

—Zoila, please don't make a scene. *No seas escandalosa.* Be dignified . . .

—*Lárgate.* Scram! I'm warning you, don't come near me!

Father clamps on to Mother's arm and tries to force her to her feet, just to show he's still the boss, but Mother jerks herself free. The little girl sitting next to Mother scowls at Father fiercely.

—*¡No me toques!* Mother says. —*Suéltame. ¡Animal bruto!* she screams at the top of her lungs.

In two languages Mother hurls words like weapons, and they thump and thud their target with amazing accuracy. Guests peer out half-naked from the windows of third-class hotels, customers at fruit-drink stands twist around on barstools, taxi drivers abandon their cars, waiters forget their tips. The corn-on-the-cob vendor ignores his customers and moves in for a better view, as if we're the last episode of a favorite *telenovela*. Vendors, townspeople, tourists, everyone gathers around us to see who it is Mother is calling a big *caca*, a goat, an ox, a fat butt, a shameless, a deceiver, a savage, a barbarian, *un gran puto*.

At the sound of bad words, the Grandmother orders Aunty to take the girls to the car. Aunty scoops me up in her arms and tries to herd us back, but by now the crowd is pressing up against us, and she's forced to put me down again.

—Zoila, just get back in the car. Look at the scandal you're creating. This is no place to discuss family matters. Let's go back to our rooms and talk calmly like decent people.

—Ha! You must be nuts! I'm not going back anywhere with you. Forget it!

—What are you saying?

—You heard me. Forget it! As of now, we're through. Finished. *Finito. Se acabó.* Understand? Then she sticks her tongue out and gives him a loud raspberry.

Father stands there humiliated, dumbfounded. My brothers look scared. By now the crowd about us shifts nervously, like an audience watching an actor painfully trying to remember his lines. Father has to say something, but what?

—All right. All right! If that's what you want, Zoila, that's what you'll have. You want to break up our family, go right ahead. Lalita, who do you want to go with, your mother or me?

I open my mouth. But instead of words, big gulpy sobs hiccup out of me laced with cobwebs of spit. Rafa suddenly remembers he's the oldest and shoves his way over to my side, picking me up and hugging me.

—*Ya ves. Ya ves,* Father says. —See? I hope you're happy.

—*Mijo,* the Grandmother intervenes. —Let her be. You're better off without her kind. Wives come and go, but mothers, you have only one!

—Who are *you* to get involved in our affairs, *metiche!* Zoila snaps.

At this, some people cheer, some jeer. Some side with Mother. Some with Father. Some with the Grandmother. Some just stand there with their mouths open as if we're the greatest show on earth.

—*¡Atrevida!* You climbed up in life marrying my son, a Reyes, and don't think I don't know it. Now you have the nerve to talk to me like that. My son could've done a lot better than marrying a woman who can't even speak a proper Spanish. You sound like you escaped from the ranch. And to make matters even more sad, you're as dark as a slave.

The Grandmother says all this without remembering Uncle Fat-Face, who is as dark as Mother. Is that why the Grandmother loves him less than Father?

—*¡Vieja cabrona!* Mother hisses.

The crowd gasps in *susto,* and in disbelief. —What a blow! —And to an elder!

—Listen, you raise-heller, Mother continues. —You've wanted

nothing better than to break up this marriage since day one! Well, guess what? I don't give a good goddamn what stories you've got to tell me, I'm not going to give you the satisfaction, and you know why? 'Cause that's exactly what you want, ain't it? Comes what comes, like it or not, late or early, you're going to have to get used to it. I'm Inocencio's wife and the mother of his kids, you hear. I'm his legal wife. I'm a Reyes! And there's not a damn thing you can do about it.

—¡*Aprovechada!* the Grandmother counters. —Trash! Indian! I won't stand here and be publicly insulted. Inocencio, I insist you take us home. To Mexico City! Now!

—Inocencio, if you let that cow turd in our car, you can forget about ever seeing me or your kids again. Put her on a bus with her address pinned on her slip for all I care.

—What stupidities you talk. My son would never dare to put his own mother on a bus, you little *cualquiera*. That's how much you know!

—Well, I'm not getting in that car with you even if they tie you on the luggage rack. You're a witch, I hate you!

—Quiet! Stop already. Both of you! Father orders.

—Do whatever the hell you want, I don't care anymore, Mother says. —But I'm telling you, and I'm telling you only once. I'm not going *any-where* again with *that vieja!*

—Nor I with . . . *ésa*. Never, never, never! Not even if God commanded it, the Grandmother says. —*Mijo*, you'll have to choose . . . Her . . .

The Grandmother's fat finger points toward Mother, who is trembling with rage.

—Or me.

Father looks at his mother. And then at our mother. The mob around us circles tighter. Father raises his head skyward as if looking for a sign from heaven. The stars rattling like a drumroll.

Then Father does something he's never done in his life. Not before, nor since.

PART TWO

When I Was Dirt

•

"When I was dirt" . . . is how we begin a story that was before our time. Before we were born. Once we were dust and to dust we shall return. Ashes to ashes, dust to dust. A cross on our forehead on Ash Wednesday to remind us this is true.

For a long time I believe my first moment of existence is when I jump over a broom. I remember a house. I remember sunlight through a window, sunlight with dust motes sparkling in the air, and someone sweeping with a corn broom. A pile of dust on the floor, and I jump over it. Feet jumping over a dust pile; that was when the world began.

When I was dirt is when these stories begin. Before my time. Here is how I heard or didn't hear them. Here is how I imagine the stories happened, then. When I was sparkling and twirling and somersaulting happily in the air.

21.

So Here My History Begins for Your Good Understanding and My Poor Telling

*O*nce in the land of *los nopales,* before all the dogs were named after Woodrow Wilson, during that epoch when people still danced *el chotís, al cancán,* and *el vals* to a *violin, violoncelo,* and *salterio,* at the nose of a hill where a goddess appeared to an Indian, in that city founded when a serpent-devouring eagle perched on a cactus, beyond the twin volcanoes that were once prince and princess, under the sky and on the earth lived the woman Soledad and the man Narciso.

The woman Soledad is my Awful Grandmother. The man Narciso, my Little Grandfather. But as we begin this story they are simply themselves. They haven't bought the house on Destiny Street, number 12, yet. Nor have their sons been born and moved up north to that horrible country with its barbarian ways. Later, after my grandfather dies, my grandmother will come up north to live with us, until she suffers a terrible seizure that freezes her. Then she's left without words, except to stick the tip of her tongue between thin lips and sputter a frothy sentence of spit. So much left unsaid.

But this story is from the time of before. Before my Awful Grandmother became awful, before she became my father's mother. Once she had been a young woman who men looked at and women listened to. And before that she had been a girl.

Is there anyone alive who remembers the Awful Grandmother when

91

she was a child? Is there anyone left in the world who once heard her call out "Mamá?" It was such a long, long time ago.

¡Qué exagerada eres! It wasn't that long ago!

I have to exaggerate. It's just for the sake of the story. I need details. You never tell me anything.

And if I told you everything, what would there be for you to do, eh? I tell you just enough . . .

But not too much. Well, let me go on with the story, then.

And who's stopping you?

Soledad Reyes was a girl of good family, albeit humble, the daughter of famed *reboceros* from Santa María del Río, San Luis Potosí, where the finest shawls in all the republic come from, *rebozos* so light and thin they can be pulled through a wedding ring.

Her father, my great-grandfather Ambrosio Reyes, was a man who stank like a shipyard and whose fingernails were permanently stained blue. To tell the truth, the stink was not his fault. It was due to his expertise as a maker of black shawls, because black is the most difficult color to dye. The cloth must be soaked over and over in water where rusty skillets, pipes, nails, horseshoes, bed rails, chains, and wagon wheels have been left to dissolve.

Careful! Just enough, but not too much . . .

. . . Otherwise the cloth disintegrates and all the work is for nothing. So prized was the black *rebozo de olor*, it was said when the crazed ex-empress Carlota* was presented with one in her prison-castle in Belgium, she sniffed the cloth and joyously announced, —Today we leave for Mexico.

Just enough, but not too much.

Everyone in the world agreed Ambrosio Reyes' black shawls were the most exquisite anyone had ever seen, as black as Coyotepec pottery, as black as *huitlacoche*, the corn mushroom, as true-black as an *olla* of fresh-cooked black beans. But it was his wife Guillermina's fingers that gave the shawls their high value because of the fringe knotted into elaborate designs.

The art of *las empuntadoras* is so old, no one remembers whether it arrived from the east, from the *macramé* of Arabia through Spain, or from the west from the blue-sky bay of Acapulco where galleons bobbed weighted down with the fine porcelain, lacquerware, and expensive silk of Manila and China. Perhaps, as is often the case with things Mexican, it came from neither and both.[†] Guillermina's signature design, with its intricate knots looped into interlocking figure eights, took one hundred and forty-six hours to complete, but if you asked her how she did it, she'd say, —How should I know? It's my hands that know, not my head.

Guillermina's mother had taught her the *empuntadora's* art of counting and dividing the silk strands, of braiding and knotting them into fastidious rosettes, arcs, stars, diamonds, names, dates, and even dedications, and before her, her mother taught her as her own mother had learned it, so it was as if all the mothers and daughters were at work, all one thread interlocking and double-looping, each woman learning from the woman before, but adding a flourish that became her signature, then passing it on.

—Not like that, daughter, like this. It's just like braiding hair. Did you wash your hands?

—See this little spider design here, pay attention. The widow Elpidia will tell you different, but it was I who invented that.

—Hortensia, that shawl you sold the day before yesterday. Policarpa knotted the fringe, am I right? You can always tell Policarpa's work . . . it looks like she made it with her feet.

—*¡Puro cuento!* What a *mitotera* you are, Guillermina! You know I did that myself. You like weaving stories just to make trouble.

And so my grandmother as a newborn baby was wrapped within one of these famous *rebozos* of Santa María del Río, the shawls a Mexican painter claimed could serve as the national flag, the very same shawls wealthy wives coveted and stored in inlaid cedar boxes scented with apples and quinces. When my grandmother's face was still a fat cloverleaf, she was seated on a wooden crate beneath these precious *rebozos* and taught the names given each because of their color or design.

Watermelon, lantern, pearl. Rain, see, not to be confused with drizzle. Snow, dove-gray *columbino,* coral *jamoncillo.* Brown trimmed with white *coyote,* the rainbow *tornasoles,* red *quemado,* and the golden-yellow *maravilla.* See! I still remember!

Women across the republic, rich or poor, plain or beautiful, ancient or young, in the times of my grandmother all owned *rebozos*—the ones of real Chinese silk sold for prices so precious one asked for them as dowry and took them to the grave as one's burial shroud, as well as the cheap everyday variety made of cotton and bought at the market. Silk *rebozos* worn with the best dress—*de gala,* as they say. Cotton *rebozos* to carry a child, or to shoo away the flies. Devout *rebozos* to cover one's head with when entering church. Showy *rebozos* twisted and knotted in the hair with flowers and silver hair ornaments. The oldest, softest *rebozo* worn to bed. A *rebozo* as cradle, as umbrella or parasol, as basket when going to market, or modestly covering the blue-veined breast giving suck.

That world with its customs my grandmother witnessed.

Exactly!

It is only right, then, that she should have been a knotter of fringe as well, but when Soledad was still too little to braid her own hair, her mother died and left her without the language of knots and rosettes, of silk and *artisela*, of cotton and ikat-dyed secrets. There was no mother to take her hands and pass them over a dry snakeskin so her fingers would remember the patterns of diamonds.

When Guillermina departed from this world into that, she left behind an unfinished *rebozo*, the design so complex no other woman was able to finish it without undoing the threads and starting over.

—*Compadrito*, I'm sorry, I tried, but I can't. Just to undo a few inches nearly cost me my eyesight.

—Leave it like that, Ambrosio said. —Unfinished like her life.

Even with half its fringe hanging unbraided like mermaid's hair, it was an exquisite *rebozo* of five *tiras*, the cloth a beautiful blend of toffee, licorice, and vanilla stripes flecked with black and white, which is why they call this design a *caramelo*. The shawl was slippery-soft, of an excellent quality and weight, with astonishing fringe work resembling a cascade of fireworks on a field of sunflowers, but completely unsellable because of the unfinished *rapacejo*. Eventually it was forgotten, and Soledad was allowed to claim it as a plaything.

After Guillermina's sudden death, Ambrosio felt the urge to remarry. He had a child, a business, and his life ahead of him. He tied the knot with the baker's widow. But it must have been the years of black dye that seeped into Ambrosio Reyes' heart. How else to explain his dark ways? It was his new wife, a bitter woman who kneaded dough into ginger pigs, sugar shells, and buttery horns, who stole all his sweetness.

Because, to tell the truth, soon after remarrying, Ambrosio Reyes lost interest in his daughter the way one sometimes remembers the taste of a sweet but no longer longs for it. The memory was enough to satisfy him. He forgot he had once loved his Soledad, how he had enjoyed sitting with her in the doorway in a patch of sun, and how the top of her head smelled like warm chamomile tea, and this smell had made him happy. How he used to kiss a heart-shaped mole on the palm of her left hand and say, —This little mole is mine, right? How when she would ask for some *centavos* for a *chuchuluco*, he'd answer, —You are my *chuchuluco*, and pretend to gobble her up. But what most broke Soledad's heart was that he no longer asked her, —Who's my queen?

He no longer remembered—could it be? It was like the fairy tale "The Snow Queen," a bit of evil glass no bigger than a sliver had entered into his eye and heart, a tender pain that hurt when he thought about his daughter. If only he had chosen to think about her more often and dissolve that evil with tears. But Ambrosio Reyes behaved as most people do when it comes to painful thoughts. He chose not to think. And by not thinking, he allowed the memory to grow infected and more tender. How short is life and how long regret! Nothing could be done about it.

Poor Soledad. Her childhood without a childhood. She would never know what it was to have a father hold her again. There was no one to advise her, caress her, call her sweet names, soothe her, or save her. No one would touch her again with a mother's love. No soft hair across her cheek, only the soft fringe of the unfinished shawl, and now Soledad's fingers took to combing this, plaiting, unplaiting, plaiting, over and over, the language of the nervous hands. —Stop that, her stepmother would shout, but her hands never quit, even when she was sleeping.

She was thirty-three kilos of grief the day her father gave her away to his cousin in Mexico City. —It's for your own good, her father said. —You should be grateful. Of this his new wife had him convinced.

—Don't cry, Soledad. Your father is only thinking of your future. In the capital you'll have more opportunities, an education, a chance to meet a better category of people, you'll see.

So this part of the story if it were a *fotonovela* or *telenovela* could be called *Solamente Soledad* or *Sola en el mundo,* or *I'm Not to Blame,* or *What an* Historia *I've Lived.*

The unfinished *caramelo rebozo,* two dresses, and a pair of crooked shoes. This was what she was given when her father said, —Good-bye and may the Lord take care of you, and let her go to his cousin Fina's in the capital.

Soledad would remember her father's words. *Just enough, but not too much.* And though they were instructions on how to dye the black *rebozos* black, who would've guessed they would instruct her on how to live her life.

*The doomed empress Charlotte was the daughter of King Leopold of Belgium and wife to the well-meaning but foolish Austrian, the Archduke Maximilian of Hapsburg. Emperor Maximiliano and Empress Carlota were installed as rulers of Mexico in 1864 by disgruntled Mexican conservatives and clergy who believed foreign intervention would stabilize Mexico after the disastrous years of Santa Anna, who, as we recall, gave away half of Mexico to the United States. The puppet monarchs ruled for a few years, convinced that the Mexican people wanted them as their rulers—until the natives grew restless and France withdrew its troops.

Carlota left for Europe to seek Napoleon III's assistance, since he had promised to support them, but France had enough problems. He refused to see her. Abandoned and delirious, Carlota suffered a mental collapse and began to suspect everyone of trying to poison her. In desperation, she tried to enlist the aid of Pope Pius IX, and is the only woman "on record" to have spent the night at the Vatican, refusing to leave because she insisted it was the only safe refuge from Napoleon's assassins.

Meanwhile, back in Mexico, Maximiliano was executed by firing squad outside of Querétaro in 1866. Carlota was finally persuaded to return to her family in Belgium, where she lived exiled in a moated castle until her death in 1927 at the age of eighty-six.

I forgot to mention, Maximiliano was ousted by none other than Benito Juárez, the only pure-blooded Indian to rule Mexico. For a Hollywood version of the aforementioned, see Juarez, John Huston's 1939 film with the inestimable Bette Davis playing—who else—the madwoman.

†The rebozo was born in Mexico, but like all mestizos, it came from everywhere. It evolved from the cloths Indian women used to carry their babies, borrowed its knotted fringe from Spanish shawls, and was influenced by the silk embroideries from the imperial court of China exported to Manila, then Acapulco, via the Spanish galleons. During the colonial period, mestizo women were prohibited by statutes dictated by the Spanish Crown to dress like Indians, and since they had no means to buy clothing like the Spaniards', they began to weave cloth on the indigenous looms creating a long and narrow shawl that slowly was shaped by foreign influences. The quintessential Mexican rebozo is the rebozo de bolita, whose spotted design imitates a snakeskin, an animal venerated by the Indians in pre-Columbian times.

22

Sin Madre, Sin Padre, Sin Perro Que Me Ladre

*A*unty Fina lived in a building that would appear lovely only after demolition, surviving in a nostalgic hand-colored photograph by Manuel Ramos Sánchez, the Mexican Atget. In rosy pastels it seemed to rise like a dream of a more charming time . . .

It was never rosy, and it certainly wasn't charming. It was smelly, dank, noisy, hot, and filled with vermin.

Who's telling this story, you or me?

You.

Well, then.

Go on, go on.

It had withstood several centuries of epidemics, fires, earthquakes, floods, and families, with each age dividing its former elegance into tiny apartments crowded with ever-increasing inhabitants. No one is still alive who remembers where this building stood exactly, but let's assume it was on the Street of the Lost Child, since that would suit our story to perfection.

Nonsense! It wasn't like that at all. It was like this. At the back of a narrow courtyard, up a flight of stairs, in the fourth doorway of a wide hallway Aunty Fina and her children lived. To get there you first had to cross the open courtyard and pass under several archways . . .

. . . that gave the building a bit of a Moorish feeling?

That gave the building a bit of a dreary feeling.

Although the walls were damp and rust-stained, the courtyard was made cheerful with several potted bougainvillea plants, rubber trees, camellias, and caged canaries.

How you exaggerate! Where you get these ridiculous ideas from is beyond me.

Lined up along the walls were large clay water urns filled daily by the walking water carriers. And abandoned in front of a doorway or on the stairwell—that Mexican obsession, the pail and mop. The roof housed a skinny half-breed watchdog named el Lobo, several chickens, a rooster, and rows of clotheslines fluttering with bright laundry. Here on the roof, in that holy hour between light and dark, just as the stars blinked open, it was possible to find a little respite from the chaos of the world below, and here it was most often possible to find Soledad Reyes examining the horizon of the city.

Exactly! In that era, the capital was like the natives themselves, *chaparrita*, short and squat and hugging the earth.

Only the volcanoes and church towers rose above the low roofs like the old temples in the time of the many gods. There were no skyscrapers, and the tallest buildings did not exceed eight stories.

If you wanted to kill yourself you had to find a church.

In much the same way that victims had been sacrificed at the summit of a temple pyramid, they now sacrificed themselves by leaping from temple bell towers. At the time of Soledad's arrival, so many women had sought out churches for this express purpose that a proclamation was signed by all the bishops in the land and an edict issued that absolutely prohibited anyone from taking their life on church property. As a result, access to bell towers was strictly prohibited, except for bell ringers, masons, and priests, but even these had to be closely watched for signs of excessive sighing and dramatic outbursts. But let us take a look at this Soledad.

It's about time!

If this were a movie from Mexico's Golden Age of cinema, it would be black-and-white and no doubt a musical.

Like *Nosotros, los pobres*.

A perfect opportunity for humor, song, and, curiously enough, cheer.

—*L*et children be children, Aunty Fina says from behind a huge mountain of ironing. Aunty Fina is a huge mountain too. She has the face of a Mexican geisha, tiny feet and tiny hands, and everything she does she does slowly and with grace, as if she were underwater. —Let children be children, she says, the thin, high brows of her pretty geisha face rising even higher. She remembers her own childhood, and her heart becomes wide for these *pobres criaturas* she has brought into this world. This is why her children are allowed to do what they desire, and why she has room in her home and heart to take in Soledad.

One of her *pobres criaturas* is wearing nothing but a soiled sock, one is under the table breaking eggs with a hammer, one is lapping water from the dog's water bowl, one, old enough to chew, is demanding and receiving *teta,* and all whimpering, whining, squealing, squalling like a litter of wild things. Aunty Fina doesn't seem to notice or doesn't mind.

—Hey, hey, lady.

—That's not a lady! That's your cousin Soledad.

—Hey, hey, you. What's your favorite color?

—Red.

—Red! That's the Devil's favorite color.

This strikes them as terribly funny. A girl drinking a mug of milk spits it up from her nose and starts them on another fit of grunts. They all look the same to Soledad, these cousins, big heads, little pointy blue teeth, hair as raggedy as if they'd chewed it off themselves. At first they stand close to the wall and stare without speaking, but once they get over their shyness, they poke and pinch and spit like children raised by wolves. Soledad doesn't want to be poked at with a finger that's been who knows where.

—Go play, go on.

But they don't want to leave her.

—Hey, hey, Soledad.

—Don't you know you're supposed to call me "aunty" before saying my name? I'm older than you.

—Hey, you, aunty. Why is it you're so ugly?

Aunty Fina has so many children, she doesn't know how many she has. Soledad counts twelve, but they all have the same fat face, the same rosary bead eyes; it's difficult to tell them apart.

—But how many children do you have in all, Aunty Fina?

—Sixteen or nineteen or eighteen, I think. *Sólo Dios sabe.* Only God knows for certain.

—But how is it you don't know?

—Because some were dead before they were born. And some were born *angelitos*. And some were never born. And some disappear until we forget about them as if they *are* dead. One, a boy with hair like a hurricane, sent us a postcard once from Havana, and another time, a little ship made of coral and seashells that I still have somewhere, but that was years ago. The others? *Sólo Dios*. Only God.

This is the way Aunty Fina explains it, though later Soledad will hear about the baby who died from swallowing the poison set out for the rats, the one whose head was sliced at the neck when he fell off the back of a tram, the one who had a child of her own and was sent no one knows where, the one run off for doing pig things with the baby sisters. And so it goes. But who can blame Aunty Fina. Stories like these are not for a mother to be telling.

At Aunty Fina's there is a fury of smells doing battle with each other. In the beginning Soledad takes to breathing through her mouth, but after a while she gets used to the stinging cloud of laundry boiling in tubs of lye, the scorched-potato-skin scent of starched cloth steamed taut under the iron, the sour circles of cottage cheese stains on the shoulder from burping babies, the foggy seaside tang of urine, the bile of chamber pots.

Every day there is a never-ending hill of laundry to wash and iron, because Aunty Fina is a laundress. This is her penance for marrying for love. Her husband is a *morenito* with a moonlike face as smooth as a baby's butt and a long Mayan nose with a little drop of meat at the tip like rain. —It's that he's an *artista*, my Pío, Aunty Fina says proudly, as Pío shuffles through the kitchen in his underwear and slippers. Pío plays the guitar and sings romantic ballads with a traveling show; his art calls him often to the road. On her dresser altar Aunty Fina has a sepia postcard of this Pío wearing an embroidered *charro* outfit studded with silver and an enormous *sombrero* cocked at an angle that shadows an eye, the striped cord of his hat just under his pouting lower lip, a cigarette between the V of a thick hand sporting a gold lady's ring on the pinky finger. In a handwriting that looks like *The Arabian Nights*, Pío has personally dedicated the postcard "To the enchantress Anselma—affectionately, Pío." But Aunty Fina's name is Josefina.

It's during the time just before the revolution. Mexico City is known as the City of the Palaces, the Paris of the New World with its paved streets and leafy boulevards, its arabesque of balconies and streetlamps and trams and parks with striped balloons and fluttering flags and a military band in uniform playing a waltz beneath a curlicue pavilion.

Ah, I remember! Music from my time! "The Poetic Waltz," "Dreamer Waltz," "Love Waltz," "Caprice Waltz," "Melancholy Waltz," "Doubt," "Sad Gardens," "To Die for Your Love," "The Waltz Without a Name."

But what does Soledad know of all this? Her world ends and begins at Aunty Fina's. The only song her heart knows is . . .

"I Am So Alone."

There was the mailman with his mailman's whistle, shrill, filled with hope. Perhaps. That little leap the heart made when the whistle sounded. Perhaps. But there was never a letter for her. Not a note her father could have written himself, but at least something the scribe in the town square would've written for him. *My beloved daughter— Receive these salutations and kisses from your father. Hoping this letter finds you well and in good health. If God wills it, we will see each other soon. We are doing miraculously well and are ready to have you come back home to us immediately* . . . But there was no such letter. At times she would say, I am sad. Is my father perhaps sad and thinking of me at this moment too? Or, I am hungry and cold. Perhaps my father is hungry and cold at this very moment.* So that her own body by extension reminded her of that other body, that other home, that root, that being whom she could not help but think of whenever her body tugged her for attention.

In the daytime it was easy for the pain to dull itself, what with the children, and Aunty Fina's commands, and having to lock the door against Uncle Pío's funny ways, and make sure he wasn't around when she undressed, and always pulling the younger children near her for protection when she fell asleep. But after their whistled breathing began, that's when the things one does not want to think about rise, those things kept under lock and key, even in the dark they rose, and it was then she said, —Mamá. And the word startled her because it sounded both familiar and strange.

There. On the rooftop. Between the pillowslips and sheets and socks and string of dripping underwear, that one, that's her. Not much to look at really.

But not too bad either!

Long clown's face, thin lips, eyes like little houses, but who can see them beneath the sad collapse of eyebrows. Poor Cinderella tired of fetching water for this one's hair, bringing in the potted rubber tree, helping a child undo his pants to make *pipí*, running to the herb shop for a bit of *manzanilla* for this one's bellyache, for this one's ear infection, for this one's colic, for this one's head full of lice, well, there you have it. No wonder she is on the rooftop watching the night stars appear, the twin volcanoes, the electric lights of the town opening like stars, and all the things inside her opening too.

One day while watching the passersby walk down Aunty Fina's street, she said a prayer, —*San Martín Caballero, trae al hombre que yo quiero.* Then she leaned out over the wall and held her breath. —The next person who walks down the street will be my husband.

You have no idea what it was like to be so alone, to be left like the saying "without a mother, without a father, without even a dog to bark at me."

And just as she said, —The next one is . . . No sooner said than there he was, the one Divine Providence had sent to be her companion for life. There, walking down the street in his smart military cadet uniform, ringing the bell, walking across the courtyard tiles she had swept and mopped that morning, her cousin Narciso Reyes. And she ripe for the taking as a mango.

Later she will learn there is no home to go back to. The Mexican revolution begins, and Ambrosio Reyes is conscripted by Obregón's troops and never heard from again. Whether he was shot, or deserted as they say and began a homeopathic pharmacy in Bisbee, Arizona, or perhaps the rumor that he was strangled with one of his own black rebozos *is true (by his second wife, the baker's widow, no less!), or committed suicide by hanging himself from the rafters with an especially beautiful silk* rebozo de bolita—*well, who knows and* ni modo. *But* that *is another story.*

23.

A Man Ugly, Strong, and Proper
or Narciso Reyes, You Are My Destiny

*I*t was the cultural opinion of the times that men ought to
be *feos, fuertes, y formales*. Narciso Reyes was strong
and proper, but, no, he wasn't ugly. And this was unfortunate for reasons
we will later see.

What was fortuitous was his timely appearance. —The next one who
walks down the street . . . He came to deliver the money owed for the
week's laundry, because the week before, "the girl" had been let go and
no one else would go. If, at that moment, a *borracho* with nine layers of
piss had suddenly stumbled out of Orita Vuelvo—I'll Be Right Back
pulquería downstairs, who knows what a different story we would have
here. But it was Soledad's destiny to fall in love with Narciso Reyes. Like
all women with a bit of the witch in them, she knew this before Narciso
knew it himself.

So let us take a closer look at Narciso Reyes, a beautiful boy blessed
with a Milky Way of *lunares* floating across his creamy skin like arrows
instructing, —On this spot kiss me. Here I must insist on using the word
lunares, literally "moons," but I mean moles, or freckles, or beauty spots,
though none of these words comes close to capturing the Spanish equivalent with its sensibility of charm and poetry.

However, what was most striking about Narciso Reyes were his
eyes   all darkness with hardly any white showing, like the eyes of
horses, and it was this that fooled the world into believing him a sensitive
and tender soul. Fastidious, demanding, impatient, impertinent, impul-
sive, he was these things, but never sensitive and seldom tender.

Ay, but Narciso Reyes could be enchanting when he wanted to be. He was always clean, punctual, organized, precise, and expected no less from everyone around him. Of course, like those hypersensitive individuals quick to censure others, he was blind to his own habits that others found disgusting.

—You there, Narciso said to a woman bathing her children in the courtyard with a tin of water, a woman much older than himself who should've been addressed with more respect, except her poverty made her his inferior. —Tell me, you, where can I find the washerwoman Fina?

—In the back, back, back, back, back, little sir. *Ándele.* That's right. Up that flight of stairs. Where all the noise is coming from. Correct. Go right in, they can't hear you knocking.

Just as Narciso stepped in the door, *¡zas!* A bowl whizzed past his head, shattering in a hail of milk and clay shards.

—*¡Ay, escuincles!* Aunty Fina said in a tone both disgusted and resigned. She dabbed at Narciso with a diaper. —I am sorry. Look what a mess they've made of you. But you know how children are, right? Soledad! Where is that girl? Soledad!

If this were a movie, a few notes of a song would follow here, something romantic and tender and innocent on the piano, perhaps "The Waltz Without a Name"?

Enter Soledad from behind a flowered-curtain doorway, her hair freshly brushed with water. Soledad has draped herself in her *caramelo rebozo* as if she is one of the hero cadets of Chapultepec wrapped in the Mexican flag. The wolf-cousins start to snicker.

—Don't just stand there! Soledad, look at this *pobre.* Help me clean him up. Apologies, please pardon us, little sir. I do the best I can, but sometimes a mother's best isn't good enough, am I right?

Soledad cleaned Narciso with her *caramelo rebozo,* wiping that beautiful face as gently and as carefully as if he were the Santo Niño de Atocha statue at the corner church. She would've washed him with her tears and dried him with her hair if he asked.

—Many thanks, my queen.

—¡Papá!

—?

—Excuse me, please. I meant, of course, *pá-pa.*

—Potato?

—It's that . . . it's my favorite food.

—Potato?

—Yes.

She was ashamed she was ashamed. The house was throbbing with noise, bubbling over with unpleasant smells, and oh, such an elegant young man!

Young man? But they were cousins. That is, cousins of cousins. They were related the way the llama and the camel are related, I suppose. Some wisp of Reyes-ness could be detected in their physiognomy, but they had long ago evolved into separate branches of being. So separate, they did not know they were *familia*. Because "Reyes" is a common enough name, this was easy enough. And even Narciso, a proud and vain boy who considered himself well educated, did not ever suspect that Aunty Fina and her wolf cubs were Reyes too.

Just like a good *fotonovela* or *telenovela*.

Because she didn't know what else to do, Soledad chewed on the fringe of her *rebozo*. Oh, if only her mother were alive. She could have told her how to speak with her *rebozo*. How, for example, if a woman dips the fringe of her *rebozo* at the fountain when fetching water, this means —I am thinking of you. Or, how if she gathers her *rebozo* like a basket, and walks in front of the one she loves and accidentally lets the contents fall, if an orange and a piece of sugarcane tumble out, that means, —Yes, I accept you as my *novio*. Or if a woman allows a man to take up the left end of her *rebozo*, she is saying, —I agree to run away with you. How in some parts of Mexico, when the *rebozo* is worn with the two tips over her back, crossed over her head, she is telling the world, —I am a widow. If she allows it to fall loose to her feet, —I am a woman of the street and my love must be paid for with coins. Or knotted at the ends, —I wish to marry. And when she does marry, how her mother would place a pale blue *rebozo* on her head, meaning, —This daughter of mine is a virgin, I can vouch for it. But if she had her lady friend do it for her in her name, this meant, —Unused merchandise, well, who can say? Or perhaps in her old age she might instruct a daughter, —Now, don't forget, when I'm dead and my body is wrapped in my *rebozos*, it's the blue one on top, the black one beneath, because that's how it's done, my girl. But who was there to interpret the language of the *rebozo* to Soledad?

No one!

There was no one, you see, to guide her.

What a funny girl, Narciso could not help thinking to himself. But she was charming too, maybe because she would not look him in the eye, and there is some charm, even if it is a vain charm, in knowing one has power over another.

—Sir, you bring back that uniform, and we'll have it nice and tidy for you. Of that, I swear to you. Just bring it back, no charge, Aunty said.

What followed was a great deal of groveling and apologies and God-be-with-yous, because Spanish is very formal and made up of a hundred and one formalities as intricate and knotted as the fringe at the end of a *reboʐo*. It took forever, it seemed, for Narciso to convince Aunty Fina that he was fine, that no, the suit was not damaged, that a little milk is good for wool, that he only came to deliver some money and had to go now, thank you.

—Please have the kindness to accept our apologies for this inconvenience.

—There is no need for it.

—I beg you to be so kind as to forgive us.

—It could not be helped.

—We are eternally grateful. Know our humble home is always yours. We are here to serve you.

—A thousand thanks.

Et cetera, et cetera. And so, by and by, Narciso Reyes was able to make his escape. All this while the mute Soledad watched enraptured by his elegance, formality, and good manners. He was already out in the courtyard making his way down the steps and trotting out of her life forever when Soledad realized this truth. We are all born with our destiny. But sometimes we have to help our destiny a little.

—Wait! The word erupted from who knows where. Did she actually say that? On the first landing, Narciso obeyed as commanded. He waited.

And it was at this propitious moment that Soledad did what she did best, and did it with a fury. She started to cry. A bull's-eye of a coyote yowl that pierced Narciso in the heart.

—What's this? What's the matter? Who hurt you, my little queen? You tell me.

Such kindness only made Soledad cry even harder. Big, greedy gulps with her mouth like a dark cave, the body hiccuping for air, the face clownish and silly.

Now, what happened next one could interpret many ways. Because he hadn't been raised with women, Narciso didn't know what to do with women's tears. They confused him, upset him, made him angry because they stirred up his own emotions and left them in disarray. What Narciso did next was done impulsively, he would later reflect, out of a sincere desire to make things better, but how was he to know he was simply following the red thread of his destiny?

He kissed me.

Not a chaste on-the-forehead kiss. Not an on-the-cheek kiss of affection. Not a kiss of passion on the mouth. No, no. He had meant a kiss of consolation, a kiss on the eyebrow, but she moved suddenly, frightened by his closeness, and the kiss landed on her left eye, blinding her a little. A kiss that tasted of ocean.

Had the kiss been more lust-driven, Soledad would have been frightened by this sudden intimacy and fled, but since it arrived clumsily, it gave a suggestion of tenderness and immediate familiarity, of paternal protection. Soledad could not help but feel safe. A feeling of well-being, as if God was in the room. How long had it been since she felt like that? She mistook Narciso's mouth on her eye as meaning more than he had meant, and like a sunflower following the sun, her body instinctively turned itself toward his. It was just enough encouragement, but not too much. Oh, the body, that tattler, revealed itself in all its honesty. Hers, a hunger. His a hunger too . . . but of another kind

—Now will you tell me why you were crying?

—It's that . . . well. I don't know, sir. Have you ever been to Santa María del Río in San Luis Potosí?

—Never.

—How strange. It's as if I've always always known you, sir, and to see you walking away, it filled my heart with such sadness, I can't tell you. But I swear to you, it was as if my own father was abandoning me, understand?

Narciso started to laugh.

—Please don't make fun of me.

—I mean no disrespect, forgive me. It's that you say such curious things . . . What do they call you?

—Soledad.

—Well, now, Soledad, won't your family scold you for talking to boys on stairwells?

—I haven't anyone to scold me. My mother is dead. My father's people are in San Luis Potosí. And my aunty up there, well, it's as if she
wasn't my aunty. There's no one, see? I can do what I choose if she
doesn't notice I'm gone too long . . . and right now, well, I feel like talking to you, sir.

—Don't keep calling me "sir" as if I was an old man. My name's
Narciso.

—Ah, Narciso, is it? How elegant.

—Do you think so?

—Oh, yes. It suits you. A very fine name. Very fine.

—Yes, I suppose. I've often thought so myself, but it's much better to
hear someone else say it.

—A name fit for a king!

—That's very funny. Because my name *is rey*. Narciso Reyes del
Castillo, that is.

—Oh, and are you a Reyes too? Because I too . . . am surnamed
Reyes.

—Really?

—Yes.

—Well, well. How curious.

—Yes, how curious.

And here Soledad started to laugh, a bit too forcefully because she
didn't know what else to say. —You have very small feet. I mean, for a
man.

—Many thanks.

—There is no need to thank me.

—Well, good day.

—Good day. May things go well for you.

—And for you.

—Mister Narciso!

— . . .

—It's that . . . it's that . . .

And because she couldn't think what else to say, again she started to
cry, this time more violently than the first time.

—There, there, there. What is this? What's the matter with you?

At this point Soledad told him her whole life story. From as far back
as she could remember, sitting on her father's lap in the doorway of their

house in San Luis Potosí until her most recent nights here in the capital with her constant fear of Uncle Pío, who liked to lift her dress when she was sleeping. She talked and talked as she had never talked, because it's the stories you never talk about that you have the most to say. The words came out in a dirty stream of tears and snot; fortunately for Soledad, Narciso was a gentleman and offered his handkerchief and silence. When she was through delivering the long, sad story of her short life, Narciso felt somehow obligated to save her. He was, after all, a gentleman and a soldier, and this is what he said.

—Look, you can come and work for us. Why don't you? I'll talk to my mother. It's all right. The girl's been run off and we need somebody. Come right away if you like. There—it's settled.

Soledad said neither yes nor no. It was dizzying to decide one's fate, because, to tell the truth, she'd never made any decision regarding her own life, but rather had floated and whirled about like a dry leaf in a swirl of foamy water. Even now, though she thought she was making a choice, she was in reality only following the course already set out for her. She would go live with the Reyes del Castillo family.

Soledad leaned over the balustrade to watch Narciso skip down the stone steps two at a time and sprint across the sudsy courtyard where the neighbor woman was still bathing babies. The damp smell of wet stone rose in the air, and Soledad shivered from a chill that had nothing to do with the coolness of the morning. She shouted down to Narciso just as he reached the heavy Mexican colonial doors and uncorked the little door within a door.

—But where am I to present myself?

Narciso stood hunkered in that tiny door frame a moment, one foot on each side of the high wooden threshold. Behind him that shimmering white light of a Mexico City morning; in that epoch it was still transparent and silver as a polished coin. The racket of the street bustle—street cleaners, merchants with all of their merchandise on their back, chairs, baskets, brooms, the fruit vendor, the sherbet vendor, the charcoal vendor, the butter vendor, whistles and shouts, rattle of wheels, *clip-clop* of horses, hum of electric trams, hoarse, sad cries of the mules hauling streetcars, slap of *guaraches*, *click-click-click* of hard boots, the unmistakable Mexico City morning smell of hot oatmeal, orange peel, fresh-baked *bolillo* bread, and the ripe tang of sewer foulness. He stood half in that world and half in the cool shadow of the courtyard, a pretty profile in his military cadet uniform, hesitated for a second, and she thought, though she couldn't be sure, he puckered his mouth into a kiss. Then he reached over to tug the little door behind him, and only just before it thumped shut, tossed his reply over his shoulder like a white flower of hope . . .

24

Leandro Valle Street, Corner of Misericordia, Over by Santo Domingo

*S*oledad Reyes arrived on the 24th of June. She remembered the date because it was the feast day of Saint John the Baptist.

The day one customarily wakes before sunrise and bathes in the river.

At least it was the custom in the provinces back then. Nowadays, the citizens of Mexico City no longer bother with the river, but bring the river to you, dousing each other with water buckets or even water balloons.

In my day they cut one's hair with a hatchet, and everyone with their rosaries and scapulars chanting, San Juan, San Juan, *atole con pan* . . .

The Reyes del Castillo family lived in the *corazón* of the capital, off *la plaza de* Santo Domingo in an apartment with two balconies overlooking Leandro Valle Street, apartment number 37, building number 24, corner of Misericordia. In other times the building was a monastery for friars from Santo Domingo Church.

The very ones who directed the Santa Inquisición in the time of the colony. No, it's true, I swear to you. May the Devil come and yank my feet if I'm lying. Ask around if you don't believe me. And before it was a monastery, it was the site of an Aztec temple. They say the building stones came from that original building. Look how the walls are a meter thick after all. It might be true. Just as the stories of some *pobre*

111

buried inside them might be true too. Well, who knows, that's what they say. But I don't like to tell stories.

What was certain was the building's convenient location, only a stone's throw from the main plaza, the Zócalo. Tailors, printers, stationers, dry goods shops, jewelers, businesses of all kinds were housed in the street level of the old mansions built by the *conquistadores* and their children. Once Indians dressed in livery had stood at attention in front of these colonial doors. Once the pearl-and-diamond-adorned daughters and wives of *las familias buenas* had traveled to church in tasseled sedan chairs carried by West African slaves. Long ago, the finest days of these residences were already history. Slouched from the spongy shifting of the earth and scuffed from centuries of neglect, they still showed something of their former opulence, though seasons of rain and sun had faded their original brilliance like a gilded dress washed ashore in a tempest.

The Reyes' quarters were on the third floor, a huge apartment with high ceilings and too many bedrooms. Later in life Soledad would remember it as having so many bedrooms she couldn't remember how many. What she never forgot, however, was her first meeting with Narciso's parents. Señor Eleuterio began by making polite inquiries, but it was obvious who was the boss when la Señora Regina burst into the room, a woman dark and feral, with eyes that seemed to burn.

—I thought you said you were bringing someone to help me with the house. This *escuincla* looks like I have to help her put on her *calzones*. I bet she still wets the bed. You, do you wet the bed?

—No, ma'am.

—Well, you'd better not even think of it, little girl. Don't make more work for me. How old are you?

—Almost twelve.

—Almost? You mean one day you'll be twelve. Turn around. Your chest is as flat as your back, and your belly more curved than your ass. If they didn't see your face, people would think you were walking backwards! Ha-ha! Poor thing. *Pobrecita*. You can't help it you're not a beauty, right? Well, that's all right. We just need somebody who's willing to work. God can't be kind to everyone, no?

But God had been kind to la Señora Regina. As dark as a cat, she was no taller than Soledad, yet she held herself like a queen. Though Señora Regina had grown thick through the years, it was easy to see she had always been beautiful and used to being treated accordingly. Even now

Soledad felt a little afraid having that ferocious woman watch her so intently. If Regina had a *nagual,* an animal twin, it would have to be a jaguar. It's the same face you see in the Mayan glyphs and everywhere in the Mexican Museum of Anthropology. Snarled lips and slanted jaguar eyes. Often this face is seen even now driving an M&M-colored taxicab or handing you a corn-on-the-cob on a stick. This face, ancient, historic, eternal, so common it doesn't startle anyone but foreigners and artists.

And so, Narciso's mother found herself obliged to take in this little mosquito Soledad, since she had just run off "the girl" for pilfering cookies.

—Well, you certainly don't look like you would eat too much, you're all bones. And so, *niña,* tell me, what do you know how to do?

—I'm good at braiding hair. I can count, add, subtract, and divide; this I learned from braiding and unbraiding the fringe of a *rebozo.* And everyone says I'm excellent at picking head lice. I can peel potatoes and cut them into little squares. I helped my aunty with the children and with hanging the wash. I mop and sweep, and I know to scrub the patio with a bucket of suds and the broom. I make beds. I empty chamber pots. I can clean and trim the lamps. I was also taught to iron and to mend. I wash dishes and fetch water, and can run errands by myself. And I can write and read, but only if the words are small words. I know a little bit of simple embroidery, my basic Catechism, and all of a poem called "Green, White, and Red," which I recited once at an assembly when the governor came to our town. Well, I know just enough of everything.

—But not enough of anything.

—Just enough, but not too much.

—Ask her if she can sing.

—You keep out of this. Pay no attention to my husband. He thinks only of wasting his time on the piano while I slave away. That's how all los Reyes are. They live in the clouds. Always dreaming away their lives while the rest of us toil like *burros.*

It must be remembered that Soledad was a Reyes too, although of that backward, Indian variety that reminded Regina too much of her own humble roots,* a peasant Reyes from the country filled with witchcraft and superstition, still praying to the old gods along with the new, still stinking of *copal* and firewood. All the same, Regina took pity on her.

—*Pobrecita,* you can have the girl's room off the kitchen. And pull your weight by helping to keep the house in order. And doing occasional errands. And cleaning, it's nothing really, just me and my husband. And Narciso. When he's home from military school, which is hardly ever. Now, let me show you around. You're to change the linen weekly. And remember to air the pillows and blankets on the balcony thoroughly, make sure they're properly sunned. And if I find any dust under the bed . . .

—And when do you expect your other children to arrive, Señora Regina?

—My other children? I have no children other than Narciso.

Even with all those empty bedrooms, Soledad found herself without a real room of her own. She was given a cot in the pantry off the kitchen, behind a metal door with frosted glass divided into six panes, but only four of them were intact, and one of these was cracked. The door itself, once white, had yellowed to the color of Mexican sour cream, except along the edges where it was rusted. Because the house had shifted, the door couldn't be shut entirely without scraping against the tile, but at the slightest grating sound Señora Regina would begin to howl that she was suffering one of her migraines. That was why Soledad was always careful to lift the door a little when opening or shutting it, though after a while she found it easier just to leave it open.

I remember the apartment had a big, dark salon with dusty striped drapes very much in fashion then, called the *castillo* style, and a dining room with a red-tiled floor that had to be mopped every day because la Señora Regina liked the tiles to shine, but it didn't matter if you mopped them six times or sixty-six, as soon as they dried, they still looked dirty. And the kitchen! Big enough to dance in. The oven alone had six *hornillas* for coal! One of those old-fashioned types that had to be lit with an *ocote* stick bought from a street peddler.

Compared to Soledad's, Narciso's family lived in splendor. They preferred to think of themselves as one of *las familias buenas* whose coat of arms had once adorned the doors of these colonial buildings. After all, Señor Eleuterio was from Seville, as the family liked to remind anyone and everyone. But if the truth must be mentioned, though it seldom was—who would want to mention it?—los Reyes were far from wealthy, and just as far from real poverty. Although the Reyes accommodations were spacious, they paid rent and did not own the rooms they called home.

Señor Eleuterio Reyes was simply a piano player, who made his living as a music teacher at an elementary school—I once played for the president of the republic!—his wages no better than those of an unskilled laborer. But Regina was a clever woman.

—Let's just say I have my little commerce. Friends brought her used items to sell, and on weekends she had a stand in el Baratillo market, though she did not like to talk about this. But it was Regina's "little commerce" that enabled them to keep the apartment and keep the appearance that they were *gente adinerada,* especially during the harsh years to come when no one could afford to be proud.

The worst thing about living with Narciso's family wasn't the bones buried in the walls, or the too-many bedrooms, or the floor that never looked clean, or the room off the kitchen without any privacy, no. The worst thing was Señora Regina's kindness.

Regina was so pleasant it was terrible. —Well, Soledad, how lovely that dress fits you. It suits you. Like if it was made for you, really. Too bad you need a haircut. But otherwise you look perfect, I swear to you. You and the girl before you must be the same size. No, of course she won't be coming back for it. Because she's too fat now. She called herself *señorita,* but who knows. Think nothing of it. You're welcome. There is no need to. Thanks to la Virgen we're rid of that lice-ridden, backward girl. *Pobrecita.* Poor thing.

The clothes, the gifts of things la Señora Regina didn't want anymore made Soledad feel worse for having to accept and wear them. —Now, Soledad, you'll see. There's no need to thank me. You can't help it if you were raised wiping your ass with corn shucks and wandering about without shoes. A girl of your category is unaccustomed to any other way of life. How lucky you must feel now, living here like a queen.

Of course, sadness always arrives in greater doses after dark. Can crying help one get past a grief? A little perhaps. But not for always. After crying the room was still there with the clubfoot door, the six panes with two missing glass, the crack in one shaped like a question mark. Everything as it ever was, ever had been, and ever would be. Now and forevermore. Amen.

Because a life contains a multitude of stories and not a single strand explains precisely the who of who one is, we have to examine the complicated loops that allowed Regina to become la Señora Reyes.

Regina liked to think that by marrying Eleuterio Reyes she had purified her family blood, become Spanish, so to speak. In all honesty, her family was as dark as cajeta *and as humble as a* tortilla *of* nixtamal. *Her father made his living as a* mecapalero, *a man whose job it is to be a beast of burden, an ambulatory porter carrying on his back objects ten times his weight— chifforobes, barrels, other human beings. Today their equivalent are the bicycle taxi-rickshaws of the* Zócalo, *inhumane and degrading, but, it may be argued, an honest labor, and practical in this polluted and overcrowded age. Back in Señora Regina's times, however, it was sometimes necessary in the season of rain to hire someone like her father who strapped a chair on his back and for a small fee carried you across the flooded streets of the capital as safely as Saint Christopher transporting the infant Jesus across the raging stream. Regina should not have looked down too excessively on her neighbors, after all, since she had only risen in social standing by riding on the back of her husband, the Spaniard, in much the same way that her father's customers had crossed to safe ground by riding on his.*

Pobrecita *Señora Regina. She had not married for love. Once and long ago there had been a certain Santos Piedrasanta, a Judas-maker who killed himself for love of her. He made the papier-mâché Judas effigies burned on Sábado de Gloria, the Saturday before Easter, Judases to be strung up in the courtyard and exploded with fireworks into smoky bits of newsprint. During the rest of the year his business was* piñatas—*bulls, lyres, clowns, cowboys, radishes, roses, artichokes, watermelon slices—whatever you wanted, Santos Piedrasanta could make it. He was, in Señora Regina's own words, "... muy* atractivo, muy, muy, muy atractivo, pero mucho, ay, no sabes cuánto."[†]

To tell the truth, she loved and still loved this Santos Piedrasanta. She had even lost a tooth once in an ugly beating, but if asked, she would say, —It's that I fell from a eucalyptus tree when I was little. Only Narciso knew the truth. —Only you have heard this story, Narciso, only you.

How Regina had broken the Judas-maker's heart when she ran off and married the Spaniard. How, for love of her, Santos had put a gun to his own head, how Regina had watched as he destroyed that unforgettable beauty. Then she would unlock her walnut-wood armoire, and there in a drawer, inside a lacquered olinalá *box painted with two doves and a heart bound in a crown of thorns, there wrapped in cotton wool and a scrap of bottle-green velvet, a cheap black button, a keepsake from Santos Piedrasanta's jacket.*

And to see his mother chattering so animatedly, so stupidly, so childishly about a ghost who had once and long ago knocked out her tooth made Narciso realize how love makes a monkey of us all, and made him feel sorry for this woman, his mother, too young to be old, tethered to a memory and an aging husband who looked like the little brush used to scrub the pots.

When Regina first met her husband he was already old. She was just a fruit vendor at the San Juan market, sucking the sweet juice of a purple sugarcane stalk when he first laid eyes on her. —¿Qué va llevar, señor? What will you take, sir?—not realizing he would take her. Who knows how it was she fell under the spell of the piano player's waltzes. I can't pretend to invent what I don't know, but suffice it to say she married this Eleuterio even though she didn't love him all that much. He was like a big grizzled vulture, but so pale and hazel-eyed, Mexicans considered him handsome because of his Spanish blood. She, on the other hand, thought herself homely because of her Indian features, but in reality she was like la India Bonita, that Indian girl, wife of the gardener, whose beauty brought Maximilian to his knees as if he was a gardener too and not the emperor of Mexico. In other words, Regina was like the papaya slices she sold with lemon and a dash of chile; you could not help but want to take a little taste.

†*These words were actually Lola Alvarez Bravo's, the great Mexican photographer, but I loved them so much I had to "borrow" them here.*

25

God Squeezes

And then, because I was an orphan, or, at least a half-orphan, that is, I lost my mother, which everyone knows is as good as being a full orphan since you have no one to advise you, especially if one's father remarries. And so there I was, a good girl of good family, left just like the saying goes—*sin madre, sin padre, sin perro que me ladre*—after a typhoid epidemic swept through the town and left me motherless at an age when I still had trouble combing my own hair, and that's why I went about *despeinada,* with my hair in terrible knots, so terrible it was impossible to comb and had to be cut off on the feast of Saint John the Baptist, which is the 24th of June, and on this day they wake you early to bathe you in the river before sunrise, and they cut your hair with a hatchet, and everyone with their rosaries and scapulars chanting, —San Juan, San Juan, *atole con pan,* —and the flowers for Saint John the Baptist Day are white-white like jasmine, but with a scent of vanilla, but what was I telling you?

Look, so it happened that I, a girl of good family, though not wealthy, I, the poor relative, the Cinderella cousin of the family, one could say, because my stepmother had farmed me out just as if I was *una cualquiera,* an anybody, a country servant girl, oh, really, it makes me want to cry to tell you this part of the story, just as if I was a nobody nothing, my father allowed his own flesh and blood to be farmed out to service on account of his new wife, the wicked stepmother, who had him enchanted by some strong magic and who convinced him it would do me good to be in the capital, but in reality she just wanted to get me out of the way, you see, because I forgot to tell you she had her own children, this woman.

How can I tell you? Before my father remarried I lived the provincial life, yes I did, in Santa María del Río, where I studied catechism and embroidery. Well, it was a town where everyone went about smelling like horses, and so I was not at all opposed to going off to the city, you see, but how was I to know my situation would be no better than that of a servant's, even if it was the kitchen of my own father's cousin. What a barbarity! Well, here's a broom, they said, and there you are. My life no better than that of the rooftop dog that barked all night or the clucking chickens scraping among the orange peels.

Sometimes before nightfall, after everyone was through shouting for me to do this or that or who knows what, well, there I would be, on the rooftop watching the lights of the town opening like the night sky. I don't know, I've always been, well, the things I think I keep inside me. Only you have heard this story, Celaya, only you. It's that sometimes my heart's like a little canary in a cage, leaping back and forth, back and forth. And when that nervous canary won't keep still, so as not to feel so alone, I talk to God.

Because I wasn't bad, understand? I'd never been bad to anyone really. What had I done to deserve being locked up in that madhouse called a home? My Aunty Fina with her too many children, too exhausted to notice I was *una señorita* and well, there were things I needed to talk to someone about, and there I was living my hard times, but like the saying goes, God squeezes, but he doesn't choke. And well, I was so young and alone in that epoch, under that foreign sky, you can't imagine, so . . . how can I tell you?

Sometimes if I said I needed to confess myself, they'd let me run off to church. The coolness like the coolness inside the mouth of a mountain, like when one drives through a tunnel, understand? The stillness like the stillness before the world was born. And I remember a very odd memory that has no home and nook in which to shelf it. I was very young and sitting on someone's lap, and someone was putting my shoe on my foot and buttoning it, because you had to have a hook in those days to put on a shoe, and this someone, buttoning me, babying me, looking after me, well, I don't know for certain, but I think this someone was my mother. And if it was not my mother, it was God, which is the same as mother, as are all things good that happen to you, that feeling of being loved, being looked after, that feeling of absolute safety, absolute happiness, someone's arms around me, and feeling as if no one could ever hurt me. That was Mother. And God. Of this I am convinced.

Mija, remember, when you're most alone, God is nearby. And that time, before I met your grandfather, that was the most alone time in my memory, me a young *señorita* in the Paris of the New World, a city of grand balls and music and wonders to look and be looked at, but what did I know? The world ended and began at my Aunty Fina's, where no one said my name except to give me an order.

They buried my mother in one of her famous black shawls. They say the knuckles of her fingers were still black when they placed her rosary between her hands, because the only way to lessen the dye's hold is to soak the skin in vinegar, but my mother died on the hottest day of the year, and there was no time for formalities.

And me, all my life something of that habit of knotting and unbraiding has stayed with me, especially when I'm nervous. A rosary, or my braids, or the fringe of the tablecloth, I don't know. The fingers never forget, isn't that so? For several years, when I was most desperate, most alone, those years at my Aunty Fina's and later on in life as well, I would comfort myself by rubbing vinegar in my palms, and cry and sniff and cry, the smell of vinegar, the smell of tears, one as bitter as the other, no?

Because you have no idea what it was like to live with my Aunty Fina and her sixteen creatures. You can't imagine it. You've never been abandoned by your father. Your father would *never* do a thing like that.

Ah, but don't think my life was all sadness. After I married your grandfather, how happy we were.

You're getting ahead of the story, Grandmother.

Well, it was all very *divertido.* Like something out of a beautiful movie, you could say, even though we were never wealthy . . . I'm talking after the war, because in that epoch before the war, the family Reyes was considered *adinerada*—moneyed, that is. The men never dirtied their hands with work, and the women never had to dip their hands in soapy water except to bathe themselves. Because your great-grandfather Eleuterio was a musician, and teacher, remember. He even played the piano at the National Palace for President Porfirio Díaz and for families like los Limantour, Romero de Terreros, Rincón Gallardo, Lerdo de Tejada, *las familias popoff,* as they say. I remember Narciso had a box of his father's papers with many waltzes composed in his own hand. I have some of them, but who knows where they all are now.* Are you sitting on one of them?

I married into a family of category. At first I couldn't bring myself to eat in front of my husband. I'd eat in the kitchen. And since Mexican food requires you to wait hand and foot on the person eating, it was easy to wait until he was through. I'd say, —I'm not hungry, I already ate when I was cooking, or, —Eat, eat, before it gets cold, do you need any more *tortillas*? And there I'd be heating *tortillas* on the *comal*.

Which is why, in my opinion, the greatest culinary invention is the microwave oven, where one can heat *tortillas* a dozen at a time and sit down to eat like *la gente decente* instead of eating standing like horses.

Qué microwave oven, *ni qué nada*. You talk like a little fool. *Tortillas* never taste like *tortillas* unless they're scorched from the *comal*. *Tortillas* and a bowl of beans in their broth with a few spoonfuls of rice stirred in, the corn *tortilla* rolled tighter than a cigarette. Delicious! *Ay,* but Narciso made such a fuss, —Rice and beans mixed together! How vulgar! Then he went on for an hour about how you were supposed to bring out each course on a separate plate, and this is how he ate, as if he didn't think twice about who was washing the dishes. All his life Narciso would brag, —I don't even know what color the kitchen walls are, which is to say he never went in there.

Which is to say he was a real man.

Because here is where one can most tell what class a person is. By the way one eats. And by one's shoes. Narciso ate like the well-to-do, as if he was sure where his next meal was coming from, not gulping it all down in a hurry and not eating too much, and not picking things up with his hands, but holding his knife and fork exquisitely and cutting the food into small portions without dropping his utensils, and he didn't talk with his mouth full, or make smacky noises, or use a toothpick at the table, and, of course, he was accustomed to each course being served on a separate plate. He did not hold his knife and fork in a fist, or scoop up his food with *tortillas* in place of silverware as they did at Aunty Fina's. His manners at the table were very elegant. And his shoes? These were elegant too. Polished military boots, or lovely leather British wing tips. Well, he liked good things.

Look, I can truthfully say ours was a marriage of love. That is, Narciso and I married not as was accustomed in that epoch by arrangement, but because we fell in love. That is, I was taking care of the kitchen of the house of my Aunty Fina, who was also your grandfather's aunty, well, we were distant cousins. And then I was invited to work for your great-grandmother. And I think your grandfather felt sorry and sad for me, because back then I was pretty. And just like in the fairy tales, he fell in love with me, even though I was dusty from the house chores. All the same, he could see I was his love of loves. So, quick as could be, he arranged to have me stolen, and, well, we married, and there.

And because my Narciso was very clever, they gave him a little paper that certified he had been loyal to the Constitutional Government during the Ten Tragic Days of 1914 and assigned him a nice comfortable position with the National Roads Commission because of his war wound. A wound he suffered from a terrible *susto*. Which is why your grandfather could never bathe in the ocean when we went to Acapulco. Ah, but that story is another story, inside another story, inside a story.

Soon we shall see.

"A Waltz Without a Name" because I lost that paper but I remember it went . . .†

(Composer—el Señor Eleuterio Luis Gonzaga Francisco Javier Reyes Arriaga, born in the year 1871 and baptized that year as per records found in the rectory of Saint Stephen of Seville. This document proves without a doubt the family Reyes is directly descended from Spanish blood.)

I.
Tenía tal distinción
Que era de aquel salón.
Tal distinción que verla
y amarla todo fue en mi
y amor ardiente le declaré.

II.
Ella sonrió, mi ruego oyó.
También me dijo: Te quiero yo.
Pues si me quieres, le respondí,
un beso dame y seré feliz.

Si con un beso feliz te haré
después del baile te lo daré.

III.
(This is the page that was lost but it went more or less . . .)
En el salón un ruido atonador se escuchó,
un tiro fugaz que en el pecho de su amada dio,
y ya no pudo cumplir su palabra y hacerlo feliz.

Tan tán

†*This song was actually written by the author's great-grandfather, Enrique Cisneros Vásquez.*

26

Some Order, Some Progress, But Not Enough of Either

What was going through your head, Grandmother? You don't remember or you don't want to remember the details, and for a story to be believable you have to have details. You forgot to mention that the year of your arrival to the Reyes household was the centennial of Mexican independence, "the era of order and progress." Then as now, the president spent huge amounts of the national treasury to impress the world with how truly "civilized"—European— Mexico had become. You could've said, —I remember every building, avenue, plaza, and boulevard was flooded with tiny lights like pearls that made me happy. You must've noticed them along the Plaza of the Constitution, the Cathedral, the National Palace. The capital hadn't looked so splendid since the time of the emperor Maximiliano. While you slept in the kitchen pantry and ate rice soaked in bean broth, there were magnificent new public buildings under construction, the Venetian/Florentine-style post office, the opera house of Carrara marble, as ornate as wedding cakes. Guests from each "civilized" nation were invited, all expenses paid, and feted with nightly banquets where the imported champagne and the thick steaks never ended. Golden statues were commissioned and erected at prominent intersections so that future generations would always remember 1910. Each evening fireworks like a field of poppies hissed and whirled and popped above your rooftop twilights, while in the distance, plazas throbbed with sentimental waltzes and pompous military airs.

Grandmother, you always want to tell stories and then when you should tell them, you don't tell. What about the 16th of September, the day of the Centennial celebrations? Parades, bullfights, rodeos, receptions, balls, all to celebrate Don Porfirio's birthday as well as Mexico's Independence Day. Indians and beggars were routed from the downtown streets where you lived so as not to spoil the view. Thousands of pairs of machine-made trousers were handed out to the poor with instructions to wear these instead of those peasant cotton-whites. The parents of the shoeless were scolded into buying their children footwear or else face terrible fines, while the little girls of the well-to-do were recruited to toss rose petals in the Centennial parade before a phalanx of Indians dressed as "Indians."

In their finest splendor and riding the most sumptuous carriages, the invited ambassadors paid their respects escorted by a squadron of hussars in gala dress. Next, the Mexican calvary cantered by on tasseled horses as proud and handsome as the riders. You forgot the doomed Moctezuma carried in a gilt litter by sixteen sweating *infelices*, or the draped chariot filled with *chaparrita* Mexican Greek nymphs. In their hands, scrolls with wonderful words—*Patria, Progreso, Industria, Ciencia*—their meanings lost to most of the city's citizenry because they could not read.

Then as now, people voted for peace, and then as now, nobody believed their votes made a bit of difference. The government, run by los Científicos, sincerely believed science would and could lead them to the solution to the Theory of Everything. But the Theory of Everything would have to wait. By the time 1911 rolled in, the little revolution began. For the next decade, brother fought against brother, governments were toppled and replaced, soldiers were patriots one day, rebels the next.

Who could believe the petty violence in the countryside would mean anything to a girl in a kitchen? Hadn't the dictator-president, Don Porfirio, established order and progress, elected himself eight times for the good of the nation, and civilized the Mexicans so that they were the envy of other nations, so that boys like Narciso dreamed patriotic dreams of defending Mexico against U.S. invaders and dying an honorable death cloaked in the Mexican flag, like the "child heroes" of Chapultepec, young military cadets who threw themselves off the ramparts of this Mexico City castle rather than surrender to the advancing American troops in 1847. He could not know that by 1914 the Marines would again invade Mexico, and once again in 1916. By then Narciso Reyes would be involved in his own U.S. invasion by immigrating to Chicago. But now *I'm* getting ahead of the story.

Like the Pedro Infante movie *Los tres García*, let us spin the camera like a dizzy child in a *piñata* game and look at the story you would not, or could not tell. It happened during the Ten Tragic Days when President Madero found himself a prisoner in his own presidential palace. Some of the troops were loyal to the president, some were on the side of the rebels, and the million citizens of Mexico City found themselves caught in the crossfire. For ten days the streets were a battleground. Who would've thought the capital would be paralyzed? But life is always more astounding than anyone's imagination . . .

27

How Narciso Loses Three of His
Ribs During the Ten Tragic Days

—You? You wouldn't know where to find food if your life depended on it. And your life does depend upon it!

—If you're not satisfied with my services, *señora,* you can dismiss me.

—I most certainly will not. You owe me for that set of china you broke. And if you think you can walk out with a debt owed to your employer you had better light your candles to Saint Jude.

—In the name of God, leave her alone already, Regina. She's just a child.

—A week. Over a week we've been locked up in here. Like rats. Worse than rats. I'm sick of hiding under mattresses. How long can this go on? Who would dream this could happen in the capital? Never in my life . . . *Ay,* my head feels like it's struck with a *machete* every time that cannon goes off. How can anyone sleep in this hell? And how am I supposed to feed us with only a clove of garlic and two tomatoes in the pantry, tell me. But look how happy you two fools are. How pretty. One busy playing with the fringe of her shawl, and the other playing the piano.

Eleuterio said nothing. How could he defend himself? His wife didn't understand about art, how by creating something you can keep yourself from dying. Regina only understood *pesos,* not the mathematics of the heart.

—Enough, enough, enough, Eleuterio sighed. —I've had it with you shaming me. I'll go out and find us something to eat.

—Oh, no, you won't. If you don't know where to find food when there isn't a war, how are you going to learn now? How? Soledad, bring me a sheet. And not one of my good ones. From the rag pile.

Then Regina made them shove aside the piano they had braced against the door, and she went out into the deserted streets of Mexico City armed only with a white flag made from an embroidered pillowcase and the broom. From the shattered windows in the dining room, her husband and servant watched her marching down the center of Leandro Valle Street just as proud and as regal as if she were one of the flag bearers in last year's Centennial parade.

On the other side of town, Narciso was loyally making his way home to the apartment on Leandro Valle. —Mamá, he hiccuped under his breath. He had run most of the way, and now his side hurt. —Mamá. Calling her made him feel safer. —Mamá, Mamá. There is nothing Mexican men revere more than their mamas; they are the most devoted of sons, perhaps because their mamas are the most devoted of mamas . . . when it comes to their boys.

All his life Narciso had wanted to be a hero. And now here was his opportunity, and the smell of death made him feel like vomiting. The cadets had been assigned the worst jobs. Instead of the fighting they dreamed of, defending their country against a common enemy, now they were witnessing Mexicans fighting against Mexicans.

The dictator Porfirio Díaz had been ousted and forced to flee, and like many fleeing Mexican presidents before and since, he left for Europe with a good deal of the treasury in his suitcases. Then Madero was elected president. But a military coup led by one of his own generals upset his victory. The Mexican armed forces were divided. Some backed General Huerta in his attempt to take over the government, while some remained loyal to the new president. For ten days the capital and its citizens were caught in this scramble for power.

The boy cadets were given the details no one had time to deal with. Like burning the dead. Narciso was to go through the pockets for identification while two classmates doused the bodies with gasoline. It was heartbreaking to see the children lying in the streets as if they'd fallen asleep there, the old women and young mothers, the shopkeepers who should not have been caught in this business. What was happening to the country?

There were fires everywhere, it seemed, a string of sticky smoke stinging his eyes. Narciso covered his nose and mouth with his handkerchief. There was no time to bury anyone. Under orders, they were to burn the dead where they fell, otherwise epidemics could start. Sometimes the bodies jumped and squirmed like crackling in the pan. *Ay, qué feo.* It was horrible to watch. They sizzled and snapped, the fat running off them in streams. Narciso felt nauseous, his head light and dizzy, his eyes smarting.

Now he was making his way home as fast as he possibly could. He would only be gone from his work duty for a little while, he reasoned. Who would miss him? In the distance along a church, Narciso saw a desperate woman scuttling across a courtyard with a white flag tied to a broom. Somebody's mama, he thought. *Pobrecita,* and his heart contracted.

On a corner in front of a photographer's studio, an unfortunate in *campesino* whites lay jerking on the ground, black blood trickling from his eyes and mouth and ears. *Mamá,* he thought he heard the dying man cough before letting go life. Narciso shuddered and stumbled on. The shadows were long and slanted now and made him aware he needed to get home before dark. After sunset the city was totally dark except for the funeral fires.

How desolate the city looked. Every shop was closed, the metal curtains pulled shut over the entrances. Broken glass from upper windows lay scattered everywhere. It frightened Narciso to see the familiar streets so heavily damaged. Stay close to the walls, he told himself. Snipers were hiding on rooftops. When he reached the Zócalo he wanted to cry, but he reminded himself he was too old to cry. The plaster on several of the building facades was pocked with bullet holes and in some places a window opened to a piece of sky. *Feo, fuerte, y formal.* A man has got to be ugly, strong, and proper, he kept repeating to himself in order to keep from buckling under.

—*¿Quién vive?* a voice called out from under the darkness of the *portales.* The question meant—Whose side are you on? Madero? Or Huerta? Narciso paused for a moment. The wrong answer would surely be followed with bullets.

—Who lives, I said.

—I do, if God wills it.

Laughter.

—Shoot him first, talk politics later.

—¡¡¡ . . . !!!

—Stand him up against the wall.

—I say we execute him under the law of flight. Let him run and we say he was trying to escape.

—We might miss. Better he stand up against the wall.

Two soldiers escorted Narciso by either arm, because by now he could barely walk. He had to be dragged and forced to stand, since his legs had turned to rags and no longer obeyed him. His captors were arguing again as to how best to do away with him when, as Divine Providence would have it, at that very moment an officer passed by.

—What happened here?

—A prisoner attempting to escape, my captain.

—Let him go. I know this boy. His father and I visit the same barber.

After a very long time, long enough for Eleuterio to worry about his wife's health and regret he hadn't gone out himself, Regina appeared as joyous as if she'd just come back from a Sunday promenade in the Alameda park.

—*¡Viejo!* What luck is mine! Who do you think I ran into? Remember Agapito Molina? Agapito. You know the one. The fatty who works in the stables of *los ingleses.* That's him. Well, you can't imagine. He promised to deliver two sacks of oats tonight in exchange for the piano!

—No, not my Bosendorfer!

—Now, don't you start with one of your *berrinches, viejo.* This is no time for sentiment over a silly piano. I promise I'll get you another one later.

—My Bosendorfer for two sacks of oats? Regina, in the name of God, you have no idea of the value of this instrument. It isn't just a piano, it's a Bosendorfer, made by one of the oldest and finest piano makers in the world, the choice of European kings. Why, Franz Liszt owned a Bosendorfer. They say the young Liszt ruined several instruments in a single performance, so powerful was his playing, until a Bosendorfer was introduced and survived his fury!

—I don't want to hear another one of your stories. I've spent all morning risking my life looking for food while . . .

—But consider this, *señora*, Soledad interrupted. —Consider how the piano has served as a barricade against the door. In these times of trouble we may need it for more than music.

—Well . . . true enough. I hadn't thought about that. Let me see what else Agapito might like.

Narciso found his legs running and his body being dragged along following. He ran along the deserted streets like a madman. He stumbled, crawled, rolled, slid along walls, scraped his knuckles, dove into doorways, and scurried off with his bladder about to erupt, but he did not stop running until he could see the corner building on Misericordia and Leandro Valle. Clambering up the stairway two steps at a time, Narciso did not stop until he stood before the huge doors of his apartment, which he thumped savagely with his foot.

It was Regina who opened the door, startled and slightly annoyed. Before her stood her son, sweaty, filthy, exhausted.

—I knew it, I knew it. I knew I couldn't depend on you. You're just like your father. Don't worry about me. Who cares if I starve, I'm only your poor mother . . .

Narciso opened his mouth. He opened his throat, he emptied his lungs, he pushed and pushed, but no sound came out except a little hacking like when one has swallowed a chicken bone. He was not able to produce a syllable beyond letting go a weak cackle just before slumping to his knees and collapsing onto the red tiles that were never quite as clean as Regina would've liked them.

All the cathedral bells in the city were ringing when Narciso opened his eyes. For a moment he thought he was in heaven, but no, it was only the infirmary, and the ringing bells were welcoming the new president, General Huerta. Narciso had suffered a collapsed lung and had to be admitted at once to the army hospital, where they removed three of his ribs as easily as if they were sawing off three rungs of a ladder. They sent him home with a hole in his chest from which they say he breathed—I don't know how this is so, but this is the story told—and with the three pieces of bone that had once been his ribs wrapped in a gauzy bundle, like lunch knotted in a handkerchief. Thereafter the opening had to be daubed daily with iodine and bound in clean bandages, so that for the rest of his life Narciso Reyes could no longer enjoy the pleasures of soaking in a hot tub or swimming in the frothy bay of Acapulco.

The diagnosis was a collapsed lung, but the real cause of Narciso Reyes' trouble, as Regina never tired of explaining, was *susto*, fear, a Mexican malaise responsible for centuries of harm:

—It happened during the Ten Tragic Days when they stood him against the wall. My son Narciso expected a bullet, but it was *puro susto* that lodged itself inside him like a bit of metal.

28.
Nothing But Story

$\mathcal{L}$ater in life Narciso would brag how he'd lost three ribs in the decisive battle at Celaya, but, of course, this was nothing but story. Long before that historic battle he was already waiting out the end of the war in the United States. Narciso was just a kid with more acne on his face than facial hair. But he would remember his bachelor days in Chicago with fondness. He'd outgrown the patriotic notions about dying wrapped in the Mexican flag after the Ten Tragic Days. He'd seen enough of war to realize it was all senseless.

All his life Narciso would remember the bodies he'd been ordered to burn during the Ten Tragic Days, the dead children and women and *ancianos*. Just the thought of them made him feel like vomiting. He wondered if all soldiers felt that way, but were too cowardly to say so. It made him shudder. Any pang of guilt he felt for deserting his country fled the moment he touched the hole in his chest. He'd done his part, hadn't he? His mother didn't deserve to have her only son reduced to three ribs.

—I don't want my son reduced to three ribs, Regina said. —There. It's decided. Narciso, I'm sending you to your father's family in Chicago.

—But didn't Uncle Old commit unforgivable sins that have the whole family not speaking to him?

—Believe me, you're in less danger with your Uncle Old than if you stayed here in your own country, *mijo*.

Then she retreated to her bedroom and proceeded to light candles to all her saints, to la Divina Providencia, and especially to a huge gilded statue of la Virgen de Guadalupe ransacked from who knows where that dominated an entire wall of her room.

—Virgencita, I promise if you send my boy back to me whole, I'll do whatever is your will, do you hear me? she said, shouting to the wooden statue of Mexico's patroness. —Well, what? Have we got a deal? La Virgen de Guadalupe seemed to nod her head meekly.

Satisfied, Regina let her son wait out the revolution with a scoundrel who had run off to Cuba and later to the States after stealing the Mexican army payroll. I wish I could tell you about this episode in my family's history, but nobody talks about it, and I refuse to invent what I don't know.

It was a good thing Narciso left when he did. By the end of 1914 any man between the ages of fifteen and forty caught wandering the streets was rounded up, uniformed, and given a gun. Hunchbacks, invalids, vagabonds, street peddlers, *borrachos,* no one was safe. They caught them coming out of the bullring, or *cantinas,* or the movies. After dark everyone took cover or the draft wagons would collect you and you were in the army. If you were not good enough to kill, you were good enough to be killed. Even Eleuterio had to hide and stay indoors; well, even the old ones were being taken.

Water and light were hard to come by during the war. The *azoteas* of every home were filled with vessels of every type catching rainwater. Electricity was turned on intermittently and never when you expected, and candles were exorbitantly expensive. Due to their demand, people had to resort to making their own candles or returning to oil lamps, though oil was in short supply too.

Often the city was plunged in total darkness, which gave the false appearance of safety from snipers, bullets, and cannonballs. The whole population scurried about like mice grazing the walls. On some moonless nights one moved about discovering the world by hand, sometimes stumbling into doorways where couples were involved in peaceful pursuits. —Oh, pardon me!

As in the case of wars, those who benefited were not the most devout but the clever ones, and Regina was clever. She sold what came her way as people slowly parted with their possessions, but what she became famous for, what people knocked on the door for, day and night, night and day, was her cigarette business. She and Soledad rolled homemade cigarettes, because cigarettes are what people need most when they are afraid.

The years Narciso was away, so many unbelievable things happened to the citizens of Mexico City, they could only be true. The servant girl Soledad Reyes, in her kitchen kingdom, witnessed many things. A dog carrying away a human hand. A Villista shot dead while squatting to put on his *guaraches*. A cross-eyed *soldadera* leading a troop of soldiers. The fearsome Zapatistas marching into Mexico City, dusty as cows, humble and hungry, politely begging for hard *tortillas*.

Soledad Reyes saw cannons, and mausers, and neighbors hiding horses in upstairs bedrooms to keep them from being stolen. She saw a man waltzing across the Zócalo with a crystal chandelier bigger than he was tall. She saw a dismembered head mumble a filthy curse before dying. She saw a mule enter the main cathedral and genuflect when it reached the main altar. She saw the magnificent Zapata riding on a beautiful horse down the streets of the capital, and just as he crossed in front of her, he raised an elegant hand to his face and scratched his nose. These things she saw with her own eyes! It was only later when she was near the end of her life that she began to doubt what she'd actually seen and what she'd embroidered over time, because after a while the embroidery seems real and the real seems embroidery.

What she could vow was true was the hunger. That she remembered. During the war they'd eaten nothing but beans, *atole*, and *tortillas*, it seems, and, when they could get it, a bit of greasy bad-tasting meat that was supposed to be beef but was probably dog, a watery milk, coffee spiked with bread crumbs and chickpeas, lard and butter with cottonseed oil, and bread that tasted like paper.

In the meantime, Narciso wandered the streets of Chicago, where recruitment posters shouted: WE MUST HAVE VILLA, CAPTURE VILLA, WHO DO WE WANT?—VILLA, LET'S GET HIM. But even if they could catch the man who spat in the face of America and thumbed his nose at the red, white, and blue, what would they do with Villa if they caught him?

The invasion at Veracruz, the invasion sent to capture Villa. This was when the Mexicans began to name their dogs after Wilson.*

---

*In 1914 President Woodrow Wilson authorized the Marines to invade the port city of Tampico after American sailors entered a restricted dock and were arrested. At the time the U.S. was trying to bring about the destruction of General Huerta's government by encouraging the selling of American arms to northern revolutionaries like Pancho Villa. (This is interesting, since Wilson had supported this same General Huerta when he ousted President

Madero from office with a military coup. Madero and his vice president were arrested at the National Palace and under mysterious, or not-so-mysterious, circumstances were shot point-blank while being taken to the penitentiary for "safety." Newspapers reported he died during an attempt by his supporters to free him, but nobody believed this even then. Thanks to Woodrow Wilson's and the world's lack of protest, Huerta became president of Mexico. But I digress.)

Although Mexico released the detained U.S. sailors within the hour, on April 21 the U.S. Marines landed in "the halls of Moctezuma," and what resulted was a bloody battle with hundreds of civilian casualties. This "invasion" created strong anti-U.S. feelings, with the Mexican press urging citizens to retaliate against the "Pigs of Yanquilandia." Riots in Mexico City occurred. Mobs looted U.S.-owned businesses, destroyed a statue of George Washington, and scared the hell out of American tourists.

Of course, later Pancho Villa would counter with an invasion of his own. In March 1916, Villa and his men crossed the U.S. border and attacked Columbus, New Mexico. One of the first shots stopped the large clock in the railroad station at 4:11 a.m., and by the time the skirmish was over, eighteen Americans had been killed. President Wilson sent General John J. Pershing and six thousand American troops into Mexico to find Villa. But Villa and his men eluded them to the end. Wilson withdrew the forces in January of 1917, $130 million later.

29.

Trochemoche

—And so, I wound up here in Chicago, a city cursed with not one but two bad words for a name: "the fucked one" and "the one who shat," said Uncle Old, the frailest branch in that furious Reyes tree.

At seventy-three, Uncle Old was still laboring like a tired Sisyphus, though everything hurt him, even breathing. Uncle was at that stage in life when the body is a nuisance and one longs and looks forward to being dust again. He dragged this nuisance of a body about like someone wearing a winter coat on the hottest day in summer.

Poor thing. To tell the truth it gave one *lástima* to look at him. Pitiful, Narciso thought. Uncle Old and his sons, Chubby, Curly, and Snake, were wheezing out a living in an undersized upholstery shop on Halsted Street filled with oversized furniture, rotund chairs and sofas that produced great clouds of dust when punched. Maybe the Reyes ancestors and descendants were twirling about in those dusty galaxies. Maybe Destiny had paid Uncle Old back for all the pain he had created in one lifetime. Was the story true that when Uncle was still a young accountant in the Mexican army, he had stolen the payroll and run off to Cuba? They say in less than three months time he had exchanged the salary of 874 Mexican *federales* for Cuban rum, Cuban women, and Cuban gambling. —Isn't it amazing how fast you can spend money! Then he had hobbled about like a hobo until he found himself at his *destino*.

—And then what happened, Uncle?

—Who remembers and who cares, the fact is I'm here.

Isn't it funny, Narciso thought. Back home he had heard nothing but bragging about the family Reyes. But here he was having coffee with one of the stories, and the tale was far from heroic. Maybe there are some stories not worth mentioning.

—And what of the *mulatas*? Narciso asked. —Are they as sensational as they say?

—Sensational? said Uncle. —Exquisite is more like it.

Narciso waited for elaboration, but none came.

—Well, Uncle, aren't you the least bit homesick for your *patria*? I bet with the revolution you could try and go back to Mexico and no one would be the wiser.

—Go back? said Uncle. —I'm better off here. Once, when I was passing through Raymondville, Texas, I almost stayed there. There was a little shorty who wanted me to marry her, but when I met her family, a whole room full of shorties seated on wooden fruit crates, and the front lawn nothing but a little square of dust, and the chickens pecking on this dust, and my own hair full of that dust too, I saw my future, all my children pecking like chickens in that miserable square of dust. No, thank you. I'm not a rich man, but at least I'm not scratching dirt.

Narciso thought there was enough dirt and dust in Uncle's shop to make anyone scratch, but, of course, he didn't say this.

—And now look. With everything you read in the papers, Uncle continued, —well, it's better I didn't stay in Texas, or the Texas Rangers would've chased me home, right?*

Because Uncle Old's wife had died a long time ago, his house was a house of men, and as such there was no attention to things of the spirit. No tablecloth or napkins, no flower garden growing from an empty lard tin, no stack of clean pressed linen, no pretty plates. Items were spartan, utilitarian, makeshift, thrifty, and filthy. Newspapers served as a doormat, seat cushions, or tablecloth. *Fotonovela* pages sufficed as toilet reading and toilet paper. A bent nail on the bathroom door was the only defender of privacy. A coffee can and a galvanized tub were the bath. And so on and on. A helter-skelter, *trochemoche*, come-what-may, *venga lo que venga* style of living.

—There are three pleasures in the world, Uncle Old said, and laughed. —Eating, shitting, and fucking, in that order! He made fried bologna *tacos*. He used American cheese for *quesadillas*! What a barbarity! He scrambled eggs and wieners and served them on homemade flour *tortillas*. Each morning Uncle rolled out huge dusty towers of fresh flour *tortillas* for his boys and served them hot with butter and salt for breakfast, or if he was feeling daring, with peanut butter. —Nothing like a hot peanut butter *taco* and a cup of coffee, Uncle said.

Uncle Old was badly dressed and, worse, bad-smelling. This affected the sensibilities of Narciso greatly, who had taken such pride in his lineage, and now to be confronted with his family "living like Hungarians," meaning gypsies.

He wrote to his mother: *Why, they are no better than barbarians. I believe this is the influence of living in the United States, don't you think? They live in the very upholstery shop, with walls made from fabric scraps partitioning the workspace from the kitchen, if it can be called a kitchen. A camp stove is how they cook and a wooden door placed across two sawhorses is their table. The beds are any available furniture awaiting upholstery, a sofa or possibly two chairs pushed together, or the kitchen table. This is how they live, worse than soldiers camping in the field, for at least soldiers have order. The saddest part is that neither my uncle nor my cousins think it strange or want for anything better. It is astonishing!*

—And how did you learn to make the flour *tortillas*, Uncle? Narciso asked, since los Reyes were accustomed to eating corn *tortillas*.

—The army, Uncle said. —And necessity.

Narciso wrote: Tacos. *That's all they eat here. Or hot dogs, which is like an American* taco. *You would think they'd forgotten a delicious squash blossom soup, or* chile en nogada *in walnut sauce and pomegranates, or red snapper Veracruz-style, or any and all the other sublime delicacies of Mexican cooking. And what the Mexican restaurants here call Mexican food, it's truly sad!*

Narciso had arrived with hats, suits, linen shirts, and silk handkerchiefs with matching ascots. And here he was, expected to sweep the shop and strip furniture down to its frame! He'd never held a hammer, much less a broom. His imported British wing tips were ruined within a week, the leather scuffed, the soles pocked with tacks. Each night he plucked them out with pliers, counting as he worked while the cousins laughed at him behind his back.

What was truly barbarous was the schoolroom map of the United States his uncle had glued to the bathroom wall with corn syrup. It depicted the states in different colors with their capitals marked with a star. Each time he entered the bathroom, Narciso made it a point to memorize one state and its capital. He thought this knowledge might keep his memory sharp and distinguish him from the lowlifes called his cousins.

—But tell me, Uncle, why did you put the map up with corn syrup?

—Because there wasn't any glue on hand when we thought to hang it.

All in all, Uncle Old seemed satisfied with what the United States had given him. It wasn't a luxurious life, but it was a life and it was his. He had picked up a little of this and that over the years, and the this and that had paid a living. So, unlike his cousin Eleuterio of the piano hands, Uncle Old's hands were covered with the calluses and blisters of his craft, the art and labor of making sofas and chairs. *Awful work,* Narciso thought, *thank God I don't have to do this forever.* His own hands with their perfect Palmer penmanship were not used to the hammer, and standing all day on hard concrete was giving him corns as stout and sturdy as the shells on the backs of turtles. —My feet are very sensitive, Narciso complained, soaking his feet nightly in a tub of hot water. *What a prince,* Uncle thought, but didn't say this.

The condition of Prince Narciso's feet did not improve during the seven years he lived with his Uncle Old. They were as abused at the end of his U.S. stay as they were in the beginning, not from labor by then, but from pleasure. Narciso danced all weekend at the black-and-tan clubs on South State Street. This was during the time the Charleston was outlawed in some U.S. cities.[†]

In those days the most beautiful women were the stars of the silent screen. Women everywhere copied them and painted their mouths like valentines. But the woman Narciso Reyes fell in love with not only had a mouth like a cupid's heart, but an ass like one upside down.

He'd seen her live onstage, a girl with beautiful legs and a behind like no one else's. The woman was like the milk with a drizzle of coffee his mother served him as a boy before bedtime, coffee with lots of sugar, a woman who made him happy just by looking at her. She was happiness, a born comedienne. The audience was hers the moment she entered the spotlight. Her act was part pantomime, part acrobat, part dance. She laughed and winked, crossed her eyes, put her hands on her hips, pouted, pirouetted, stuck her butt out and shook it, did a Charleston, then a split, a somersault, then waddled off the stage only to cartwheel back and finish with a shimmy that shattered the house and nearly killed Narciso.

Narciso came to every show, made a pest of himself backstage, and fancied himself in love. He could not believe his good fortune when she plunked herself down on his lap one day, all arms and wiggling tongue. Oh, to have such a woman as this. When he pressed his mouth to hers, he was filled with joy too. The laughter gurgled and overflowed and entered him, and energized and filled him with life. He decided he would marry this Freda McDonald who called herself Tumpy, who went by the stage name of Josephine Wells, showgirl with caramel skin. He would take care of her, he would tame her and make her his. He wept to hear her tale of how she had had to fight for everything that was hers. How she had run away from her hometown of Saint Louis in 1917, the same year as the race riots. How whites worried Southern Negroes were taking away their jobs even though most whites wouldn't work for $2.35 a day in the sewer-pipe factory if you paid them!

—Freda McDonald, please do me the kindness of accepting . . .

—I told you, nobody calls me Freda but my mother. Can't you read the marquee? My name is Jo. Jo Wells. But you can call me Tumpy. Which Narciso pronounced as "*Tom-pi.*" His English made her laugh.

—Tompita, heart of mine, I must ask you this . . .

—Honey, you name it.

—Please will you . . . ? The capital of Idaho, what is?

—Shit, hell if I know.

—Oh, you *keed*!

And they wrestled and laughed and squealed, he trying to impress her with the names of all the U.S. states and their capitals—Springfield, Illinois; Sacramento, California; Austin, Texas—and she laughing and laughing at his funny way of talking.

In his arms her body glittered and shimmered and squirmed. It was like making love with a river of mercury, a boa constrictor, a weasel. It was lovely, *bruto*, tender, *bonito, bonito.* He'd had women pink as a rabbit, and dark as bitter chocolate, and all the *caramelo* shades in between. He'd had and had, and he was never filled up, never.

Until now.

Narciso wrote a letter home to his father: *Father, she is Spanish like you. Well, Spanish on her father's side. Her mother is half Cherokee and half Negro. But all together she is a real American and wonderful, and when you meet her . . .*

¡Qué! What! *Una negra* to be his daughter-in-law! *Una negra* to become a Reyes! But this was too much. Eleuterio forgot that his own family would've disowned him if they'd met Regina. Of course, like everyone, his memory was selective and he didn't think of this.

It happened that Narciso's letter arrived while his father was eating breakfast, but Eleuterio was never able to finish the meal. The news in his son's letter caused Eleuterio his own death shimmy. Regina wired her SON: FATHER DEAD RETURN HOME.

—My sky, I tell you in all confidence, for you I will die, but I have compromises now. You will wait? Promise, Tompita, my queen.

—Chili pie, I'll do nothing but cry till you send for me.

As Destiny would have it, Narciso was boarding a train south to the border when Freda Josephine Tumpy McDonald Wells was also standing on another track in a felt cloche and a raccoon-collar coat, a cardboard suitcase with all her belongings beside her. Freda left Chicago with the company that same afternoon en route to Philadelphia to marry Billy Baker, abandon Billy Baker for New York, abandon New York for Paris, dance with a banana skirt, and well, the rest everybody knows is history.

In 1915 more than half of the Mexican-American population emigrated from the Valley of Texas into war-torn Mexico fleeing the Texas Rangers, rural police ordered to suppress an armed rebellion of Mexican Americans protesting Anglo-American authority in South Texas. Supported by U.S. cavalry, their bullying led to the death of hundreds, some say thousands, of Mexicans and Mexican Americans, who were executed without trial. The end result was that Mexican-owned land was cleared, allowing development by Anglo newcomers. So often were Mexicans killed at the hands of the "Rinches," that the San Antonio Express-News said it "has become so commonplace" that "it created little or no interest." Little or no interest unless you were Mexican.

†The Charleston was named "the Dance of Death" after a Boston tragedy that claimed 147 lives when a Charleston-throbbing dance floor collapsed in a heap, causing the building to do the Charleston too. Variety reported: "The offbeat rhythm of the Charleston, reinforced by the indulgence in things alcoholic is said to have caused the Hotel Pickwick to sway so violently that it fell apart."

30.

A Poco—You're Kidding

$\mathcal{E}$leuterio was finishing a boiled egg and the heel of a toasted *bolillo* when he read his son's letter. The shock proved so great, he suffered *un fuerte coraje,* that national syndrome known as a terrible rage, and on October 12, 1921, he was declared dead from a cerebral embolism. Because it isn't the custom in that country to embalm the dead, Eleuterio's corpse was simply displayed in the living room in his best suit, a black rosary laced in his hands, four candles lit at each corner, and on his belly a fan of red gladioli, the collective gift of his wife's flea market customers.

This next part of the story I know sounds as if I am making it up, but the facts are so unbelievable they can only be true. The room was filled with the respectful murmur of a novena when Eleuterio's niece let out a shriek like a dagger. Everyone thought she cried from grief. —What a good girl, that one, you can see she loved him the best. But it was because of what she noticed when she kissed the corpse good-bye. —He's still warm! Look, his eyelids are twitching! It was true, even in death something behind his eyelids seemed to dance as nervously as it had when he was alive. —*Virgen Purísima,* he's alive!

Immediately the doctor was summoned, the body moved to a bed, and all the hangers-on and relatives were first politely and then rudely requested to leave, because by now there were a lot of curious people about, neighbors and those walking down the street to see what they could see, *metiches,* busybodies, *mirones,* oglers, and *mitoteros,* liars/gossips/ storytellers/troublemakers all rolled into one. These the doctor ordered out. Then with a stiff brush and rubbing alcohol, the doctor scrubbed Eleuterio back to life.

Little by little the body began to regain its color, and little by little Eleuterio Reyes began to breathe normally; accordingly, the doctor amended his final diagnosis from cerebral embolism to a cataleptic attack. Everyone was overjoyed, and a bottle of *rompope* was opened and glasses of that thick rum eggnog passed around.

It was an exuberant moment, perhaps the only epiphany in that decade of deprivations, until it was discovered that God had a wicked sense of humor.

Eleuterio was only half alive. Only the right half of his body awoke from the dead. The left half remained as sleep-filled as the day of his wake. From then on Eleuterio dragged himself about the apartment with a cane and mumbled a curious language made up of grunts, gestures, and spit that no one but Soledad could understand.

That evening the family celebrated Eleuterio's half-resurrection. Then all the blood relatives signed a will. I, so and so, do hereby request that upon death I have my veins opened, or have my heart stabbed with a hat pin, or both, before burial to avoid being buried alive in the sad event I have inherited Eleuterio Reyes' rare and unfortunate condition, et cetera, et cetera. Something like this, more or less, because that paper was lost among all the other items of no consequence that no one can remember exactly and no one can entirely forget.

31

The Feet of Narciso Reyes

All his life Narciso never knew what was happening to him when it happened. As if his life was a pair of dice, and the world a cup that shook him about and let him drop at odd moments. Only after the rattling and rolling did he realize what numbers life had cast him. That is how it was love flourished without his being aware of it. He had only to feel the sharp pain in his chest to be reminded he was alive. And love is like that, too, constantly reminding us with its sharp delights and sharp pains, that we are, alas, alive.

When Narciso came home, Regina took one look at him and realized her baby was gone. In his place was *un fanfarrón,* a young peacock, a man with glints of the boy gleaming here and there, now and then, depending on the angle or the light. His neck was thick and powerful, there was a buoyant spring to his walk now, and his body had grown taut and strong. But there was something else. Something throbbing in his eyes, or perhaps something no longer there. He had that look people have when they've experienced a disappointment in life.

Why do people delight in inflicting bad news? Even before Narciso's train pulled into Mexico City, a telegram from his Chicago cousins arrived that promptly and joyously reported his jilting. A pain wheezed from that little wound above the little wound—the hole in his heart where Narciso had once harbored *la negrita* Tompi. *Ah,* Regina thought to herself, *he has the look of a man deprived of a mother's love; I'll fix that.*

Among her other duties, Soledad was now assigned to help keep Narciso clean. Never mind that he had taken care of himself just fine when he had lived in Chicago all those years. Now that he was home, Regina insisted that Soledad act as his nurse, and Soledad was now obliging with a washbasin and a kettle of hot water she had heated on the stove.

—When they put me against the wall, I thought they'd shot me even before I heard a gunshot, because I felt a little heat trickle out from my body and run down my leg. Only later when I began to stink with fear, because fear stinks, did you know? Only then did I realize it wasn't blood, but urine.

—You're lying! Soledad said.

—I swear to God it's the truth. It's almost like the story of Adam when God borrowed his rib to make Eve. They had to saw through three of my ribs, put your hand here. That's what they did to get to the lung that collapsed, because that's what happened to me, Narciso explained.

—What a barbarity! And is it true you can never swim anymore?

—Never, Narciso said, hanging his head and pretending to feel sorry for himself.

Narciso's displays of sadness only endeared him to his nurse. Such a helpless thing, and with eyes as tender and dark as *café de olla,* as if at any moment he was about to cry. He looked sadder than she remembered him. More alone. This made him even more attractive. Sweet, Soledad could not help noticing, and those feet—too small for a man.

Such delicate feet! Soft as doves, as pale as the behind of a nun, luminescent as the wings of moths under the nacre moon, as delicately veined as marble and as transparent as a teacup. Once they had been smooth as river stones, but now they were calloused like her own.

—Corns, Narciso explained. —Up north I had to work *como un negro.*

Which is to say he worked very hard. The truth, the corns were from dancing the Charleston all night, not from hard labor.

In that instant Soledad's heart flooded with pity. She wanted to bless those feet with kisses, caress, cradle, bathe them in milk. But as always, she was afraid of her feelings and simply said, —You've got hooves like a girl's. This was meant as a compliment but taken as an insult.

Narciso Reyes let out a laugh as if he was used to being ridiculed. The girl Soledad brought out strange feelings in him. He remembered the first time he'd felt like this, a long time ago that first day he talked to her, on the stairwell of her Aunty Fina's. He had tried to comfort her with a kiss, but missed; a crooked kiss of childhood that had landed on her eye, blinding her a little. They'd been kids. And now here she was all filled out with a nice little behind and a sweet bounce in her blouse every time she moved. He'd show her a thing or two he'd picked up in Chicago.

Then Narciso Reyes tugged Soledad toward him and kissed the woman who would become the mother of his children. In that kiss was his destiny. And hers.

32

The World Does Not Understand Eleuterio Reyes

*E*ven with a lifetime of experiences, life takes one by surprise. So Eleuterio Reyes was astonished not only to have died but to be alive again and to have his only child at his bedside. Here was his Narciso, a little lizard strutting about in a tight suit and patent leather shoes, a red carnation in his buttonhole. He was nothing but a baby-faced dandy, a mama's boy, a frightened spoiled brat, a snot-nosed kid disguised as a man, crying real tears, promising on his knees, —I'll do anything you say, Father, name it, just don't die on me again.

What else could Eleuterio do but laugh, since any words he tried to speak came out sounding like gargling. He laughed, then—a hacking fit that frightened his relations into thinking he was having another attack. Because he no longer had a language to explain himself, Eleuterio's laughter arrived at what appeared to be odd moments. The family thought him a little senile since his resurrection, though inside that sluggish sea of body, he was stranded on an ice floe, hopelessly alert.

Fortunately, Eleuterio Reyes retained his ability to play the piano, if only with his right hand, and this perhaps saved him from jumping off a church tower. He composed some uncomplicated, entertaining pieces, and it was here he found solace from the world that did not understand him. His music was quick, elegant, lithe, and as overly romantic as ever. It didn't matter if he wasn't. With the gentlemanly manners of another era, a pencil, and imagination, Eleuterio Reyes composed several waltzes that revealed, if anyone had taken the time to listen, how explicitly naive and youthful he still was. The soul never ages, the soul, ball of light tethered to that nuisance the body.

Eleuterio Reyes was trying his best to rise from the ashes of his near-death, and the Mexican nation was doing the same. So it happened that Narciso returned at a time when Mexico City was busy with balls, benefits, and fundraisers, as if reconstruction began by filling a dance card. Who could blame the citizens? Men were tired of jumping over dead bodies. Women were sick of grieving. The city, like its troops, was exhausted, sad, and dirty, disgusted with seeing ten years of things they wished they hadn't seen, ready to forget with a *fiesta*.

In the decade of war, Mexico City had cheered a great confusion of leaders. The morning that Madero marched triumphantly into the city, the citizens shouted *vivas*. When the Ten Tragic Days ended and Huerta assumed power, the church bells rang and high masses were said in his honor. A short time later, when Huerta fled, they rang again as if to say, —Good riddance. Women stood on balconies throwing kisses and flowers to the victorious Villa and Zapata,* who marched in like caesars, and the city whooped again when it was Carranza, and just as sincerely for his rival, the one-armed Obregón. It wasn't that they were fickle. It was peace they were welcoming, not leaders. They'd had enough of war.

For Regina the war had meant an opportunity at finding her true calling. As in all wars, those who flourish are not the best people but the most clever and hard-hearted. Regina's little commerce not only sustained the family through difficult times, but prospered and moved them up a notch in economic status. Now their apartment was packed with enough furniture to make it look like La Ciudad de Londres department store. Narciso had to climb over brass cuspidors, musical birdcages, obscene mirrors bigger than beds, Venetian finger bowls, crystal chandeliers, candelabras, carved platters, silver tea sets, leather-bound books, past paintings of nude chubbies, and portraits of chaste teen nuns taking their vows.

All the beds served as counters for displaying linens, even the one Regina slept in; she simply made a little room for herself at the foot of it, beneath velvet antimacassars, Oriental pillows, fringed draperies of satin and chintz and brocade, towers of embroidered sheets, towels, and pillowslips with monograms of the original owners. Every room was mobbed with furniture in the popular colors of the time, royal reds and purples—a suite of Louis XVI furniture, high-back wing chairs, horsehair love seats, damask chaises, Queen Isabella carved sideboards, brass beds complete with silk curtains and canopy, caned Art Nouveau settees and Victorian chairs.

On the hour a variety of fragile clocks chimed, some with dancing figurines, some with cuckoos, some with a few notes of a popular waltz, like an aviary of noisy birds. Fringed piano shawls, carved wooden trunks, punched-tin lanterns, musical instruments, fluted glassware, engraved cigarette cases, crocheted bedspreads, hand-painted fans, plumed hats, lace parasols, dusty tapestries, ivory chessboards, gilt sconces, bronze and marble statuettes, gilded vitrines, Sèvres china chamber pots, glazed urns, silverware and crystal and porcelain, jewel inlaid boxes, lacquered Chinese screens, Aubusson carpets, zinc bathtubs, and, under glass domes, tortured saints, weepy madonnas, and pudgy baby Jesuses. More is more. It was a style of decorating that was to figure prominently in this and succeeding generations of the family Reyes.

—Look how we live now, son. Like kings!

—You mean like Hungarians, Narciso said.

—What are you saying, my life?

—I said *precioso*, Mother.

When Regina had instructed Narciso to take off his shoes on entering the apartment, he'd thought she meant it so as not to disturb his father, but then realized it was to save wear and tear on the carpets and furnishings.

—Be careful. Everything's for sale, Regina said.

All day people knocked on the door to deliver items or to take them away. Indians arrived with *ayates*, slings strapped around the forehead and hanging on the back, and with this they were able to carry away items ten times their weight, just as Regina's daddy had once done. Under monstrous loads, humble as worker ants, they ambled off to deliver an armoire or a couch or a bed at a given address. Regina did better business than El Monte de Piedad, the national pawnshop. The desperate came to pawn their inheritance. Quite a few left welted by an ugly lash of bad words or in the misery of tears, and some of these were men!

A great deal had changed while Narciso was gone. His mother, Regina, counted her earnings nightly and hid them in a shoe box in the walnut-wood armoire next to the red bandana housing his three ribs and the box with Santos Piedrasanta's button. His father, Eleuterio, had turned into a half-mad invalid whose drooling speech everyone ignored except Soledad. And Soledad? The homely housegirl had grown up into a slender young woman with stingy breasts and a stingy ass, but sweet all the same to look at, really. Ah, those funny Charlie Chaplin eyebrows and the dark little eyes beneath them. She was cute, almost pretty, honest, she was sweet, he had to admit. How was it he hadn't remembered?

Soledad had become especially talented at translating Eleuterio's tantrums and tears to his family. —He says he has a craving for a bowl of sweet potatoes and milk. He says you'd better not even think of selling his piano, or he'll smash everything in sight. He says you have the manners of a Pancho Villa.

—He told you all that?

—More or less.

Poor Soledad. She understood Eleuterio because she was as mute as he was, perhaps more so because she had no piano. It was best to say only what one absolutely had to, just enough but not too much, better to not get in the way if the *señora* was suffering her migraines. All she had was the *caramelo rebozo*, whose fringe she plaited and unplaited, which was a kind of language.

Poor Eleuterio. A great grief filled his heart each night, and he suffered helplessly, witnessing his son, Narciso, sneaking into the kitchen pantry after dark. Eleuterio grunted and hit the wall adjoining his wife's room with his cane. Regina arrived with a cup of *manzanilla* tea.

—What is it, old man?

She had called him this as a joke when they first married because of their age difference, but now it was the truth and said out of affection.

—Thirsty, *viejo?* Here you go, then.

Eleuterio warbled, yelped, and whined.

—There, there, you go to sleep now. Is it because I sold your old mattress today to the postmaster's family? No, don't think anything of it, my fatty. I'll get you a nice new mattress tomorrow, and you'll sleep just like a baby, right? *Pobrecito.* Drink up your tea.

She gathered him squirming like a child, swaddled him tight in her *rebozo,* and fed him her *manzanilla* tea with a spoon.

—That's my good boy. Don't you worry, everything's going to be just fine.

What else could Eleuterio do but swallow.

*There were many revolutions within the revolution, so that at times certain factions were patriots and at other times were dubbed rebels, hounded by the very same government they had once supported. Case in point, Emiliano Zapata, who led the indigenous forces from Morelos, the subtropical region just south of Mexico City, a group fighting for their ancient land rights. Pancho Villa was an outlaw turned rebel leader who controlled the desert border states. These two powerful chieftains, "the Attila of the South" and "the Centaur of the North," and their followers met in a historic encounter in Mexico City midway through the war. In any good Mexican restaurant today you'll see a sepia photo documenting the event—a cheerful Villa sitting in the presidential chair while a feral Zapata glowers suspiciously at the camera.

For a Hollywood version of the Mexican revolution, see Elia Kazan's Viva Zapata. John Steinbeck wrote the screenplay. His choice for the lead role was none other than the Mexican movie star Pedro Armendáriz, featured in The Pearl. Armendáriz had the sexy, indigenous looks for the job, and, more importantly, the acting skills, but was unknown in the States. Kazan, however, wanted and got Marlon Brando for the part, who, in my opinion, looks ridiculous with his eyes taped slant trying to pass as Mexi-Indian.

33

Cuídate

*P*eople said, —Now that you're a *señorita, cuídate.*
Take care of yourself. But how was Soledad to know
what they meant? *Cuídate.* Take care of yourself. Hadn't she taken care of
her hair and her nails, made sure her underclothes were clean, mended
her stockings, polished her shoes, washed her ears, brushed her teeth,
blessed herself when she passed a church, starched and ironed her petti-
coat, scrubbed her armpits with a soapy cloth, dusted off the soles of her
feet before getting into bed, rinsed her bloody rags in secret when she had
"the rule." But they meant take care of yourself *down there.* Wasn't society strange? They demanded you not to become . . . but they didn't tell
you how not to. The priest, the pope, Aunty Fina, la Señora Regina, the
wise neighbor lady across the street, *las tortilleras,* the pumpkin-seed vendor, *las tamaleras,* the market women who gave her back her change with
this added *pilón,* —Take care of yourself. But no one told you how
to . . . well, *how* exactly.

Because wasn't a kiss part of the act of loving? In truth? Honestly,
now? Wasn't a kiss the tug of a string, a ribbon, a dance, a thread looped
and interlocked that began with the lips and ended with his thing inside
you. Really, there was no way once it began for her to find where or how
to stop, because it was a story without beginning or end. And why was it
her responsibility for her to say *enough,* when in her heart of hearts she
never wanted it to end, and how sad she felt when it was over and he
pulled himself away and she was just herself again, and there was nothing
left of that happiness but something like the juice of the maguey, like cold
spittle on her thighs, and each person went back to being just themselves.

For a little, for a moment as fine as *una espina de nopalito,* she felt as if she could never be lonely, she felt she was not herself, she was not Soledad nor was he Narciso, nor rock nor purple flower, but all rocks and purple flowers and sky and cloud and shell and pebble. It was a secret too beautiful, to tell the truth. Why had everyone kept such a marvel from her? She had not felt this well loved except perhaps when she was still inside her mother's belly, or had sat on her father's lap, the sun on the top of her head, her father's words like sunlight, —*Mi reina*. She felt when this man, this boy, this body, this Narciso put himself inside her, she was no longer a body separate from his. In that kiss, they swallowed one another, swallowed the room, the sky, darkness, fear, and it was beautiful to feel so much a part of everything and bigger than everything. Soledad was no longer Soledad Reyes, Soledad on this earth with her two dresses, her one pair of shoes, her unfinished *caramelo rebozo*, she was not a girl anymore with sad eyes, not herself, just herself, only herself. But all things little and large, great and small, important and unassuming. A puddle of rain and the feather that fell shattering the sky inside it, the lit votive candles flickering through blue cobalt glass at the cathedral, the opening notes of that waltz without a name, a clay bowl of rice in bean broth, a steaming clod of horse dung. Everything, oh, my God, everything. A great flood, an overwhelming joy, and it was good and joyous and blessed.

34

How Narciso Falls into Disrepute Due to Sins of the Dangler

Well, how do you like it so far?

Some parts not so good. But not so terrible either. Go on, go on.

Honest to God, there's no pleasing you. Look, if I would've known telling this story would be this much work, I wouldn't have bothered. What a whole lot of *lata*. Nothing but trouble from start to finish. I should've guessed it. A tangled string, I'm not lying. So what was I telling you?

You were telling about how happy Narciso and I were.

Ah, yes . . . happiness.

It could be said, and quite accurately, too, Narciso Reyes came replete with his twenty-two-volume histories, like a set of encyclopedias. He was, after all, *un hombre bonito*. You might ask what a pretty man like Narciso Reyes saw in his not-so-pretty cousin Soledad.

But not so ugly!

But in his sexual preferences, Narciso was not fussy. He was neither heterosexual nor homosexual exactly. He was . . . how shall I put it? . . . omnisexual. That is, he was a normal man. However, if you told him this, he would be mortified. Like most men, he did not know his own truth. If truthful we must be, then it must be said he found everything in the universe sexually inviting. Woman. Man. Boy. Papaya. Crocheted potholder. The Milky Way. Any and all were possibilities, real or imagined.

Before her induction into love, Soledad had been as neuter as a stone . . .

I hate when you do this to me.

. . . as pure as a silk *rebozo*, and as innocent as if she had been castrated before birth. And she *had* been. Not by any knife except an abstract one called religion. So naive was she about her body, she did not know how many orifices her body had, nor what they were for. Then as now, the philosophy of sexual education for women was—the less said the better. So why did this same society throw rocks at her for what they deemed reckless behavior when their silence was equally reckless?

Why do you constantly have to impose your filthy politics? Can't you just tell the facts?

And what kind of story would this be with just facts?

The truth!

It depends on whose truth you're talking about. The same story becomes a different story depending on who is telling it. Now, will you allow me to proceed?

And who's stopping you?

*L*ike all novitiates, Soledad sincerely believed the *piropos* Narciso tossed her, a word in Spanish for which there is no translation in English, except perhaps "harassment" (in another age, these were called "gallantries"). —*¡Ay! Mamacita*, if I die who will kiss you? —How sad there isn't a *tortilla* big enough to wrap you up in, you're that *exquisita*. —Virgen de Guadalupe, here is your Juan Dieguito! She'd never had anyone say such things to her. Who could blame her for feeling grateful to the man she looked up to as honorable and well educated, her social superior.

—Don't tell anyone, but you're my favorite!

It made her heart *ping!* How was she to know it was just a *piropo*? Something a man says to one, and then to several others.

—Don't tell anyone, but you're my favorite!

It was not a lie exactly, but an untruth. She was his favorite. At that precise moment. A moment can be eternal, can't it?

Soledad could not have known Narciso was not singling her out among all women, but simply enjoying her as his birthright. Was she not "*la muchacha*," after all, and was it not part of her job to serve the young man of the house?

That Narciso. It was as if Destiny had assigned the universe to *echarlo a perder,* to indulge him and cast him to rot, but no, that's not true. It was as if he'd arrived at birth marked "Damaged Goods," ruined beyond reparation, a route begun before the first kiss his mama planted on him when she'd inspected what she'd ejected and turned and admired her good piece of labor, her fine jewel, her delectable handiwork. Delighted his mama was to see he was born lighter than herself. She pinched the mauve genitals to test if it was true, —This is how you can tell. Yes, he would be *güero,* fair. The world would be kind to him.

It was a shame Narciso had not read that illustrious and educational book of his great-great-grand-other Ibn Hazm and paid close attention to the chapter "On the Vileness of Sinning."* Had he been fortunate to have been schooled by his early ancestor, then perhaps Narciso Reyes would have saved himself a lifetime of grief. But it is true we are but an extension of our ancestors, our several fathers and many mothers, so that if one thinks about it seriously and calculates, at one time hundreds of years ago, thousands of people were relatives-to-be walking across villages, passing each other unknowingly in and out of tavern doorways or over bridges where barges rolled quietly beneath, without knowing that in years to come their own lives and those of contemporary strangers would merge several generations later to produce a single descendant and twine them all as family. Thus, in the words of old, we are all brothers.

But who listens to what is said of old? It was youth, that amnesia, like a wave sliding forward and then sliding back, that kept humanity tethered to eternal foolishness, as if a spell was cast on mankind and each generation was forced to disbelieve what the previous generation had learned *a trancazos,* as they say.

So it was when Eleuterio decided to intervene and give his son some much-needed if too late advice. He could see his son coming and going into the kitchen at night even if Regina pretended not to. He was not blind. But he *was* mute. After the supper dishes had been collected, when he and Narciso were alone drinking their milk coffee, Eleuterio looked across the table at his son.

My son, listen to me, Eleuterio thought, looking at his boy. *The Devil knows more from experience than from being the Devil.*

Narciso sipped his coffee and read a sports newspaper.

Your mother. Your mother and I were once very young, just like you. And we used to think like you, believe it or not. Yes, we did. But your behavior is like a dog, worse than a dog, not befitting a Reyes.

You know about your grandfather Hipólito Eduviges Reyes, don't you, mijo?

Narciso cleared his throat.

Good, I knew you would remember me telling you about him. He would always say a man has got to be feo, fuerte, y formal. Yes, your grandfather always said that. A man's got to be ugly, strong, and a gentleman. Above all else he must be a gentleman.

Now this happened some time ago, remember, when I was not the old man you see sitting here now. I was quite elegant back then . . .

Narciso snickered at something he was reading.

It's laughable, I know, only because it's true. I don't like to take a bath now, but back then, well, I was un catrín, if you can believe it.

Narciso bowed his head and burped.

You can believe it? Good. Well, your mother and I have stayed together as man and wife for over twenty years because we gave our word to each other we would do so, which sometimes seems like a silly reason. Especially if someone is accustomed like your mother to her peasant habits. There are bound to be problems. But that's how she came to me, your mother, with her ranch ways.

Of course, there are fights. There have to be fights. There are always fights. But at least we believe in honor. Not like now when no one believes in anything. Back then, all of us, wise and foolish, we believed in something, which is what kept us from turning into dogs.

Something I've never told you . . . When I met your mother I couldn't think of anything but my own pleasure. And in this blindness, son, you were conceived. When your mother told me she was with child, I packed up my things and took to the road without looking back, and eventually headed back to the country of my birth, Spain. I ran off and abandoned your mother.

Narciso slouched on the table, burying his face in his arms.

Oh, I should've expected you'd react like this, son. I'm as ashamed of myself as you are. But wait, the story gets better. Don't give up on me.

Propped up on one elbow, Narciso was now concentrating on a huge mosquito whining in the room.

When your grandfather learned I had left a woman with child, he waited till we were alone after dinner, just like we are, and he told me this.

Narciso plucked himself up, nervously twisting his newspaper.

He said, Eleuterio, we are not dogs! That is all he said. We are not dogs. His words filled me with so much shame I knew immediately what I had to do.

Narciso's newspaper came crashing down on Eleuterio's shoulder.

Don't abuse me, son, though I deserve it. It wasn't easy convincing a proud woman like Regina to marry me. At first she wouldn't have me, and who can blame her? But perhaps she realized that if she did not marry the father of her child, nothing but a life of difficulty would be her destiny.

Satisfied, Narciso eased back into his chair and buried himself in his newspaper again.

But thanks to God she finally forgave me, and that's how it was we married. And years later, years and years I'm talking, because I never told her, years later she would learn it was her father-in-law whom she had to thank for saving her honor, a man whom she never met, on the other side of the ocean. How ironic is life. Her father-in-law, who would've forbidden the marriage if we were living in Seville.

A huge yawn erupted from Narciso's throat.

We are not dogs. We are not dogs, Eleuterio continued. *That was all that was needed to be said, and I turned around and came back and fulfilled my obligation as a gentleman. And that is how I turned, that day, from a dog into the gentleman I was raised to be.*

Suddenly Narciso looked up and locked eyes with his father.

The Devil knows more from experience, Eleuterio repeated in his thoughts. Narciso blinked. He was getting through to the boy! *We are Reyes and must behave like Reyes. Promise me you will always remember this, son. Promise?*

When his father stared at him like that so intensely, Narciso almost believed there was still a small fire of intelligence left in him. But on second thought . . . No, he was probably just suffering from indigestion.

What I mean to say is shall I tell your mother what I've witnessed . . . ? Eleuterio Reyes stopped in midthought and blinked excessively, a nervous habit since the Seville days of his youth. He remembered only too well how his own clacker had gotten him into trouble. Permit me to take a detour in our story, because the detour often turns out to be one's true destiny . . .

"It was said of old, 'He who is preserved from the evil of his clacker, his rumbler and his dangler, is saved from the evil of the whole sublunary world.' The clacker is the tongue, the rumbler is the belly, and the dangler is the privy parts." The Ring of the Dove, *Ibn Hazm*

The Detour That Turns Out to Be One's Destiny

Till the end of his days Eleuterio Reyes had the nervous habit of clenching his eyes into tight stars as if he had soap in them. But that was because of what his eyes remembered. A murder. Yes, a murder! A long time ago, in his other life, when he still lived in that country of his birth . . .

In that Seville of his times, not ours, more dusty, less tourist-filled, yet just as blindingly hot, the young Eleuterio Reyes worked the bars playing piano tunes that made the patrons alternately happy and sad. As often happens on days of murder, it was a payday, and again as often happens, the murderer and the victim were friends. They had been laughing and hugging each other, buying each other drinks, and then, just as Eleuterio was beginning a cheerful mazurka, the two leapt at each other like cats, rolled, danced, and sparked across the room, burst out the door like a flamenco act, and tumbled onto the cobbled street with a trail of chairs, tables, and glass crashing behind them.

Everyone else had the good sense to duck or run for help. Only Eleuterio watched transfixed as a sleepwalker; he was by nature a nosy man. This was why all his life he was able to remember so clearly the murderer's face. He had seen it all, from the beginning embrace, from the round of drinks, the jokes, the laughter, the sudden explosion of anger, the startling glint of the knife blade, the dark blood the color of autumn dahlias bubbling from the nose and mouth.

It was only when a crowd of onlookers began to gather that Eleuterio came to his senses and, like an injured animal, suddenly had the instinct to run. But it was too late, the police arrived.

—Who did this? Did anyone see anything?

—No, said the wise. —I don't know nothing, I saw nothing, don't even ask me.

But Eleuterio, who was not gifted with wisdom, spoke up. —Yes, it was him, pointing to the one who had done it, because by now the murderer had come back and was standing there among the curious. In an instant the police were on the fellow, forcing him into horrible contortionist positions and adding a few extra *thumps* to his body, that human drum, for good measure. Then they ordered Eleuterio to accompany them to the station, since he was the star witness.

There was a lot of commotion, everyone walking over to the police station, the murderer, Eleuterio, the police, and a huge crowd, since by then it was like a parade, and by the time they arrived to the chaos of the station house, Eleuterio, who was simply a musician, was so terrified by the prospect of being yanked into history, his mind began to panic and then doubt whether this man was truly the murderer, and this frightening thought brought on a fierce urge to pee.

As providence would have it, at that very moment two women entered the station who had been hauled in for fighting, one still grabbing the other by the hair, and the other without one shoe, and an even bigger mob had come in to watch these two, because two women fighting are more exciting to men than two *pobres* killing each other, and with the excitement and commotion of all those people, the murderer and Eleuterio took advantage of the situation and ran out without anyone noticing.

And that is why my great-grandfather Eleuterio could no longer live in Seville, you see, but to be fair to the truth, I must explain his other motive. He had married into a family too good for him. His first wife, a woman of exceptional memory, was especially adroit at reminding Eleuterio of his humble origin and his subsequent mediocrity. It was with no regret and only the clothes on his back that Eleuterio abandoned this wife, Seville, and that life without life. —I'll be right back, I'm going for cigarettes. Then, like countless partners who have gone out for cigarettes before him, he marched to where the land met the sea, boarded the first vessel headed across an ocean, and began his life anew.

His destination—Tierra del Fuego, the end of the earth, where no one would ever find him, or at least to Buenos Aires, where everyone has a past they'd just as soon forget. But it was Eleuterio's destiny to stop first at Veracruz, Mexico, to work a little and raise funds. Eleuterio was not proud. He worked at what he could find, playing the piano in the "cabarets of the bad death" and the houses of assignations. The *carpas*, too, he knew, accompanying a mismatched chorus line of ladies with short legs and wide tree-trunk waists outfitted in terrible costumes—little Mexican flags, coconut shells, strings of *papel picado*—getups so cheap and pathetic they gave one *lástima* to look at. Once Eleuterio even accompanied an indecent version of the *jarabe tapatío* performed with a Tenancingo *rebozo* the colors of the Mexican flag, a hermaphrodite, and a *burro*—a filthy finale that brought down the house.

Like all immigrants, Eleuterio Reyes did what he had to do, working the worst shifts in the roughest parts of towns at public bars and private parties where someone was sure to die, though no one would notice till the next morning when they came to clean. And so with necessity prodding him forward, Eleuterio meandered his way through the sleepy provincial villages, some mere mirages of civilization so forgettable and forlorn there was only one way to enter and one way to leave.

Eleuterio Reyes was not a handsome man, but he was born under a good star. He had a fine little mustache that twisted up nicely when he thought to wax it, and small, even teeth, as tiny and square as if he were still a baby. The hands, too, were sweet and childlike, even though the rest of him was huge and rumpled, as if the clothes he wore were not his, or as if he roomed in places without a mirror, which often was the case. This is not to say Eleuterio Reyes was without appeal. Women like men like this, to tidy and take home for improvement. So it was with this lumbering flour-sack body and his soft piano player's hands that Eleuterio Reyes made his way finally toward that city in the middle of the world, halfway between here and there, between nowhere.

The move to the capital raised his social standing. By the time he finally sent word to brothers in Spain as to his whereabouts, he held the respectable position of teacher of music at an elementary school. He became a family example. Younger unsuccessful siblings, good-for-nothing cousins, and layabout godsons were sent in hopes the New World would allow them to begin their lives over again. So that when Narciso Reyes was born, there were already several rotten branches of the family Reyes scattered across the Republic of Mexico, some reminding los Reyes too much of their lowly beginnings. Say what they say, their blood was Spanish, something to remember when extolling their racial superiority over their mixed-blood neighbors. And even if these ne'er-do-well Reyes had not inherited anything but an overdose of pride, the family Reyes was still *española*, albeit mixed with so much Sephardic and Moorish ancestry, all it would have earned them in an earlier Mexico was a fiery death at the Plaza del Volador.

So, as is always the case, a detour turns out to be our destiny. That is how Eleuterio Reyes arrived in Mexico City, where he taught at an elementary school and once played the national anthem when the president dictator, who had elected himself to office eight times, came to the inauguration of a new building. Except the descendants would remember it wrong and say it was at the Presidential Palace that great-grandfather Eleuterio played, though he wasn't a brilliant composer and had only mediocre skills as a musician. Like all chronic *mitoteros*, los Reyes invented a past, reminding everyone that their ancestors had been accustomed to eating oysters with mother-of-pearl forks on porcelain plates brought over on the Manila galleons.* It was a pretty story and told with such fine attention to detail, neighbors who knew better said nothing, charmed by the rococo embroidery that came to be a Reyes talent.

The truth was they had only recently learned to eat with knives, spoons, forks, and napkins. Their ancestors had eaten food cooked with sticks, served on clay dishes, or on that edible plate, the tortilla.

36

We Are Not Dogs

A very telling statement of the times came from the mouth of that philanderer painter Diego Rivera, who, after learning of his wife's vengeances, exclaimed, "I don't want to share my toothbrush with anybody!" By which we can infer women were toothbrushes. If that be the case, when Soledad's belly began to swell, there was no doubting whose toothbrush was whose.

It so happened that Narciso returned to his homeland at a time when Mexico was trying to build itself into a modern nation. So much of the railroads had been destroyed in the war, there was an urgency to unite the country with paved highways for the newly invented automobile. The government created the National Roads Commission, and the National Roads Commission created a desk job for Narciso as bookkeeper to its Oaxaca unit, thanks to his perfect penmanship, a Reyes aptitude for mathematics, and the excellent qualification of having a godfather who was the director-in-chief. The little paper that certified Narciso had been loyal to the Constitutional Government during the Ten Tragic Days of 1914 and a note from a physician who owed Regina a favor allowed Narciso's reentry to Mexico with no disgrace or suspicion, and his bandaged chest only attested to his patriotism.

It was a time of intense nationalism, and Narciso caught the patriotic fervor of the nation. He remembered his childhood history lessons. Oaxaca was where the last strongholds of the Zapotec and Mixtec royal houses had held out successfully against the Spanish invaders, their resistance assisted as much by their own ferocity as by that of the terrain, with its cold in the high mountains and its steamy isthmus jungles.

No paved roads existed in the state then, only dirt paths pounded hard by oxcarts. To make matters more difficult, the Oaxacan landscape was overwhelmed with tropical canyons, valleys, rivers, and mountains. It is said that when the king of Spain asked Cortés to describe the terrain, Cortés crumpled a sheet of paper, tossed it on the table, and said, —Like that, Your Majesty. Like that.

Similarly overwhelmed with canyons, valleys, and mountains was the state of Regina's nerves. She was a confusion of emotions now that Narciso was home. What good was having the love of her life back if he was to be sent away again? Her migraines returned, as did the shadow of grief—rage. And rage, unlike grief, will make do with any convenient target. This was most often Soledad. A knuckle, a fist, a wooden spoon, a bad word, all these were *thwacked* against the poor girl without a second thought.

It's amazing how blind Mexican sons are to their mothers' shortcomings. A meddlesome, quarrelsome, difficult, possessive mother is seen only as a mother who loves her child too much, instead of the thing she is—an unhappy, lonely person. So although Regina made Soledad's life hell, Narciso saw in his mother only an example of absolute devotion. She was weepy and cross, she locked herself in her room and refused meals. Her boy was home but being taken from her again. It wasn't fair. At the oddest moment she burst into rages and then into tears. *Ah, see how much she loves me*, Narciso thought, *and who can fault her for that?*

In his honor, Regina decided to organize an elaborate farewell supper to demonstrate to all how much she loved her boy. It gave her something to do and, though it doubled Soledad's chores, at least it lessened the beatings.

Soledad's body was already showing changes. Like a dusty house cat, she stretched often and rubbed her lower back, and when she was lost in thought, she stroked her belly unaware she was stroking her belly. The body spoke and said just enough, but not too much. Only Señor Eleuterio took the time to listen. Like him, she was a sad, frightened creature whom everyone was so used to seeing they didn't see her. Least of all his wife, Regina, who was busy with *mijo*'s farewell party, oblivious to anything but the preparations.

On the night of the party, the table was arranged with treasures that could rival Cortés' plunder—porcelain vases overflowing with flowers, handmade lace tablecloths, silver candelabras, etched crystal, gold-rimmed Sèvres china, and linen napkins monogrammed with a rococo "*S*." They were, after all, objects from Regina's inventory.

A prestigious list of nobodies was invited. The relatives and important acquaintances of Regina's commerce. People she wished to impress more than people who were close to Narciso. In fact, most of them hardly knew the guest of honor. But that never stopped anyone from attending a Mexican feast.

And what a feast! All of Narciso's favorites foods. Pickled meats, sweet *tamales* and hot *tamales;* roast leg of pork; stuffed *chiles;* black, yellow, and red *mole;* creamy soups; *chorizo* and cheeses; roasted fish and roasted beef; fresh *ceviche* and red snapper Veracruz style; platters of rice the colors of the Mexican flag; *salsas* of several hues and potencies; and drinks of all kinds—punch, wine, beer, *tequila*. All through the meal the girl Soledad served platters and took away plates, a pathetic creature with a sad face made sadder by her circumstances. No one took notice of her except Eleuterio, who watched her dragging trays of food in and dragging them back out again.

Soledad was serving the last course when Eleuterio decided enough was enough. Soledad had just finished placing a bowl of *capirotada* in front of him and was moving on to the next guest when Eleuterio grunted and tugged her back. He rose slowly from his chair. At first Soledad thought he was tired and needed her help getting up. The guests jabbered and laughed and ignored him, as they had all evening, until he raised his cane and brought it smashing down over Regina's expensive merchandise.

Crystal shattered, wine spilled on the carpet, *café de olla* permanently spattered the guests' clothing. Eleuterio was a madman, launching silverware, unsettling coffee cups, smashing the punch bowl, hacking away at the over-the-top floral arrangements, swinging at the crystal chandeliers as if they were *piñatas*. He did not stop until every dish, glass, and platter was broken, bent, or destroyed. And when he finally was through, with women sobbing and men outraged, Eleuterio stood there, a grizzled heap of flesh gasping and sputtering and foaming at the mouth, frightening the guests who had anticipated a nervous disorder, an epileptic fit, a heart seizure, anything but this . . .

Eleuterio spoke. All those months after his near-death words had twisted inside him, a stew of emotions without the means to say. And now, finally, he said something.

—We are not dogs! he said, looking directly at his astonished son, Narciso. Then he gathered the terrified Soledad out from under the table and pulled her to his side. —We are not dogs!

It was not much, but it was enough of a miracle, one he was never able to repeat. God had granted Eleuterio the ability to speak at the decisive moment, or perhaps God had spoken through Eleuterio. —We are not dogs! God said.

Until that moment, it was as if Narciso could not really see Soledad. She looked so pitifully absurd and small shivering next to Eleuterio, with her round *panza* and all. He regained his humanity at that moment and realized what his father was telling him. He was a Reyes, a Reyes, and los Reyes, although they were many things, were most certainly not dogs! Reminded of this, Narciso Reyes fulfilled his obligation as a gentleman.

It would be untrue to say everyone lived happily ever after, because ever after is very long and happiness rather on the short side. But church bells did ring exuberantly on the morning of Soledad and Narciso's wedding, although only in the imagination, because church weddings were strictly prohibited in the years following the war due to the anti-Church provisions of the new Constitution. So let us imagine the bells, and imagine the *mariachis*, and imagine a beautiful reception that never happened, because to tell the truth, Soledad's belly made Regina ashamed to look at her. No, she wasn't the daughter-in-law she would've picked, but she had to accept her husband's miraculous speech as God's will. She had made a promise to la Virgen de Guadalupe to do whatever she commanded, if only she would keep Narciso safe during the war. And here he was, after all, delivered safe and sound.

And so this is how it came to pass that Narciso Reyes, who never left his home without a hat, a clean handkerchief, and a sharp crease in his trousers, took for his wife his cousin Soledad Reyes, she of the kingdom of kitchen.

37

Esa Tal por Cual

Ay, Zandunga,
Zandunga, mamá, por Dios.
Zandunga, no seas ingrata,
cielo de mi corazón.

— *"La Zandunga"*

Exaltación Henestrosa, like Nohuichana the fish goddess, in all the isthmus of Tehuantepec there is no other. One gold-capped tooth with a cutout star, eyes dark and alive as the belly-button of the stormy *mar*, sea eyes tilted slightly and shaped like fish. A wide, lustrous face. Two gold coins dangling like drops of water from the shells of her ears. A conch-dyed purple skirt. Arms akimbo. Woven belt. Brown bare feet. Big bare sea breasts. A necklace of fish vertebrae. And wild sea of hair covered with a clean white square of cloth with *caracol* stripes, knotted at the nape like a pirate.

A woman of a woman. As big and splendid as a boat with full sails. Voluptuous. Graceful. Elegant. Voice *ronca* like the sea, a voice squeezed with lemon. Skirt knotted so as to allow a glimpse of that valley without a name between the globe of belly and bone curve of hip. Woman of smooth arms and smooth hips. Wide-waisted as the Tula tree Cortés is said to have slept under. With a luxury of thick hair "down there," which in the isthmus is the same as saying—a woman ferocious.

She sold baskets of shrimp, fresh turtle eggs, sun-dried fish, *iguanas*, and embroidered cloths. These she traded for corn, bread, chocolate, fruit, and hen eggs. And since she was a good saleswoman and knew the merit of attracting attention, tied her stock of live *iguanas* together by the tail, and arranged them on her head like a headdress. This she wore as she walked the road to Tehuantepec, and this was how Narciso Reyes first saw her, resplendent in the season of rain, with her crown of *iguanas* and her banana-leaf umbrella, though she did not see him.

—That woman, the one with the hat of *iguanas,* he said asking one of the laborers, —ask where she is from. The answer given and brought back, —San Mateo del Mar Vivo, San Mateo of the Live Sea.

San Mateo. In that epoch, there was no road to San Mateo del Mar. To arrive one had to travel by oxcart, by horse, or on foot. But since Soledad, surrounded by mountains, was seasick with the unborn Inocencio, she stayed behind in Oaxaca, Oaxaca, with the green mountains undulating around the city like a sea of waves that made her dizzy just to step outdoors.

This was how it was Narciso Reyes found himself without Soledad in that season of rain, in the Isthmus of Tehuantepec, 1922. The sky blue as happiness would suddenly turn pewter after the afternoon meal, the air heavy like the hand of God on your lungs. —You go on, Soledad said, panting and sweating like a *perra.* —I'll be fine here. All the while the veins in her legs complaining.

Her refuge was a room across the *zócalo* Narciso had found for her in a colonial building that was once a convent and now a boardinghouse. It was the room above the store that sold popcorn, candy, gelatins, and fresh fruit drinks—*horchata, chía, tamarindo, piña, jamaica.* —This way you'll never be lonely. You just lean out the balcony, he instructed, —and you have all the world to amuse you.

But on weekdays Soledad couldn't bear the noise of the schoolchildren. —Go to hell, you *changos.* Worst of all were the lovers groping each other in the plaza, oblivious to all humanity, indecently happy. She tossed the water from her washstand down on them, —Show yourselves in front of your mother's house, you sons without shame. She watched with disgust the widow walk to and from church in her lascivious black garments sashaying her fat cow's behind. —Filthy queen mother of the goddess of whores! She wished she could boil a washtub of water to shower on them all and cleanse them from her sea of troubles.

¡Virgen Purísima! At all hours she was plagued by the corn man's sad steam-whistle, the green banana man, the —*¡Exquisitos carrotes!* of the sweet potato vendor, the *ixtle* seller advertising ropes and fine hammocks

and *petates* of all sizes and qualities, the dawn patrol of the street cleaners with their branch brooms *scratch-scratching* across the flagstones of the plaza, the woman with a voice like a crow shouting — *¡Aquí hay atoleeeee!* —the *sombrero* vendor wearing all his merchandise, the knife sharpener's shrill two-note whistle, the blind beggar man bellowing — *Bendita caridad.* Heartless vultures of the kingdom of hell!

She was not well. She threw up everything she swallowed, including her own saliva. At night she suffered cold chills and then a fever, her tongue dry and her bones as sore as if a fat man had sat on her. The housekeeper announced "*dengue*" because a wind had entered her, or perhaps she'd eaten something hot when she should have eaten something cold. Or the other way around, she couldn't remember. That on top of her pregnancy seasickness.

Soledad could neither bear the sweet smell of popcorn rising from downstairs nor the sweeter scent of gardenias that floated from across the *zócalo*. The girl who swept the rooms but always forgot to sweep under the bed brought her a fist of mauve flowers with petals so translucent they looked like . . . well, they looked like . . . Holy Mother of God! They looked just like the color of a man's erect penis, but with thick hairy centers like the coarse hair that grows from men's ears and nostrils or on the legs of flies. In her delirium she wound up tossing them against the armoire, vase and all.

—It's the baby inside me, she explained. —Won't let me rest, turns and twists all night, well, I'm afraid he will be born too early or too late.

The housekeeper's grandmother gave this prediction: —It's that the child is destined to be a poet, only artists have souls like that.

But this did not calm the woman Soledad. She could not admit it was Narciso who turned and twisted in her heart those days and nights, the wide, sandy stretches of weeks like the lagoons where Narciso found himself without her. She dreamt a dream of red seagulls, red pelicans, red ducks, red deer, red goats, and red butterflies. She did not know she was dreaming the fingers of Exaltación Henestrosa embroidering with red thread the seagulls, pelicans, ducks, deer, goats, and butterflies on squares of white cotton she sold in the market of Tehuantepec.

Don't you think we need a love scene here of Narciso and I together?

Why?

Just something in the story to show how happy we were?

Nobody wants to read about happiness.

All I'm asking for is one little love scene. At least something to remind people Narciso and I loved each other. Oh, please! We really only have that vulgar love scene overheard by Eleuterio. And isn't it important to understand that Narciso and I were in love, really, I mean before he met the so-and-so? Especially after his fling with the little tramp in Chicago.

No! Now let me get on with the story. The world was filled with wind the day Narciso Reyes met Exaltación Henestrosa.

Ha! That shows what you know. The winds in Oaxaca arrive only in the winter.

Well, let's pretend it's winter.

But you just finished saying it was the rainy season. Really!

All right. Just for poetic purposes, we'll allow the wind to arrive in this scene. It suits the story better.

*T*he world was filled with wind the day Narciso Reyes met Exaltación Henestrosa, as if it wouldn't be satisfied until it set everything upside down, put everything on its head. The palm trees swirled, the women's skirts, the clouds were windswept, as if someone had run a comb through them. On this day when the sand stung one's face and the children ran chasing after the palm-tree-like figures of women with baskets of fish on their heads, on this day with its howl of church bells and yelping dogs, this day of all topsy-turvy days, Narciso's blindness was turned into vision.

He was suffering a terrible eye infection, my grandfather. By Thursday it was so bad, they had to lead him with his eyes shut to the home of a certain Exaltación. From a clay bowl she mixed dry white powder, spat on it till it was a paste, and this she rubbed on his inner eyelid.

—What is that?

—Better you don't know. You'll just complain.

—What do you take me for, a woman? Tell me.

—*Iguana* shit, she said.

But before he could protest, his eyes cleared themselves from their milky fog, and he saw before him the fish goddess Nohuichana. It was the woman of the *iguana* hat.

—Where did you come from? Land, sea, or heaven?

—From hell, she said. —From here, San Mateo del Mar Vivo.

As opposed to the sandy salt lagoons they call Mar Muerto.

—I mean from what half shell did you rise? Of all the creatures in all Tehuantepec, I swear, you are the most exquisite.

She gave a little shrug and sighed. —I know.

Some would say there was some witchcraft in that spit and *iguana* shit, because Exaltación was known as a crazy woman, that is, she knew of plants and herbs and other things which people did not like to say but said anyway, well, she could do things. But say what they say, it's not true. Her magic was that she didn't care to put a man at the center of her life, and this, for any man, is aphrodisiac enough.

—Well, now, what are you doing? Exaltación said. —Where do you think you're going?

—Well, I suppose they still think I'm sick, said Narciso.

—Well, then, have some coffee with me. I'm afraid you'll have to drink it cold, I can't light a fire today, too much wind, too dangerous, she said, meaning the walls of dusty thatch.

He was a victim of the right time and place. And because she felt like it, she slept with him. Because she felt like it. And what of it?

Celaya, why are you so cruel with me? You love to make me suffer. You enjoy mortifying me, isn't that so? Is that why you insist on showing everyone this . . . dirt, but refuse me one little love scene?

For crying out loud, Grandmother. If you can't let me do my job and tell this story without your constant interruptions . . .

All I wanted was a little understanding, but I see I was asking for too much.

Just trust me, will you? Let me go on with the story without your comments. Please! Now, where was I?

You were telling *cochinadas*.

I was not being filthy. And to tell the truth, you're getting in the way of my story.

Your story? I thought you were telling *my* story?

Your story *is* my story. Now please be quiet, Grandmother, or I'll have to ask you to leave.

Ask me to leave? Really, you make me laugh! And what kind of story will you have without me? Answer me, eh?

Well, for one thing, a story with an ending. Now calm down a little, and let me go on with the story. We were in the home of Exaltación, remember?

Remember? After all these years, I'm still trying to forget.

The woman Exaltación had chosen the Grandfather as her plaything, but she wasn't very satisfied.

—You shouldn't begin what you can't finish, Exaltación said. —The problem with you pretty men is you don't know how to make love. All you're good for is fucking.

—Teach me, then, said Narciso.

—*¡Ay!* my heaven, don't be a fool. To make love one must use this, she said, tapping her heart —and that can't be taught.

Love or not love, Exaltación Henestrosa *lo salpicó*. That is to say, his heart was left spattered with a million and one sand flies, like the sandy stretches of that land called San Mateo del Mar.

How was Soledad to know she held in her belly, in that being no bigger than an amaranth seed, the great love of her life. In turn, at that very same moment, Narciso held in his secret heart his own seed of love. Each beginning their furious fight for life.

38.

¡Pobre de Mí!

And then he fell in love with her.
I don't know why people march into disasters of
the heart so joyously. Somehow in the darkness before sleep, the truth
must arrive with its sharp little teeth. It's almost as if being the tragic hero
is a poetic indulgence, a public penance, a luminous grief. Perhaps it was
like this with Narciso Reyes and his nemesis Exaltación.

When Narciso was working in the isthmus,* he felt disconnected
from all the world, as if he could run away and no one would ever find
him again. It was a great relief to not have to be Narciso Reyes, to let go
the world's demands and expectations. And like the tropical plants that
grow in excess there without anything stopping them, a lushness, an over-
abundance, a luxury, he allowed his passion to grow as well, unkempt and
untamed, and he knew for the first time joy.

So it was that when Narciso Reyes came to have his infected eyes
cured he saw before him the brilliance that was Exaltación Henestrosa,
but he could not see inside her heart.

During the winter, a northern wind snaps in, swirling dust across the
isthmus for miles. Wind bending the palm trees, wind blasting the blue
sky clean, wind pumping the skirts of women, wind billowing across the
skin of the curly sea, the sound of the wind in your ears for months and
months.

And in the summer, no wind at all; a sticky airlessness that leaves
everyone in a terrible mood with *ganas* to do nothing. A silence like the
maw of sorrow. Until night, when the mosquitoes arrive.

It was the wind of desire that blew the circus toward San Mateo del
Mar, a sight to sting the hearts of even the deadest citizens of that dead-

sea muck of rotten fish, though it was an exaggeration to call them a circus; they were but defectors of other trades. The Circus Garibaldi consisted of a zebra-striped mule hauling an ancient oxcart overloaded with canvas backdrops of airplanes, madonnas, and invented Tibetan landscapes. The company included a lady photographer, a Mayan family of acrobatic clowns, a gypsy accordionist/percussionist, a dancing raccoon that told fortunes, and the singer Pánfila Palafox. The day they arrived you could not speak without the melodramatic accompaniment of the wind.

How many months do you expect a woman to be with child? Your father was born in the summer, remember? And here you have the story shift to winter. You take such liberties!

Indulge me. I need the wind for this part of the story.

With a flourish of instruments from another age, shells, gongs, *marimbas*, bamboo flutes that smelled of smoke, and a drum made from a turtle shell, the Circus Garibaldi announced itself. The gypsy played a magnificent waltz while the raccoon clapped, Pánfila sang, the clowns dazzled the crowd with cartwheels and contortions, and the lady photographer passed out flyers announcing the next show as well as an advertisement for: *Artistic Photography, the achievement of the century!* ¡Un bonito recuerdo! *Preserve a memory! A souvenir! Conserve your beauty, your strength. Allow your children to remember you in your glorious youth. Allow us to take your picture. We have splendid palaces, magnificent gardens, and modern airplanes that will serve you as background. Or select the sacred image of your patron saint if you so desire. President Obregón himself has declared our photographs "so real and lifelike they are astonishing!"*

And though the Circus Garibaldi yelped and played with all their might, the wild air rushed about them rudely, swirling and swallowing them up like a frothy sea. The announcement flyers printed on cheap newsprint fluttered out of their hands, and in this way made their way over the town like a flock of pigeons. Dust devils whirled the flyers in dizzy circles in the square. Everywhere you walked you could not help but notice the circus flyers with a pyramid of clowns balanced on a magnificent painted elephant, though the Circus Garibaldi had no elephant.

Dirty squares of paper tangled themselves in the palm trees, fluttered out to sea, were caught in the fishnets left out to dry, as well as in the hammocks of those taking their afternoon nap. They clogged the barrels left out to collect rainwater. Pigs ferreted them out from the brush for months and ate them. Flyers descended in droves, batting citizens on the head like a plague of locusts. One slid easily under the wide space beneath the makeshift door of the barracks of the employees of the National Roads Commission, who were overjoyed at the possibility of some new entertainment. This gave Narciso Reyes the excuse to set out toward the town square, where the very old and the very young assembled daily waiting patiently and impatiently for something to happen.

A faded tent was struggling to come to life, and in front of this confusion, Narciso waited. The lady photographer calmly set up an outdoor photo gallery and was doing excellently despite the wind that made the subjects look as if their hair were fire. When Narciso arrived, there was already a long line of people waiting their turn, almost all the town it seemed, but no Exaltación. Families with their freshly combed hair still wet from the bath arrived dressed in their good clothes, almost everyone barefoot, except for the exceptionally vain or those a little better off than most, which were only the mayor and the mayor's godchild. Widows with their string of children and their children's string of children lined up their tribe for intense inspection. Babies were dressed in fancy lace shirts, but with nothing covering their bare bottoms. A few citizens brought along their prize possessions—a trumpet, a baseball uniform, a piglet. One cradled in her arms her recently dead infant dressed as an angel wearing a crumpled paper crown.

And when the powder flashed, no one smiled. It's not the custom to smile for the camera over there. The citizens of San Mateo del Mar looked directly into the lens with that same serious gaze found in tombstone portraits. Young, old, mothers, beauties, sons, husbands, wives, brothers, sisters draped in the arms of a loving sister, children, alone or in a group, all looked directly into the camera as if looking severely into a mirror. That was the way it was done, then and now.

For a backdrop, there were several choices. That new invention, the airplane, which Lindbergh was just then testing at an aviation field on the plains of Balbuena between Mexico City and Puebla; the ever-popular Virgen de Guadalupe; or a palace garden. —Look how pretty!

Narciso Reyes waited and waited, busying himself buying candied sweets—*obleas*, pastel wafer sandwiches filled with goat-milk caramel;

tri-color coconut bars with the colors of the Mexican flag; pumpkin-seed brittle; candied oranges.

When he was almost ready to give up, his jaw aching from so much sugar, he finally saw Exaltación crossing the town square.

—Exaltación Henestrosa! Narciso shouted. He came running up to her like a child. —I bought you some *chuchulucos*.

It was fortunate for Narciso he had brought along the candies. There were many things Exaltación could resist, including this silly boy in front of her in his *fanfarrón* striped suit, but she could not resist candy.

To make small talk, Narciso reported the most recent gossip he'd gathered waiting for her. —Have you heard the scandal? It's about the photographer and the circus singer. They say these two women are sharing a hammock.

Exaltación Henestrosa burst out laughing, covering her mouth with her hands, a habit perhaps from the days before her gold tooth with the cutout star. —Ah, is that so? she said. —Well! All I can say is I'd never do anything like that.

No sooner said than . . . duck! The whipped cream pie is coming! Which whipped cream pie? The whipped cream pie Divine Providence likes to throw in one's face when we say, —Oh, I'll never . . . And whatever you say "I'll never" to, believe me, you will. Some years there are so many whipped cream pies flying about, crisscrossing each other like meteorite showers. *Whoosh, whoosh!* Whatever you don't expect, *¡ahí viene!* Watch out, here it comes! Right around the corner your whipped cream pie awaits you.

Narciso trailed behind Exaltación like a child and talked her into taking her portrait with him.

—Please. How about a souvenir, *un recuerdo*, something to remember this evening by?

—If that's what you'd like to waste your money on, who am I to stop a fool.

They were seated on a bentwood settee and the moment before the powder flashed, Narciso bent toward Exaltación. It was a very telling gesture, like a flower growing toward the sun.

They spent the rest of the evening at the circus. Even if the Circus Garibaldi was anything but excellent, it brought to a hungry town a great deal of nourishment. The acts consisted of some forgettable skits, corny and without charm, with only the animals coming off with any grace, but the show was saved by the big finale, the singer Pánfila, who entered the empty ring with her Paracho guitar. She was dressed like a *campesino* in humble cotton whites, and she sang and sang, songs so simple and true it hurt your heart to hear them.

That voice. Like the quivering grief of a guitar. It might be true the woman Pánfila was often filled with evil thoughts, but when she sang she confirmed without a doubt the existence of God. I am God, if only for a glimmer of a moment. But, ah, that moment was like the heart being squeezed when one saw a school of dolphin leap up from the sea.

Everyone cried. Everyone was overjoyed. And then, weeping, the citizens of San Mateo slouched toward their homes hugging each other.

The secret was this. Pánfila sang *con ganas*, as they say. With feeling. It gave everything she sang authenticity, and authenticity of emotions engendered admiration, and admiration—love. Singing, she said what the public could not say, what they did not know they felt. And what she sang she sang so sincerely, with such heartfelt emotion, it wobbled even the stoic Exaltación to tears.

Narciso was overjoyed. He believed the tears were tears of emotion meant only for him. It's just as well. It was a beautiful night, and the universe was not in any hurry to cheat him of this pleasure.

That night Narciso was invited to Exaltación's bed. Well, that's not precisely right. He made a pest of himself until the only way she could get rid of him was by inviting him in, servicing him haphazardly, and then getting him to leave only by promising she'd see him again tomorrow.

—Tomorrow?

—I promise.

—Do you?

—Yes, tomorrow, tomorrow, for certain. Now go away and let me be!

But when he came back the next night her house was empty. All he found was a few skinny chickens and some dogs rummaging through the trash. The children said she had left with her belongings in a big bundle.

—But how?

—She left with that woman.

—Which woman?

—You know. The one from the circus. The one who sings.

It was true. She had vanished with Pánfila Palafox.[†] It was as if they were spirits dissolving into air, because no one could say in which direction they'd left. The roads were as fine as talc in that dry season, and the wind so furious, they left no tracks.

A few days later, the Circus Garibaldi hobbled out of town. To make matters worse, the cardboard portrait arrived to smack him into fresh pain. The photographer was as despondent as Narciso, after all, since she too had been abandoned, and she could not bring herself to deliver it in person. She left it behind with the mayor's godchild to deliver, which the child dutifully brought to Narciso with a great deal of babbling, as if he were bringing good news and not grief.

The photo broke Narciso's heart. The photographer had taken the trouble to cut out the image of her rival so that only Narciso's image remained. Narciso Reyes stared at what was left of the sepia photo. He leaned like a clock at ten to six, his head tilted toward a ghost. *Ay,* heaven of my heart!

If Mexico was a Gibson girl, then the isthmus of Tehuantepec would be her hourglass waist. The locals still boast one can bathe in the Gulf of Mexico before breakfast and swim in the Pacific by sunset, but this is true only if one has a car. Before the invention of the automobile, in the childhood times of Narciso and Soledad, trains ran as often as twenty times a day uniting the two oceans and testifying to all the world the modern nation Mexico was fast becoming. But the Panama Canal of 1906 put an end to this transcontinental efficiency, and eventually the area was lucky if even one train passed daily.

Because of love, the railroads ventured into that furious savagery called Tehuantepec. It was here, while stationed as a soldier during the French occupation, that the future dictator Porfirio Díaz met the great love of his life, Juana Romero, or Doña Cata, and became her lover until death. The railroads, thanks to this eternal passion, were built on Díaz's orders and her request, and that is how the tracks arrived almost at the door of Doña Cata's resplendently gaudy house. This not only helped to expedite the sweethearts' visits, but the train whistle added a charming melancholy to their liaisons.

Since the time of Cortés, since the Spanish Viceroy Bucareli, since the German naturalist Humboldt, countless investors, conquerers, engineers, and inventors had failed to bridge the two oceans, defeated by lack of funds, insurrections, or infestations of mosquitoes. It was during the California gold rush that the Tehuantepec Railway Company of New Orleans operated a route to San Francisco even though no railway trains were involved.

Once a month passengers boarded a freighter from New Orleans to the Mexican gulf coast, then sailed lazily up the Coatzacoalcos River on a Mississippi side-wheeler named the Allegheny Belle. *They feasted on fruits exotic to the typical* norteamericano—plantains, papayas, mangos, *guavas, star apples, and custard apples, not to mention the meat of animals they'd never seen before—monkey,* iguana, *and* armadillo. *The comforts of the Confederate steamboat ended in the town of Suchil, where passengers were packed on jolting carriages, then made to ride muleback, and finally carried on box chairs strapped on the backs of Indians before arriving gratefully to the Pacific Coast and a ship bound to San Francisco if no storm deterred them. By scrupulous accounts, 4,736 gold-seeking forty-niners made the trip to California like this, enduring malaria, dysentery, regret, and a mysterious disease that left their skin blue.*

†*Pánfila Palafox was a woman famous for running off with everyone's wife. Her real name was Adela Delgadina Pulido Tovar, and she was of a* familia adinerada y decente. *Pánfila was raised by French nuns in the Convent of the Sacred Heart and remembered for her passionate verses written in excellent French and her watercolor miniatures painted with her own tears. But after the revolution it was no longer fashionable to be fashionable. Adela rebaptized herself under the name of the housekeeper's daughter and took to escaping at night to those bars where the music is good and the neighborhood bad.*

They say Pánfila Palafox had affairs with the most talented artists of the day—Lupe Marín, Nahui Olín, and the young Frida Kahlo—before the papers denounced Pánfila for her "libertine attitude against public decency and good customs." Every town in Mexico, little or big, had a Pánfila Palafox story. True or not true, Pánfila sang in a mahogany vibrato, a voice that defied imitation by woman or man, and her train of scandal only made her more sought after by a curious public that was both shocked and fascinated by her bravado.

At the time of this story Pánfila Palafox was living like a muleteer, on the road with her Paracho guitar on her back and an ixtle *bag containing everything she owned. She sang on corners, under stars, beneath balconies, and in bars, where the scandalized public, out of curiosity and longing, thronged to hear her. Pánfila was used to traveling across the dustiest roads of the republic living the life of the peasant artist; she came from a wealthy family and could afford to be poor. That is how it was she found herself in the Isthmus of Tehuantepec, that land of extremities, during the season of wind.*

39

Tanta Miseria

Júrame	Promise Me
Todos dicen que es mentira que te quiero porque nunca me habían visto enamorado, yo te juro que yo mismo no comprendo el por qué tu mirar me ha fascinado.	Everyone says it's a lie I love you because no one's seen me in love, I swear I don't understand why your gaze has me so fascinated.
Cuando estoy cerca de ti y estás contenta no quisiera que de nadie te acordaras, tengo celos hasta del pensamiento que pueda recordarte a otra persona amada.	When I'm close to you and you're happy I don't want you thinking of anyone else, I'm even jealous of your thoughts that might remind you of another.
Júrame, que aunque pase mucho tiempo no olvidarás el momento en que yo te conocí,	Promise me though time passes you won't forget the moment we met,

mírame, pues no hay nada	look at me, there's nothing
más profundo	deeper nor
ni más grande en este mundo, que	greater in this world than the love
el cariño que te di.	I give you.
Bésame, con un beso enamorado,	Kiss me with a lover's kiss,
como nadie me ha besado desde el	like no one's kissed me since the
día en que nací.	day I was born.
Quiéreme, quiéreme hasta	Love me, love me till
la locura,	madness,
y así sabrás la amargura	and that's how you'll know
que estoy sufriendo	the bitterness I'm suffering
por ti.	for you.

—*composer, María Grever*

To be accompanied by the scratchy 1927 version of "Júrame," as recorded by José Mojica, the Mexican Valentino, who would later renounce fame, fortune, and the adulation of millions of female fans by taking vows and becoming a priest.

His life makes a wonderful story and was adapted into that unforgettable film . . . What was its name again?

If you've never heard Mojica, imagine a voice like Caruso, a voice like purple velvet with gold satin tassels, a voice like a bullfighter's bloody jacket, a voice like a water-stained pillow bought at the Lagunilla flea market embroidered with "No Me Olvides," *smelling of chamomile,* copal, *and cat.*

Doubt begins like a thin crack in a porcelain plate. Very fine, like a strand of hair, almost not there.

Wedged in between the pages of the sports section, in the satin puckered side-pocket of his valise, next to a crumpled bag of pumpkin seeds, a sepia-colored photo pasted on thick cardboard crudely cut down the center. The smiling Narciso seated leaning toward the cut-out half.

—And this?

How many have started trouble with just these two words? If you poke under the bed expect to find dirt.

—Oh, that. It was just a joke. We took a portrait the day a traveling photographer came to town. One of the fellows and I were bored and thought it would be fun. What do you think! We only had enough money between us for just one picture, that's why we had to cut it in half. Throw it away. I don't even know why I kept it.

—Of course I won't throw it away. I'd like to keep it. Especially since you're gone so much.

—Do as you like. It's all the same to me.

How is it my grandmother knew to know? How is it a woman knows what she knows without knowing it, I mean. So that while my grandfather Narciso was enjoying the pleasures of the woman with the *iguana* hat, that sweetheart from the hotlands, my grandmother Soledad was at that very second haunted by some crazy but real fears.

She would wake in the middle of the night, disoriented, a sick feeling swirling in her heart. Where was her Narciso at this moment? Perhaps loosening the lazy strap of a woman in a once-white slip? Kissing the moon of a shoulder, the instep of an arched foot, the wrist with its little flicker of life, the sticky hotlands of the palm, the soft web of the fingers? At this instant was he sucking the salt off an earlobe, or placing his hand on the valentine of a woman's back, or maybe sliding himself off the rippled flesh of a big woman's big hips? No, no, too terrible to think about, she couldn't stand it when he was away. And what if he left her? Worse . . .

What if he stayed? A fever like this. She suffered, *ay,* she suffered the way only Mexican women can suffer, because she loved the way Mexicans love. In love not only with someone's present, but haunted by their future and terrorized by their past. Of course, each time Narciso returned from the coast, Soledad attacked him with accusations, a flurry of brilliant colors like the wings of jungle macaws.

—You're crazy!

—*Júrame.* Swear, swear to me it's only me you love, my life, *júrame.*

—*Te lo juro.* I swear.

—Again!

—Only you, he said. *Sólo tú.*

Only you. This would satisfy her. For a little. There is a saying: Drunks and children tell the truth. One afternoon when the sky was sorrel-colored, as if the world was about to come to an abrupt end, the nosy child of the cleaning woman was visiting Soledad's room and touching everything he could get his hands on, including the photo of Narciso, which Soledad had placed on a bedside table.

—And who's that?

—That's my husband.

—No, I mean who's the lady sitting next to him?

—What are you talking about? Here, give me that, you little snot! Don't you know better than to touch things that aren't yours?

Soledad shooed the child out of the room and took a closer look at the bottom of the photo. She took it out to the balcony and looked again. She looked and she looked, said nothing, tucked the photo in her pocket, put her shawl on, marched over to the plaza, waited on a wrought-iron bench in front of the kiosk till the jewelry shop opened, then asked the watchmaker if she might borrow his jeweler's eyepiece. —Just for a second, I promise I won't drop it, of course, what do you take me for, if you would be so kind, thank you please, please give me a little privacy if you would please!

What she saw next to her husband's boot was this. A dark shadow of flowered calico. The hem of a skirt! *¡Virgen Purísima!* A long thin pin in her heart.

When she came to, there was a crowd of busybodies pressing around her screaming, —Give her water! Give her air! Put her feet up. Someone pull down her skirt! And there was mixed in as well the angry shouts of the watchmaker, who was more concerned about his jeweler's glass than the welfare of Soledad.

But how can one live like that, with a pin in one's heart? How? Tell me.

Soledad sought out the only person she could confide in, the *anciana* who sold *atole* and *tamales* on a wooden table outside the church. Inside, the priest was hearing confession and sending out the guilty with a long list of useless prayers as penance. But outside, the *tamal* vendor gave out only sound advice, which was so sensible as to be mistaken for foolishness.

—Help me, I'm suffering, Soledad said after explaining her story.

—Ah, poor little creature. What wife hasn't had your troubles? It's just jealousy. Believe me, it's not going to kill you, though you'll feel like you're dying.

—But how much longer will I feel like this?

—It depends.

—On what?

—On how hard you love.

—Holy Mother of God!

Soledad started to cry. People often mistake women's tears for defeat, for weakness. Hers were not tears of surrender, but tears for the injustice of the world.

—There, there, my sweetness! That's enough. Don't even think terrible things. It's not good for the child in your belly. He'll remember later when he's born and keep you up nights with his crying.

—It's just that . . . So much . . . Soledad managed to hiccup, —So much misery in the world.

—*Sí, tanta miseria,* but also so much humanity to make up for the cruelty.

—Enough, but not too much.

—Not too much, but just enough, the old woman said.

She sent Soledad home with *hierba buena* tea and instructions to drink a cup in the morning, a cup at night, and to bathe herself in it as often as she felt sad.

—Patience. Have a little faith in la Divina Providencia, why don't you. The fearful are those who don't trust God's plans. There is, after all, one cure for jealousy, you do know that, right?

—And what would that be?

—Oh, it's very easy. Fall in love again. Like they say, one nail drives out another.

—Yes, and the second bullet dulls the pain of the first. Thank you. I must be going.

When one is young and just beginning one's marriage, how can one believe the wisdom of someone as dried up and ugly as a roasted *chile poblano?*

—God closes doors so that another may open, the woman shouted. —When you least expect it, love will arrive with its Gabriel's trumpet. Then you'll forget all this sorrow. You'll see. *Ánimo, ánimo.*

But by now Soledad was scuttling across the cobbled churchyard toward the wings of filigreed gates, pushing her way past resilient beggars and insistent rosary vendors, beyond the hobbled bundles of humanity seated placidly on the cool stone steps still and solid as gray river stones, hurrying without pause past a chorus of chirping voices calling out to her to take a taste of their cool drinks and hot meals, shoving through the throng of the faithful and faithless clumsily tumbling in front of her to complicate her route to her room.

Ánimo, ánimo. Soledad saw nothing, no one in that rush to regain her solitude. She was lost in her own thoughts, which were not thoughts of *ánimo* at all but of its opposite. That ugly squashed hat—despair.

I Ask la Virgen to Guide Me Because I Don't Know What to Do

*L*ies, lies. Nothing but lies from beginning to end. I don't know why I trusted you with my beautiful story. You've never been able to tell the truth to save your life. Never! I must've been out of my mind . . .

Grandmother! You're the one who was after me to tell this story, remember? You don't realize what a tangled mess you've given me. I'm doing the best I can with what little you've told me.

But do you have to lie?

They're not lies, they're healthy lies. So as to fill in the gaps. You're just going to have to trust me. It will turn out pretty in the end, I promise. Now, please be quiet, or I'm going to lose my train of thought. So where were we? And then . . .

*A*nd then, each time Narciso returned to Oaxaca, he found Soledad suffering from a sadness without a name. Which is why he dreaded returning and avoided her when he did. She had gained so much weight her face was puffy, her neck thick and pink, and her chin had doubled. She had changed from a woman to a fat child dressed in baggy dresses with white embroidered baby collars. She had also done something strange to her hair, cut her bangs across the forehead so she looked like an overgrown toddler. *Why did pregnant women do this?* he wondered.

This is how Narciso found his wife, weepy, bloated, and barefoot because she said her shoes no longer fit. Since her husband's departure,

Soledad swore her feet had grown a size bigger. In private, she took to walking about barefoot, but this made her husband angry. —You look like an Indian, he'd scold. —Don't insult me by being seen like that; as if I didn't have money to buy my wife shoes.

—Are you hungry?

—No, I'm not hungry. Would you stop that!

—What?

How could he explain?

How could she? His body was her body now. She worried whether he was tired, was he hungry, did he need to sleep any more, a sweater to keep him warm. It was as if her body extended itself to encompass his, another body with all its needs. Because this is the way women love. How could she explain even if she knew herself?

But men love in a different way. They don't understand. They don't set out a glass of water for their lover when they themselves are thirsty. They don't hold a spoon to the lover's mouth, and say, —Taste! —so close you can't see what's in it. They don't. Unless they fall in love with their own child, as is often the case. —Who loves you?

It seemed to Soledad her husband forgot she was there. He walked in front of her lately, as if she wasn't with him. What would've made her mad before drove her to tears now. Didn't a man know? Did he have any idea how important it is to hold a woman's hand when walking down the street with her? Did he realize when holding a woman's hand his body was saying, —World, this is my *querida*, the woman I love, I am proud to be walking beside her, my hand in hers the flag of our love.

If only he would whisper a cariñito *in my ear*, she thought, a sugary sweet, a word made holy by his warm breath on her neck. A kind word made the skin shiver. Did he know this, her Narciso? She didn't know to tell him. He didn't know to ask.

The final nightmare was her body. Holy Mother of God! A body that didn't look as if it belonged to her. She was a disaster of buttocks and hips, as wide and heavy as the stone goddess Coatlicue. When she looked at herself in the mirror, it gave her a little shudder.

How to begin? Soledad could not explain without overexplaining. Her spine hurt, her ribs hurt, she was tired all the time, she couldn't go out without always constantly feeling as if she had to pee, and:

—Did I tell you about my problems sleeping? I can't rest, I can't rest. She would moan all night and then have to get up in the middle of the night and sit down to catch her breath. She tried sleeping on her side, because when she slept on her back she felt she was choking. She was so big she could not sleep. She was frightened of childbirth, she confessed to the housekeeper:

—It's because I don't know what to expect.

But the housekeeper who had given birth eighteen times said, —Believe me, it's worse when you do.

Her husband said, —You'll be all right once you have the baby. Everyone said motherhood was sacred, but all the everyones who said it were men. Soledad did not feel sacred. She felt more human than ever. She prayed the baby would hurry and be born so that she could have her body back. To this end, Soledad tried the women's remedies, hot baths or walking all day through the town. Scrubbing floors on one's hands and knees was also guaranteed to induce labor, but since it was the lazy girl who cleaned the rooms who suggested this, Soledad ignored the advice.

What was it? Lately when she entered a room Soledad found herself frantically searching the ceiling beams, always staring upward like the church paintings of the Madonna ascending into heaven. —What are you looking at? —Oh, nothing, nothing. She didn't know when she began this habit, but it was something she did now automatically, as if she was looking for . . . What was she looking for? As if somewhere in those rafters and cobwebbed corners was an answer, a secret, an angel, a vision, that might descend from heaven and rescue her from herself.

It seemed as if her sense of smell was never as acute as during this period when she was waiting for the unborn Inocencio. In the mornings, when the street cleaners arrived with their branch brooms, there was such a coolness as day broke, a stillness just for a moment, when Soledad would be fanning herself on the balcony and just as suddenly drop to sleep there in her chair. The night that smelled of night, a velvety moistness that would give way to light and gradually the perfume of the laurel trees, and with this a terrible pain behind the bridge of her nose like the throbbing of a tooth, that wouldn't go away until *siesta*. But any scent, the smoke from a cigar, the oatmeal boiling for breakfast, the damp-dog smell of the back streets, church incense so sweet it stank like urine, the steamy cooked-corn aroma of the corn-on-the cob man, all these left her dizzy. Once in the market while bending down to pick up a coin, she even fainted at a stall of *cilantro,* green onions, and *poblano* peppers.

Besides the heartburn, the taste for Manila *mangos,* the gagging phlegm in her throat, the cramps in her legs, feet, toes, hands, added to all this calamity were the crying spells.

—*¡Ay, caray!* said Narciso. —Not again. How could she explain to her husband it was more than a loss of control of her body, but also, her life.

In the dark coolness of the church of la Soledad, Soledad Reyes prayed daily to the wooden statue of the Virgin of Solitude draped in velvet and gilt edged robes housed in a glass case behind the main altar. Soledad was so big now she could hardly genuflect, and had to content herself with a half-squatting, half-sitting position in lieu of kneeling. She looked at the Santo Niño de Atocha housed in his own little glass case along the side, the Santo Niño with his shepherd's staff and funny hat trimmed in fur, his lace dress embroidered with gold thread, the seed pearls that had no doubt dimmed a nun's eyes blind. If her baby was a boy, Soledad vowed she would love him like la Virgen and name him Inocencio. She could not name him Jesús, unfortunately, because Jesús was the name of the lecherous man at *la farmacia* who wiggled his middle finger indecently in your palm when he gave you back your change. No, Inocencio was what she would name her baby if he was a boy, and she would love him with a mother's pure love like la Santísima Virgen de la Soledad mumbling and grieving all alone while Joseph, well, where the hell was he when she needed him? Dependably undependable, like all husbands.

And when the pains began and the midwife was sent for, there it was, that feeling, that search in the rafters for, —Oh, my God, I don't know. She did not call out to her husband, nor to God, la Virgen, or a saint.

When the labor began she felt her body lurch forward of its own accord like a piece of machinery, like a chariot, like a wild horse and she dangling from a stirrup. There was no going backward and no changing your mind. And your life a little flag fluttering in the wind. Your life nothing but a ragged bit of cloth. —*Muh.* Like all orphans and prisoners condemned to death, she heard a voice she recognized as her own call out from someplace she didn't remember. —*Muh, muh, muh,* with every breath like a dagger. —*Ma,* she heard herself say, and it was as if she were all the women in history who had ever given birth, a cry, a chorus, the one and only, never-ending alpha and omega yowl of history, guttural and strange and frightening and powerful all at once. —*Ma, ma, ma* . . . Ma-má!

41

The Shameless Shamaness, the Wise Witch Woman María Sabina

All women have a bit of the witch in them. Sometimes they use it for ill, and sometimes they use it for good. One who used it shamelessly for good was the woman called María Sabina,* and though she was still young at the time of this story, already she had gained a reputation as a shamaness. So it was that Narciso Reyes working on the roads of Oaxaca came to hear of this woman with her great powers, and finally, because he could not bear his sleepless nights, twisting and turning in the net of his dreams and waking tangled in his hammock like a sad caught fish, was ripe to listen to what he would not have heard otherwise.

—Oh, it's that you're *embrujado*, that's what it is. Bewitched, that's all.

—Ah, is that it. He wanted to laugh but did not, because the village mayor was telling him this. The mayor was very, very old and said to be knowledgeable in these things.

—And what does one do about such bewitchings in these parts?

—You'll have to seek out the witch woman María Sabina. Up in the cold lands, in Huautla de Jiménez, where the clouds catch in the crags of the mountains, up there you'll find her. María Sabina Magdalena García is her name. I can't help you.

Narciso Reyes set out on a mule in search of this María, a journey that took him higher and higher into the wildest parts of Oaxaca, furiously beautiful but furiously poor country. He pushed his way past violent thickets and streams with water so clear and cold it hurt his teeth to take a drink. He scrambled up trails that tottered on the lips of precipices and through tropical forests tangled in knots of greedy vines. He rode past the laughing, ruffled leaves of banana groves and over brittle cow pastures, beyond lemon and orange trees and clearings of coffee plantations. The air was hot and moist, then cool, then hot again as it rose and rained, and the light, a lazy green color, alternately dimmed and brightened as he traveled under canopies of vegetation so thick the leaves let loose a soft talc of dust as he brushed past.

Along parts of the way Narciso followed the Río Santo Domingo upstream, swollen and rowdy from the downpours. Now and again at the clearings he saw black butterflies as big as bats fluttering in sleepy figure eights above blue flowers. Hot and steamy air made him cross at times, and then all at once an intense rain would begin so suddenly it gave him no time to seek shelter. Narciso sliced off gigantic heart-shaped leaves from the path without even getting off his mule, and these served as rain *poncho* and umbrella as well as a hat.

When the rain lifted into a fine drizzle and then stopped altogether, and the earth turned this into steam, hummingbirds darted nervously over dripping blossoms and then flickered off. The world smelled of mud, mule shit, flowers, rotten fruit, and far away of wood smoke, *nixtamal*, and refried beans. Wind from across the ravines, from across water, from across hot flatland, across tropical forests, across endless rows of sugarcane, through the ruffled banana trees, across all of Oaxaca, mixed itself with the sweet stink of Narciso's own skin.

There in the mountains in a lopsided hut of crumbling clay with an uneven floor also made of earth, in a dark that stank of pig manure and smoke, he found his witch woman. The house was empty except for a pitiful table that served as an altar and a bunch of naked children running about chasing the chickens.

She was dressed in rags. A skinny woman not much older than himself, her belly big with child.

—God is an immense cloth that contains the universe, she whispered.

This girl is crazy, Narciso thought and almost turned around to leave, but the trip up the mountain had taken eight days, by foot and by mule. He was filled with despair and doubt, until she began again.

—I'll tell you what it is you've come for, you, Narciso Reyes. You want a love medicine. Is that right?

—Yes, that's how it is.

—So that the woman who wears the crown of *iguanas* will come back and love only you, no?

—How did you know?

—You want her to fall under your spell?

—With all my heart I desire it.

—Well, then, it's obvious what you have to do. Forget her.

—Forget her!

—Yes, forget her. Abandon her. The more you let someone go, the more they fly back to you. The more you cage them, the more they try to escape. The worse you treat them, the crazier in love they are with you. Isn't that so? That's all. That's my love medicine for you today.

Of course, Narciso could not forget Exaltación. He was too much of a man. And because he would not forgive her preference for Pánfila over him, this only caused him to remember Exaltación even more. The pain overwhelmed him, caused him to say, —I hate you, Exaltación Henestrosa, which could only mean he loved her very much, otherwise, why bother. Because failures are much more memorable than successes, she was constantly in his thoughts. Forget Exaltación Henestrosa? No. That he could not do. And because he could not forget, she was lost to him, he was lost to her.

A person of independence, who does not need nor want us, inspires our admiration, and admiration is a love potion. A person who needs us too much, who is weak with neediness, inspires pity. And pity, the other side of admiration, is the antidote to love.

Remembering is the hand of God. I remember you, therefore I make you immortal. *Recuerdo.* I remember. *Un recuerdo.* A memory. A memento.

Years later, driving behind a truck full of brooms on the *periférico,* the memory of Exaltación Henestrosa would arrive, and with it, all the love Narciso had hoarded in a lifetime flooding the heart valves and heart chambers like a *zandunga,* and causing him great pain. *¡Ay, mamá, por Dios!*

In hand-painted pink letters, the bumper of the truck in front of him boasted this truth:

PODRÁS DEJARME, PERO OLVIDARME—¡NUNCA!

YOU MIGHT LEAVE ME, BUT FORGET ME?—NEVER!

*In the times of love and peace, an invasion of illegal aliens descended into Oaxaca, land of the siete moles, and ascended into the clouds of Huautla de Jiménez because of the magic mushrooms Ndjixito, "that which makes one become," which the locals had used in their religious ceremonies and healing rituals for thousands of years and which took one to trippier trips, it was said, than LSD. Hippies and vagabond anthropologists, artists, students, foreigners, the spoiled children of the rich, the Beatles, the Rolling Stones, Bob Dylan, the wives of politicians, the devout and the curious, anyone who was somebody and a whole string of nobodies came to see María Sabina and gain a shortcut to nirvana. Some leapt from the windows of hotels lost in the Age of Aquarius, some became a public nuisance, getting evicted from their hotels or falling asleep in the market like lopsided sacks of sugar, some chased each other around the zócalo bandstand naked, causing such a scandal, ay, what a nuisance, and some camping carelessly in the woods caused a terrible fire that burned thousands of acres of forests and fields and threatened half a dozen Indian villages, and all because that María Sabina gave those fools the mushrooms, the townspeople said. As a consequence, María Sabina became infamously famous, so famous that the sister of a Mexican president would come and visit her, and everyone would have their picture taken beside her as if she were a holy relic, and restaurants named "María Sabina" with even napkins carrying her name would profit from her celebrity, but María would live just as poor after everyone from professors to writers and politicians to television crews, absolutely everyone ran off, and would die penniless and almost naked as the day she was born, thanks to a lot of good-for-nothing offspring, not to mention the evil from the envy of neighbors—because her fame made them terribly aware of their own unhappy lives—who raised a ruckus because the confidentiality of the spiritual mushrooms had been betrayed to strangers who did not understand that the mushrooms were medicine and, like any medicine, only to be taken when ill, and therefore muddied their purpose on this planet, which in turn lessened María's powers, until finally she was acabada, finished, worn, done, so that at the end of her remarkable life, María Sabina was quoted as saying, — Was it all right that I gave away the mushrooms? Tú, what do you say?

Tú, reader, she is asking you.

42.

Born Under a Star

The baby was as bald as a knee, with a head like a peanut
and limbs like *chorizo*, but to Soledad he was exquisite.

—Isn't he beautiful? *Mi rey*, my king, she cooed, smacking one fat
foot with a loud kiss. —Someday you'll grow up to be a person of category, my fatty. Yes, my life, you were born under a star. You won't go
barefoot like I did when I was little. No, not you. You're a Reyes, right?
Aren't you? Aren't you, my heaven. You're destined to be a king. You'll
see. Right, *mi chulito*, right? Who's my beauty? Who's my little treasure?
Who loves you the best? I'm going to swallow you up, you fat little sweetness. You little tum-tum of *caramelo*. Yum, yum, yum, yum. What's the
matter, my heaven? Don't cry. Mamá loves you, and you're going to be a
king.

Baby Inocencio wore a lace bonnet with a huge fluted trim like a sunflower, like a star, and scowled as if he knew just how silly he looked.
—*Precioso*, his mama said to him and to no one in particular. —*Precioso*.

Once, a long time ago it seemed, Soledad had lain awake watching
Narciso sleep, marveling at her husband's profile, his sweet snoring, the
thick eyelashes, the delirious constellation of moles sprinkled on his man
shoulders, the sensuous down on the nape of his neck. —*Precioso*, she'd
whispered to herself, fascinated by the very elements that made Narciso a
man. His stiff whiskers, the swirl of sideburns, the strength in his wrists,
his jaw, the hard shield of his chest. She made an inventory of his charms.
People complained and complained about marriage, it seemed, but no one
mentioned the gift of sleeping beside another. —*Precioso*.

Now she watched Inocencio sleep beside her. *How is it God could pour
so much beauty into one little being*, she wondered. Maybe God made

babies beautiful because they needed so much care. Maybe God parceled out equal portions of beauty and of trouble, and that's how it was Narciso arrived with his enormous beauty and his equally enormous load of need.

Moths fluttered against the glass of the balcony doors, but they could not get in. The old man in the room next door coughed and spit up, as he always did before sleeping. A street vendor's whistle moaned from the plaza. In the distance a dog *yap-yapped*. The yellow eye of the moon peered through one pane of the French doors. It was night. Where was Narciso? Somewhere vague and far away, but it no longer mattered. She had made this little human being. This little human had grown inside her and now here he was, just as perfect as you please. *How do you do? Oh, I'm very well, very fine indeed.*

Very fine. Very. She looked and looked at her son, not remembering once what the *tamal* vendor outside the church had said about falling in love again that day she had been so sad. *Tanta miseria.* So much misery in the world. But so much humanity too. Just enough. Not too much. Just enough, thank God.

𝓗e was never happy unless he was sad. To tell the truth, his name should have been el Sufrido. But, no, it was Inocencio Reyes. In another life, he might've been a philosopher. Or a poet. He liked to think and think, a skinny youth who enjoyed examining life at length. He would walk around the block if things he saw were worth looking at more than once. A waitress with a thick forest of underarm hair. A black man with a white woman. A drunkard who had shit in his pants. These items deserved consideration. So taken was Inocencio with his thinking, he forgot he was mortal and not invisible to the eye, and was always startled whenever anyone stared back.

—He's a daydreamer, complained his schoolteachers.

—He's a thinker, said his mother in his defense. She liked to remind them how as a baby he had been colicky. —Cried and cried, day and night, crying and crying and crying, as if even then he knew his destiny. Not like my other babies.

True. Unlike his younger siblings—Fat-Face, Light-Skin, and the Baby—Inocencio's head was filled with too much remembering. Things he thought he remembered, and things invented for him to remember. —Before the revolution, when the family Reyes owned railroads . . . his mother would begin.

The Mexican revolution had tossed and tumulted everything, including everyone's memories. It was as if the revolution gave everyone from the most beggarly and poor an excuse to say, —Before the revolution when we were moneyed, and thus, to excuse their humble present. It was better to have a gallant past, because it made one's present circumstance seem all the more wretched and allowed one the liberty of looking down condescendingly on one's neighbors. Or, if there was no recent wealth, one could always resort to the distant past, —Remember our great-great-great-great-great-grandfather Nezahualcóyotl, the poet king? No such thing, but it sounded *bonito*.

Inocencio's family was neither rich nor poor, but part of a wide middle class that flourished in Mexico City while the U.S. suffered through the Depression. Boys like Inocencio were encouraged to strive for an education at the national university, especially if their fathers wanted them to avoid a military career. But a career of any kind, military or civilian, seemed the last thing on Inocencio's mind.

God had been kind and bestowed an aura of melancholia about Inocencio Reyes, and this coupled with his intense eyes, dark as Narciso's but shaped like his mother Soledad's, like slouching houses, would bless Inocencio with the air of a poet or a martyred Sebastian without having had to undergo either torture.

He did not choose to be unhappy. Who would choose to be unhappy? He was simply a boy without the words for what he was feeling, someone who felt most comfortable in the company of his own thoughts.

It would be a lifelong habit. When he wanted to become invisible, when he felt like leaving a room, when he couldn't bear being around the people he was around, the house he was housed in, the city where he was citizen, he left the premises without leaving the premises. Into the he, within-the-he, within-the-he. Without the body, that bad actor. Simply his soul, pure and unencumbered, oh!

It could be said Inocencio Reyes lived the life of a person in self-exile, happiest when he could devote himself to his daydreams. Love inspired him to think, as it inspires so many fools. He dedicated his life to this interior inquiry. He did not know he was continuing a tradition that traveled across water and sand from nomadic ancestors, Persian poets, Cretan acrobats, Bedouin philosophers, Andalusian matadors praying to la Virgen de la Macarena. Each had in turn influenced their descendant Inocencio Reyes. A low-ranking Baghdad vizier, an Egyptian cheesemonger, an Oulid Naid belly dancer wearing her dowry of coins around her hips, a gypsy holy man, a goose herder, an Arab saddle-maker, a scholar nun carried off by a Berber chieftain the day Córdoba was sacked, a Sephardic astronomer whose eyes were put out in the Inquisition, a pockmarked slave girl—the sultan's favorite—couched in a gold and ivory seraglio on the shores of the Abi Diz. Tunis. Carthage. Fez. Cartagena. Seville. And like his ancestors he attempted his own treatise on that enigma of enig-mas. What is love? How does one know one is in love? How many differ-ent kinds of love are there? Is there truly a love at first sight? Perhaps he was going as far back as our graffiti-artists grand-others of Altamira who painted on the walls of caves.

While other young men busied themselves with serious preparations for their profession, Inocencio took to staying up late at night, —Like a vampire! his father complained, and in these hours of darkness and light he indulged himself in what he loved to do most—dream. Asleep dream-ing or awake dreaming, this is what Inocencio did best.

He was thinking how is it a woman can collapse so comfortably with her legs folded beneath her like a cat. The seduction of the eyelids droop-ing when someone lit a cigarette. The charming *tac tac tac* of a high-heel shoe across tiles. Or a million and one observations cataloged as either nonsensical or brilliant, depending on your point of view.

To tell the truth, his mother sometimes thought him a little crazy, and in reality he was. A little crazy to be so happy alone putting thoughts together and taking them apart, and thinking over and over of what he should've said, and what someone meant by what they didn't say, the minute details of life, living his life turned around backward, living his life, reliving life and examining it to an unhealthy indulgence.

His first obsessions were about those things that overwhelmed and frightened him precisely because there was no language to name them. And he would seek out a quiet space and think until that smudge of emo-tion clarified itself. The fear and allure of the wind that set the trees and the arteries in his body trembling. The sunsets watched from the *azotea* when Mexico City was still smog-free and one could watch a sunset. The face of a blond, three-quarter profile, with the sun behind her and the down of her cheek ablaze.

Things like this filled him with a joy akin to sadness or a sadness akin to joy, and he found himself unable to explain why he was blinking back tears with an uncontrollable desire to laugh and cry all at once. —What? —I don't know, nothing, he might've said. But that was a lie. He should have said, —Everything, everything, ah, everything!

44.

Chuchuluco de Mis Amores

I don't know, but I keep asking myself, don't we need to see Narciso and me together more? To feel the passion we had? To believe in it? Don't you think? Just a little love scene? Something sweet would be nice. Come on, don't be bad.

Ay, qué fregona. All right. All! Right! Just one scene, but you've got to promise to quit interrupting. After this, no more noise from you! I can't work like this. Not another word until I'm finished no matter how the story turns out.

Not even if God commanded it! You won't even know I'm here. *Te lo juro.*

A dream is a poem the body writes. Even if we lie to ourselves in the day, the body is compelled to speak its truth at night. And so it was with Narciso, who cluttered his daytime hours with so much noise and distractions he didn't know his own heart, but was plagued with listening to its babbling all night.

—*Abrázame,* he'd say to his wife when she climbed into bed with him. —Hug me.

And hug him she would. That's how he was accustomed to falling asleep.

One night he dreamt this dream. They were asleep the way they always slept, his body nested inside hers, her arms around him. This is why the dream frightened him, because he wasn't aware he was dreaming. He was asleep with her holding him. At first it was a pretty feeling to be asleep inside the circle of someone's arms. But here is when he realized there was a third arm wrapped around him, and that's when he began to scream. On his side of the dream he was hollering and screeching, flailing and yelling, but on the other side, the body simply wheezed and whimpered as if it wanted to sneeze.

—There, there, it's only a dream. I'm here. Then Soledad snuggled closer and wrapped her arms around him tighter. A knot of frustration and fear, like a woolen sweater neither on nor off but tangled on one's head. She tugged him toward her, heat of her words in his ear. —There, there, there, I'm here.

It made him miserable, cranky, and mean toward her. Long after the stint in Oaxaca was over, and he had a family and was living in the capital, suddenly he dreamt a dream that surprised him. A dream of the other one, the sweetheart from the hotlands.

—You betray me every night, he heard himself tell her.

—Betray you? she said laughing. —You're married! Who are you to hold the word *betrayal* to my throat?

Then he tried to strangle her, but when he reached for her she turned into a fish and slipped through his fingers. When he woke he found himself filled with sadness.

He'd fallen in love with a mermaid. With her scent of the sea. The sweaty, gritty stew of lovemaking he loved. Her silver laugh. The purple orchid of her sex. That heat he remembered, even the sand flies, because they reminded him of her, the woman who did not care for him, unlike his mother and wife, who adored him. Men take women's love for granted. All his life he'd been cooed and coddled. It startled him to find this mighty, huge, and holy woman who didn't care for his approval. Of course, because of this, he loved her even more.

He could not forgive her. To forgive her for sex is bad enough, but it was not the sex that he could not let go. It was the love. After how many moons and suns had waxed and waned, plunged and plummeted into blackness, worn themselves bony and empty, and fattened themselves full again, yet the pain was still there, leaving him sharp-mouthed and cross and thin-eyed. The horn of a Guadalupe moon, the whalebone of the word lodged itself in the soft, fleshy part of his heart. *Love.*

Day sleeping or night sleeping, he lived his life like this, plagued by some annoyance he couldn't name, like a hair on his tongue. One day walking the streets of the capital he found himself suddenly with a craving for sweets. He couldn't explain why he felt an urge for *chuchulucos*. He was like a man sleepwalking until he came upon the candy shop Dulcería Celaya on Cinco de Mayo Street. He bought pumpkin-seed-studded *obleas*—transparent pastel wafers, pink, white, yellow, pale green, Ave María blue. He bought marzipan hens, *cajeta* from Celaya, guayaba paste, sesame seed candy, burnt-milk bars, candied limes filled with coconut, candied sweet potato with cinnamon and cloves, glazed orange rinds, candied pumpkin, tamarind balls, coconut bars, those cone-shaped suckers called *pirulís*, lassos of *membrillo*, almond nougats, Mexican delicacies dubbed Fatties, Harlequins, Queens, Joys, Alleluias, Glories, and those sublime meringue drops named Farts of a Nun. He bought everything he pointed to, and stumbled out of the shop with his sugary purchases, toward where?

It was an extraordinary day, sun-dappled, tepid, as clean and soft as a cotton dish towel used to wrap the fresh *tortillas*. He wished he had a room alone he could go to to wash his face. Perhaps he should rent a hotel room? But the thought of a hotel room. Hotel rooms depressed him. They were filled with memories of other bodies, of sadnesses, of joys no amount of *copal* or pine-scented disinfectant could flush out. No, he could not bring himself to rent a room filled with someone else's emotions.

Narciso meandered toward the green of the Alameda and in the curly flutes and spirals of an iron bench he finally found refuge. The ashes and willows never seemed so transparent and cool as at that moment, as if the world were underwater and everything set in motion by distant whirlpools and currents.

A street dog with rusty fur sniffed at his left shoe, and instead of kicking it away, he watched himself feed it a yellow marzipan chicken. *Membrillo*, burnt milk, pink-edged coconut bars, Narciso and the rusty dog ate it all. He filled himself up with sugar, oblivious to the splendors of pork rind vendors, indecent lovers, and the exuberance of clouds.

Narciso ate the *chuchulucos*, but they tasted like the food in dreams, of air, of nothing. He wasn't even aware he was eating in just the same way he was not aware the light was dimming, clouds tearing into gauzy shreds across the sky, the dog trotting away satisfied.

Sadness was gathering where it always gathered, first in the tip of the nose, and then in the eyes and throat, and in the twilight sky running like a ruined cloth, not all the sugared sweets in the world could stop it. He chewed slowly the last bit of *caramelo*, carefully, the molars grinding, the jaw working, great gobs of saliva washing down his throat. His teeth hurt, but, no, that wasn't it. His heart hurt. And something else. Exaltación Henestrosa. He said her name. A deep root of pain. The little wall he had built against her memory crumbling like sugar.

45

'Orita Vuelvo

Why did I think I could expect any understanding from you? You have the sensitivity of an ax murderer. You're killing me with this story you're telling. *Me maaataaas.*

Please. Quit the theatrics.

That's what comes from being raised in the United States. *Sin memoria y sin vergüenza.*

You're mistaken. I do too have shame. That's how I know where the stories are.

Don't you have any self-respect? I'm never going to tell you anything again. From here on, you're on your own.

The less you tell me, the more I'll have to imagine. And the more I imagine, the easier it is for me to understand you. Nobody wants to hear your invented happinesses. It's your troubles that make a good story. Who wants to hear about a nice person? The more terrible you are, the better the story. You'll see . . .

With such fierce love uniting mother and son, Inocencio Reyes should've been the type of boy who never strayed from Soledad's side. But it's precisely because she loved him so much that he was destined to be her cross. God loves an interesting plot.

Like the Chinese blessing-curse, Inocencio Reyes had the misfortune to grow up in interesting times and witness the beginning of Mexico's Golden Age. While the U.S. suffered its Depression, Mexico was undergoing its finest decade. President Cárdenas threw out the foreign investors and nationalized the oil companies to the cheers of all the nation. Assisted by the new government, the arts flourished, creating a new *mestizo* identity proud of its Indian heritage, though in reality Indians were still treated like Indians everywhere, like dirt. National industries were created to fabricate the imported goods no longer available because of the war. Franklin Roosevelt's "Good Neighbor Policy" invited Mexican workers to harvest U.S. crops, since the U.S. labor force was depleted by the draft. And young men like Inocencio could even brag that Mexico had done its part to aid the Allies by sending a small but brave air unit, Squadron 201,* to assist General MacArthur in the Philippines.

Let's be honest. Soledad Reyes was not an educated woman. So how could she be blamed for neglecting her children's education? She hardly had any schooling herself and was in no position to supervise theirs. Her husband should have been the one to advise his wife in this matter, and advise he would have, if he had noticed his offspring. But the truth is, Narciso hardly knew they were alive. His job kept him traveling to backwater outposts, and traveling back home was often difficult. To tell the truth, he was happier alone, lost in his own concerns. He hardly knew his family and they hardly knew him. He was shy and awkward with these strangers. He would've liked to have been warmer with them, but he didn't know how. So much time had lapsed.

Order. He relied on his military upbringing to create some kind of discipline, some kind of affection with his children.

—Sergeant Inocencio, are these my troops?

—They are, my general.

It had been a long time since he played with his children. He no longer knew how to play.

So when Inocencio brought home mediocre grades, Narciso shouldn't have blamed anyone but himself. Of course, it was not himself he blamed. He hoped his son could have the opportunities he did not. Inocencio was coerced into applying to the national university, but unfortunately, he did not apply himself to his studies.

One semester later, Inocencio's final grades terrified him into realizing he'd spent more time with women than with books. What could he do? His father was a strict man who came home seldom and who was seldom understanding. Narciso had already run off Fat-Face for being *un burro*, and now Fat-Face was vagabonding the U.S.

—You're nothing but a *burro*, you'll never amount to anything, Narciso had too often said to Fat-Face, and because the power of words spoken by those we love is so strong, they stung Fat-Face's heart. If he was never going to amount to anything, why bother trying, right? Fat-Face hopped on the back of a flatbed truck filled with corn husks and shivered all the way through the Desert of the Lions until he found his way to the border, and meandered through the United States.

Inocencio admired his younger brother's audacity. Inocencio had always been the good boy, while Fat-Face had been the adventurer. Now that Inocencio was in trouble, he chose to take to the road and join his brother Fat-Face hitching trains and picking up women. At least this is how Inocencio imagined it.

And so, Inocencio Reyes set off with Chicago as his eventual goal. He had relatives there. The sons of Uncle Old. It would only be for a few months, he reasoned. —When Father calms down, he promised his mother, —I'll come right home.

*During World War II, a squadron of Mexican fighter pilots, Escuadron 201, helped liberate Luzon and Formosa. Created by Mexican president Manuel Ávila Camacho in 1944, the squadron of 38 fighter pilots and 250 ground personnel serving under U.S. orders logged 59 missions and 1,290 hours of combat flight time.

For a super-sentimental story of Squadron 201, see Indio Fernández' splendid Salon México, a classic. Note the Mexican matriarchy scene between the injured returning pilot and his angelic mother. This scene alone will explain everything.

46

Spic Spanish?

*T*he old proverb was true. Spanish was the language to speak to God and English the language to talk to dogs. But Father worked for the dogs, and if they barked he had to know how to bark back. Father sent away for the Inglés Sin Stress home course in English. He practiced, when speaking to his boss, —*Gud mórning, ser.* Or meeting a woman, —*Jáu du iú du?* If asked how he was coming along with his English lessons, —*Veri uel, ɀanc iú.*

Because Uncle Fat-Face had been in the States longer, he gave Father advice. —Look, when speaking to police, always begin with, "Hello, my friend."

In order to advance in society, Father thought it wise to memorize several passages from the "Polite Phrases" chapter. I congratulate you. Pass on, sir. Pardon my English. I have no answer to give you. It gives me the greatest pleasure. And: I am of the same opinion.

But his English was odd to American ears. He worked at his pronunciation and tried his best to enunciate correctly. —Sir, kindly direct me to the water closet. —Please what do you say? —May I trouble you to ask for what time is? —Do me the kindness to tell me how is. When all else failed and Father couldn't make himself understood, he could resort to, —*Spic Spanish?*

Qué strange was English. Rude and to the point. No one preceded a request with a —Will you not be so kind as to do me the favor of . . . , as one ought. They just asked! Nor did they add —If God wills it to their plans, as if they were in audacious control of their own destiny.

It was a barbarous language! Curt as the commands of a dog trainer. —Sit. —Speak up. And why did no one say, —You are welcome. Instead, they grunted, —Uh-huh, without looking him in the eye, and without so much as a —You are very kind, mister, and may things go well for you.

47

He Who Is Destined to Be a Tamale

*L*ike the Mexican saying goes, he who is destined to be a *tamal* will find corn shucks falling from the sky, and Inocencio is one lucky *tamale*. In Little Rock Inocencio is finally recognized for the royalty he is. He's not a wetback. He's a Reyes. Mr. Dick understands this.

It's during the time Inocencio is shucking oysters. He works in a big seafood restaurant called Crabby Craig's Crab Kingdom with a neon crab opening and closing its pincers. It's a step up to be shucking oysters. In Waco he'd been a dishwasher, in Dallas a busboy. In San Antonio he had coughed up dust and sneezed black for weeks after collecting pecans. And now here he was in a nice white jacket, almost as nice as his own tuxedo hanging in his closet at home.

For a time Inocencio enjoys his job shucking oysters. But after a while his hands sting from the nicks and cuts. The ice doesn't help. The wounds keep getting irritated from the lemon juice. Inocencio takes to wearing white cotton gloves, and Mr. Dick, the boss, is impressed by this added touch, which he mistakes for elegance instead of practicality.

Inocencio *is* very elegant in his white jacket and black bow tie, his white cotton gloves and his face of a young Errol Flynn. He could be el Catrín in the Lotería cards, the Mexican bingo. He could be Claude Rains with his pencil-thin mustache. He could be the debonair Gilbert Roland with his wavy dark hair and dark eyes. When he opens his mouth and asks, —May I serve you? he says it in such a charming way, the women customers are sure to ask, —Are you French? Or, —I've got it—you're Spanish, right? They don't say "Mexican," because they don't want to insult Inocencio, but Inocencio doesn't know "Mexican" is an insult.

At the end of the day, before Inocencio walks back to the room he rents at the hotel around the corner from the bus station, he announces to the Puerto Rican busboy, —Today I worked *como un negro,* which is what they say in Mexico when they work very hard. When a white man says, —I worked like a black man, he means he hardly worked at all. But Inocencio is not a white man, although his skin is white. Today I worked like a black man, to the one other white man who is not white—the Puerto Rican busboy.

Mr. Dick and his wife take a special liking to Inocencio. Mrs. Dick thinks it a shame Inocencio has to go home each night to that awful transient nest full of riffraff, a young man of such good manners. —You come with us, you don't belong there. And so Inocencio goes home with Mr. and Mrs. Dick and he lives with them for a time almost like a son. —Thank you, Inocencio, says Mrs. Dick, patting his hand with her speckled twig of a hand when he brings her her gin and tonic. —With pleasure, Inocencio says. —Yes, truly a good man, says Mr. Dick when Inocencio lights his cigarette. Inocencio cannot believe his good fortune and is grateful to excess, polite as a Mexican ought to be, famous for his compliments and grandiosity.

Once when Inocencio is serving highballs, Mr. Dick says, —The Mexicans know how to live. Do you think they care who is president or what is going on outside their small villages? These people live for the now. The past and the future mean nothing to them. They are a people who live in the clouds and are better off for it.

—Sir, I am of the same opinion, said Inocencio. He could not think what else to say. And even if he had, he couldn't say it.

—Let's drink to you, Inocencio, said Mr. Dick. —And to your happy race.

—You are very kind, sir. If Inocencio had had a *sombrero,* he would've taken it off and bowed.

48

Cada Quien en Su Oficio Es Rey

Uncle Old was already dust by the time Inocencio tumbled off a Greyhound bus in downtown Chicago, and with many please, most kind, and very thank-yous, arrived finally at the address of his Uncle Snake's upholstery shop on South Halsted. Chubby, Curly, and Snake had all inherited their father's trade, but only Snake had inherited his father's business. Uncle Snake, like Uncle Old before him, was only too ready to take in lost kin and to offer him all he had, even if all he had was not much.

It was the same storefront where Inocencio's father had stayed when the country was gripped in an earlier world war, and the shop was just as dirty as ever. The smoky windows were covered with pieces of fabric scraps, and in a rustic shelf unit were bolts and bolts of grimy old material stacked like scrolls in an ancient library. Overstuffed chairs shaped like grandmothers in flowered Sunday dresses, couches huge and rotund as fighter airplanes, cupcake footstools, and fringed chaise lounges all were piled one on top of the other like Aztec pyramids. But unlike his fussy father, Inocencio found the chaos of his uncle's shop an opportunity; something for him to improve and, therefore, make himself useful.

—Do you remember when my father came to live with your family, or were you too little, Uncle Snake?

—Remember? I'm the one who taught your father everything he knows. But he was never cut out to be an upholsterer. I tried, but he just didn't have it in him. I hope to God you don't take after him. Let's see. Let's look at your hands, *mijito*. Have you ever lifted a hammer before?

—I once demolished a chicken coop my mother wanted removed from the roof after all the chickens died. Does that count for something?

—Sure, why not. The important thing is to have *ganas,* and you've got necessity biting you on the ass, I can see that. Your father's problem was he didn't feel like learning a trade. Didn't have any respect for upholstery. So how can you do a job right if you don't respect it, right? Got to have pride in your labor, Inocencio. Put your heart and your soul into it. You don't want to be famous for making junk, do you? After all, your work is your signature, remember that.

Uncle Snake lived in the upholstery shop because his wife wouldn't let him come upstairs. She'd been angry at him since 1932. That's the truth. Gradually he took to adapting his workspace into a home.

It began with cutting his nails with the upholstery scissors. Then a hot plate. Then a homemade shower rigged from a garden hose, a washtub, and an old screen. A jagged triangle of mirror above the sink to shave. And finally trimming his own hair and sucking away the clippings from his neck with the compressor.

—Well, no wonder I look like I do. He'd run his hand over his scalp, laughing.

He was not exaggerating. His hair looked like a coyote had chewed it. His joints and muscles sagged, slack and tired like an old mattress. And his clothes were as rumpled as if he'd slept in them. He had. Over everything, tufts of lint and pieces of string—hair, day-old beard, eyelashes and eyebrows, raggedy undershirt, baggy trousers, socks, even his shoes with the tips that curled up because they were too big for him.

—I'm turning into a chair, he'd say, and laugh.

—Upholstery is simple, Uncle Snake began. —It's all a matter of getting the taste of it, see? A taste for the Italian twine when you lick it like so before threading the curved needle. The iron flavor of a handful of tacks in your mouth and the cold hammer pressed to your lips when you kiss it to pick up a tack. The dust fibers from the ripped batting swirling in the air and in your nose, the cotton stuffing, the fabric scraps, the endless sweeping up all day like a barber's assistant, the bent tacks stuck on the soles of the shoes, the *crkkk, crkkk, crkkk* of scissors cutting fabric, the rolling Spanish "r" of the sewing machines. You've just got to get the taste of it, that's all. In no time at all you'll be a master upholsterer, Inocencio. Take my word for it. But first you've got to start at the bottom.

This said, he handed Inocencio the broom, and with the broom as partner, Inocencio Reyes began his royal profession.

49

Piensa en Mí

1945. The holding tank. The Chicago police station, Homan and Harrison. Lights bright and blazing like a supermarket, chipped pea-green paint, benches too narrow to sit on and too crowded to sleep, a latrine in the center of the room stinking of urine and vomit and shit, cement floor as sticky as a movie theater's. But worst of all, the echo of doors slamming shut.

—Lord, lord, lord, this place is a fucking hellhole. This place is a fucking hellhole. This place is a fucking hellhole.

—Would you please be quiet.

—Jeez! This place is a fucking hellhole. This place is a fucking hellhole. This place is a fucking . . .

—Can't someone make that cat pipe down?

—Lordy, lord, lord. Hellhole, man. Fucking . . .

—You try. He's been at it for over half an hour. Like the hiccups. He's driving us all nuts.

—Fucking hellhole, my God. This place is a fucking fucking hell . . .

—Shut up already! a voice like a cartoon ordered from inside the latrine.

—Who said that?

—I did!

—Who? Ain't no one in the stall.

—Me! That's who, you big stupid! Me! A piece of turd, you piece of turd. It takes one to know one, and I said shut the hell up!

—!

A nervous laughter rippled through the room, a reflex like muscle twitching off a fly; it made everyone feel better, if only for a little while.

They were ugly, all right. It hurt to even look at one another. Bruised and shivering like dogs left out in the rain. They'd been hauled in for fighting, for pissing, for cussing, for shoving sharp edges into flesh, for sneezing, for spitting, for cracking skulls or cracking knuckles, for picking pockets or picking fights, running when they should've walked, walking when they should've run. For having the misfortune of calling attention to themselves at the wrong place at the right time. Whether guilty or innocent, they all whimpered, —I didn't do nothing, I didn't do nothing. Wherever they came from, they sure as hell didn't want to belong here.

Inocencio Reyes felt like crying and puffed on his last Lucky trying not to. He'd never felt worse. He had a big yellow swelling on his left eyebrow, one eye sealed shut like Popeye, and a lip split an octopus color. His face felt oily, and he could smell himself on himself, a sharp metallic scent to his flesh. There was a film over his good eye that made him keep blinking, and a bitter taste on his tongue and teeth. His nostrils and mustache were crusted with blood. And though he'd hardly eaten anything, he kept belching up bile and couldn't control his farting. Each time he thought about how he got here he felt his stomach cringe like a dog being kicked. His kidneys throbbed. And he couldn't sit down without his back hurting. Everything hurt, every bone and muscle, even his dirty, stiff hair.

The only one who didn't appear to belong to this *inframundo* was an older fellow dressed in a dapper tuxedo and tails. To make matters even more comic, he was wearing a top hat. He looked like an aging Fred Astaire.

Maybe because of the cold, or the fear in his throat, or all the things he'd been holding in since they dragged him in, Inocencio started to cough and couldn't stop coughing. The man in the top hat whacked him on the back until he could breathe again.

—*Zaw-rright*, my friend?

—*Zaw-rright*, Inocencio answered. —Thank yous. Many thanks.

—You are most welcome, the tuxedo man said with a curious accent, like a broom sweeping across a stone floor.

—*Spic Spanish?* Inocencio ventured.

—Finally! Someone who speaks the language of God! Wenceslao Moreno* to serve you, the tuxedo man said proudly and tipped his top hat, flashing for a moment a bald head.

—Inocencio Reyes at your orders, Inocencio replied, relieved to find himself in the company of someone who was his equal. —I regret this is my last cigarette, but, please, take half.

—No, no, I would not even think of it.

—I insist. Don't offend me, Inocencio said.

—As you wish. Many thanks.

—There is no cause for it. It's a pleasure to find someone who speaks Castilian in this dog pit. Are you Spanish? Inocencio asked.

—Yes. I think it's not an exaggeration to say there are more Spaniards living in other countries than back in Spain.

—I understand you. I am a Mexican national by birth, but my father's father was from Seville.

—Is that so? Wenceslao said, studying Inocencio's face.

—That's how it is. Look at my nose.

—But it's obvious, man. You have the profile of a Moor. And the same ill fortune. What brought you here, my friend?

—Honor, said Inocencio. —They mistook me for a drunk and an irresponsible and hauled me in with a carload of criminals. And you?

—The same, Wenceslao Moreno said, sighing. —So what's your story?

—Well, look, Inocencio said, pausing for effect. —I don't want to bore you with a lot of talk, but since you ask. It all began rather innocently. You won't believe it! At a soccer match.

—A soccer match? Wenceslao said. —I believe it.

—Well, let me tell you, how it happened was like this. I often frequent Grant Park to watch the Mexican team, and, as Destiny would have it, our team was playing against a local team of Mexicans from over here, American Mexicans, I mean. People think because we carry the same blood we're all brothers, but it's impossible for us to get along, you have no idea. They always look down on us nationals, understand? And so whenever we scored, some *pocho* would shout an insult, "Sons of the fucked whore," or something or other, terrible things.

Worse was their lack of respect during the Mexican national anthem. They started tossing a lady's stocking filled with piss and sand. They swung it over their heads like this, like David and Goliath, and let it go flying over to our side, where that filth rained all over us. You can imagine what a bunch of animals I'm talking about, right?

The last straw was when some monkey started insulting Mexico. That's even worse than someone insulting your mother. That this thing, and this, and that. Well . . . some of the things he said are true. But it hurts to have them said all the same! Especially because they *are* true, understand? And then they started with, "We didn't come to this country because we were starving to death," that's what they said. "No," I said. "You came because your fathers were a bunch of cowards and deserted their *patria* during its time of need." That's when they answered with their fists, even the players joined in. An entire field of tangled arms and bodies, and the next thing I know the police are rounding us up and clubbing us both, Mexican Mexicans and American Mexicans, herding us like cattle into their wagons, I'm not lying. And that made us all mad as hell, you can imagine. And the Mexicans from over here more American than anything, and us Mexicans from over there even more Mexican than Zapata. And, well, what more can I tell you? Here I am.

—But you were only doing your patriotic duty, Wenceslao added.

—Correct.

—You wouldn't be a true patriot if you didn't defend your country. These *norteamericanos* don't understand about honor.

—That's how it is, my friend, Inocencio sighed. —*Qué suave* your clothes. Very elegant. I've always wanted a tuxedo with tails. And the white tie and cummerbund. Sharp.

—Thank you, but I'm afraid these aren't mine. Borrowed from a colleague. Though I really think they suit me.

—*Fíjese nomás.* It looks as if it was tailored for you, Inocencio said.

—You don't think the hat makes me look too foolish?

—Not at all, a true gentleman is what you look like. It gives you class, if you ask me, and class, in my experience, always opens doors. With your permission, may I ask what is your profession?

—Better I show you, Wenceslao said, —if you will permit me.

—But of course.

Wenceslao Moreno looked inside the latrine door, called inside the toilet, and shouted, —*Zaw-rright?* And a voice from deep inside the toilet bowl gurgled back, —*Zaw-rright!* He walked about, found a match on the floor, and drew a pair of eyes with dark eyebrows on his fist.

The fist said in a high wobbly voice, —*Señor Wences, tengo miedo.*

—Are you afraid, Johnny, my friend?

—*Sí, señor. Y la verdad, tengo muchas ganas de llorar. Llorar y orinar.*

—There's nothing to be afraid about, Johnny. Don't worry. I know exactly how you feel. Would you like a little entertainment? Perhaps a song to cheer us up, then? I know just the thing. How about a nice Mexican *bolero* for our Mexican guest here? He pulled his pocket inside out a bit and had his pocket sing, "Piensa en mí," a sad song guaranteed to make you cry, even when you're happy.

—*Si tienes un hondo penar, piensa en mí.*

Si tienes ganas de llorar, piensa en mí.

Inocencio swallowed back his own grief, but just then Wenceslao's bologna sandwich began to complain about the singer. And the cockroaches scurrying across the ceiling hurled funny insults as well. Laughing, Inocencio forgot he was waiting in a miserable cell. He was fed with laughter, and this nourished him a little. When Wenceslao stopped, Inocencio broke into furious applause.

—*Maestro*, you're a genius!

—Not so much a genius, just an artist. And these days that's genius enough. I work in the theater. Traveling. Maybe it's Chicago today, tomorrow it might be Nashville. This tuxedo is my magician friend's. I borrowed it for a wedding. But at the reception some fellows got too drunk, and before you know it, a fight broke out. Isn't that how it always goes? I was out the door and down the block before the police even got there. Then I remembered I'd left my puppets at the hall, because I was supposed to perform at the reception. That was my gift to the bride and groom. Of course, I was obliged to return, they're my livelihood. And that's when the police mistook me for one of the troublemakers and pounced on me. So there we were, understand? I had my puppets under each arm and was making my way out when *whoosh!* One big gorilla tried to yank them from me. I wouldn't let them go, of course. Next thing I know he had me by the neck like this, and another gorilla bends my arms behind my back like so, as if I was a puppet, and then to add insult to it all, they banged my puppets into chalk dust right before my eyes. You have no idea. It was like seeing my own children being murdered. I can't tell you how it breaks my heart. I'm still sick when I think of it.

Wenceslao paused to blow his nose. —You must think I'm a big fool. But that's my wonderful life for you. I'd do anything for just a little luck.

I've been on the stage for twenty, more than twenty years and have nothing to show for it yet. Look at me. I'm not young anymore.

—Nonsense! You're well conserved, *maestro*.

—Well conserved or not, if something doesn't happen soon . . . I just don't know. Of course, going back to Spain is out of the question. The war.

—Well, of course.

Wenceslao sighed. And then, as if to fight off sadness, he made the fist-puppet talk:

—And you, Señor Inocencio, what about you? What do you wish for?

—Me? Well, right now two things. One, to get out of here. The other, to fix my papers. There's sure to be trouble for me after this arrest. It's that I'm not here legally, see. I'll be deported for certain. And, like you, I can't go home either because . . . well, because of my father. He and I . . .

—Don't see eye to eye? Wenceslao finished the sentence for him.

—That's how it is.

—I understand. So. You wish only for two things? To get out of here and to fix your papers?

—You can't imagine how much.

—I think I can, I think I can. Well, leave it to me. I'm a bit of a magician myself. Watch.

They waited until the next officer walked past and then a little voice erupted from out of Inocencio without his even moving his lips. It said this:

—Officer! Pardon the trouble, but I do not have the English.

—What did you say, wise guy?

—Excuse, Wenceslao interrupted. —My friend here says he wishes to enlist.

—Oh, is that so?

—Yes, sir, Wenceslao continued. —I beg you to be so kind. Let me present my friend Inocencio . . .

—Reyes, Inocencio said.

—Yes. Inocencio Reyes here, who desires very much to become an enlisted man.

—!!! Yes, Inocencio stammered. —With all my heart, officer my friend. Please please.

—Oh, yeah? So, you want to join up, eh? Seems to me the whole bunch of yous should be sent to the front line. Uncle Sam ain't picky these days. I'll ask someone up front to personally escort you to the nearest enlistment station, buddy. Hold on.

After he'd left, Inocencio said, —What, are you crazy? I don't want to enlist.

—You said you wanted to get out of here and fix your papers, right? And unless you have money, my friend, this is the easiest way, believe me.

—Well, my father *was* a military man. Maybe he'd be proud of me finally if . . .

—Of course. Don't worry. You're young. You've got nine lives. You can do anything. But look at me. Here I am at midlife going nowhere. I'm tired. How many times can a man reinvent himself? I've got absolutely nothing, no energy, no money, no family, not even my puppets. I'm finished, I tell you, I'm dead.

—But, *maestro*. Don't exaggerate. As long as God keeps loaning you life, you'll do well. I'm certain. You're a genius. You make everything come to life. In my opinion you don't need toys. It seems to me you're excellent with what God gave you, your imagination and your wit.

—Think so?

—Absolutely. Trust me.

—Well . . . they may have destroyed my instruments, but not my music!

—That's it!

Just as Wenceslao Moreno was expounding on the nature of art, a police officer unlocked the door and shouted:

—Moreno! Out!

—How?

—You're free. Some clown just paid your bail. Says he's a magician.

—Ah! My friend the escape artist, of course! The greatest since Houdini, in my opinion. An excellent man! But look what time it is! If I hurry I can just make it to the theater. No time to change. I'll have to go just as I am. No harm in that, is there? I'll make do without my puppets. Improvise, as they say. After all, the show must go on!

—*¡Bravo, maestro!*

—Inocencio, my friend, it's been a true pleasure. I'm off. So long. Wish me shit.

—*¡Mierda!* said a voice from inside the toilet bowl.

Inocencio laughed, and his spirit squeezed between the bars of his jail cell, somersaulted in a shaft of sunlight, floated past the armed policemen, ascended into the starry heavens, and escaped on the wings called hope.

Spanish ventriloquist Wenceslao Moreno, Señor Wences, became a big success in the fifties and sixties, appearing many times on The Ed Sullivan Show. *Like Desi Arnaz and Gilbert Roland, he was one of the first Latinos we ever saw on television. Then, as now, there were hardly any Latinos on TV who were actually Latino and not some* payaso *pretending to be Latino. In his elegant tux and with his elegant accent, Señor Wences thrilled us and made us feel proud of who we were. I wonder if he ever realized this gift he gave us. He died April 20, 1999, in New York City at the age of 103.*

Neither with You
Nor Without You

A fanfarrón, nothing but a big show-off, she'll confess in disgust, first to the best friend, Josie, and later and always to us. She's talking about Father, what she thinks when she first meets him. How he's full of the sweet scent of Tres Flores hair oil and full of shit. But she never says why she kept seeing him. Zoila Reyna couldn't tell her sisters or herself. She's not the kind to tell someone her feelings. She's not one to think about *those* things.

Better to not think. *Ni contigo ni sin ti*—tumbling and repeating itself in her head, like a jingle from the radio. *Neither with you nor without you . . .*

Friday. 8:49 when a skinny private with a face like Errol Flynn steps in with eight of his friends and a cigarette in his mouth. He never goes anywhere without a cigarette and a whole bunch of hangers-on hanging on. His army buddies. And you can bet he pays when they haven't got a dime. He's a good sport like that.

—It's that I'm a gentleman.

—A fool, mumbled she.

Better than sitting at home, Zoila thinks, with the clock ticking toward and then past the hour Enrique* used to telephone. The clock, the calendar, the hours, weeks, months. The silence. The silence like an answer. The silence an answer. There was a little hole in her heart where he'd once been, and when she breathed, the air hurt her there, there. Before. And then after. Before. After.

The dance hall smelling of the men in uniform, of Tres Flores hair oil, of Tweed cologne. The wooden floor old and stained like a pissy mattress. Women wearing hair snoods, silk flowers bought at the five-and-dime bobby-pinned behind one ear like Billie Holiday.

The Reyna sisters. Aurelia, Mary Helen, Frances, Zoila. In flowered crepe and open-toed platform shoes. The best friend, Josie. The swish of skirt and lipstick pressed on toilet paper. Nylons that cost a whole dollar. —An hour of standing at the cookie factory these cost me!

—Full of himself, she'll say. —A big talker. Nothing but talk. A mile a minute. Can't fool me.

Wants to go to Mexico. —Ever been there? Never? I'll take you there. I've got a new car. Not here. Over there. Miss, would you care to dance?

—Get a load of her.

Looked after a redhead with big floppy breasts. —*Chiches* Christ! Looked at a *morenita* with a heart-shaped ass. —*¡Nálgame Dios!* Did the jitterbug with a flirtatious *tejana* with a dress so tight you could see the mound of her *panocha, te lo juro.*

Zoila Reyna dressed in a crepe skirt and a pink see-through blouse she borrowed from her older sister Aurelia after three days of begging. —*Huerca,* you'll ruin it! —I won't, I promise—please—I'll wash it by hand. A pink blouse with rhinestones and pearls sewn around the collar. Hair brushed a hundred times each night and draped over one eye like Veronica Lake. Zoila has a way with hair, does all her sisters'. Her sister Frances won't let anyone touch her hair but Zoila.

—Comb me like Betty Grable.

First you put a rat in, and comb the hair over it like this. Then you dip the comb in that clear green gel, and you use plenty of bobby pins, and then you finish with a hairnet. She takes her time. She likes doing hair. Maybe she'll even take classes at the Azteca Beauty College on Blue Island. Zoila, who studies the magazines—*Mirror, Hollywood.* She can tell you anything. Who Linda Darnell was married to before she got famous. How Gene Tierney paints her eyebrows into a perfect arch. The secret to Rita Hayworth's shiny hair.

Zoila Reyna looking in the crowd for his face. Enrique. The crowd of black-haired men. *Enrique. Enrique,* she had said to herself, and every cell inside her filled with light.

She couldn't admit that she still telephoned, would hang up before anyone answered. Once she had let it ring and someone answered, but the voice on the other end was a child's voice and said no one with that name lived there. Some nights, she still walked past the house, *that* house, though she knew Enrique no longer lived there. Even the street name made her shiver. *Hoyne. Silly, ain't it? Silly, just plain goofy. A silly girl. That's me.*

Records starting before the band. Peggy Lee's sassy voice singing "Why Don't You Do Right?" Bodies pressed against each other, sad swishing sounds of feet dragging across dance floor.

When she was little and had a wound on a hand or knee, some place that broke the body's symmetry, she would look at the unharmed twin and compare it with the limb that was now swollen and plum-colored. This is how my hand had been before the fence tore it open and this is how my hand is now. Before. And after. Before. And now this.

Something like this happened to Zoila Reyna when she met Enrique Aragón. There was her life before him, smooth and whole and complete, without her ever being aware or grateful for its well-being, and then her life after Enrique Aragón, taut and tender. Forever after.

Dressed in a borrowed pink blouse and skirt too big for that skinny girl's body, hangs on her hips, pinned it with a safety pin. Bring-me-luck blouse, and a pair of gold earrings bought on layaway.

Not Hank. Not Henry. "Enrique," *he'd said. Enrique Aragón, in Spanish.* And not a crooked Spanish either, like her own. A Spanish luxurious as gold silk wrapped in tissue, an English crisp and creased as a pocket handkerchief. A tongue that leapt from the whir of one to the starched linen of the other with the ease of an acrobat on a flying trapeze. Enrique, this name with its tongue trill, with its patent leather shoes and toe taps clacking down an ivory stairway built by Ziegfeld, this name in tux and tails, began its reign of terror. She had taken to writing the name beside her own a thousand times in ballpoint pen, on napkins, in between the lipstick print of her lips on toilet paper. Enrique Aragón. Enrique Aragón. Enrique Aragón. And sometimes if she dared, Zoila Aragón.

"Mi reina," *Enrique had said once.* "Neither with you nor without you," *he'd told her. That's what he'd said. And it's as if love is some kind of war.* "Are you brave enough to sacrifice everything for love? Are you?" *he'd said.*

Enrique Aragón. Mr. Aragón's son, who traveled and was here in Chicago for a little, and then there, Los Angeles. Because los Aragón owned a lot of movie theaters in Chicago and L.A.—Teatro San Juan, Las Américas, El Tampico, La Villa, El Million Dollar—all raggedy and run down, with a flickering version of some old black-and-white Mexican western. *Jalisco, no te rajes. Soy puro Mexicano. Yo maté a Rosita Alvírez. Ni contigo ni sin ti . . .*

The Reyna sisters, always loud. Making so much noise in English, so much noise with their crooked Spanish. Winking over the shoulder of this sister being taken out to dance, the others giggling, —Not if you paid me! —Want him? *Te lo regalo.* —*Tú que sabes de amor, tú que nunca has besado un burro.* —*¡Un burro!* Do you know what that means? —Your mind's in the gutter. —Want that one, Zoila? I'll give him to you after I'm through. —I'm telling you, you can have him, I don't want him.

Her sisters nudging Zoila when the private with eyes like little houses and a pointy mustache comes over and asks Zoila to dance, in Spanish, and how the Spanish reminds Zoila of Enrique Aragón. And how she shrugs and joins him out on the dance floor, with a couldn't-care-less attitude. He does all the talking. —Inocencio Reyes at your orders. Mexico City is where I'm from. My family very important. My grandfather a composer who played for the president. Me, my, my, have you ever been there? I'll take you. I have a car. Not here. Over there. And her eyes glazed over his shoulder. The language taking her back to Enrique.

Enrique had held her face, drew it up like water, drank from it, drank from it and let it go empty as a tin cup. How she had wanted to jump out that window, like a sparrow found in the snow, wouldn't that have been hilarious? The sisters would've had to gather her in a blanket and carry her home, like a fairy tale she read about. All the fractured little bones. How she wanted to jump out of that window of his flat on Hoyne Street. She would've liked to have jumped and bubbled in her own juices, wouldn't that have been cute?

But it's this one who's talking a mile a minute. —Do you smoke? Would you like a cigarette? Putting out one cigarette and already lighting the next. —What? *¿Qué?* Yeah, I mean no, I mean I don't know. Inocencio Reyes so close she can hardly see him. And she tired, exhausted, dragging the body around the dance floor, this body, with its nagging need of washing and feeding all its necessary hungers, this *her* inside the borrowed pink blouse with its stained armpits and the skirt held together with a safety pin. This human being talking and talking right in her face, she has to lean back. For sure her sisters are watching and laughing. A strange face. Mustache thin as Pedro Infante's, those sad little eyes like if he just finished crying.

Neither with you nor without you.

How she'd gone back to the scene of the crime, over and over, circling that house, those rooms, those corridors, that house that haunted, that held and gripped and bit her in two. Voodoo house that hypnotized her. *"I do not love you,"* he'd said. *Here I am again. Here I am. And I come back.* Same late-night compulsion.

The way Inocencio Reyes looks at her. More than that, the way he holds her, moves her across the dance floor. He's not clumsy like other men her age. He dances like he knows where he's going, like he knows what he is doing with his life. With that confidence that lets you close your eyes and you know nothing bad will happen to you ever. No matter how tangled and muddy everything else, Inocencio Reyes dances with a self-assuredness. A tug to say this way, turn that, a light nudge to direct her in the other direction.

He'd said, "I do not love you." I do not love you. I do not love you. And my heart opened its mouth into an "oh," into a wound, a bullet, a circle big enough to push a finger through. "I do not love you," Enrique said. You said. I said nothing.

You don't like me when I don't talk. Of what good am I if I won't talk. It's not nice when I don't talk. You might as well be alone. You might as well call a taxi and put me in it and send me home. You don't like me when I begin. You won't stand for this again. It's not as if we're married or anything. And what kind of nonsense are you muttering now? Of course, you're not mine. It's a new world and a new love and I don't own you and you don't own me and we're free to come and go and love as we please. A modern age, right?

Except last night, Tuesday or Thursday, or either or both, any day so long as it's not the weekend, you call and ask me to come and visit you. And I do, but it makes it so hard to get out and travel and take the streetcar and worry when I'm waiting for it, you say come and I do, worrying at night, walking that half block from where it leaves me off to that half block to your house in the dark, not a long ways, not very, it's no trouble, sure. Not very, but bleak and lonely and me humming so I won't be afraid of the night. And my shoes hard against concrete, taking me to you, taking me. But I don't talk. That is, I talk less and less. In the beginning I talked all the time, right? And you talked with me and we laughed and you opened a cognac, a good one—one you paid a lot for, because you know all about cognacs—and played the phonograph—not the kind of cheap music of the dance halls, the kind I used to like before I met you, but music like Agustín Lara and Trío Los Panchos, and Toña La Negra, "High-class music, not trash," you said, and we danced under the soft light of a lamp with a thick carved glass that shot light up to the ceiling. Me and you dancing, that soft light of your apartment there on Hoyne. And it didn't matter if we both had to go to work tomorrow, Enrique, right? You just had to see me. I just had to see you. We were a couple of crazies like that, right? Todo por amor. You'd telephone and say, "Zoila," and even though I told myself I hated you, I can't explain why I'd hop right over. I can't explain it very well. Never mind, never mind. Only I'd hear it as "never mine."

We'd dance and then you'd undress me, and I didn't mind, because what I wanted and waited for was afterward when I held you in my arms. And we're loving each other, softly, quietly, as if we'd just invented it, as if we never had to go out into the world again, right? And I rock you, hum a little song, rock and rock you and hum, like if you were mine.

And it's as if love is some war. And are you brave enough to battle all the world, to defy everyone, and what the world says is right, what they think of you? Are you brave enough to sacrifice everything for love? Are you?

He asks how a girl as young as me got to be so brave. How he knew from the first moment he saw me I was the type of woman who . . . "Who what?"—a little too angrily. "The type of woman who would appreciate love," he says, and suddenly I'm as soft as snow. I'm anything he wants. Don't let me go.

Ni contigo ni sin ti . . . ni contigo porque me matas, ni sin ti porque me muero. Neither with you nor without you. Because with you, you'd kill me. Because without you, I'd die.

—What? What'd you say? Zoila asks Inocencio, because to tell the truth, she's been daydreaming again. Hasn't heard a word he's said.

—I said you have the cleanest fingernails I have ever seen, mi reina.

Instead of the smart-alecky reply she usually tossed, only a little sound came out of her mouth, like the sound one makes in a dream when one is trying to shout. And this little sound with its curly fluted spiral pulled all the other sounds lined together like a train, an animal braying tangled in the strands of her black-blue hair, so that at first Inocencio Reyes thought she was laughing at him. Mi reina. Those words in that language of tenderness and home. It was only until she raised her head to the light that Inocencio realized his mistake.

Twenty-five years later he'd still be telling the story. —Because I am a gentleman I told her something nice—how pretty her hands were.

That's nice, no? Instead of saying thank you, she started howling like a baby. Like a baby, I'm not lying. She was a mystery then, and she's a mystery to me now. That's how she's always been, your mother. You tell her something ugly, she just laughs. But just give her one kind word, and *¡zas!*

---

*Enrique Aragón was what you would call un hombre bonito. *A pretty man. He had fulfilled his obligation and chosen a profession honorable to his family. That was all they asked.*

—Cualquier cosa, que no sea mesero o maricón. *Anything, so long as you aren't a waiter or a fag. This was what his grandfather Enrique Aragón had said to his son, Enrique Aragón Junior, by way of benediction before departing north to find fame and fortune in los Estados Unidos. His grandfather had had the good fortune of coming across President Venustiano Carranza and his party fleeing from Mexico City with all the country's gold in their pockets and saddlebags. So much so that it was impossible for them to outrun the pursuing Obregón forces. They'd had to dump treasury bags this way and that, exchanging fortunes for their lives, and it had been the destiny of this elder Aragón to encounter on the road to Veracruz one morning, a Carranza[†] crony at a desperate and decisive moment. For hiding him under a clay* maceta, *the elder Aragón had been paid a* sombrero *full of gold coins. With this, he was able to flee the sleepy heat of the town of his birth and begin his enterprise as the owner of the first air-conditioned cinema house in Tampico.*

The son had heeded his father's counsel, and with some of his father's fortuitous fortune as capital, arrived first in Chicago, and later in Los Angeles on the same train that brought Rudolph Valentino's corpse, in October of 1926. Chicago, Los Angeles, Los Angeles, Chicago. With several important contacts, he'd been able to open a few movie houses in the Spanish-speaking barrios. He counted among his acquaintances the young Indio Fernández, who in those days was still a mustached Hollywood extra in tight pants and sombrero, the beautiful Lolita del Río— "Just another escuincla trying to break into Hollywood,"—and the sons of Al Capone. Well, that's what he said. It was impossible to know what was true and what not so true, because Enrique's father had told the story so many times over he could no longer remember which truth he was telling.

What was certain was the advice he'd been given by an aspiring Mexican filmmaker: "Art is stronger than war, Enrique. Greater than a stampede of horses. Bigger than a mauser, an airplane, all the Allied forces combined. You have no idea what a tremendous weapon the cinema is."

It was true. Hadn't he fallen in love with Greta Garbo's stand-in, a little Cuban thing named Gladys Vaughn (née Vasconcelos),‡ taken her as his wife and put her in a golden pumpkin shell in Tampico replete with enough seedlings to have caused her body to prematurely age from the shock of too many too soon births. Her eldest, Enrique, however, was her consolation, especially since her husband was never home, or often oblivious to her when he was home. It was remarkable to look at this boy's face and see her own, those pale silver eyes the eyes of a white wolf, the high cheekbones and long, thin nose that proved without a doubt the Vasconcelos aristocratic ancestry, the transparent skin pale as an onion, the same as Greta Garbo's. She loved Enrique Junior as she loved herself, but as soon as he was old enough, his father took him from her and had Enrique enrolled in schools in the States.

Enrique Aragón Junior had inherited no extraordinary aptitude for anything but spending money. His father had taken it upon himself to train his son in managing the theaters. It was important, after all, that he have a career, something with which to support a family, and after a few failed attempts at acting, Enrique had learned it was important to be something, something, anything, although he hadn't a clue what that anything was. In the meantime, he would fill in the waiting period as his father's apprentice. —Anything, something, anything, Enrique Senior said. —So long as it isn't a waiter or a fag.

†*How ironic is history. The cousin to this same Carranza had to flee the country as well, because he was a Carranza. He ran away to San Antonio, Texas, and there he opened a butcher shop, Carranza's Grocery and Market, which his grandsons ran, until recently, as a restaurant under the family name. Thus, Venustiano Carranza, the butcher of the Zapatistas, would have a cousin who would become a famous butcher too, but not for skewering Zapatistas. Instead, the Carranza family of San Antonio became noteworthy for their excellent brisket and smoked sausages, which I recommended highly until a fire snuffed them out of business.*

‡*Gladys Vasconcelos was one of the Vasconcelos sisters of Mexico City, all of them famous beauties. After her marriage to Enrique Aragón, she threatened divorce unless he installed them in a two-story Art Deco building across the street from her family's house in Mexico City. This was in the Colonia Roma. They lived there during the time Fidel Castro had to flee Cuba and found refuge in Mexico City, and since all the Cubans in Mexico knew each other, it was easy for Fidel to be introduced to and befriended by the Vasconcelos family. It is said that the young Fidel was so in love with Gladys's youngest child, Gladys the younger, he would beg her mother to be allowed to watch her sleep. Just that. So in the family's good graces and confidence was he, he was allowed this tender privilege. All without Gladys the younger ever knowing this until years later. She was blond and blue-eyed and incredibly lovely, they say. I imagine the young Fidel passionately in love, bent over the sleeping Gladys like a sunflower. Supposedly he wrote her desperate love sonnets, which he published under a pseudonym and titled* The Gladys Poems, *but I'm afraid that nothing came of the affair, and Fidel left Mexico to write his name in Cuban history. As for young Gladys, she married a pharmaceutical king and went away to live in Pasadena, where she lived long enough to see the disastrous collapse of her beauty. In her old age, she moved in and out of Beverly Hills beauty hospitals having her face lifted more times than María Félix. My friend's mother, who still lives in the Colonia Roma and was neighbors with the Vasconcelos family in the forties and fifties, told me this story but made me promise never to tell anyone, which is why I am certain it must be true, or, at the very least, somewhat true.*

51

All Parts from Mexico, Assembled in the U.S.A.

or I Am Born

I am the favorite child of a favorite child. I know my worth. Mother named me after a famous battle where Pancho Villa met his Waterloo.

I am the seventh born in the Reyes family of six sons. Father named them all. Rafael, Refugio, Gustavo, Alberto, Lorenzo, and Guillermo. This he did without Mother's consultation, claiming us like uncharted continents to honor the Reyes ancestors dead or dying.

Then I was born. I was a disappointment. Father had expected another boy. When I was still a spiral of sleep, he'd laugh and rub Mother's belly, bragging, —I'm going to create my own soccer team.

But he didn't laugh when he saw me. —*¡Otra vieja! Ahora, ¿cómo la voy a cuidar?** Mother had goofed.

—Cripes almighty! Mother said. —At least she's healthy. Here, you hold her.

Not exactly love at first sight, but a strange *déjà vu*, as if Father was looking into a well. The same silly face as his own, his mother's. Eyes like little houses beneath the sad roof of brow.

—Leticia. We'll name her Leticia, Father murmured.

—But I don't like that name.

—It's a good name. Leticia Reyes. Leticia. Leticia. Leticia.

And then he left. But when the nurse came to record my name, Mama heard herself say, —Celaya. A town where they'd once stopped for a mineral water and a *torta de milanesa* on a trip through Guanajuato. —Celaya, she said, surprised at her own audacity. It was the first time she disobeyed Father, but no, not the last. She reasoned the name "Leticia" belonged to some *fulana,* one of my father's "histories." —Why else would he have insisted so stubbornly?

And so I was christened Celaya, a name Father hated until his mother declared over the telephone wires, —A name pretty enough for a *tele-novela.* After that, he said nothing.

Days and days, months and months. Father carried me wherever he went. I was a little fist. And then a thumb. And then I could hold my head up without letting it flop over. Father bought me crinolines, and taffeta dresses, and ribbons, and socks, and ruffled panties edged with lace, and white leather shoes soft as the ears of rabbits, and demanded I never be allowed to look raggedy. I was a cupcake. —*¿Quién te quiere?* Who loves you? he'd coo. When I burped up my milk, he was there to wipe my mouth with his Irish linen handkerchief and spit. When I began scratching and pulling my hair, he sewed flannel mittens for me that tied with pink ribbons at the wrist. When I sneezed, Father held me up to his face, and let me sneeze on him. He also learned to change my diapers, which he had never done for his sons.

I was worn on the arm like a jewel, like a bouquet of flowers, like the Infant of Prague. —My daughter, he said to the interested and uninterested. When I began to accept the bottle, Father bought one airline ticket and took me home to meet his mother. And when the Awful Grandmother saw my Father with that crazy look of joy in his eye, she knew. She was no longer his queen.

It was too late. Celaya, a town in Guanajuato where Pancho Villa met his nemesis. Celaya, the seventh child. Celaya, my father's Waterloo.

---

*Tr. *Another dame! Now how am I going to take care of this one?*†

†Tr. of Tr. *How am I going to protect her from men like me?*

PART THREE

The Eagle and the Serpent

or My Mother and My Father

•

For a long time I thought the eagle and the serpent on the Mexican flag were the United States and Mexico fighting. And then, for an even longer time afterward, I thought of the eagle and the serpent as the story of Mother and Father.

There are lots of fights, big and little. The big ones have to do with money, the Mexicans from this side compared to the Mexicans from that side, or that trip to Acapulco.

—But, Zoila, Father says, —it was you and the kids I drove home, remember? I left my own mother in Acapulco. *Pobre mamacita.* She's still *sentida* over it, and who can blame her! It was *you* I chose. Over my own mother! No Mexican man would choose his wife over his own mother! What more do you want? Blood?

—Yeah, blood!

—*Te encanta mortificarme,* Father says to Mother. Then he adds to me when she's out of earshot, —*Tu mamá es terrible.*

—I'm talking to you, Mother continues. —*Te hablo.* Which sounds like the Spanish word for *Devil.*

—Ma, why you calling him *diablo?* I say to be funny.

—Aw, he just likes to pretend he can't hear me.

Te hablo, te hablo—at the beginning and end of every phrase, so, of course, he never listens. Father is a little deaf from the war. Things exploded too close to him, he says, or maybe the story's true he grew deaf from jumping too many times out of a plane for fifty dollars a jump. At the most convenient hour he can't hear what's being said around him.

Mother begins. —*Te hablo, te hablo* . . .

Father watches television. Boxing, an old Pedro Infante movie, a *telenovela,* a soccer match. *A la bío, a la báo, a la bim, bom, bam* . . . If this doesn't work, he opens the orange La-Z-Boy to reclining, crawls under a nubby blanket, and goes to sleep.

Finally, when Mother has had it with Father ignoring her, she picks up the biggest rock she can find and flings it:

—*Tu familia* . . . Your family . . .

It's enough to ignite wars.

235

52

Cielito Lindo

> Ese lunar que tienes,
> cielito lindo,
> junto a la boca,
> no se lo des a nadie,
> cielito lindo,
> que a mí me toca.
>
> ¡Ay, ay, ay, ay!
> canta y no llores,
> porque cantando se alegran,
> cielito lindo,
> los corazones . . .

This is the song the Grandmother teaches us on the trip to Chicago. The whole van is belting it out. Grandmother, Father, Mother, Toto, Lolo, and Memo. Loud as their lungs will allow.

Except me. You couldn't get me to sing that corny old song if you paid me.

Not my family, they love corn. Especially the *ay-ay-ay-ay* parts, which they screech like a cage of parrots. The words thunder out the windows, thud over the trailer hauling the Grandmother's walnut-wood armoire, and roll down the bleached desert hills of northern Mexico, startling the vultures in the scrub trees.

Father twists the ends of his Zapata mustache with his fingers the way he does when he's lost in thought. He's watching me through the rearview and can tell I'm pissed.

We're riding in the metallic-blue shop van with the windows rolled down because of the heat. TAPICERÍA TRES REYES—THREE KINGS UPHOLSTERY—the doors read. FURNITURE FIT FOR A KING. Father sold the red Chevy station wagon the year he and the uncles went into business for themselves. During the work year, the rear seats are taken out to make room for deliveries, but in the summer, they're hauled out of storage and bolted back for the trip south. When Father's legs turn into lead, he moves to the back and lets Toto drive, or, if the road is clear, Lolo takes his turn, but only when supervised.

—What's the matter, Lala? *¿Estás* "deprimed"? Father says, chuckling.

It's an old joke, one he never gets tired of, changing a Spanish word into English, or the other way round, just to be a wise guy.

I think to myself, *Yes, I'm* deprimida. *Who wouldn't be depressed in this family?* But I don't say this.

When I don't answer, Father adds, —*Ay, que* Lalita. You're just like your mother.

I'm nothing at all like Mother!

—It's hot back here, I say. —It's like malaria. It's like a laundromat. It's like Maxwell Street in August. How come Toto gets to sit up front next to you, Father?

I say this just to bug Toto, not because I want his seat. Ever since Toto's birth date placed number 137 in the draft lottery,* he's been treated like a little prince.

—I need Toto up here, Father says, knocking on the hot box of the motor between his seat and Toto's. —You forget Toto's my navigator. And besides, he knows how to drive.

—I can help you with that, Father. Isn't it my turn to drive now? Memo asks.

Everybody shouts—No!—at the same time.

Memo's been trying to get behind the wheel since he was a kid. Father gave in on the trip down and let him drive in the country, but somewhere before San Luis Potosí, Memo ran over a chicken. We had to stop the car, look for the owner, and pay her five American dollars, which Mother said was way too much. Father felt sorry for her. —She was just a kid, he explained. —And she was crying. Now nobody trusts Memo behind the wheel except Memo.

I'm stuck in the back row next to the Grandmother. Mother, Memo, and Lolo always get the middle row. There's no questioning this. Just the memory of Acapulco stops any argument. Father doesn't even like to say the word "Acapulco." Why get Mother and the Grandmother all worked up and bothered?

Forget it! Just as soon the singing and the good times quit, the Grandmother starts up again with her elephant's memory.

—I'll have to buy new clothes when we get to Chicago. Black, of course, now that I'm a widow. Nothing too fancy, but not cheap either. None of my old things fit anymore. Well, I've gained so much weight this summer, it's amazing. It's to be expected. The same thing happened to la Señora Vidaurri when she lost her husband. Ballooned up from grief, remember? Her son bought her boxes and boxes of *chuchulucos*. And not the cheap kind either, the expensive imported sweets, from France! What a good son, that one. So attentive. Remember how Señor Vidaurri came to Acapulco to fetch us. You can bet *he'd* never leave his mother stranded . . .

—Mamá, I didn't leave you stranded, Father explains. —It was *I* who arranged for Vidaurri . . .

—Such a good man. A gentleman. He was always so very proper, so very correct, so Mexican. Your father used to say a man ought to be *feo, fuerte, y formal*, that's what he'd say, but nowadays . . .

Right. She forgets to mention how a "gentleman" like Señor Vidaurri forgot to marry our Aunty Light-Skin and let her move away to Monterrey, Nuevo León, where Antonieta Araceli studied at the Tech and earned her degree in matrimony . . .

—Too young, perhaps, but at least married, the Grandmother always says when the subject comes up. —And better to find her married respectably than getting into trouble.

I know she means Aunty Light-Skin, and the thought of Aunty makes me sigh. Poor Aunty. Did Señor Vidaurri get tired of Aunty, I wonder, or did she get tired of being called his daughter? I don't know and it's too late to ask. Aunty lives in Monterrey now. It was supposed to be temporary, just to help Antonieta Araceli when she was expecting her baby. And later to help her while her stitches were healing. And then Aunty just . . . stayed. She came back to help us close up the house, but then the Grandmother and Aunty got into it and had a big fight. If it wasn't for the Grandmother and Aunty arguing at the last minute, we'd be able to stop in Monterrey and visit overnight. We could be eating *cabrito tacos* by now, avoiding the afternoon heat, and maybe even napping or swimming in the pool. But no, forget about it. The Grandmother can't even mention Aunty without having a heart attack.

Aunty is shoving all her clothes into her white Samsonite suitcases, snapping bags shut, the toes of pantyhose and lace of slips sticking out of the sides. She's blinking back tears, blowing her nose loudly into a handkerchief. Aunty has me sitting on top of the biggest suitcase with her, and we're trying to get the lid to shut when Father knocks gently on the door.

—It's no use, brother, you can't change my mind. I already told you, I'm going back to Monterrey tonight!

—Come on, sister. What would Father say if he were alive? Let it go. Please! You can't be angry with Mother forever.

—That's what you think, Inocencio. You weren't here when she beat me with her fists. With her fists! As if I was a door! And that's not all. She had the nerve to say she hated me! Me, the one who stayed and took care of her while all of you moved up north. What kind of mother tells her child she hates her? She's really crazy! I'm never going to talk to her again as long as I live!

With one sweep of her arm Aunty slides all the bottles and jars off the dresser into her matching Samsonite makeup suitcase.

—*Ay*, sister, please! Don't talk that way. Imagine what Father is thinking watching all this from heaven. For his sake, forgive. Think of the family.

—It's easy for you to talk about forgiveness. You moved away! I've been stuck with her all these years. But now that Father's gone and the house sold, she's all yours. Look, are you driving me to the station, or do I have to take a taxi?

The Grandmother is brushing her frizzy permed hair with a pink plastic hairbrush. She brushes and brushes with a fury, pieces of her wiry gray hair fly over my clothes.

—Dandruff! That's what I get for not washing my hair. But with the border and all, I thought it best to wait until we got to the other side. So much dirt! Nothing but dust, dirt, and desert around here. If I'd known it was going to be so horribly hot . . . *¡Fuchi!* If you ask me, they should've given this all to Pancho Villa.

She looks at me sharply, as if I only just came into focus, and then adds, —Celaya, can't you do something about those bangs? No wonder your forehead is full of pimples. What is it with young people and their hair these days? Inocencio, we really should stop at a barber as soon as we get to Nuevo Laredo. You look like Burrola's husband, Don Regino,[†] with that broom of a mustache. And your children, just look at them. Like a bunch of hippies *greñudos.*

Father says, —It's that they're teenagers, Mamá. They don't listen. Nobody listens to me anymore.

—But Lala just got a haircut. Especially for this trip, Lolo has to remind everybody. —Isn't that right, Celery?

—Leave me alone!

I blame Mother. She's the one who complained and made me go get this dorky haircut. I wanted a shag, but because my hair is coarse and thick, the top sticks up like celery when it's humid.

—Don't pick on Lalita, Father reminds Lolo. —She's your only sister and the baby.

—You mean Baby Huey, Memo adds, snickering.

The boys act like jerks, like it's the funniest thing they ever heard in their life.

—So? So I'm not Twiggy, so what! I'm . . . Father, what's that word for big-boned?

Eres fornida, Father says, defending me against my goofy brothers.

—*¿Fornida?* says the Grandmother. —Are you sure Celaya hasn't got a worm? What this girl needs is injections. She's turning into a man.

This makes the boys roar even harder. They're hopeless.

—Lala takes after her mother's family, Father says. —The Reynas are all built like a mountain range. It's their Indian blood. Pure Yaqui. Right, Zoila?

—How the hell should I know? Mother says, annoyed. She doesn't like to be called Yaqui in front of her mother-in-law.

—Lalita, did I ever tell you the story of how I bought you?

—Only a million times, I say, sighing.

—Because I already had too many boys, I wanted a little girl. With all my heart. I want a little girl, I kept praying.

—Ha! Mother says. —Since when do you pray? And you did not want a little girl. You were mad at me for a week.

Father continues his story as if he didn't hear her. —I went into every hospital in Chicago looking for just the right little girl. I was almost ready to give up. Finally, at Presbyterian Hospital I found a whole maternity ward filled with beautiful baby girls. Rows and rows. But the prettiest one there was, who do you think? That's right—you. *¡Ay, qué bonita!* That one! I'll take that one. And after paying lots of money for you— because you cost me a lot, my heaven—after going to the cashier, they let me take you home!

—Oh, brother, Lolo groans. —I think I'm getting carsick.

—Father, did you save your receipt? Maybe we can still get you a refund, Memo adds, howling at his own corny joke.

Toto doesn't say anything, but he's the worst because he laughs the loudest.

They're like the Three Stooges, my brothers. If there was a way to start divorce proceedings for siblings, believe me, I'd be there.

Mother is fixing a bandana over the window so the sun won't hit her so hard and she can nap.

—Forget about it, Mother says, glaring over her shoulder at me.

—I wasn't . . .

—Well, whatever you were going to ask for, forget about it, Mother says, making her eyes bigger before she tilts her head back and shuts them completely.

How could Father say I'm like her! Even she admits I take after him. Says even as a baby I was *una chillona*. How she had to wear me on her hip like a gun, and even then I wouldn't stop crying. I drove her crazy.

Now she drives me crazy.

When I was little, Mother would tell me this story to make me behave. Once there was a girl who couldn't stop crying. She cried and cried and cried, until her eyes got tinier and tinier and tinier. Until finally her eyes were just two apple seeds, and the tears just washed them away. Then she was blind. The end. That's the kind of stories Mother used to tell me. I mean, what kind of story is that to tell a kid?

Honor thy mother and thy father.

I wonder if the Grandmother really hates Aunty? The Grandmother is bending over her knees and brushing her hair from the bottom up. There is no commandment that says honor thy daughter.

Memo and Lolo are arguing over the road atlas, trying to calculate how many kilometers translate into how many miles, and Toto won't let up with asking Father about the war.

—I mean, did you ever kill anyone, Father? Toto asks.

—Only God knows.

—Ha! What a brain you are. Man, you're way, way off, Memo! No wonder you almost flunked math.

—It wasn't just me, ninety-five percent of the class almost failed, no lie.

—Grandmother, did you know they make a powder hairspray in the U.S. that you can use so that you don't have to wash your hair?

—But, I mean, did you see any action, Father?

—Action? I saw Death this close, Father says, holding his hand near his Berber's nose.

—A spray so you don't have to wash your hair? How terrible. Sounds like something that's sure to give you head lice.

—Where? Was it on the Pacific beaches, or in the island jungles?

—Neither. In a bar in Tokyo. Two Mexicans killed each other in a knife fight. This was *after* the war was over. By the time I got shipped over, the Japanese had surrendered.

—It's new. They announce it on the radio a lot. It's called Pssssssst.

—And what were two Mexicans doing in Tokyo?

—Same as me, fighting with the U.S. Army.

—What kind of name is that? That's what loose women on corners say to men. You wouldn't catch me asking for that product even if they gave it away.

—But if they were on the same side, why'd they kill each other?

—Those are the ones who hate each other the most, Father says and sighs.

—Who hates each other the most? the Grandmother asks.

Mother opens her eyes and snaps to attention.

—We were talking about the war.

—Wars! Now that's something I know about firsthand. You can always tell who's seen war, the Grandmother says, pausing for effect.

—Well, at least *I* can tell.

—How?

—Simple. It's in the face. Something in the eye. Or better said, something no longer there. It's from the things one witnesses in wartime, believe me. Your Grandfather, may he rest in peace, saw things during the revolution, and oh, the stories I could tell you about what I saw!

The Grandmother waits for someone to ask her what she saw, but nobody directs a word toward her except a fly buzzing near her face.

—And did *you* see things, Father? In the war, I mean, I ask.

—Well, yes, but no. That is. Not much.

—Like what?

—Like abuses.

—What kind of abuses?

—Abuses of women.

—Where?

—In Japan and in Korea.

—By whom?

—The barbarians.

—Who?

—*Los norteamericanos.*

—But why didn't you do anything?

—Because that's how it is in war. The winners do what they like.

—But why didn't you stop them? Why didn't you, Father, if you're a gentleman you're supposed to, right?

—Because I was just a *chamaco,* he says, using the Mexican-Aztec word for "boy." —I was just a *chamaco* then, he says.

—But why did you enlist, Father, if you weren't a U.S. citizen? Toto asks. —Did you feel it would make a man out of you?

—It's that they took me.

—Who?

—Well, the police.

—Here we go again, Mother mutters, slumping in her seat and crossing her arms.

—But how did the police take you, Father?

—Look, I was working in Memphis, and since there were hardly any young men about who weren't in uniform, they spotted me right away and took me with them to the enlistment office.

—But what were you doing in Memphis, Father? Weren't you living in Chicago with Uncle Snake?

I look at Father with his face from Seville, Fez, Marrakech, a thousand and one cities.

—On my way I stopped and worked when I could find work, Father says. —In Memphis they were hiring at a casket company. They needed upholsterers to sew the satin linings of the coffins, and I needed bus fare to Chicago. "Do you have any experience upholstering?" "Yes, sir, at my Uncle's shop in Chicago I practically run the whole business." "Well, show us what you can do."

At that time I was just beginning, understand? But the dead must not care if the sewing looks like you did it with your feet. "Okay, you're hired." So that's how it was I was working in Memphis when the police picked me up and escorted me to the enlistment center. When I got to my *destino*, to Chicago, a letter was waiting for me from the government. Report here and here and here. So you see, I was obligated to serve as was my duty as a gentleman. After all, this great country has given me so much.

—Great country, my ass! If they ever get to Toto's number, I'm taking him personally to Mexico, Mother says, disgusted. —You don't know it, Ino, because you never pick up a newspaper, but believe me, all the brown and black faces are up on the front line. If you ask me it's all a government conspiracy! You can't pull the wool over my eyes, I listen to Studs Terkel!‡

Memo and Lolo start singing *"Mi mamá me mima . . ."* to tease Toto, who is mother's favorite.

—Quit it, morons! Toto says. —I said shut up already!

—What are you going to do? Memo asks. —Demote us to donkey-privates?

—Wait till you guys get shipped to Vietnam, then we'll see who's laughing!

—Fat-Face is to blame for everything, the Grandmother says, not having understood a word of Mother's rantings because Mother said it all in English. —I don't know how he does it, but Fat-Face has always convinced your father to do horrible things!

—What kind of horrible things, Grandmother?

—Yeah, what kind of horrible things?

—Like running away from home, and then sending for Baby to go north too. That's how they all wound up so far from me, getting involved in business that was none of their business in my opinion.

Mother just snorts, but the Grandmother doesn't notice, or pretends not to.

—I was working here and there, Father explains. —Philadelphia, Little Rock, Memphis, New York City. Shelling oysters, wiping tables, washing dishes . . .

—Why he's never even washed a dish in his own house! the Grandmother adds as if boasting.

—You can say that again, Mother says in English.

Father just laughs his letter "k" laugh.

—But why didn't you stay in Philadelphia, or Little Rock, or Memphis, or New York, Father?

—Because it wasn't my *destino.*

And I wonder if he means "destiny" or "destination." Or maybe both.

—And then what? Tell more *cuentos* of your life, Father, go on.

—But I keep telling you, they're not *cuentos,* Lala, they're true. They're *historias.*

—What's the difference between *"un cuento"* and *"una historia"*?

—Ah! . . . now that's a different kind of lie.

During the Vietnam War, a draft lottery based on birthdates was instituted beginning in 1969. It aired on national TV. Whole families watched this lottery of death in terror, as 365 Ping-Pong balls came down the chute and announced if you were a "winner." The birthdates of men between eighteen and twenty-six were drawn and posted in order of sequence. If you were one of the first 200, it was almost certain Uncle Sam would call on you.

†*Burrola and Don Regino Burrón are characters from the excellent Mexican comic book* La familia Burrón, *a chronicle of Mexico City life created by Gabriel Vargas. In a country where books are expensive and often out of reach for the masses, Mexico's comic books and* fotonovelas *are aimed primarily at an adult audience, among them Mexican Mexicans and American Mexicans, as well as Mexican Americans and some 'Mericans trying to learn Mexican Spanish.* La familia Burrón *is remarkable because of its longevity. It began in 1940 and is still sold today in kiosks across Mexico. Every Tuesday—or is it Thursday?—a new issue appears on the newsstands, but if you*

don't get there early, you're out of luck. Copies of La familia Burrón *are sold in Mexican grocery stores throughout the U.S., though the issues are not as current. Thus, a popular request to someone venturing south is to bring back the latest issues of* La familia Burrón*!*

‡ —*Lies! All lies, Mother says.* —*Nothing but a bunch of lies. He doesn't exist.*

—*Who doesn't exist?*

—*God, Mother says.*

She's staring at stacks of her precious magazines she's piled in a plastic laundry basket.

—*I can't believe I saved this shit, she says.*

There are volumes of Reader's Digest, McCall's, Good House-keeping, *and a year's worth of* National Geographic, *a gift subscription from her sister Aurelia.* "Apollo 15 Explores the Mountains of the Moon." "Those Popular Pandas." "Lady Bird Johnson's White House Diary." "Julia Child/28 Great New Vegetable Dishes." "The Skirt-Length Problem/Ten Ways to Solve It!" "Do-It-Ahead Holiday Ideas/Food, Fashion, Beauty, Gifts, Needlework." "Ralph Nader/Are Baby Foods Safe?" "A Guide to Christmas Gifts under Twenty Dollars." "The Kahlil Gibran Diary." "Adorable Animals to Crochet and Deco-rate." "Fifteen Ways to Trim That Tummy." "Twenty Scrumptious Dessert Recipes."

—*You, Mother says to me in her that's-an-order voice,* —*help me get this junk outside.*

The laundry basket is filled to the top and bulging, too heavy to pick up. We have to slide it to the back door, then thump it down two flights of porch steps to the backyard. I thought Mother meant to haul everything to the alley, but she heads for the garage, unlocks the padlock, and wheels out the Weber kettle she bought at the Wieboldt's with her S&H green stamps. Mother feeds the Weber the first batch, douses it all with lighter fluid, and, with a little sigh, lights a match.

It takes a while before the fire catches. The magazines are thick and let loose a pale, ashy smoke that makes you cough. Satisfied, Mother puts the lid on and then goes back inside. She makes her bed, washes the breakfast dishes, starts several loads of laundry, before we sit down to egg and hot-dog tacos. Every once in a while she plucks the kitchen curtains aside and makes me go outside to feed the kettle more magazines. Mother isn't satis-

fied till she can see the smoke unspooling steadily from the lid, a thin gray string.

—*Cripes, she mutters while peeling potatoes.*

When the boys come home later that evening they ask, —*What's burning?*

—*My life, Mother says. Every time she talks like that, kind of crazy, we know to leave her alone.*

Memo wants to go out and take a look, but our mama grabs him by the hood of his sweatshirt. —*Oh, no, you don't. You eat your dinner, boy, and finish cleaning up your room, she says. And by the time he's finished, he's forgotten about the Weber kettle.*

There are unfinished embroidery projects she's abandoned. There are paint-by-number sets. There are plants to repot and television shows to watch. But Mother doesn't feel like anything. Nothing. Not even lying on her back and staring at the ceiling.

It all started when December 20th popped up on a Ping-Pong ball, number 137 in the draft lottery, Toto's birthday. Mother stops putting on her makeup, gives up setting her hair and plucking her eyebrows. She lets the Burpee seed catalogs pile up with the Chicago Sun-Times, *and then throws them all out. She gains weight once she stops doing her daily exercises. Nothing interests her.*

Until the older boys bring home their college textbooks. She reads Freire, Fromm, Paz, Neruda, and later Sor Juana, Eldridge Cleaver, Malcolm X, and Chief Joseph. She begins a subscription to Mother Jones *and* The Nation. *She tears out pages of political poetry and tapes them to our refrigerator. She listens faithfully to Studs Terkel on WFMT and pastes Spiro Agnew's face on our dartboard. Mother clips the slogan of a national ad campaign and tapes it on the bathroom mirror: "A mind is a terrible thing to waste."*

53

El Otro Lado

*T*he Little Grandfather died on a Tuesday in the time of rain. He had an attack of the heart while driving on the *periférico* and crashed into a truck filled with brooms. The Grandfather's face looked startled. This was not the death he had imagined for himself. An avalanche of plastic brooms of all colors spilling onto the windshield like crayons. The *thwack* of brooms under car wheels. The *thunk-thunk* of their tumbling on metal. Brooms twirling in the air and bouncing. The Grandfather, who never lifted a broom in his life, buried under a mountain of plastic brooms, the ones Mexican housekeepers use with a bucket of sudsy water to scrub the patio, to scrub the street and curb. As if Death came with her apron and broom and swept him away.

At first the family thinks they can outrun Death and arrive in time to say their good-byes. But the Little Grandfather dies in his automobile and not in a hospital room. The Grandfather, who paid so much attention to being *feo, fuerte, y formal* in his life, backed up traffic for kilometers; a *feo* diversion, a *fuerte* nuisance for the passing motorists, a sight as common as any yawning Guanajuato mummy, as *formal* as any portrait of Death on the frank covers of the *¡Alarma!* scandal magazine.

When they dug him out from under the brooms, they say he mumbled a woman's name before dying, but it was not the name "Soledad." A garbled swamp of syllables bubbled up from that hole in his chest from the war. That's what the *periférico* witnesses said. But who can say whether it was true or simply a story to weave themselves into that day's drama.

He had a bad heart, it will be explained when explanations can be given. —It's that we have a history, we Reyes, of bad hearts, Father says. Bad hearts. And I wonder if it means we love too much. Or too little.

The brothers Reyes hurry to make their reservations south. In our family it's Father and me who fly down for the funeral. Father insists I go with him even though it's almost the end of the school year and the week of my finals. Father talks to the school principal and arranges for me to make up my exams later, so I can be promoted to the eighth grade. I'll miss the end-of-the-year assembly where my class is to sing "Up, Up, and Away." —I can't go without Lala, Father keeps saying. Father and me on an airplane again, just like in the stories he likes to tell me about when I was a baby.

The Grandmother is already beyond grief by the time we get there. She busies herself making great pots of food nobody can eat and talking nonstop like a parrot that has bit into a *chile*. When she's exhausted her stories with us, she talks on the telephone to strangers and friends, explaining again and again the details of her husband's death, as if it was just a story that happened to someone else's husband and not hers.

It only gets worse at the burial. When the time comes to pour dirt on top of the coffin, the Grandmother shrieks as if they'd put a pin through her heart. Then she does what is expected of every good Mexican widow since the time of the Olmecs. She tries to throw herself into the open grave.

—Narcisooooooo!!!

All three of her sons and several husky neighbors have to hold her back. How did the Grandmother become so strong? There's a commotion of huddled bodies, shouts, yelps, screeches, and muffled sobs, and then I can't see.

—Narcisooooooo!!!

Please. Too terrible. The Grandmother collapses into a trembling heap of black garments, and this bundle is tenderly lifted and loaded into a car.

—Narcisooooooo!!! the Grandmother hiccups as she is led away. The last syllable stretched out long and painful. Narcisooooooo, Narcisooooooo!!! The "o" of a train whistle. The longing in a coyote's howl.

Maybe she's seeing into the future. Maybe she can foresee selling the house on Destiny Street, packing up her life, and starting a new life up north *en el otro lado*, the other side.

To tell the truth, the Grandmother didn't realize how much she loved her husband until there was no husband left to love. The smell of Narciso haunts her, his strange tang of sweet tobacco and iodine. She opens all the windows, but can't get the smell out of the house. —Don't you smell it? You don't? A smell that makes you sad, like the ocean.

Days later, when everyone who has tried to help has gotten out of the way and events have settled to a startling solitude, the Grandmother decides.

—The house on Destiny Street must be sold, she says, surprising everyone, especially herself. —There is no changing my mind.

The Grandmother decides everything, same as always.

—And why do I need such a big house in the center of such a noisy neighborhood? It was different when my children were children. But you have no idea how Mexico City has changed. Why, our old neighborhood La Villa is no longer La Villa anymore! It's flooded with a different category of people these days. I'm not lying. It's not safe for a woman alone, and with my only daughter abandoning me to be a burden on her daughter, do you think she'd invite me? Of course, I wouldn't think of imposing on her even if she did, I'm not that kind of woman. I've always been independent. Always, always, always. Till the day I die my children will know I never imposed on any of them. But my sons, after all, are sons. And with the three of them up in the United States, what else can I do but suffer one more calamity and move myself up there to be near my grandchildren. It's a sacrifice, but what's life if not sacrifices for our children's sake?

And so that's how it is that Aunty Light-Skin is summoned back to Mexico City to help the Grandmother say good-bye to the past. And that's how it is we go back, after the Grandfather's burial, recruited as involuntary volunteers to help move the Grandmother up north. At least the half of the family still young enough to have to obey Father. The older ones have perfect excuses; summer jobs, graduate school, summer classes. Father, Mother, Toto, Lolo, Memo, and me are stuck with her. That's how it is we lose another summer vacation and head one last time to the house on Destiny Street.

By the time we arrive, the house has already been sold to the family who rents the downstairs portion, the apartments where Aunty and Antonieta Araceli once lived. The rooms closest to the street, where we always stayed, will be rented to strangers. All that's left is for the Grandmother to pack up her things and come up north with us to Chicago. She plans to buy a house in the States with the money from the Destiny Street house and its furnishings.

The Grandmother insists on overseeing every little thing, and that's why everything takes twice as long. Father has to make sure she is given something to keep her busy, and now she is sorting through the walnut-wood armoire, the doors standing open exhaling a stale breath of soft apples. She pauses at her husband's favorite flannel robe, holds it up to her face, and inhales. The smell of Narciso, of tobacco and iodine, still in the cloth. She had avoided sorting through his clothes. And now here she is, holding her husband's ratty old robe to her nose and relishing the smell of Narciso. A pain squeezes her heart.

What does she miss most? She is ashamed to say—laundry. She misses his socks swirling in the wash, his darks mixed with her florals, his clean undershirts plucked stiff from the clothesline, folding his trousers, steam-ironing a shirt, the arrow of the iron moving across a seam, a dart, the firm pressure along the collar, and the tricky shoulder. Here, this is how. That silly girl! Leave my husband's things. Those I'll iron myself. Cursing all the while about how much work it was to iron undershirts and underpants, men's shirts with their troublesome darts and buttons and stitching, but she did them all the same. The complaining that was a kind of bragging. Scrub out the sweat stains—by hand!—with a bar of brown soap and the knuckles stropped raw, scrub with lots of suds, like this. Put the shirts to the nose before soaking them in the outdoor sink with the ridged bottom, the smell of you like no one else. The smell of you, your heat I roll toward in my sleep, your wide back, your downy bottom, the curled legs, the soft, fat feet I embrace with my feet. Your man shirts puffed with air, your trousers hooked on the doorknob, your balled socks shaken out of the sheets, a tie lying on the floor, a robe draped behind a door, a pajama top slouched on a chair. I'll be right back, they said. I'll be right back. I'll be . . . right . . . back.

And she misses sleeping with somebody. The falling asleep with and waking up next to a warm someone.

—*Abrázame*, he'd demand when she came to bed. Hug me. When she did wrap her arms around her husband, his fleshy back, his tidy hipbones, the furry buttocks tucked against her belly, the bandaged chest, his wound with its smell of iodine and stale cookies, this is when he would sandwich her plump feet with his plump feet, warm and soft as *tamales*.

The talk in the night, that luxurious little talk about nothing, about everything before falling asleep: —And then what happened?

—And then I said to the butcher, this doesn't look like beef, this looks like dog cutlets if you ask me . . .

—You're kidding!

—No, that's what I said . . .

How sometimes he fell asleep with her talking. The heat of his body, furious little furnace. The softness of his belly, soft swirl of hair that began in the belly button and ended below in that vortex of his sex. All this was hard to put into language. It took a while for the mind to catch up with the body, which already and always remembered.

Everyone complains about marriage, but no one remembers to praise its wonderful extravagances, like sleeping next to a warm body, like sandwiching one's feet with somebody else's feet. To talk at night and share what has happened in a day. To put some order to one's thoughts. How could she not help but think—happiness.

—Father says I'm to come and help you, I say, entering the room and startling the Grandmother from her thinking.

—What? No, I'll do it myself. You'll only make more work for me. Run along, I don't need you.

All over the floor and spilling out of the walnut-wood armoire is a tangled mess of junk impossible not to want to touch. The open doors let out the same smell I remember from when I was little. Old, sweet, and rotten, like things you buy at Maxwell Street.

In a shoe box full of the Grandfather's things, a photograph of a young man. A brown sepia-colored photo pasted on thick cardboard. I recognize the dark eyes. It's the Grandfather when he was young! Grandfather handsome in a fancy striped suit, Grandfather sitting on a caned bentwood settee, his body leaning to the side like a clock at ten to six. Somebody's cut around him so that only the Little Grandfather exists. The person whose shoulder he's leaning on is gone.

—Grandmother, who was cut out of this picture?

The Grandmother snatches the photo from my hand. —Shut the door when you leave, Celaya. I won't be needing your help anymore today.

The key double-clicks behind me, and the springs from the bed let out a loud complaint.

Behind a drawer of stockings, rolled in a broomstick handle, wrapped in an old pillowcase with holes, the *caramelo reboţo,* the white no longer white but ivory from age, the unfinished *rapacejo* tangled and broken. The Grandmother snaps open the *caramelo reboţo.* It gives a soft flap like wings as it falls open. The candy-colored cloth unfurling like a flag— no, like a hypnotist's spiral. And if this were an old movie, it would be right to insert in this scene just such a hypnotist's spiral circling and circling to get across the idea of going into the past. The past, *el pasado. El porvenir,* the days to come. All swirling together like the stripes of a *chuchuluco* . . .

The Grandmother unfolds it to its full width across the bed. How nice it looks spread out, like a long mane of hair. She plays at braiding and unbraiding the unfinished strands, pulling them straight with her fingers and then smoothing them smooth. It calms her, especially when she's nervous, the way some people braid and unbraid their own hair without realizing they're doing it. With an old toothbrush, she brushes the fringe. The Grandmother hums bits of songs she doesn't know she is humming while she works, carefully unworking the kinks and knots, finally taking a comb and nail scissors to snip off the ragged ends, holding the swag of cloth in her arms and sniffing its scent. Good thing she thought to burn dried rosemary to keep it smelling sweet all these years.

When the Grandmother had slept in the pantry of Regina Reyes' kitchen, she'd tied her wages in a knot in one end of this *reboţo.* With it she had blown her nose, wiped the sleep from her face, muffled her sobs, and hiccuped hot, syrupy tears. And once with a certain shameless pharmacist named Jesús, she had even used it as a weapon. All this she remembers, and the cloth remembers as well.

The Grandmother forgets about all the work waiting but simply unfolds the *caramelo reboţo* and places it around her shoulders. The body remembers the silky weight. The diamond patterns, the figure eights, the tight basket weave of strands, the fine sheen to the cloth, the careful way the *caramelo reboţo* was dyed in candy stripes, all this she considers before rolling up the shawl again, wrapping it in the old pillowcase, and locking it back in the walnut-wood armoire, the very same armoire where Regina Reyes had hid Santos Piedrasanta's wooden button until her death, when someone tossed it out as easily as Santos had knocked out her tooth. As easily today as someone tossing out a mottled-brown picture of a young man in a striped suit leaning into a ghost.

54

Exquisite Tamales

—Sister, please, I can't help it Mother wanted me to settle all this. *Pobrecita*. You know how she depends on me. Father says this as he ties another box shut with twine.

The Grandmother, Memo, and Lolo have been gone all morning running errands, and the house is finally quiet. Because the dining room is almost empty, Father's voice has a strange tinny echo. The big blond dining room table and heavy chairs were sold and carted away before we even got here. The walls are empty. All the Grandmother's fancy dishes and glassware are gone too. There's nothing left in the room except the chrome chandelier, a beat-up end table, and some wooden folding chairs.

—And what am I? Painted? Don't I count for something around here? Aunty Light-Skin says, reappearing from the bedroom with another armload of linen. —I made sacrifices to be here too, but do you think she ever says thank you? I don't know why I even bother. I should've taken off to Veracruz with Zoila and Toto. Zoila has the right idea.

—Don't be like that. The only reason Zoila agreed to come was because I promised her a vacation. But you and I, we're blood. Mother expects us here. Don't take the things she says so hard. And, if it makes you feel any better, I appreciate you. I couldn't close up this house without you, little sister. Too many—Lala, bring me a knife or scissors—too many memories.

—It's just that you don't know. No sooner do I step in the courtyard than I remember why I left. She's terrible. She won't throw anything away. Look at these old sheets. Mended over and over; they look like Frankenstein. But what do you think? I found brand-new sheets in the closet! I swear to you! Brand-new. Still wrapped in their store packaging! What's she saving them for? Her funeral? Look, I try to help, and when I do, she snaps at me, "This is *my* house, not yours!" Remember those stories Father used to tell us about how his mother hoarded things? Well, that's the disease Mother's got. You're not going to believe this, but I found a slice of birthday cake in the freezer that she'd been saving since your last party, the year the ceiling fell down, I'm not lying. Antonieta Araceli was thirteen then, so that means . . . seven years ago! What a barbarity!

—*Ay, qué mamá,* Father says, shaking his head and laughing. —*Pobrecita.*

—Don't start. There's nothing *pobre* about her.

You're just like your father. He wants everything he sees, the Grandmother says, scolding me as we dodge, shove, and stumble through the *Zócalo* crowds.

—It's because it's been a long time, I explain.

To tell the truth, every trip back it's like this, whether I've been away a long time or short.

What I want is a balloon. The Mexican kind herded in front of plazas or in the parks. Balloons the way I remember them, wearing a paper hat, balloons painted with pretty swirls, or with a clown face. The balloon vendor whistling his shrill balloon-vendor's whistle. The sound of that whistle calling kids outdoors like the Pied Piper.

—Really, Celaya, don't you think you're too old for a balloon? Look at yourself. You've got the body of a man and the mind of a child. I bet you're taller than your father. How tall are you? How much do you weigh?

—I'm the same height as Father, except he's shrunk a little with age, I say. —And as far as weight, I don't know how to explain it in kilos.

I do so, but I'm not about to get the Grandmother started on that. I bet I could pick up Father and carry him on my back if I had to. The Grandmother says it's the milk we drink in the U.S. that makes us all giants.

—Well, make sure I'm not with you when you buy that balloon, the Grandmother adds, huffing and puffing because she walks as if she's running. —You'll make a fool of yourself, believe me. That's for certain.

I've been waiting for the right moment to escape to La Villa. In front of the *basílica* there are pumpkin-flower *quesadillas*. Milk gelatins. Hot-off-the-griddle "fatties" wrapped in bright twists of "Chinese paper." Mexican pink. Circus yellow. Orange. Royal blue. All of this I've been dying for since we first started our trip south.

But now the Grandmother can't be bothered with my *antojos*. My cravings don't count.

The Grandmother is anxious to find *tamales* for Father's *tamal* sandwich, *tamales* wedged in between a crusty *bolillo,* a meal so thick and heavy it hurts when you swallow.

—Mother, all I want is two things, Father says moments after we arrive. —A breakfast bowl of *nata*. And. A *tamal* sandwich.

—*Ay, mijo.* Why didn't you say so? I'll run downtown and get you the most exquisite *tamales* in all of Mexico. I know an old woman who cooks divinely. Like an angel. You won't believe it.

—Mother, don't bother. I'll get *tamales* here at La Villa. I can send Memo and Lolo.

—Memo and Lolo! Are you joking? With their *pocho* Spanish nobody will understand what they're saying. No, I'll go downtown myself, tomorrow, I insist. The *tamales* I mean to buy are *exquisitos*. And as for the *nata,* you shall have it for your breakfast, God willing. Inocencio must have his *nata*. Inocencio will get his *nata,* with a nice knob of fresh *bolillo* bread to scoop it up with—no, my king? When you were little you could never finish your breakfast. I'd wait till you left for school and then I'd finish your breakfast for you, and the food always tasted sweeter because it was yours. I swear to you! What a sentimental old lady your *mamá* has become, telling you her secrets. Oh, don't laugh at your *mamá,* come here and let me hug you! Who loves you? That's right, *tu mamá*. You have no idea. Why, when I have you sleeping under my roof, I finally get some sleep. Even my dreams are more beautiful when you're here. When I die, then you'll realize how much your *mamá* loved you, right?

A *tamal* sandwich.

The Grandmother takes me with her to fetch the exquisite *tamales*. It's Father's idea, not hers, not mine. We have to ride a bus downtown and walk a few blocks too. The Grandmother walks like she always does, trotting in front of me, always in a hurry, pulling me by the wrist instead of by the hand. Every once in a while she turns around and snaps at me for dawdling, but when I try to keep up, she complains I'm tripping on the heels of her shoes.

I lope about as if I'm invisible, until somebody stares at me and reminds me I'm not a ball of light, a dust mote spiraling in a sunbeam. Lately the Grandmother has taken to talking to me only to complain. —Stand up straight, Celaya. I can't stand looking at you walking about like the hunchback of Notre Dame. Why do you insist on wearing your hair like that? Can't you at least pin back your bangs? You look like a sheep dog. The last time I saw you, you were a normal little girl. And now look. You're as big as a Russian. Don't you think you should exercise and try to look more feminine?

Leave me the hell alone. But of course I don't say this. I say, —All the girls in my class look like me.

Not true. It's bad enough Mother won't buy me a bra yet.

—But Maaa! Everybody in eighth grade wears a bra except me, some since the fourth grade even. And I start high school this fall! It's disgusting!

—Forget it! I'm not wasting good money on something you don't even need! And quit your moping. You're not changing my mind!

When it comes down to it, I guess I inherited the worst of both families. I got Father's face with its Moorish profile, a nose too big for my face, or a face too small for my nose, I'm not sure which. But I'm all Reyna from the neck down. A body like a *tamal*, straight up and down. To top it off, I'm way taller than anyone in my class, even the boys. The last thing I need is the Grandmother pointing out my charms. No wonder I'm always depressed.

Thank God there's enough freaks downtown to make even me look normal—so many strange sights, you don't know where to look. On a cardboard-box table at the curb, a stocky little cigar of a man is whipping up a huge mound of what looks like shaving cream. *Concha nácar*, abalone cream. He whips it up with a plastic playing card, whipping and whipping, and it seems crazy to see a big pile of white whipped cream plopped out on the counter like that, naked, without even a bowl.

—*Para curar barros, espinillas, manchas, cicatrices, paño negro, jiotes, acné, quemaduras, y manchas de varicela.* Guaranteed to make your skin whiter, more beautiful, more brilliant. Volunteers? How about you, doll? But the Grandmother yanks me when I pause.

Downtown is changed from how I remember it, or could it be I remember it all wrong? Walls are dirtier, more crowded, graffiti painted on buildings like in Chicago. Mexico City looks more like cities in the U.S., as if it suddenly got sick and tired of keeping itself clean.

And the sidewalks, buckled and crooked. You have to watch where you're going. There are huge, dangerous holes like underground caves, some with pieces of metal pipes snaking out. If you don't look out, you could have an accident. I think this must be why almost every other person I see downtown has an eye patch, or a big gauze Band-Aid on his face.

At a certain corner that smells of roasting corn, the Grandmother turns and tugs me down a dark courtyard. In a doorway, an old woman in a speckled black *rebozo* is standing over a smoky aluminum brazier. The Grandmother loads up the basket we brought with us with enough tamales to last us a week.

The afternoon rain arrives just as we hurry and make our way to the bus stop. The Grandmother and I have to wait under a CANADA shoe store awning to keep dry. A big crowd of tired-looking people getting out from work waits with us. It's getting darker and darker, later and later, and buses marked LA VILLA come and go, but they don't even stop because they're already clogged with people, some hanging from the open doors and back bumpers like in a Familia Burrón comic.

Finally a bus stops.

—Push, push, the Grandmother instructs.

A jowly man with bad skin gets in front, waits till the doors open, then shoves everyone aside. — Let *la señorita* get on first, he commands. Some people look disgusted, some people shove back, but the man holds firm, parting the crowd like Moses parting the sea. —*La señorita* first, he repeats. The Grandmother pushes me forward, and it's only then I realize he means me!

La señorita! I can't believe it. Even though the bus is crowded and smells of wet wool and *tamales,* all the ride back I can't stop thinking that somebody held a mob full of wet, grumpy people aside so I could go first! And called me *la señorita!*

The blood arrives in the daytime when Aunty isn't home. Nobody's home except the Grandmother. And Father. The blood isn't a story you can tell your father. There's no one else to tell but her.

—You mean to say your "rule" hasn't descended yet? A big lug of a girl like you? What was your mother thinking? She should've taken you to the doctor ages ago like I told her and gotten you injections!

Then the Grandmother makes little clucking noises like an angry hen and goes off to look for something for me to wear down there.

When I asked my friends what it would be like, they said to expect a nervous drip like a leaky faucet. Or something skittish like kite string. Or a slow trickle like tree sap. Lies. The blood's like the body swallowing backward. But from down there.

It's in the pink bathroom of the house on Destiny Street that the blood first appears, the bathroom with the huge tomb of a tub big enough to drown in, the floor of white octagons, the hundred times I've balanced on the tub ledge pushing the windows of pebbled glass open when the balloon vendor went past whistling his balloon-vendor whistle.

I don't know why, but the Grandmother doesn't come back with a box of sanitary pads. She hands me a plastic bag of Red Cross cotton, a box of Kleenex, and two safety pins.

—Here. This is much better, believe me. Make yourself a cotton sandwich and wrap a tissue around it. Don't start with your faces. You don't know how lucky you are. At least you don't have to wash out rags like I did when I was your age. But did I complain?

In the old apartment Father, Mother, and I slept in when I was little, the one upstairs, closest to the street, Aunty Light-Skin and I share a room. The room smaller than I remember, the big double bed replaced now with two twins.

How long is the blood supposed to last? Five days? Six? Seven? On day ten, I get scared and ask Aunty. —Don't worry, my soul. It'll stop soon. She brings me *manzanilla* tea and a hot water bottle wrapped in a towel, and talks to me from her twin bed, talking and talking until I fall asleep and dream she is talking to me.

A balloon. All I want is a balloon, for crying out loud. Is that too much to ask for? Everyone's too busy with the closing up of the house to go with me. I tell Father I'll go alone.

—*¿Sola?* Alone? How, Lala? Take the girl with you at least.

—No, the girl's been sent to fetch more boxes. Let Celaya go, the Grandmother says, —Better she's out of our way.

Finally! I thought they'd never let me out of that prison. I think of the Grandmother's warnings when I cross over the courtyard and let myself out the gate. *Don't play out in the street, something could happen to you!* And I laugh thinking how hysterical the Grandmother was with us when we were kids.

Destiny Street seems smaller than I remembered it, too. Noisier. Could it have gotten noisier, or could it be I forgot the noise? Huge trucks rumble and belch down our street and cut across to Misterios, tanks of gas on the back flatbed clanking dangerously, the stink and dust making me glad to reach the avenue.

At the corner, I turn and walk down the route Candelaria and I used to walk toward the *tortillería*, and I look at the doorways and try to remember where I would abandon Cande and where she would abandon me in the blind man's game we played. Here is the shop where the Grandfather always stopped to talk to the tailor, and here's the kiosk where he picked up his newspapers, and here the store where I bought the milk gelatins with the *pesos* Grandfather gave us. I pause at the doorway. An old man behind the counter with the same pelt of white hair and scent of a good cigar like the Little Grandfather. Suddenly I feel funny, a sadness and tenderness all mixed together. Until the old guy looks up and starts making smacky kisses at me. I forget about buying anything and hurry toward La Villa.

Men in the street, alone and in groups, look at me and say things to me. —Where are you going, my queen? Only not the way Father says it. I walk fast like I'm late, and keep my eyes on the sidewalk.

In the gutter, the bone of a mango with wisps of golden hair. A half-eaten corncob. Satellites of green iridescent houseflies. How come I never remembered being scared?

From far away the lopsided figure of the church that leans into the *basílica* like a *borracho*. On the corner before crossing to the church plaza, a man more raggedy than Cantinflas, *un borrachito* slouched like a sack of dirty laundry. What *is* that bulging out from his belt? I don't think anything of it until I get closer.

Ay, it's his *thing.* Worse—a green fly is sitting on it like a big green sequin!

¡Córrele, córrele! Run, run! My heart racing several steps ahead of me. *Ay, qué feo, feo, feo.* A little shudder goes through me when I make my way around the corner and turn back to the Grandmother's house on Destiny Street. I forget about the balloons, the milk gelatins, the cookie vendors in front of the church, the pumpkin-flower *quesadillas,* the sandwich of cotton wadded between my legs. I forget everything on the way to the Grandmother's house except what I wish I could forget, that man's ugly pipi with the fly on it.

When I get back, I throw myself on the bed, and pretend to be sick from my period, and that's how I get out of having to eat a plate of *mole* the Grandmother has waiting for me. —No, thank you.

Curl myself into a question mark and pull the blanket over my head. I try not to think, but the things I try not to think about keep bobbing to the surface like drowned people. A green, white, and red gelatin with a dead bug curled on it. A corncob in the gutter. A hairy mango bone. A fly on a drunk man's pipi. A thick wad of cotton like a *tamal* sandwich between my legs. A river roaring in my brain. Muddy water sweeping everything along.

— $\mathcal{S}$ he says she's not hungry. Can you imagine! She's always been finicky, that one. If you ask me, Inocencio's to blame.

—Maybe she's suffering a fright, Aunty says. —That's how girls behave who've had some harm done to them.

—How would you know? Nothing like that's ever happened to you.

—How do you know what's happened to me?

It's true, the Grandmother hasn't a clue. All those years living with someone, and she's never noticed her daughter except to say, —Pass me that plate. She's been too busy with Narciso, with Inocencio. Well, how could she help it? They needed her, and her daughter is independent, can always be counted on to take care of herself.

—How do you know what's happened to me?

The silence in the room is thick. Dust motes eavesdrop, pirouetting and somersaulting in the shafts of sunlight.

A rumble like a growl rolls out from the Grandmother's throat. And then she comes at her daughter like a small animal charging, like the Devil himself sent to fetch her.

—You're selfish, you've always been selfish, the Grandmother says, banging both fists on her daughter's body. *Thunk, thunk, thunk.* —You've always done what you wanted with your life, always, always, always. I hate you!

Stunned, Aunty runs into the bathroom and locks herself in, her body heaving into tears.

—Come out of there, you spoiled *escuincla.*

—No, I won't. Never!

Never. Forever. Never. But life is very short, and "never" long.

The Grandmother feels as if her daughter has stabbed her with a fork. *Cruel daughter! Vice-ridden, selfish girl!* Aunty feels as if her mother has knocked her out with hammers. *Scandalous crazy old woman!* After a while, Aunty can hear the Grandmother stomping over to her bedroom, the door slamming, keys turning in the tumbler, doors from the walnut-wood armoire creaking open, drawers shuffling, then the bedsprings groaning like a sigh. Aunty had only wanted what the Grandmother had wanted. Love. Is that too much to ask one's mother?

The Grandmother throws herself on the bed and draws the *caramelo rebozo* over her face to still the pain behind her eyes. *Ungrateful girl!*

At the same time on opposite sides of the house they each swear never to talk to the other as long as they both live. But life is very short and anger long.

55

The Man Whose Name No One Is Allowed to Mention

— *L*ook, I kiss the cross I'm telling the truth, Aunty says, kissing her thumb and index finger. The little green dial from the alarm clock bright. The wall fanned with light every once in a while from the headlights of passing cars. Aunty Light-Skin anchored in her twin bed, me in the other. Soft hiss of rain, and the windows filled with rain, too. On the wall the shadows of raindrops skittishly falling, as if the walls are crying.

Aunty has just clicked off an old black-and-white movie. —Not an *old* movie, Aunty corrects. —A movie from my times. Tin Tán in *Chucho el remendado*. And it wasn't *that* long ago.

Aunty putting her nightgown on with her back to me. Mexican women never dress or undress unless they have their back to you and the room is dark. The shape of Aunty's body like a mermaid. On the swan of her spine, a big black mole as lovely and perfect as an elevator button. When I was little I once asked if I could touch it. How is it ugly things can be so beautiful?

—So there we were, it was 1950, and he and I finally married. Aunty Light-Skin calls him "he" or Antonieta Araceli's father. She never says his name. No one says his name. Ever. To say his name would wake the grief asleep inside her heart and cause too much pain. To spare Aunty, we don't mention him either. That's why I never ask. Tonight, without asking, Aunty is telling her story.

—I'm telling the truth. May the Devil come and yank my feet tonight if I'm lying. We were legally married. Married. I have a ring and papers to prove it. Lalita, you believe me, don't you? We weren't married by the Church, of course. Because he was married in a church the first time, understand, so we couldn't marry in a church. But we were married by the court before we started to live together. We weren't like the young people now, do you follow me? In those days a woman wouldn't think of being with a man just like that.

Those times were different. Even to go out in the day a woman had to be accompanied or it wasn't proper. Your Uncle Baby would always come up with some plan so I could escape and enjoy myself a little. If it wasn't for him, I wouldn't have gone anywhere. But, *ay,* what vagabonds we were, your uncle and I. We lived to visit *los* shows. It was all very *divertido.* And *sano.* Healthy and innocent fun, not like now.

Aunty brightens remembering the names of the clubs, the performers from her times. La Carpa Libertad, where she saw first saw Tin Tán.

—You mean the little guy we just saw on TV?

—The very one. Before he became famous. And Cantinflas, Pedro Infante, Jorge Negrete, and who can forget the unforgettable Toña la Negra with her beautiful night orchid voice. *Veracruz, rinconcito donde hacen sus nidos las olas del mar . . .*

—Hey, Aunty! I didn't know you could sing. You're pretty good.

—Once maybe, but not anymore.

—But what does this have to do with Antonieta Araceli's father?

—Wait, I'm getting to that part. There were *carpas* all along the streets of San Juan de Letrán and las Vizcaínas back then, tents with gaudy painted backdrops, just rows of hard benches for seats, like a poor man's circus. But a lot of the big stars got their big break there and moved up to the fancier theaters like el Lírico and el Follies, el Tívoli, el Teatro Blanquita. It was at el Blanquita that I met . . . *him.*

She almost says his name, but then she doesn't say it.

—He said that when he saw me he knew. That's what he said, I don't know. I didn't see him in that way at first, but he says he knew the instant he saw me, I was *el amor de sus amores.*

Aunty looks both thrilled and embarrassed when she says this, and to see her so "emotioned" makes me feel sad for her. When the man whose name no one is allowed to mention used to telephone, Aunty would take the phone into the closet under the stairs to talk to him. That's how the Grandmother knew she was talking to a man.

—Who do you think introduced us? Guess!

Before I can even answer . . .

—Tongolele!

—The shimmy dancer from the movie?

—The same. *The* Tongolele. You can't imagine!

But I do imagine. A grainy black-and-white movie. The spotlights swirling across a smoky nightclub, the conga drums drumming when Tongolele enters dancing barefoot.

—*Rumberas* and exotic dancers came and went, Aunty adds.

—Kalantán, Rossy Mendoza, María Antonieta Pons, Ninón Sevilla, Rosa Carmina. But after Tongolele, Tahitian dances became the rage.

—Coming to you direct from Papeete!

—But that's not true, Aunty says. —She arrived Yolanda Montez from Oakland, California, but how would that sound? Yolanda Montez direct from Oakland, California! It doesn't have *chiste*. They invented all kinds of stories about Tongolele. That she was Cuban. That she was Tahitian. But that was just *puro cuento*. She was like you, Lala, a girl born on the other side who speaks Spanish with an accent.

—I didn't know you knew any movie stars, Aunty. How come you've never taken me to see her movies?

—Movies? You mean *churros*, Aunty snorts. —Not movies. Just excuses for a movie. But, oh, to have seen her dance!

I imagine a Mexican fifties musical like the one we just saw, a good thirty minutes devoted to Tongolele's cabaret scene, lots of smoke rising through the silver spotlight, and the unforgettable body of Tongolele to save the cheesy film. Cardboard palm trees on a big blank stage with dancers in silhouette, the stage too huge to be believable, drinks called "highballs" wearing paper umbrellas, and the tropical nightclub decorated with bamboo wallpaper, sparkly beaded curtains, tables with soft little lamps, and here and there African masks, even though this is supposed to be Polynesian, because that's just how movies are. In a black-and-white bikini with a chiffon train, the young Yolanda Montez with a face like my first Barbie doll—slanted eyes, heavy eyeliner, and a big waterfall of a ponytail. Hair dyed a hard black except for her trademark white streak above her right eyebrow.

—Yolanda Tongolele was just a teenager, only a little older than you are now, Lala, when she first came to Mexico, climbed up on a conga drum and danced her way to fame and fortune in a leopard-skin bikini.

—For real? Only a little older? Maybe there's hope for me after all.

—The night they took me to see her, Aunty continues, —Tongolele was already famous and had been dancing for years, even though she was still just a kid. I was *una escuincla* too, nothing but a kid. That was during the times when brassieres were pointy, because the night I saw Tongolele's show at el Blanquita, I was wearing one of those pointy brassieres with circles stitched round and round like a bull's-eye. I remember this detail because I was so young I didn't have anything to fill them up with but air. I had to be extra careful no one hugged me.

Your Uncle Baby and one of his girlfriends took me. If it hadn't been for your uncle I don't think Mother would've let me go. "Why do you want to go there? Don't you know a lot of Indians hang out at el Blanquita, they vomit in the aisles and throw stockings filled with sand and urine, and oh, who knows what, well, why do I even tell you?" But finally your uncle, who was a real *lambiache* with Mother, always, "*Ay*, Mamá, you look so beautiful with your hair permed," and, "How young that dress makes you look," this, and this, and that, you can't imagine how terrible Baby was! So finally your uncle gets her to let me go.

—I thought Grandmother was only strict with us. So what did you wear, Aunty?

—I was *estrenando,* wearing a new outfit, a beautiful painted skirt with sequins, a night scene of Taxco, black with purple and green sequins. I still have that skirt, remind me to show it to you. Unbelievable. No, sweetness, I can't fit into it anymore.

But let me tell you! The night we went to see Tongolele there was a riot! No, I mean *inside* the theater, with chairs being smashed and bottles breaking and everything. It was delightful! Well, not at the time, but now thinking back.

God, I wish exciting things happened to me.

—Imagine a wave. No, an ocean of people pushing and shoving. And to make matters worse, some *bruto* taking advantage of the situation and rubbing himself on your behind. Well, that was me. How ugly! *¡Fuchi!* That part of the story I don't even like to think about. But, oh! Imagine, this sea of madness rushing to get at Tongolele.

—And then what happened?

—What do you think? They climbed up on the stage and stormed through the curtains.

—You're lying!

—They did! They were like cannibals, that crowd. The theater stank,

I remember, from so many bodies pressed together. Like Japanese peanuts, like stale cigarette smoke and Tres Flores hair pomade, like the sour tears from armpits and groins and feet, like the sweet gas of someone who has eaten too many *chicharrones,* fried pork rinds. A stew of stinks. They just went wild, clambered up on the stage, yanked down the velvet curtains, and roared all the way to her dressing room. All this happened while I was waiting backstage for Tongolele to autograph my ticket.

After the first round of applause Baby says, "Let's go backstage." The audience is stomping its feet and whistling and yelling and practically pulling down the building, because they want more, they can't get enough. They think an hour of dancing isn't enough. But you should've seen her, *la pobre,* she was covered with sweat, as slippery as a fish plucked from the sea, but oh, so stunning. I was fascinated. I'd never seen anybody dance like that. You have no idea what a beauty she was, Lala, she was divine. Those eyes of hers. Sensational. Jungle-green. Green as the wings of a parrot. That green-green like an avocado. As green as peridot, I think. A brilliant green like . . . like that Jarritos soda you like to drink. Don't laugh, I'm not lying to you. But I was telling you about the riot. What an *escándalo,* Lalita, like you can't imagine.

But I do imagine, Aunty. Everything shot in deep shadows, high contrast, plenty of profiles and silhouettes. A black-and-white *churro* of a movie with one hair on the lens flickering on the screen. Tongolele is a tropical rainstorm, a steamy jungle, a black panther in heat. Her dressing room door inhales and exhales from the pressure of 3,129 Mexican men pushing to devour, sink their teeth, lap up blood, swallow her heart whole. Ton-go-le-le! Ton-go-le-le! Ton-go-lee-leeeeeeeee!

The door dissolves into dust!

Tongolele barely has time to escape, running barefoot out a stage door accompanied by sixteen soldiers and twelve police officers down *avenida* San Juan de Letrán on a motorcade. The siren wailing like a baby squalling at the movies.

Aunty says, —And so, there I was backstage with my ticket in one hand and Baby's fountain pen in the other. Tongolele was wearing a gorgeous fur coat that smelled of expensive perfume and chewing gum, and on her feet she was wearing snakeskin shoes, the kind that were in style back then, open-toed with straps that crisscrossed at the ankle. I remember I was admiring her gold-painted toenails when the mob came shoving down the narrow corridors roaring like a herd of wild elephants.

"Jeepers! Not again!" Tongolele says.

I remember I was so frightened, I just clung to her like a monkey and found myself squeezed into the backseat of a big maroon Cadillac with Tongolele and a bunch of her friends, imagine! There wasn't time to explain. Nobody even noticed I was there until Tongolele asked, "Do you like *tamales*?" Before I could even answer, she says, "Let's all go to Café Tacuba."* "Wherever you command, my queen," the driver says. The sequin crown from the Corona beer billboard on *avenida* San Juan de Letrán glittering in the rearview mirror.

All the while Aunty is enjoying herself. She's having a wonderful time. Life is marvelous! Tossing her head back. Laughing with all of her teeth.

—Suddenly Tongolele aims those twin panther eyes on me and asks, "Excuse me, who are you?"

How can Aunty tell her she isn't anybody? How can Aunty hold out a dog-eared ticket stub and a leaky pen and say, "I'm one of your fans, I was waiting backstage to shake your hand and congratulate you with my brother Baby," because by now Uncle is gone, left behind in that roiling sea of lust called the audience of el Blanquita.

But what does Uncle Baby care? He's used to this. To him, this is nothing. He hangs out at the clubs that have signs that say, GENTLEMEN, KINDLY REFRAIN FROM DROPPING LIT CIGARETTES ON THE DANCE FLOOR, THEY BURN THE LADIES' FEET, as well as the other kind with signs in the bathroom that bark, PLEASE DO NOT VOMIT IN THE SINK. Wherever Uncle Baby is, he's not worried about his sister.

—So what did you do, Aunty?

—What did I do? I did what any woman would do in my place.

—You made up a story?

—No. Well, not yet. First I started to cry. The story came later. I don't know why, but when Tongolele asked, "Who are you?" I just started to tremble. By then everyone in the car had stopped talking and realized I wasn't anybody. "*Who* are you?" she says, just like that.

The tears wanted to come out of my eyes, Lala, I swear to you. I've always been such a fool like that. Whenever I'm excited or anyone shouts at me, I just start crying. There's no stopping me for hours. And I could feel the shame rising in my throat and in my eyes with everybody staring at me and waiting, and the car suddenly very quiet, quiet, quiet. And me in a panic, because that's what it was, Lala, an absolute panic for a moment. Just as I'm about to hiccup into tears, a voice says, "She's with me."

It was a soft voice for a man, even though the body was big, husky, a big-shouldered man like a gorilla, but such a kind voice. All I could see was the back of his hat and the big man-shoulders of his top coat, because I forgot to tell you, he was sitting in the front seat next to the driver.

"She's with me," he says.

"With you?"

"Sure. With me. Isn't that right, my soul?"

I nodded. Then everyone started yakking again, and he looks back at me and smiles and winks. That wink that says, "I know it's a lie, and you know it's a lie, but let's just keep it to ourselves, right?" I go back to being invisible to everyone but him. It's as if I was always invisible until that moment. Until he said, "She's with me," I didn't have a life, right?

With all the pushing and shoving to get out of that theater alive, half the sequins on my painted skirt fell off, and the cones from my brassiere looked like a map of Oaxaca, but I didn't care. I was so happy.

When we pulled up to Café Tacuba, he helps me out of the car and takes me by the arm, but very gently, eh? As if to say to all the world, "She's with me." And well, ever since then, ever since then . . .

But she doesn't have to finish.

—He was divine, divine, divine. Of course, he behaved very correctly. That first night I couldn't look him in the eye, he couldn't look me in the eye, without feeling . . . how do I explain? *Ay*, Lalita, the hairs on my arms stand up even now after all these years.

—So how was it he was in the Cadillac that night with Tongolele?

—Well, Tongolele had musicians that played with her, drummers, and so on. And there was a certain *conguero* . . .

—So Antonieta Araceli's father played the *congas*?

—No. He wasn't the *conguero*. He was the *conguero*'s cousin. But he was every bit the artist. And the gentleman.

—For real? What did he do?

—He was a tire salesman. But that's only how he made his living. The talent God gave him was as a dancer. And as a *payaso*, a real clown. I think that's the way to a woman's heart, don't you? By making a woman laugh and by dancing with her. You can tell a lot about someone by the way he moves you about the dance floor.

But to finish telling you the story, it was 1950 and there we were, so in love and wanting to get married, except I was too afraid to tell my parents. Your grandfather was very strict, because of the military, but your grandmother, what was her excuse? You think she was bad by the time you knew her, but back then, well, you have no idea, and why should I even tell you, but believe me, she was strict. That's why *he* said, "Normita, you know better than I your parents will never give us permission to marry." This was because he'd already been married, and *lo más triste,* in a church. Plus he was a lot older, almost twenty years older than me, and to make matters worse he was a bit chubby and much-too-much-too Indian for Mother to approve. She was always concerned with *el que dirán,* the what-will-they-say.

And so he said to me, "Normita, there's only one way for us to marry; that's for me to steal you." And I said, "Well, all right, steal me." And so I let myself be stolen and that's how it was we married finally.

—Stolen! Like kidnapped? All for love, that's too cool, Aunty. Your life would make a terrific *telenovela.* Did you ever think about that?

—And so, I was married, but what good did that do me when your grandmother found out? "What, are you stupid or just pretending to be stupid?" My own mother said this to me, can you believe it? "What, are you stupid or just pretending to be stupid? As long as his first wife is still alive, your marriage is just paper. You may think you are married, but in the eyes of God you're nothing but a prostitute." Those words, they hurt me even now, Lalita.

—Wait, Aunty. I'll get us a box of Kleenex.

—*Gracias, mija.* But I was telling you, I went to live with my husband, right? Except it was as if I went to live by myself, because my husband's work as a tire salesman took him all over the republic. Sometimes he was gone for weeks at a time. And it was after one of his work trips that everything went from bad to worse.

We'd been quarreling. It was one of those stupid arguments that begins with, "And your family . . ." "But what about *your* family!" A fight without end. He had just come back from out of town. He'd left mad and came back worse. There was something odd about him that night. Something. Almost as if he deliberately wanted to fight with me. A woman can sense these things, believe me. By the end of the night neither of us was talking, and he just threw himself on the bed like a pile of laundry and started to snore. He worked so hard. I felt terrible after a while, seeing him sleeping like that, so completely exhausted, *el pobre.*

It filled me with love to see him sleeping so soundly, I just wanted to make up with him, so I lay down and put my hands like this, under his T-shirt, just so I could rub his back and say, "I'm here, *corazón,* I'm here." And what do I feel on his back but scratches, big welts. I turn on the lights and pull up his shirt, and ask, "And this?" But he couldn't say a thing, could he?

What a howl I let go! Like if they'd put a pin through my heart. I broke everything that was breakable and cursed and cried, and how could he bring another woman's scratches to our bed, and I don't know what. The neighbors must've enjoyed that fight. He was so upset he left. For days he didn't come home, and then I get a note saying he was staying with his family in Jalisco. I went a little crazy. Oh, I suffered, Lala. I was all right in the day. In the daytime it was easy to be brave. It was when I lay down to sleep, that's when I'd let myself cry.

—Why is it sadness always comes and gets you when you lie down?

—Maybe it's because we talk too much in the day, and we can't hear what the heart is saying. And if you don't pay attention, then it talks to you through a dream. That's why it's important to remember your dreams, Lala.

That's why when I started to dream the dreams about a telephone ringing, I took it as a sign that I should call and forgive him. I even went to *la basílica* to ask la Virgencita for this strength, because by then my heart was as knotted and twisted as those rags the faithful wrap around their legs to walk to church on their knees. I lit a candle and prayed with all my soul, like this, "Virgencita, I know he's my husband, *pero me da asco,* he disgusts me. Help me to forgive him."

And I know this sounds crazy, but it was as if a big rock rolled off my heart in that instant, I swear it. I walked home from La Villa like an angel, as if I had wings and was flying. When I got to the corner where we lived, I was practically running, I knew I had to telephone him. He was supposed to be staying with his family, right? But every time I called, guess what. He wasn't there. And again, "Oh, he's not here." Each time I called his relatives, they wouldn't let me talk to him. "Well, *fíjate,* he's not here right now." "Oh, how is it he's not there?" "Well, he stepped out." And like that, and like that. Of course, I was worried. Till finally one night I got it in my head to call the only hotel in that wretched town and ask for my husband at the registration.

Oh, Lala, never phone a man in the middle of the night unless you are brave enough to know the truth. You can always tell when a man has a naked woman lying next to him. Don't ask me how, but you can. There's a way men have of talking to you, or, rather, of not talking. The silences. It's what they *don't* say that's the lie.

"Are you alone? Is there someone there with you?" "Well, of course not, my life." But, Lala, I could hear sounds in the background.

—Like what kind of sounds?

—Well, like a zipper zipping. Like coughing, like water, like what do I know? Like someone. But I just knew. There's some things you just feel right here, you know. Right here I got a sick feeling, like if my heart was a *limón* being squeezed. *¡Pom!* And I just knew.

"Do you love me?" "Of course I do." "Do you? Then say it." "... Why?" "Just say it. Say you love me. Say it, *canalla*. Say you love me, say it!" "... I love you." "Now, say my name. Say, I love you Normita." "... I love you, Normita." And me laughing a little laugh like a witch, a hee-hee-hee from I don't know where. And at that moment I was a witch, wasn't I?

Everyone knew how the story was going to end except me. Isn't that always the case with love? He'd been hanging out with too many *güeros*. That's where he got such foreign ideas. So that after we broke up he wanted to keep calling me, can you believe it? "Can't we just be friends?"

"Friends? What do you think I am, *una gringa*?" That's what I told him, Lala. "What do you think I am, *una gringa*?" Because that's how *los gringos* are, they don't have any morals. They all have dinner with each other's exes like it's nothing. "That's because we're civilized," a *turista* once explained to me. What a barbarity! Civilized? You call that civilized? Like dogs. Worse than dogs. If I caught my ex with his "other," I'd stab them both with a kitchen fork. I would!

When I went back home to live with my parents with their terrible I-told-you-so's, the first thing I did was get rid of anything and everything he had ever given me, because I didn't want any part of him contaminating my life, right? When we were *novios* we had our names written on a grain of rice by one of those *Zócalo* vendors over by the cathedral. It was just a cheap gift, but it had meant a lot to me then.

I put that grain of rice inside my pocket, and the next Sunday when I went to the Alameda I fed it to an ugly pigeon. That's how mad I was. Oh, seeing that pigeon swallow that rice gave me a pleasure like I can't tell you.

"Normita, you're better off," everyone said to me. "You're young, you find yourself another to erase the pain of the last one; like the saying goes, one nail drives out another." Sure, but unless you're Christ who wants to be pierced with nails, right?

For a long time after, I'd just burst into tears if anyone even touched me. Sometimes it's like that when somebody touches you and you haven't been touched in a long time. Has that ever happened to you? No? Well, for me it was like that. Anybody touched me, by accident or on purpose, I cried. I was like a little piece of bread sopped with gravy. So when anything squeezed me, I started to cry and couldn't stop. Have you ever been that sad? Like a donut dunked in coffee. Like a book left in the rain. No, never? Well, that's because you're young. Your turn will come.

One of my girlfriends said I needed to see *un curandero*. That would cure me. "Look, you need to go somewhere by yourself and have a good cry," he told me. "It's that I don't have any privacy," I said. "Well, why don't you go to the forest?" That's when I realized how unaware men are about the world women live in. The forest? How could I go there? A woman alone. Because that's what I was, more alone than I'd ever been in my life. I was alone, and the person who loved me was a piece of red thread unraveling. Thank you, good-bye. And when I die, then you'll realize how much I loved you, right? Yes, of course. That's how it always is, isn't it? I dreamt a dream; I opened my wallet, but instead of money, there was a row of starched handkerchiefs, and I knew I had a lot of tears to spend.

I just wish *he* would've said, "I hurt you, Norma, and I'm sorry." Just that, I don't know, I don't know. If only he'd said that. Maybe that's why I still hate him!

—But if you hate him so much, Aunty, what's the point? Why does it even matter?

—Look, I wouldn't hate him if I didn't love him. Only people you love drive you to hate, don't you know that yet, Lalita? The ones you don't give a cucumber for, who cares what they think, right? They're not worth the bother of being upset. But when someone you love does something cruel, *¡te mata!* It can kill you or drive you to kill, *¡te mato!* You know that *pobrecita* who came out on the cover of *¡Alarma!* magazine, the one who made *pozole* out of her unfaithful husband's head? *Qué coraje, ¿verdad?* Can you imagine how mad she must've been to make *pozole* out of his head? That's how we are, we *mexicanas, puro coraje y pasión*. That's what we're made of, Lala, you and me. That's us. We love like we hate. Backward and forward, past, present, and future. With our heart and soul and our *tripas*, too.

—And is that good?

—It isn't good or bad, it just is. Look, when you don't know how to use your emotions, your emotions use you. That's why so many *pobres* wind up on the cover of *¡Alarma!* Me, I put my anger to good use. I used it to make a life for myself and Antonieta Araceli. You be careful with love, Lalita. To love is a terrible, wonderful thing. The pleasure reminds you—I am alive! But the pain reminds you of the same thing—*¡Ay!* I am alive. You're too young to know what I'm talking about, but one day you'll say, "My Aunty Light-Skin, she knew about life."

—And you've never looked for him again, Aunty? Never?

—For what? A woman doesn't want a man who is going to kill her with jealousy. Believe me, better to be lonely than jealous. Loneliness is one thing. I know about loneliness. But *los celos*, Lalita, for *that* there's no cure.

But listen, I tell you in secret, Lala, after everything, after all these years, after all the humiliations, after everything, everything, everything, everything, I love him still. I'm ashamed to say it, I love him still . . . But, well, that's ended now.

Now, my queen, time to go *mimi*.

—To sleep! But how, Aunty? You were going to tell me about . . . about *him*.

—Oh, another day, Aunty's tired of telling stories. Come, kiss me, my treasure . . . Lalita. Understand, only to you have I told this story, because you're *la gordita de la perra*, Aunty's favorite, and *una señorita* now. But don't tell the others or their feelings will get hurt, promise? Now, off to sleep with the fat little angels. Remember, only you have heard this story, my heaven. *Sólo tú.*

---

* The marvelous Café Tacuba on Tacuba, number 28, still operates today, serving traditional Mexican fare, including Mexican candy desserts hard to find anywhere else in the capital, though I always ask for the same thing— the tamales and hot chocolate. Señor Jesús Sánchez, of Oscar Lewis fame, once worked there as a busboy.

56

The Man from Mars

everal kilometers before the border, the Grandmother finally falls asleep, with her head thrown back and her mouth open. Father drives without saying a word. It's too hot to talk. Same as always, whenever we're near the border, no one feels like moving. Toto, Memo, and Lolo finally shut up and give us a break, lulled by the movement of the van. Mother escapes the way she always does when the Grandmother's with us, lost in her own thoughts.

What little breeze comes in the windows just makes you feel like fighting. It's worse when we finally stop. Nuevo Laredo is dizzy, dusty, and airless. A kid with crusty eyes tries to sell us Chiclets, and the Grandmother shoos him away with a swat and a, —*Váyase, chango apestoso.* She's in a terrible mood. When we finally drive through customs, she tells the border officials what she thinks of them. And just for that, they make us get out of the car while they search everything we own, including the walnut-wood armoire sleeping in the trailer!

The Grandmother meant to be sad and weepy when crossing, to hum the Mexican national anthem, or recite perhaps that little poem from childhood, "Green, White, and Red." —Now how did it go? *Verde, blanco, y colorado, la bandera del soldado* . . . She was, after all, leaving her homeland.

Weeks before, the Grandmother, who'd always sworn Mexico was the most *burro* of all nations, suddenly turned nationalist. She kept singing "México lindo y querido" over and over. But with the heat and confusion, when we finally get to the border, she forgets to be patriotic and instead crosses the international bridge cursing the corrupt border agents, the U.S. government, the Mexican government, the last three

Mexican presidents and their wives who wear too much makeup. What upset her was the loss of her *mangos*. She doesn't quit complaining all the miles *after* we cross the border either. By the time we stop in San Antonio for dinner, a hot three and a half hours later, she's still harping about those *mangos*.

—I tried. But, *ay*, to bring across Manila *mangos* is harder than trying to bring across Mexicans. What are *mangos*, for God's sake? I know a woman who crosses practically every weekend with a brassiere full of sleeping parrots. Look, you pour a bit of mescal down their beaks, and then they snore like babies, tuck them under a loose dress and there you have it. Pocket money for Christmas.

But I wasn't so lucky with the *mangos*. They were this big, I swear to you. And heavy too. Sweet, sweet, sweet, what with it being *mango* season and all. Pity the border agents seized them. If you had put them under the dirty clothes like I told you, lazy girl! You can bet those *desgraciados* enjoyed our *mangos* for lunch. Because Manila *mangos* are sweeter. I'm not lying to you. Manila *mangos* are the best, that's why they don't let them pass. That's why you never see Manila *mangos* in the States. Those border agents, they know what's good.

Ay, what I would give for a Manila *mango* right now with a little lemon and *chile*. I myself prefer the Manila *mango* shaped like a plump fish over el Petacón, the round parrot-colored *mango* one buys here in the States, don't you? But, *ay*, the Manila *mango* can only be bought in Mexico, that country where sweets are sweeter, isn't that so? Before I left I ate Manila *mangos* day and night to satisfy my craving for them. Did I get sick? No, not at all. Imagine when I saw street vendors with their pyramids of orange *mangos* as we drove away. A wealth of *mangos* spilling out from the flatbed of trucks like Cortés' gold. "Look, *mangos*," I said to my granddaughter, but she just shrugs like the badly raised child she is. The day of my good-bye party I ate two *mangos* before lunch at my neighbor's house even though it was rude to ask if I could have them before being offered. And then I ate another at my *comadre* the widow Marquez' house, the last *mango* in the house and maybe she was saving it for her son, but it sat in a nice basket on top of the fridge letting out its sweet perfume that tells you, "Come and eat me, I'm ready."

She's talking to a man named Mars, a friend of Father's from the war. Marcelino Ordóñez is his name, a little rooster of a guy in dark glasses with a deep, raspy voice and big white teeth, the kind that could maybe pry a nail from a wall. On each sunburnt arm a tattoo. Betty Boop on one arm and la Virgen de Guadalupe on the other. Mars owns the *taquería* on South Nogalitos Street, where we've stopped for dinner.

—As a matter of fact, I started out with just this one restaurant . . . , Mars begins.

Mother sighs, and says to no one and everyone, —I'm bored . . .

—But now I own everything from here to the fire station, Mars says proudly, pointing to a strip mall of one-story shops painted so white it makes you squint.

—¡A poco! the Grandmother says, as impressed as if he is pointing to the Taj Mahal instead of a string of crumbly storefronts.

I don't see what's so special. The crown jewel is the corner shop, where we're seated, and it's nothing to brag about. A sticky bunch of Formica tables and chrome kitchen chairs, a few plastic booths that could use new Naugahyde, the smell of fried meat and Pine-Sol like a million other little taco joints. MARS TACOS TO WENT. A huge sign facing Nogalitos Street, old Highway 90, the route we used to drive to the border before they built the new interstate. Maybe Mars thought he was going to get a lot of through-traffic, and maybe in the old Highway 90 days he did. But I-35 whooshes past beyond view, just making the signboard shudder.

—The name was my idea, Mars explains, —instead of "Tacos to Go." Any jerk can think of that, right? I wanted something with a little more snap to it, little more pizzazz. Something that says speedy service. So I named it "Mars Tacos to Went." Pretty cool, eh?

Mother rolls her eyes and sighs.

—Want to know what's the secret to success around here? Real estate! Mars continues. —*Hijo 'esú,* you should see what kind of barganzas you can find in *San Anto'.* It's the best-kept secret. Here, take a newspaper with you, you'll see, Mars says, pressing a free weekly on us.

Mother perks up. Even the Grandmother is interested.

—You boys need to come to San Antonio, Mars says, addressing my brothers, who are paying more attention to their plate of *enchiladas* than to investment tips. —Make yourself a bundle, Mars continues, —I kid you not. I'll teach you cats how to be millionaires before you're thirty. Buy yourself a fixer-upper. Live off the rents . . .

Mars talks like a beatnik, a cowboy, or Dean Martin or something. It's hard to imagine he's really Father's army buddy. Even harder to believe is the way the Grandmother treats him, making a little room for him on her side of the booth, listening to his every word like he's family, as if she's known him her whole life instead of just having met him.

—In the war Mars saved your father's life, she reminds us proudly.

—No kidding! I say. —How'd you do that, Mister Mars?

—Sweetheart, you can call me Mars, he says, forgetting how rude it is to call old people by their first name without adding "mister." Maybe he doesn't know he's old.

In the end, Father is the one who tells the story, one I've never heard before, which is even better. Father begins by sipping his coffee and exhaling his cigarette midsentence, pushing his plate away, making a long story longer, stretching it out so slow you almost feel like yelling.

—When I was in the army . . .

—Where's the toilet? Mother says, getting up and disappearing.

—I used to save all the money I earned, which wasn't much, maybe about fifty dollars a week. I hardly spent anything for myself. And you can ask your grandmother, in case you don't believe me. Isn't that right, Mamá? Everybody else bought beer and who knows what . . . but not me. I only allowed myself two Milky Ways a week, a Hershey's now and then, and every once in a while, as long as I didn't have to treat anyone else, a beer. I was saving for my furloughs when I'd travel home to Mexico.

Well, it happened . . . [Here he pauses to tap his cigarette ash onto his coffee saucer.] It happened that on one trip . . . I had all the money I'd earned, about four hundred dollars or so, in the front pocket of my uniform. I was riding a train headed to New Orleans . . . From there I was going to make my way to Texas . . . then the border . . . and then home. I remember I fell asleep . . . And then the next thing I know . . . the conductor is shaking me awake and asking for my ticket! I looked in my front pocket . . . I looked in my other pockets . . . I got up and looked under the seat . . . My ticket was gone, and all my savings too . . . The conductor made me get off at the next stop, New Orleans. So there I was in New Orleans without any money.

—How did you feel, Father?

—Well, I felt like crying . . .

—Wow. For real? And did you cry?

—No, my heaven, I didn't, but I felt like it. I knew it wouldn't do any good. It's worse to feel like crying, believe me, without the relief of tears. I needed some place to sit down and think . . . I remembered from my first visit to New Orleans that there was a park . . . near the train station. I remembered because it was there where I'd eaten a peach pie. You know . . . it's funny when you're all by yourself the things you wish for. I remember I'd wished I had someone to buy a pie for, a table and chair, someplace to sit down and eat a pie, somebody to share it with . . . At home I never would've thought of buying a pie. But there I'd bought a whole peach pie and eaten it in the park by myself, imagine.

Well, it was the same park where I'd eaten the pie, and now here I was again, but this time without even a few coins to buy a cup of coffee.

—Did you ever think about making a collect phone call?

—Lala! Quit butting in with your stupid questions, Toto says, disgusted.

—Yeah, Lolo adds, —you're always blabbing about nothing.

—Leave her in peace, Father scolds. —She's your *only* sister.

—The *only* girl? And six boys? Oh, so she's *la consentida*, eh? Mars chuckles.

—*La única*. She's the one who orders her poor papa about, isn't that right, *mi cielo*?

—So then what happened, Father? Memo asks. —Then what?

—How?

—In New Orleans.

—Oh! So then . . . there I was in New Orleans with no money and with no friends. I was sitting on a park bench thinking, "Now what?" And I guess I must've looked sad, because there was a soldier sitting nearby, a Texan from San Antonio . . .

Mars looks at me and winks at this part of the story.

Father continues, —Well, he talked a Spanish like he came from another planet, but he was Mexican too, a Mexican from the other side. From Texas, that is. I tell him my story and he tells me his.

"Ordóñez, Marcelino is my name," he says to me. "West Texas is where I'm from. From Marfa, where those strange UFO lights appear. Ever hear about the Marfa lights? No, you haven't? I could talk all day and tell you stories. That's why everybody calls me the Martian. But you can call me Mars," he says.

Then he did something I never expected . . . He pulled fifty dollars from his wallet and handed them over . . . just like that. Fifty dollars! A lot of money to give to a stranger, then or now.

At this point Mars interrupts, —Aw, it's cause we're *raza, ése*.

—I remember I promised to pay you back just as soon as I got to Mexico City, Father says, reeling the story back, —and the moment I stepped in the door my father, who was very correct, very much a gentleman, wired Mars his *centavitos* . . .

Mars adds, —And what did I tell you back then? . . . Don't worry about it, buddy. Way I figured it, you paid me or you paid somebody else one day. It's all the same. Look, you give hate and you get paid back in hate. You give love and the world pays you back in love. I give you fifty bucks, and someday somebody does me a favor when I need it too, see?

—All the same. I paid back my debt. I'm a man of my word.

I look out the window and am surprised to see Mother leaning against our van smoking a cigarette. Mother hardly ever smokes, except maybe once in a while, like maybe on New Year's Eve.

—But the day I met my friend here, Father continues, —he took me to the Red Cross to get duplicate furlough papers, then the USO station, he bought me a hamburger, two cups of coffee and a chocolate donut, he bought me a train ticket, and then he walked me over to the train station, gave me the Mexican good-bye—*un abrazo* and the double pat on the back . . .

—Because we're *raza*, Mars says, shrugging. —Know what I'm talking about? Because we're *familia*. And *familia*, like it or not, for richer or poorer, *familia* always gots to stick together, bro'.

Then Mars does the funky *raza* handshake with Father, like Chicano power, and Father, who is always ranting and raving about Chicanos, the same Father who calls Chicanos *exagerados*, *vulgarones*, zoot-suiting, wild-talking, *mota*-smoking, forgot-they-were-Mexican Mexicans, surprises us all. Father handshakes the funky handshake back.

57

Birds Without a Nest

*S*in—without. *Sin compañía.* Without company. Without companion. Without compromises. Without worries.

The Grandmother was strangely quiet the rest of the trip. Mars' string of buildings impressed her. She thought about how she might invest the money from the sale of the house on Destiny Street. She didn't have to ask permission from anyone now, did she? She busied herself looking through the classifieds of the newspaper Mars had given her and ignored the chatter of her grandchildren. Since they spoke to each other in English most of the time, this was easy to do. Was it true one could become rich in San Antonio? Not that she had any intention of moving to San Antonio. Why, of course, she wanted to live near her sons and be with them in Chicago. But it doesn't hurt to look, she thought to herself. It was this column that caught her heart:

FLECHAZO

Would you like to start an interesting friendship? Are you tired of looking everywhere for that special person to share your life with? Send us your personal announcement and mention your name, age, weight, height, and hobbies.

Mexicana, white, tall, thin, 5'3", attractive, cheerful, decent, elegant, without vices, without compromises. I love dancing and all kinds of healthy diversions. I am formal and affectionate. I wish to meet a gentleman of 45 to 55 years old, light or fair-skinned, medium height (like 5'5" or taller). He must be attentive, affectionate, responsible, without vices or compromises, and should be formal. Also, he must be educated; must love dancing and serious relationships; and above all, be economically solvent.

Feel free to write me in English o español, no le hace y don't you worry! *Mex-Tex, single, 35 years old, 145 pounds,* piel apiñonada, *not too fat, not too skinny, not too bad-looking either, without vices, own my own tree-trimming and lawn-mowing business. I love* la música norteña, *dancing, accordion playing, I am without dependents, love diversions, but I am a homebody and loyal. I look for a woman between 19–30 years, any nationality, attractive, feminine above all, if you think you're compatible with me, write, you won't be sorry. Don't forget photo and telephone number. Come on,* vamos a hacerle el *try!*

I am a Mexican lady, divorced, 5'2", 157 pounds, 46 years old, white-skinned, a home person, clean, hardworking, affectionate, and they say I am quite attractive. I am a romantic. I love those things that make a person better every day. I adore all kinds of healthy diversions, and I am a believer in moral values. I desire a gentleman of 43 years to 53 years, between 5'7" and 5'10" height, weight appropriate to his height, moreno claro (no es requisito), *without vices, responsible, honest. Stable in his sentiments, please no lying. He should be a worker and without any amorous compromises.* Absténgase, no aventuras. *God willing I will find him to begin a friendship, not matrimony. When he writes, I will know him.*

My name is Rudy, I am a 61 years old widower (don't have gray hairs, they say I look 55). I am a veteran and love healthy diversions, fishing, films, camping, and visiting Natural Bridge Caverns. I am looking for a life companion. I sweep my house, iron, and mop. I bake cakes and bread. I don't smoke or drink, and I have always tried to be as sincere as possible. I would like to meet someone with good presentation, kind, with good character, to begin a clean and sincere relationship. My intentions are serious. Write or call me for friendly conversation. You won't be sorry.

Señora of 48 years seeks gentleman of 48 to 60 to establish a beautiful relationship. I am without vices, with a university degree in art and am very healthy spiritually. I am from a good family with an eye for the finer things of life. I look for a professional, no widowers or divorced please, a man of category without compromises, someone with the same qualities as I. If interested, send photo immediately.

Single, 31, shy, hardworking, honorable man of good character seeks ideal woman to form firm relationship. I am 5'6", 160 lbs., and though I have a big heart, it's patched as I had to undergo surgery recently. First we'll talk by phone, then decide the date of our meeting. I have never married, and am clean, sincere, honest, and live simply. I work as an operator of heavy equipment.

Woman of 60 years, Taurus, well conserved, active, very affectionate seeks man of appropriate age without vices. Must be cheerful, attentive, with no compromises whatever. If he's a veteran, even better. I love t.v., soft music, meditation, fresh air. I am a bit of a vegetarian and I neither smoke nor drink. Desire a man with similar interests. Color, appearance, and nationality don't matter, but qualities and thoughts do. If you are Virgo or Cancer, even better. Send telephone number.

There were so many decent men out there in San Antonio. The Grandmother thought perhaps it was Divine Providence that was leading her there. Who knows what the future would bring? She felt a little ashamed of her thoughts. Was it a sin to be thinking these things so soon after her terrible grief? But she'd always been so alone, especially *after* her marriage.

No, she could never bring herself to put an ad in the paper like a side of beef for sale. All the same, she could not help but mentally re-create herself:

> *Kind, mature woman, wronged in life too many times, seeks a stable, affectionate, tender, and above all, loyal gentleman* sin problemas. *Must be* feo, fuerte, y formal . . .

58

My Kind of Town

One would think now that she was living in Chicago, in the same city as her Inocencio, the Grandmother would find happiness. But no, that wasn't the case. The Grandmother was meaner than ever. She was unhappy. And didn't know she was unhappy, the worst kind of unhappiness of all. As a result, everyone was in a hurry to find her a house of some sort. A bungalow, a duplex, a brownstone, an apartment. Something, anything, because the Grandmother's gloominess was the contagious kind, infecting every member of the household as fiercely as the bubonic plague.

Because Baby and Ninfa's apartment had room to accommodate a guest, it was understood the Grandmother would stay with them until she could find a house of her own. This had seemed all well and fine when the plans were made long-distance with Uncle Baby shouting into the receiver that he insisted, that he and Ninfa wouldn't think of her staying anywhere else, that the girls were thrilled she was coming. But now that she was actually sleeping in Amor's narrow bed with radios and televisions chattering throughout the apartment, and doors and cupboards banging, and the stink of cigarettes soaking into everything, even her skin, and trucks rumbling past and shaking the building like an earthquake, and sirens and car horns at all hours, well, it just about drove her crazy; even the rowdy Chicago wind, a rough, moody brute who took one look at you and laughed.

Baby's family was housed in an immaculate apartment on the top floor of a ziggurat-capped three-flat facing the Kennedy Expressway, off North Avenue and Ashland. In the old days the hallways of these brick buildings had exhaled the scent of pierogi or kielbasa, but now they let go a whiff of *arroz con gandules* or *sopa de fideo*.

All day and all night the expressway traffic whooshed past, keeping the Grandmother awake. She napped when she could, even when the apartment and its inhabitants jabbered the loudest. She was tired all the time, and yet she had trouble sleeping, often waking once or twice in the early morning, and in her sleeplessness, padding in her house slippers to the living room, where the front windows looked out onto the lanes of traffic, the expressway billboards, and the frighteningly grimy factories beyond. The trucks and cars, furious to get from here to there, never paused for a moment, the sound of the expressway almost not a sound at all, but a roar like the voice of the sea trapped inside a shell.

She pressed her forehead against the cold glass and sighed. If the Grandmother had consulted her feelings, she would've understood why it was taking her so long to buy a new house and settle in Chicago, but she was not a woman given to reflection. She missed her old house too much and was too proud to admit she'd made a mistake. She couldn't go backward, could she? She was stuck, in the middle of nowhere it seemed, halfway between here and where?

The Grandmother missed the routine of her mornings, her three-minute eggs and *bolillo* breakfasts. She missed rubbing her big toe along the octagon tiles of her bathroom floor. But most of all, she missed her own bed with its mattress sagging in the center, the familiar scent and weight of her blankets, the way morning entered gradually from the left as the sun climbed over the east courtyard wall, the one topped with a cockscomb of glass shards to keep out the thieves. Why do we get so used to waking up in a certain room? And when we aren't in our own bed and wake up in another, a terrible tear for a moment, like death.

There is nothing worse than being a houseguest for too long, especially when your host is a relative. The Grandmother felt like a prisoner. She hated climbing up the three flights of stairs, and always arrived clutching her heart, convinced she was having an attack, like the one that killed Narciso. Really, once she was upstairs, she couldn't even bear the thought of coming back down. What a barbarity!

The apartment, with its glass and carpeting and knickknacks and froufrou, made her feel ill, with an inexplicable urge to pick up a chair and send everything smashing. The tufted cushions, the fringe, the brocade draperies, the spotless glass and mirrors and gleaming kitchen, it was unbearable. The Grandmother blamed her daughter-in-law. Ninfa never talked to you without doing twenty things at the same time. Loading up the washer, rinsing a glass, wiping off a counter, spraying a mirror with glass cleaner. All this while trailing a violet plume of cigarette smoke. Ninfa was as skittish as a cat. The Grandmother was convinced Ninfa's intent was to slowly drive her crazy.

To cure her homesickness, the Grandmother tried to make her borrowed room look like the one she had left behind on Destiny Street. She covered the bed with her Mexican pillows with their Mexican *cariños*. But it was no use. It was still Amor's room with the chartreuse bedspread and hot-pink shag rug, the tape marks from where the black-light posters came down still sticky on the daisy wallpaper, the white wicker bedroom set from when Amor was a child, the pink-and-green faux Tiffany petal lamp dangling like a rosary from its gold swag chain, the plastic Boston fern in its fuzzy macramé plant hanger still dusty as ever, the princess vanity table cluttered with all of Amor's things—electric hair rollers, a lighted makeup mirror, and two wigs, a copper pageboy and a blond shag. Amor left the Leonard Whiting and Olivia Hussey/*Romeo and Juliet* poster, but the Jackson Five had to go to make room for the Grandmother, who couldn't understand why anyone would want pictures of *negros*.

Amor and Paz complained the most, because they had to share a room, and there was very little they enjoyed sharing except for an intense dislike of each other. It seemed to the Grandmother the girls had too much of everything—clothes, spending money, boyfriends, and their parents indulging them further with each birthday. She tried to give them some badly needed instruction, but they were lazy, ungrateful girls, beyond reach. She wondered how much Spanish they really understood when they nodded at everything she said, even when it wasn't appropriate.

—Always, always, keep a neat bed, the Grandmother said, pinching and tugging the chartreuse bedspread until it was taut. —You can tell the character of a woman by how she makes her bed. Show me her bed, and I'll tell you who she is.

Anything the Grandmother said always made Amor and Paz feel miserable. They wondered if their father had been telling stories about how they often forgot to make their beds, because they woke up too late and had to rush off to school, and then came home after dark when it seemed pointless to make a bed for just a few hours.

—An unmade bed is the sign of *una mujer cochina*, the kind who catches lice, do you hear me? No man wants to marry a woman who can't make a decent bed.

Oh, brother! the girls thought, but they were only allowed to nod and say, —*Sí*, Abuela.

Her sons had too many children and too many things. It made their apartments crowded. And they rented, but didn't own. None had the foresight nor the resources to buy their own home. Stupid children! Why didn't they think?

Baby and Ninfa were too busy spending on home furnishings, furnishing their daughters like princesses. Fat-Face and Licha spent all the money on their flea market weekends, the way others play the slot machines, and then transporting all this junk to Mexico, spending the profits on their vacation, and coming back to buy all over again. And Inocencio, though he was a very good upholsterer, was never as excellent with figures as he was with tufted cushions. With seven children and with Zoila at home as homemaker, there was never enough for a house, though Zoila argued that if only Inocencio would let her work they could save for a down payment. —Real estate! That's the ticket, she said. But Inocencio countered with his own argument, —What! A wife of mine work? Don't offend me!

The Grandmother's sons were busy. All week long they worked, and on weekends they took turns escorting her to look at houses, a horrible business of looking into other people's bathroom cabinets. The new houses were too far away and beyond her resources. And houses within her budget were in neighborhoods with all kinds of riff and raff.

—Here you'll feel at home, they said, but she couldn't say she did not feel at home in the crowded squalor called the Mexican *barrio*. —This isn't home. This is a slum, that's what this is.

Something happened when they crossed the border. Instead of being treated like the royalty they were, they were after all Mexicans, they were treated like Mexicans, which was something that altogether startled the Grandmother. In the neighborhoods she could afford, she couldn't stand being associated with these low-class Mexicans, but in the neighborhoods she couldn't, her neighbors couldn't stand being associated with her. Everyone in Chicago lived with an idea of being superior to someone else, and they did not, if they could help it, live on the same block without a lot of readjustments, of exceptions made for the people they knew by name instead of as "those so-and-so's."

To visit Chicago is one thing, to live there another. This was not the Chicago of her vacations, where one is always escorted to the lake shore, to the gold coast, driven along the winding lanes of traffic of Lake Shore Drive in the shadow of beautiful apartment buildings, along State Street and Michigan Avenue to window-shop at least. And perhaps taken on an excursion on the lake. How is it she hadn't noticed the expression of the citizens, not the ones fluttering in and out of taxis, but the ones at bus stops, hopping like sparrows, shivering and peering anxiously for the next bus, and those descending wearily into the filthy bowels of the subway like the souls condemned to purgatory.

At first the Grandmother was thrilled by the restaurants and the big discount chains—but then the routine got to be too familiar. Saturdays in search of houses that were not to her liking. Dark brick houses with small, squinty windows, gloomy apartments, or damp little bungalows, everything somber and sad and not letting in enough light, and no court-yards, a dank, mean gangway, a small patch of thin grass called a garden, and maybe a bald tree in front. This wasn't what she had in mind.

And as the weeks and months passed, and she was still without a house, the rainy, cold autumn weather began and only made her feel worse. There was the Chicago winter coming that everyone had warned her about, and she was already so cold and miserable she didn't feel much like leaving her room, let alone the building. She blamed Ninfa, who kept lowering the heat in order to save money. The Grandmother confined herself to bed, satisfied only when she was under several layers of blankets.

The city was such a nuisance. Everything was so far away and hard to get to. She couldn't take the bus—no, no, even though she had wandered about alone in Mexico.

Now it was her sons' turn to say, —Alone? How? No, wait till the weekend. But when the weekend came, they were exhausted, and Amor and Paz for some reason were so rude to her. They grunted, they scurried off without greeting her when she entered a room. They mumbled in their atrocious *pocho* Spanish with English words minced in. She suspected they were hiding from her. —¿Y la Amor? —Amor *se fue a la* . . . library. Like that.

Her sons fought like cats and dogs. Where did they get such cruelty? Only weeks had passed since Inocencio had traveled to Mexico to fetch her, but in that short amount of time Inocencio was astonished to find the neat order and fastidious habits of the Tapicería Tres Reyes shop dissolve as easily as polished chintz ripped off an old love seat.

— *S*ince when does Tres Reyes do chrome kitchen chairs? Inocencio begins.

—Don't be such a snob, Fat-Face shrugs. —Money's money.

—I told you, Baby says to Fat-Face. —I told you he wouldn't like it, but who listens to me?

—He'll like it all right when the dough starts rolling in.

—Idiots! Inocencio shouts, a vein on his forehead throbbing. —Don't you two stupids understand anything? Tres Reyes has always stood for custom work, for quality. The day we trade in our hammers for staple guns we're ruined. We've made a name for ourselves restoring fine antiques, by hand! Not pumping out cheap kitchen chairs. I turn around and now look what you've done! Next thing you know we'll be making plastic slipcovers.

—As a matter of fact, Baby says proudly, —we've practically landed the Casa de la Raza Furniture Store on Cermak. If they agree to our proposal we'll be doing all their slipcover work!

—Please, Inocencio says, —kill me already!

—Don't create a drama, Tarzán. You know as well as I do we're running a business here.

—Well, for you it may be a business, but for me it's like a religion. I don't put my name on work that looks like . . . dirt.

—Spare me your stories. We can't rely on little old ladies from Winnetka. It may be all well and fine to make a beautiful chair, but it's not enough volume to make us rich.

—Not now, but soon, soon.

—Soon? When? I'm sick and tired of waiting for soon. Tarzán, listen to me. If you would only let go a little and let me manage things for a while. You live in the clouds. You don't have a head for business, you never have . . .

—Let you manage! I leave for a few weeks and look what you've done! You're crazy!

—You're the one who's crazy! You never let me do anything. You can't boss me around like when we were kids. You live in the past, do you hear me? You think it's easy to work with someone like you? Ha! You want the truth? Tarzán, you drive me nuts! You get on my nerves! You make me sick! Do you realize you call out Zoila's name at least twenty times an hour? I'm not lying. Like the hiccups. And that's not all. I didn't want to tell you, but we've lost more upholsterers from you making them rip up something they just did and having them do it over just because it doesn't meet your standards. And let me tell you another thing: I can't even put a hammer down without you picking it up and putting it away. You're worse than *una vieja*! I've had it with you . . .

*I*nocencio tells all his troubles to his mother. —You know what Fat-Face says, Mamá. He says he and Baby are already thinking of opening up their own business.

—Is that so? says the Grandmother. —And let them. You don't need them, *mijo*. You're better off working for yourself.

—I'd like to see them try. I give them one month, and then they'd be begging to come back. Mamá, you don't know them. They're my brothers, but they're terrible upholsterers. It's that I can't make a go of it with them. Fat-Face is always cutting corners, and Baby's sloppiness is making us lose our best customers.

—You don't need these mortifications. Listen to your mother, start your own business. The customers will follow. They know good work when they see it.

—It's that I don't have the *centavos* just now. Maybe one day. *Ojalá.*

*B*ut nothing, nothing in the Grandmother's imagination prepared her for the horrors of a Chicago winter. It was not the picturesque season of Christmas, but the endless tundra of January, February, and March. Daylight dimmed to a dull pewter. The sun a thick piece of ice behind a dirty woolen sky. It was a cold like you can't imagine, a barbarous thing, a knife in the bone, a cold so cold it burned the lungs if one could even believe such a cold. And the mountains of filthy snow shoveled in huge heaps, the chunks of ice on the sidewalk that could kill an aged citizen. —Oh, this is nothing, you should've been here for the Big Snow, the grandchildren bragged, speaking of the recent storm of '68.

Big snow or little snow, it was all the same after the novelty of snow had worn off. A nuisance, a deadly thing, an exaggerated, long, drawn-out ordeal that made one feel like dying, that killed one slowly, a torture. *Let me die in February, let me die rather than have to step out the door again, please,* the Grandmother thought to herself, dreading having to dress like a monster to go outside. —*Ay, ya no puedo.* I can't anymore, I can't. And just when she could no longer, when she could no longer find the strength, the drive, the will to keep on living, when she was ready to fold into herself and let her spirit die, just then, and only then, did April arrive with sky the color of hope and branches filled with possibilities.

59

Dirt

On Sunday mornings other families go to church. We go to Maxwell Street. —*Vamos al Más-güel,* Father announces, and starts to sing "Farolito" in a happy voice. He sings while he's shaving. He sings so loud we can't stand it. Father flicks the light on in the rooms where we're sleeping. —Wake up. *Vamos al Más-güel.* He tears open curtains and raises venetian blinds, dust spinning in his wake, the summer sunlight killing us.

The Grandmother has already had her toast and coffee by the time we pick her up at Uncle Baby's. She climbs in the van with a hairy *ixtle* shopping bag and her old maroon umbrella with an amber handle. —To protect me from the sun. Thanks to you sleepyheads it's already so hot. No doubt we've missed the best buys by now, she adds, settling in. She's wearing her market dress, a shapeless, faded shift. —The better to haggle with, the Grandmother insists. —This way they feel sorry for me.

But Father wears his good clothes even though Maxwell Street is filthy. Flies on crates of rotten cantaloupe. Rusty coffee cans filled with rusty nails. A plastic Timex box filled with gold molars. Boxed lemon meringue pies with the meringue a little squashed. Beyond the trash are real and not-so-real treasures. A man playing an accordion with a live chicken on his head. Strings of plastic pearls the colors of Easter eggs. A china shepherdess statue with a crack like a strand of blond hair, —From Paris, gimme ten dollars. The finest homemade *tamales* in the world from that Michoacán widow the police keep hassling because she doesn't have a food permit.

Father hates used things. When we bring home toys from the Goodwill and the Salvation Army, we have to lie when he asks where we got them. —This? You bought it for us, remember? But Maxwell Street is different. It reminds Father of the open-air markets in Mexico.

Mother and the Grandmother are just glad to get out of the house. They wander the streets like prisoners escaped from Joliet. Everything amuses them. The blues musicians twanging away on steel guitars. The smoky scent of grilled barbecue. The medicine man wearing live snakes. They don't care if they don't buy a thing. They're happy just to eat, to stop at 18th Street for *carnitas* and *chicharrón*, or at Taylor Street for Italian lemonade on the way home.

But Father is shopping with a purpose. He's looking for his British wing tips, the Cadillac of *zapatos*, with pinhole designs along the toe and ankle, along the lace-ups, shoes so heavy if you dropped them on someone's head, you'd kill him. But these are the shoes Father prefers, classic wing tips of oiled and waxed calfskin, a rich tobacco color.

It's over to Harold's we're headed, corner of Halsted and Maxwell, across the street from Jim's Original Hot Dogs.* Harold has been there since . . . —Since before you were born, girlie. Up a narrow, dark flight of wooden stairs. On each sagging step, a strip of aluminum so that your footsteps coming up or down announce you. *Tap, tap, tap.* The stairs creak. The walls are stained. The banister, dark from the oil of hands, is sagging. Everything is sagging like a pile of shoe boxes—building, shelves, steps, Harold.

Two hundred and forty pounds of Harold is standing with a shoe box in one hand, tissue paper gaping over, one shoe in the other hand. —Those costs you double in the Loop, Harold is saying to a black mother who is buying a pair of red high-tops for her lanky baby-faced boy.

Harold's best shoes come in strange sizes, display shoes from the windows, tiny as a Cinderella. "Good lucky" for Father he has small feet.

It smells sweet in Harold's, dusty and sweet as leather. The box window fan revolving slowly. All of Harold's salesmen are young boys in ties, the place too hot for ties, especially today. Everyone sweating. Harold, tie-less, standing among a pile of messy boxes, talking too loud. How does he find anything here? He does. It's not a fancy shop. The grime, the dirt, the sweet leather smell. Harold wiping his face with a handkerchief. He knows shoes like Father knows sofas.

There are only a few chairs, the ones with seats that lift up like in the movies. Mother and the Grandmother have already claimed the last two, Mother fanning herself with a shoe box lid, the Grandmother flicking a limp handkerchief.

Harold demands you step on a box lid when you try on a shoe. It's a bit dim and dark, and there's a real disorder that nobody minds, which makes finding a pair more exciting. At any second another Chicago fire could start, a spontaneous combustion of shoe polish and paper and shoehorns and dirty shelves. At any moment the place could collapse in a sea of flames. A speckled light enters from the windows that have been painted over in green paint. The windows yawning open. Noise of street hucksters and hawkers. The sticky scent of pork chop sandwiches rising from Jim's Original Hot Dogs.

But at Harold's Father forgets that British wing tips mean excellence. —Dirt, dirt, he says in Spanish, when examining the slippery leather soles, the fine stitching, the sweet scent of real Italian calfskin. —Trash, he keeps muttering in Spanish. —*Mugre. Porquería. ¡Fuchi!* Father feels it's his duty to insult the merchandise. He's furious whenever we pay the first price quoted for anything. —Fools! Store owners expect you to haggle.

—How much, my friend? Father asks.

—Them cost you fifty, Harold says, already talking to another customer.

—How much? as if he hadn't heard.

Harold, sweating, looks at him, disgusted. —*Amigo,* I already told you, fifty bucks. *Cincuenta. Cinco* and oh.

Father: —Fifty? Then that look he is famous for, that eye of the rooster, head tilted a little as if he has razors tied to his talons and is about to attack in a gleam of green-black feathers and bloody foam.

—Fifty dollars? For *this dirt* . . .

Harold brings his 240-pound body of businessman over and plucks the shoe box from Father's hands. —For you, *not* for sale.

—Get outta . . .

—You get out of here, Reyes. Don't bother me, I'm busy selling shoes.

—Twenty-five. I give you twenty-five.

—I already told you, forget it. They're the best, those shoes.

—*Sheet* on you. Get outta . . . Son of a mother . . . Muttering as we all step down the rickety aluminum-tipped steps that *tap-tap* with our defeat.

Father is a man possessed. We talk to him, but his eyes are spirals. We tug his sleeve and point at items we'd like to buy—popsicles, bandanas, felt-tip pens. It's useless.

After we've walked around the block and touched bunches of socks, six pairs for one dollar, after we've reached for a cold bottle of strawberry cream soda bobbing in an ice cooler with chunks of ice floating like icebergs, your hand numb when you finally fish it out, after we've heard the preacher man shouting for us to receive the Lord, *He* is coming, but he's not here today at Maxwell Street, after we've walked past the doorways with big, busty women in halter tops and purple satin hot pants, after we've eyed sacks of Ruby Red grapefruit, a plaster Venus di Milo, a geranium plant growing in a coffee can, we *do* go back, we will go back, we must go back. Must we? We must! It's terrible to have to climb the aluminum-tipped crooked stairs the second time.

Mother asks for the car keys.

Humiliating the third.

When we get to Harold's, the Grandmother camps on the first step and says, —I'll wait here.

—How much? Father asks Harold once more, as if this was the first time.

—Forty-five, Harold snorts. —And you're getting them dirt cheap, too!

—Thirty! Father says.

—Forty! That's what I paid for them.

—Thirty-five!

—I said forty and get outta here, you heard me!

Father pays his money, muttering, —Dirt, dirt, for this dirt. All the while Harold is stuffing the bills in his shirt pocket and waving him off, waving his arms as if saying, —You're nuts, get lost, forget it. Both of them terribly angry, ruined even, all day. Enraged. Disgusted.

Triumphant!

*Taquitos de *Pine-Sol*.

    Father's favorite taquería *is a place on Halsted Street called La Mila-grosa, a few blocks south from Jim's Original Hot Dogs on Maxwell. Father likes to tell the story about the first time he took Mother there. They were still newlyweds. Mother was not impressed.*

    A hungry mob stands next to a greasy steel counter and waves plastic numbers in the air to butchers who dispense orders beneath a neon Virgen de Guadalupe and a dusty bull's head with glass eyes. Curly strips of flypaper hang from the ceiling like streamers at a children's party, the steady death drone of flies making the room jump.

    —How can you bring me here? This place looks like a dump, Mother says.

    —It is *a dump, says Father. —That's how you can tell the* tacos *are good.*

    —I mean how do you expect me to eat here? Mother asks, eyeing the sawdust on the floor behind the butcher counter. —This place looks like it has bugs and mice.

    —Well, so does our house, but we eat there too, don't we?

    At this, Mother can think of no clever response. It's true. They live in the only neighborhoods they can afford, where the rent is cheap and the fauna resilient. Mother tries not to look at the seams where the floor meets the wall. She orders a chile relleno taco *and a* taco de cabeza. *Father asks for three brain tacos and two tongue, and a rice-water drink.*

    At the moment their food arrives, almost as if on cue, a man appears with the ubiquitous mop and pail[†] and starts to mop with Pine-Sol. The mop is a sweet stinky, as if it hasn't dried properly, the Pine-Sol so strong it makes you blink. That smell, the sad smell of Saturday mornings, of hallways shared with other tenants, of nursing homes, of pets or people who have had accidents, of the poor who have nothing to clothe themselves with but pride. We may be poor, but you can bet we're clean, the smell says. We may be poor. It is no disgrace to be pobre, *but . . . it's very inconvenient.*

[†]*Even Bernal Díaz del Castillo, one of Hernán Cortés' foot soldiers, cites in his wonderfully detailed chronicles the Mexican obsession with cleaning. This is true even today. You have only to arrive in the Mexico City airport, step off the plane into the waiting area, and your first encounter with Mexican culture will be to dodge someone furiously mopping. Especially if it's the middle of the day.* ¡CUIDADO! WATCH OUT!*—warns a plastic yellow sign with a stick figure of a person falling on his back.*

60

When an Elephant Sits on Your Roof

— Long distance from Texas, I say, handing the phone to Mother, —It's Papa.

—*¿Mijo?* Mother says tenderly. She always calls Father *mijo* when she's feeling kind. Father's been gone for over two weeks, long enough for Mother to miss him.

—*¡Mi vida!* *¡Ya tenemos casa!* Father says, shouting so loud even I can hear him. —We're homeowners!

Mother barrages him with questions, and finally finishes by telling Father to hang up and call back after eleven, when the rates are cheaper. Mother is as wild as if she'd won the lottery.

— Well, for once your grandmother has given us something other than headaches. She's bought us a house in San Antonio. On a street named El Dorado. And your father's found himself a shop nearby. Cheap too! A house, Lala! Think of it. Finally, after all these years.

—How many bedrooms? I ask.

—Bedrooms? Did he even tell me, or did I forget to ask? But he did say there's an apartment in the back we can rent. That guy Mars had your father and your grandmother hunting up and down all over San Antonio till they found a house for the right price. We couldn't even buy a garage for that amount of money here in Chicago. Not in a million years. You can bet we won't have to lock up the gate every night to keep lowlifes from stealing my roses. Think, Lala, a garden without rats! We can sit outside after dark, and we won't be scared, won't that be something?

Mother starts laughing and phones her sister Frances. —Pancha, guess what, you won't believe it, good news. We bought a house. Uh-huh. In Texas. That's right, San Antonio. No, there's no Ku Klux Klan there. What are you talking about? It's Mexican. Why do you think it's called *San Antonio* and not Saint Anthony? Go on. You're crazy. Go on, you've never even been there! Well, will you let me finish? If you won't let me talk, I swear I'm going to hang up.

Father and the Grandmother took off to San Antonio just to look around, because Mars lured them down. But nobody believed Father would actually buy something on this trip. We thought maybe someday, like when he got old, and we sure didn't think the Grandmother would be so generous.

It's like our family's been struck by lightning. It happens so fast we're dazed by the smell of charred wood, the spiral of gray smoke. Mother announces we're to pack and move this summer, to get there before school starts and all. That's the plan. —Only bring the essentials, Father orders. —Everything else we'll get in Texas.

—Texas? You're kidding, Toto groans. —What's in Texas?

—A house. Ours! You don't think we're going to keep throwing money at a landlord all our lives, do you? Mother says. —Your father's going to be home any day now. We've got to start packing.

Memo and Lolo start their whining. —Packing! Again? We just finished helping Abuela move last summer. Do we have to?

—Yes, we have to. Your father's orders, Mother says.

Or the Grandmother's, I think to myself. Same thing.

The older boys—Rafa, Ito, and Tikis—start a mutiny and argue they've got to stay in Chicago because they can't afford to lose their college loans and grants. There's no reason for them to move; in the past year they've been living away at dorms anyway. They can find a cheap apartment and live together during the summer.

—They're so close to finishing! It won't be long, Mother reminds Father once he's home.

Father says as long as they're in school, it doesn't matter if the older boys stay in Chicago. —So they won't have to work like me. And then he adds for the benefit of us younger kids, —Study and use your head, not your hands. He holds out his palms to scare the hell out of us. Hands as hard as shoe leather, layered and yellow like a Bible abandoned in a field.

I'm the only one who doesn't complain about this breakup of our family. I'd be changing schools anyway even if we stayed, since I start high school this fall. What I've never told anyone is this—I've wanted nothing more my whole life than to get out of here. To get out of the cold, and the stink, and the terror. You can't explain it to somebody who's never lived in a city. All they see is a pretty picture postcard. Buckingham Fountain at dusk. But take a good look. Those furry shapes scampering around the base aren't kittens.

Father promised me the next address I'd have a room of my own, because even he admits I'm *"una señorita"* now, and he's making good on that promise, I guess. There's never anywhere we've lived that's had enough bedrooms for all of us. Apartments aren't built to sleep nine people. I sleep on a twin bed in the middle room, which would be all right if you didn't have to cross through it to get to the other rooms. All this traffic, and never any privacy, and noise all the time, and having to dress and undress in the bathroom, the only room with a lock on the door except for the exit doors.

When I was a kid I slept in the living room on the orange Naugahyde La-Z-Boy, but I got too big to sleep there comfortably. Sometimes Father slept me and Memo and Lolo together. We've slept head to foot on bunk beds, on couches, on twin beds, on double beds, on cots, and on rollaways shoved in every room except the kitchen. We've slept just about everywhere except on the floor, which Father forbids. —Sleeping on the floor, like going barefoot, is low class, he says. Then he adds, —Do you want people to think we're poor?

I can remember every flat we've ever rented, especially the ones I want to forget. Their hallways and their hallway smell, dank and dusty or reeking of Pine-Sol. A heavy door blunted with kicks, carved initials, and the scars from changes of locks like appendectomies. Fingerprints on the glass. No yard, or if there is a yard, no grass. A darkness to the hallway, like a cave or an open mouth. Paint old and splintering off. A skinny lightbulb naked and giving off a sickly glow. A dirty cotton string hanging from the bulb. Dust in between the posts of the banister. High ceilings. Walls oiled with hands. Voices behind the apartment doors. People downstairs who talk too loud, or people upstairs who walk too much. Neighbors who are a pain. Manolo and Cirilo, and their bad-mouth mama. Floorboards thumping to Mexican country music early in the morning, even on the weekends when you're trying to sleep, for crying out loud.

A loose step squeaking like a mouse, or a mouse squeaking like a loose step. Holes shut over with nails and a piece of tin. A dark curve before you get up to the third flight. Delivery men scared to come up here. No one ever knocks on our door for Halloween. No need to put up spooky decorations. Our home already looks haunted just the way it is. Dust and darkness and dust, no matter how many Saturdays we clean it.

On our landing on the wall beside our door, somebody's kid drew in pencil a big chicken with a stupid-looking eye like a human's, a wall we painted over, but you can still see the lead outline of that chicken if you look close. Inside the apartment everything spackled, patched, and sanded clean. Walls painted colors as bright as the inside of a body. New linoleum to match, too, mopped every day by Ma or me.

Every apartment we've ever lived in with its cold room, a room in the back where all our wrinkled clothes sit in sacks waiting for the iron. In that cold room that nobody likes to go in, a ghost probably keeping watch over the cold sacks. Every time I go in there —Oh, blessed ghost of the wrinkled clothes, please leave me the hell alone.

Rats in the walls chirping like birds. Little rumble and scramble on the other side. Noises like gravel, like pebbles dropping. Loose plaster. I don't dare leave the bed at night. Even to pee. I'd rather wet the bed than face the dark.

Brothers snoring beside me. Mother and Father in their room far away, whispering. Elbows and warm knees. Keep off my side of the bed, or I'll clobber you. Sleep on my belly, turn the pillow over to the cool side, dust the dust off my feet. Sleep coming after me.

Old house, our house, ugly old shoe. We polish and wipe and paint and clean, fix what we can afford to fix, but it's no use. It still looks as dirty as ever.

The good news about our new house on El Dorado Street isn't good to everybody. Father and the Grandmother return to Chicago in a great mood, blind to the fact that everyone around them is pissed. Uncle Baby and Aunty Ninfa are hurt, and I don't blame them. After all, that's the thanks they get for taking care of the Grandmother all these months. Uncle Fat-Face and Aunty Licha are beyond hurt feelings. —And what are we? Painted? Don't we need help as much as Tarzán? That money came from the sale of the house on Destiny Street, which should've been split up between all of the family. Our father always said so. —What nonsense, says the Grandmother. —Inocencio has more need than the rest of you, he has "seven sons." And if you're going to quarrel about inheritances you should at least wait till I'm dead.

It's like a gas leak, the bad feelings. A slow hiss you know will end in something terrible.

But at our house, Father and Mother ignore the family feuds. At night, they whisper their plans.

—And there's the little apartment in the back, for my mother, of course.

—Your mother? I thought she was going to get her own house. You didn't tell me she was going to live with us.

—*Poco a poco*, not all at once. She needs to look for a house, and I'll need to borrow some money from her to put into the new shop. I'm starting from scratch. I have to buy sewing machines, a compressor, build tables. You don't expect me to take anything but my tools with my brothers acting like they do. After all, my mother gave us the money for the down payment of our house. *Gave* it to us. A *gift*, not a loan, Zoila. Just think, when she moves out, you'll be a landlady. A *landlady*, Zoila! Isn't that what you always wanted?

—Well . . . She's not staying forever, right?

—*Mi vida*, when have I lied to you?

I takes a long time to get rid of our things and pack up only the essentials. Some things we ship, and some things get left behind with the boys in Chicago, and some things just get lost or broken or both. Some of our furniture we sell, and lots is given away. And the rest we put in storage. —Don't worry, Father promises Mother. —I'll make you new furniture when we get there. But half the stuff we own is old anyway, and Mother's glad to get rid of it. The only thing she wants is her rosebushes, and these Toto dutifully digs up for her and packs into plastic buckets.

When finally we hitch up a trailer with the Grandmother's walnut-wood armoire swaddled in green moving quilts, we look like, as Father would put it, "Hungarians." Father keeps prodding us to let go of things. And when we don't, he gives our things away for us when we're not looking. —It's all right, I'll buy you a new one in Texas.

Our German shepherd, Wilson, almost gets left behind in Chicago with Rafa, Ito, and Tikis. Father tries to convince us he'll buy us another

one, because Wilson is already old and half lame, but there is no other
Wilson in the universe. I found Wilson in the alley years ago and put him
in our yard. He was already full-grown then, dirty and covered with cigarette burns on his muzzle; a dog with sad, watery eyes outlined in black
like Alice Cooper's. But now Wilson is ancient, though he hobbles about,
dragging himself around, still trying to protect us. Toto, Memo, Lolo,
and me decide to get organized. —If Wilson doesn't come with us to
Texas, we're not going. Mother won't hear of it, until I break into tears.
—Look at her, *pobrecita*, Father says. —Let the girl bring her dog, he's
no trouble. Finally, Wilson is allowed to come with us, and we load him
into the van with his special doggy bed made from an old couch cushion.

The trip south to San Antonio is slow, not like when we headed to
Mexico City, maybe because we're dragging the past with us. Father
doesn't let us dawdle or allow us nights at motels because of the trailer
and the risk of having everything ripped off. So the boys and Father drive
in shifts, with only breaks for coffee and food, the Grandmother snoring
heavily, waking up at every bump and asking, —*¿Ya llegamos?*

We get to San Antonio in the early afternoon, tired and cranky, ready
to get to the house on El Dorado Street, but Father insists on driving us to
his workspace first. —It's right here, right on the way, you'll see. Father
meanders west past the corner of Commerce and Rosillo Streets, where
Carol Burnett lived when she was little. We drive past streets named
Picoso, Hot and Spicy Street; Calavera, Skeleton Street; and Chuparrosa,
Hummingbird Street. It's odd to see the names in Spanish. Almost like
being on the other side, but not exactly.

Father takes us up and down and around as if he's lost, through back
streets with row houses with goats and roosters tied to a porch rail and
yards full of dogs sleeping under the shade of a tree, scratching themselves, or trotting across the street. Blackie, Snowball, Smokey, Lulu,
Pinky. Dogs that go nuts and chase our van like if they'd never seen
wheels before.

Finally Father pulls up along a chalky strip of storefronts that look
like they've been painted with nurse's shoe polish, a crumbly row of
white made whiter in the sun. It's a dusty shop on a dusty road, Nogalitos
Street, old Highway 90, which once led us south to Laredo before the new
interstate was built. We park in front on a diagonal like everyone else, the
curb a rubble of concrete and indestructible sunflowers that spring back
to life the moment after we drive over them. JEWELRY MINGO'S, WE HAVE

LAYAWAY. FINA'S WEDDING CAKES FOR ALL OCCASIONS. AZTEC UNISEX BEAUTY CHATEAU—CLASSY CUTS FOR ONLY ONE FORTY-NINE. AUTO TINT WHY SQUINT WINDSHIELD REPAIR. A notary public office advertising INCOME TAX, BOOKKEEPING, GRAPEFRUIT ONE DOLLAR A DOZEN, and SE DAN LIMPIAS/CASA/NEGOCIO. But there on the corner, at the choicest location, MARS TACOS TO WENT.

—Hey, we've been here before, Father, remember? We ate at the corner at Mars' place.

Wedged between the bakery and beauty salon, Father's shop. REYES UPHOLSTERY in red and yellow block letters with a crown on the "R." A stink of pink permanent wave solution and sugary bread. —After a while, you don't even notice it, Father says.

A short ride south on Nogalitos and then a jig jog, and we're on El Dorado Street. On a block of squat dull houses, a modern two-story brick stands out like a jewel among the junk. Clean, blond bricks and an immaculate driveway surrounded by a high iron fence painted black and gold, scary as a Doberman.

—Is that it?

—No, Father says. —It's further down. Then he adds, —*Drogas.* Meaning—you can bet the people who live there are probably dealing drugs.

—Is this it? I ask pointing to a purple Victorian with a green swing on the porch.

—Oh, no, the Grandmother says. —It's much bigger than that.

—Is that one it?

—Ha, ha, ha. Father and the Grandmother look at each other smugly and wink.

Finally Father says, —Here we are, and drives into a driveway littered with pecans that crunch under our tires.

—*This* is *it?*

I look at the house. It reminds me of a riddle from the first grade. Question: What time is it when an elephant sits on your roof? Answer: Time to get a new roof.

Rascuache. That's the only word for it. Homemade half-ass. Our house is one of those haphazard, ramshackle, self-invented types, as if each room was added on as the family who built it got bigger, when they could afford it, layer upon layer of self-improvement, somebody trying their very best, even if that best isn't very much. Some of it in wood, some in funky siding, and some parts of it in brick. A house like the excavations of Mexico City. A downstairs porch and an upstairs porch with mismatched rusted metal railings, bent metal aluminum awnings, iron window guards, last year's Christmas decorations—a wire Santa and reindeer—potted plants with shard tile or shards of mirror on the pots, *nicho* to la Virgen de San Juan, tire planters, a dull Sears chain-link fence, crooked TV antenna, a rotted wicker porch swing, a garden full of overgrown banana trees and burnt, red and yellow cannas, vines growing up over everything, taking over, choking everything, in fact. Pecan tree seedlings sprouting from the cracks in the buckled sidewalk and in the abandoned weedy pots. Pecans crunching underfoot. Little green lizards that puff their chests pink and then vanish. Iron daisies made out of plumbing pipes and the blades of a broken fan. A wooden wishing well where giant cockroaches the color of varnished wood scatter when you touch it.

Our house looks like something out of Acapulco, like Catita's house, in fact. Washed-up, rotten, rusted, falling apart. Shipwrecked. That's what we are. A huge galleon made up of this and that stranded on land.

All summer we'd been hearing about our wonderful house from Father and the Grandmother, forgetting what exaggeraters they are. With something like the optimism of realtors, Father and the Grandmother see what the house can become, but I see what's there in front of me.

All around us are houses as bad off or worse than ours. Houses like bad words meant to shock or scare you. Like *chanclas*, shoes without backs, squashed and scuffed and sad-looking.

I start to cry.

—Don't cry, Lalita, please! Father says. He cups my face in his hands and makes me blow my nose with the tail of his T-shirt. —It's that you're homesick, right? But just think, pretty soon you won't think of any other home but this.

This makes me cry even harder. I cry *con mucho sentimiento*—with feeling, as they say, like a professional. I cry carrying boxes inside the house, and I cry carrying trash out.

—Cripes, Mother says, —You were a *llorona* when you were a baby, and you're still a *llorona* now. Quit it! What this place needs is some Pine-Sol.

*My life. That's what Father calls Mother when he's not mad. —My life, where did you hide my clean calzones?

Mijo, my son. What Mother calls him when she isn't angry. —They're in the walnut-wood armoire, mijo.

Mijo, even though she's not his mother. Sometimes Father calls her mija, my daughter. —Mija, he shouts. Both Mother and I running and answering, —What?

To make things even more confusing everyone says ma-má, or ¡mamacita! when some delightful she walks by. ¡Ma-maaaaaaa! like a Tarzan yell. ¡Mamacita! like a hiccup.

If the delight is a he, —¡Ay, qué papacito! Or, —¡papasote! for the ones truly delicious to the eye.

A terrible incestuous confusion.

Worse, the insults aimed at the mother, —Tu mamá. While something charming and wonderful is —¡Qué padre!

What does this say about the Mexican?

I asked you first.

Very Nice and Kind, Just Like You

 —And then what happened?

 —And then her husband ran off with that floozy across the street and was never heard from again. And she said, "Alone at last, thank God!" *Tan tán*.

Floozy is one of Mother's words, from her time not mine, but I use it anyway to make her laugh, and it works. Mother's in a good mood. We're helping Father put some order to his shop. Mother's mopping, and I'm sweeping. Every once in a while, out of nowhere, Mother will ask, —And then what happened? Even though I haven't been telling a story. It's kind of a game between us. I have to come up with something out of the blue, the more outrageous the better. It helps pass the time.

Father was putting up a series of shelves for his fabric sample books, but now he's talking to a walk-in customer. Some of the people who come in are downright rude. Not the Mexicans. They know to be polite. I mean *los güeros*. Instead of calling Father "Mister Reyes," they call Father "Inocencio." What lack of respect! *Qué bárbaros*. *Pobrecitos*. Father says we have to forgive the ignorant, because they know not what they do. But if we know enough about their culture to know what's right, how come they can't bother to learn about ours?

 —Hey, that's right. Where you from, *amigo*?

 —Mexico. And you, my friend?

 —Oh, well, little bit of everywhere, I guess. Here. There. I was an army brat. My father was with the U.S. Army.

 —I was in the U.S. Army! This during the Second World War, my friend.

—You're kidding! I didn't know Mexicans fought with the Allies.

—Both in Mexico and here.

—My dad fought in that war. Saw enough action to get promoted to a post at Camp Blanding.

—Camp Blanding? I cannot believe! For basic training at Camp Blanding I did too.

—Well, don't that beat all! Maybe you knew my dad.

—Please, your name.

—Cummings. Dad was Major General Frank Cummings.

—Oh, my Got! I remember! Everybody loved General Cummings. He was a gentleman.

—That's no lie! He sure was a swell guy, my dad.

—More. He was very nice and very kind. Just like you, my friend. Always, he say, my son, my son. So proud he was.

—Was he now? Aw, that sure is a heck of a nice thing to hear, especially since he never told me to my face when he was alive. But Dad was like that. I kind of always knew, you know. It sure is nice to hear it, though.

Father and the big Texan talk and talk and talk for what seems forever. Oh, you're kidding. No, I swear. Well, I'll be! Like that. When he finally folds himself into his blue Mustang and drives away, the Texan *toot-toots* the horn and we all wave, except for Father, who salutes. That's when Mother lets Father have it.

—What a liar you are! Mother says. —You didn't go to Camp Blanding! You went to Fort Ord. Can't you even tell a story straight? I can't stand liars.

—It's not lying, Father says. —It's being polite. I only say what people like to hear. It makes them happy.

—*Qué lambiache*, Mother hisses, using the word that means "lick." —That's what I can't stand about Mexicans, she continues. —Always full of bullshit!

—Not *sheet*, Father corrects her. —Politeness. I am a gentleman. He tips a box of black tacks and pours them onto his palm, then pops a few into his mouth as if they were raisins.

—Well, *güeros* don't see it as polite, if you want the truth, Mother says.

Father just keeps kissing the magnetic tip of the hammer and hammering the wing chair he's working on.

—Do you hear me? Mother says. —*Te hablo,* I'm talking to you, Inocencio . . .

I click on my transistor radio and find a station playing oldies. The Supremes' "Stop in the Name of Love." Turn the volume up so loud, I can't hear a word of Father's story and Mother's history.

A Godless Woman, My Mother

In our house votive candles never flicker from bedroom bureaus night and day. No chubby statue of the baby Jesus dressed as the Santo Niño de Atocha, plumed Three Musketeers hat, sandals ragged from running about nights answering prayers, has ever paid us a call. No one burns *copal* incense for the souls condemned to purgatory or for the souls condemned to life. No dusty rosary swags across the wall above our beds. No Palm Sunday cross collects grease above the kitchen door. No guardian angel picture protects us while we dream. No silver *milagros* or braids of hair are promised to a favorite saint. Nobody murmurs a novena, and no dinner demands we say grace. We don't have "the fear" swept from us with the broom. Nobody cures us of the evil eye with an egg. We don't cross ourselves twice and kiss our thumb when passing a church, nor have we ever asked for the blessing from our parents when we say good-bye. Sunday mornings don't call us to church. Altars do not command our genuflections. We're allowed to believe or not believe whatever the nuns and priests teach us at school, and though they tell some pretty stories, what sticks is the stick God stinging across the palms of our hands, and, every month when we pay our tuition late, the horrible God of shame. The happiness God of the dandelions isn't taught in Catholic school.

Except for a framed portrait of la Virgen de Guadalupe, God doesn't visit our house. But the Awful Grandmother does. And brought with her once, along with several pieces of large vinyl luggage, la Guadalupe. This Guadalupe, purchased from a Villita vendor in front of the very hill where the Indian madonna made her miraculous apparition, blessed by the *basílica* priest, wrapped in a fresh copy of *ESTO* sports newspaper, tied taut and double-knotted with hairy twine, stuffed alongside a bottle of *rompope* rum eggnog, bags of Glorias—Father's favorite *chuchulucos*, and a year's worth of *La familia Burrón* comic books in an *ixtle* shopping bag—*By hand, by hand*, just so you know!—ascended into the heavens via Aeroméxico, descended, and was delivered to our crowded Chicago flat several years ago, and, at the Grandmother's request, hung above Father and Mother's bed. Do this in memory of me.

—Like hell, Mother muttered under her breath, but Father insisted. Father is a true devotee of mothers, both mortal and divine. Though it could be argued that Mother is a mother too, no one but Mother would argue her seniority over the other two.

Mother grew up with nothing but suspicion for anyone who represented the Church, even if they weren't Catholic.

—Don't open the door, it's the alleluia people.

So why would Mother send us to Catholic school? Not for any love of Church, believe me, but because the public schools, in her own words, are a piece of crap.

—The whole system is designed to make you fail, Mother says. — Just look at the numbers dropping out. But until it's the *güero* kids who are failing in as many numbers as us, nobody gives a damn. Listen to me, Lala. Better to be beaten by priests and nuns than to get a beating from life.

My brothers think Mother is God. They don't complain at all about the plans to send them to Resurrection High School downtown. Father says I'm to enroll at their sister school, Immaculate Conception. But if I'm to have any social life, I've got to get Mother to send me to the public school on the other side of the freeway.

This is what I'm thinking as we clean the house on El Dorado Street. The man who owned it left so much stuff for us to cart away, it's all we can do to shove aside a space to put one foot down. Some of the junk is good, a few air conditioners and window fans we're already using, because we've gotten here at the end of *la canícula*, August, the dog days, and it's, like they say here, hotter 'n hell.

On the kitchen door we've kept a 1965 Mexican calendar, a picture called *El rapto*. A white horse, a handsome *charro*, and in his rapturous arms, a swooning beauty, her silk *rebozo* and blouse sliding off one sexy shoulder. The horse raising one hoof in the air, proud as any bronze statue. *El rapto.** I wonder if that means "The Rape." And I wonder if "rapture" and "rape" come from the same word.

In the living room we've inherited a dual portrait of LBJ/Kennedy, which Mother wanted to toss out, but Father asked if we could keep it there. Father's fond of almost any president.

—Because he never picks up a newspaper, Mother says.

The sound of Mother's hammer banging as if she means to tear the house down. Mother can't rest until every hole in the house is sealed tight with the lids of tuna and coffee cans—her war against mice and Texas-size bugs. In some rooms the floorboards don't even meet the walls because of the house shifting, but that doesn't stop Mother.

—Why can't we just call an exterminator?

—Because we've got to cut corners, that's why.

It's always about cutting corners. Always about something shimmering on the wall when you turn on the lights. Or something creepy scurrying off along the floorboards. It's always, always about being afraid to get up in the middle of the night. And being scared to eat from a half-open box of corn flakes. Tell me about cutting corners.

—How's about we make a sacrifice, Ma, and you don't send us to Catholic school this year. Think of the money we'd save there.

—I already told you. No, no, and no. You give me enough trouble as it is. Besides, your brothers are going to get part-time jobs to help out. We need to make sure they get a good education for college. You don't want them to wind up in Vietnam, do you?

—But I wouldn't have to take a bus to go to the public school, because I could walk. And nobody's going to draft me to Vietnam.

—Look, we can scrimp on lots of things, but not on your education. What if you get married and something happens?

—Like what?

—Something. You never know. You might need to be able to take care of yourself, that's all. Just in case.

—In case what?

—Never mind, *metiche.* Run to the hardware store and buy me some steel wool. And a putty knife. And don't take all day coming back either.

Mars told us the guy who lived here was a junk dealer who was too old or too lazy to lift anything but a beer. He was a pack rat who dabbled in this and that, which is why none of the windows match, and why every

door in the house looks like it came from somewhere else. But the fact
that the house has three bathrooms was a major selling point for Father.
One upstairs in a big dormlike room with a pitched roof for the boys.
One downstairs, and a small one for the bedroom off the kitchen. This is
supposed to be my room, but the Grandmother nabbed it almost as soon
as she stepped in the house, because her own apartment in back isn't
ready yet. Right now it's as dusty as a barn and full of giant cockroaches,
too dirty to even put Wilson in there.

—And where am *I* to sleep? the Grandmother asked the moment we
got here, in a voice as regal as the empress Carlota's.

Maybe because it's the room farthest away from Mother and Father's
room, or maybe because it's the only room with its own private bathroom, Mother gives her my room. Without even asking me!

Instead of thank you, the Grandmother says flatly, —Oh, just like
when I lived at Regina's and had my little room next to the kitchen. She
means it to hurt Mother, that's for sure, because the room next to the
kitchen in Mexico is always the one for "the girl," only Mother doesn't
get it, or doesn't hear her.

—And me? I ask. —Now what? Do I sleep in the van?

—I'll fix you a bed in the front room. Just for tonight, Mother says.
—And no complaints. You're not the only one making sacrifices around
here.

Nothing's the way Father said. He doesn't own a shop. He rents.
From Mars, because he needs money for supplies for his shop, and later,
poco a poco, he intends to buy a shop of his own. And later, little by little,
when the Grandmother gets her own place fixed up, I'll have my room
back, the one off the kitchen where a previous tenant glued Raquel
Welch's[†] poster for *One Million Years B.C.* on the wall. It was put up with
shellac and who knows what; we can't get it down till the room's painted.
Till then, la Virgen de Guadalupe and Raquel both share a space above
the Grandmother's bed.

I sleep in the living room. Mornings there's the annoying rubber
screech of black birds called grackles. Now and then a pecan drops and
pings against the house like somebody throwing stones at us. By ten, the
sun's so solid and strong it drives awake the dead. Then there's the noise
of the Grandmother slamming cupboards in the kitchen, sneezing like a
bugle, shuffling about in her *chanclas*.

We've opened all the windows and aired the house, but it still smells like it's been closed up since forever, the smell of mold and dampness, like something creepy is growing in here. There's also a dry smell of chalk and plaster and dust from the stuff you have to climb over. Tools? Newspapers? Boots? Things that trip you up as you're climbing the stairs or walking across a room. A sad, hopeless feeling to the house, like a mouth with missing teeth. Old magazines and rubber girdles and tool bits stored in crates or slouched boxes. Wallpaper sticky and dusty. And the smell of insecticide, like someone set off a roach bomb—and that smell catching in your throat and in your eyes and making you cough up phlegm all the time.

Outside, Texas clouds—wide, loose, and light, like pajamas, but a sun so bright and hot it hurts to stand outside and look at anything. Kids in the street screaming each other's names—Victor, Rudy, Alba, Rolando, Vincent. And far off, a radio turned to Tejano music with its zippy accordion and its pessimistic bass.

I'm like that bass. Big. The only sounds coming out of me sad and deep. Mother's right, I'm never happy unless I'm sad. When night falls, I wander about like Wilson making circles, trying to find a comfortable spot to rest. After the ten o'clock news, I bring down my bed from the closet—the sheets and pillow—and kill time in the dining room by pushing two chairs together and reading until everyone's cleared out and gone off to sleep, and I can claim the couch.

Some nights, like today, the funkadelics arrive.

To tell the truth, nobody knows what I want, and I hardly know myself. A bathroom where I can soak in the tub and not have to come out when somebody's banging on the door. A lock on my door. A door. A room. A bed. And sleeping until I feel like it without somebody yelling, —Get up or do I have to make you get up. Quiet. No radio jabbering from on top of the kitchen counter, no TV thundering in the living room. Somebody to tell my troubles to. Something good and soothing to the eye. To be in love.

All this is well and nice if one day I can have them, but depress me when I think maybe I'll end up like Hans Christian Andersen, old and dying in a bed he didn't even own. What good did all that fame do him if he didn't even have his own room?

You know the Fifth Dimension? The music group, I mean. "Up,

Up, and Away" and "Aquarius." The funkadelics are like that. A harmony of voices, high and low, except instead of making you feel good, you feel sad—in five gradations. Loneliness, fear, grief, numbness, and despair.

You can't row past the funkadelics. At least I can't. I sort of drown myself in it, fall asleep, my body sodden and soggy. And when I wake, if I'm lucky, it's a relief to find the funkadelics have worn off like a fever that finally breaks.

My cousin Paz taught me how to crochet one summer, and it's a good thing too. It comes in handy when the funkadelics arrive. I buy a ball of cotton string and a double-zero needle at the Woolworth's and crochet a dirty knot of lace because my hands always sweat, and I can't keep the string clean. There's a poem by García Lorca we had to memorize once in school. It has a line that goes "Who will buy from me this sadness of white string to make handkerchiefs?" Something like that. It sounds kind of goofy in English. *¿Quién me compraría a mí, este cintillo que tengo y esta tristeza de hilo blanco, para hacer pañuelos?* This sadness of white string. That's how I feel when I get the funkadelics. An endless white string full of tiny knots.

—The trouble with you is you're too somber, a nun at school would tell me. Somber. I wonder if the word comes from the same place as *sombrero.*

Don't forget to put on your "sadness." I won't. That "sadness" suits you, was made for you, in fact!

Sadness suits me. I savor it the way some people savor good food. Sleep or sadness, it's all the same to me. Come get me. Like an ocean hungry to lap you up.

—Thanks to God we're here, and we got here safely, Father says, waking me up from my daydreaming. Then Father makes his same joke.
—*¿Qué tienes, mi vida? Sueño o* sleepy.

—*Es que tengo* sleepy. I have sleepy, Father.

I don't tell Father the truth. This house gives me the creeps, like it's haunted or something. But how can I tell him that when he's so happy?

—Go to *mimi. Noches,* Father says. —*Que duermas con los angelitos panzones.* Sleep with the fat little angels.

The fat little angels, like the ones la Virgen is always stepping on.

Like the ones shoving a saint up to heaven, carrying Mary's blue drapery, or rolling about in the clouds in holy ecstasy.

The fat little angels. I sigh and pull the sheet over my head like I did when I was little and scared of lizards. Thanks to God somebody believes in something.

---

*El rapto *is also a film directed by el Indio Fernández, starring María Félix and Jorge Negrete, 1954. It is a Mexican version of* The Taming of the Shrew.

†*According to the* Star, *Raquel Welch's real name is Raquel Tejada, and she's Latina. We would've cheered if we'd known this back then, except no one knew it except Raquel Tejada. Maybe not even Raquel Welch.*

God Gives Almonds

Who opens the door is a crooked branch, speckled, chalky, brittle as birch. I never bother to think what I look like till somebody looks at me like she does. I should've worn my good shoes.

Father begins, —Madam, I beg you, the priest, he is home?

—Father Ginter isn't seeing anyone just now. He's eating . . . You can come in and wait, though.

—Most kind.

Each time we move to a new neighborhood, Father and I have to call on the priest. Just once and never again. The sitting room of every rectory we've ever waited in just like this one. Clean. Floor tiles a beige-and-brown checkerboard, always waxed, always glossy, without a scuff mark anywhere. Walls as spotless as a museum. The whole house smelling like chalk and the holy clouds from boiled potatoes.

—Remember, Lala. Don't say anything when *el padrecito* appears, Father whispers. —Not a word, understand? I'll do the talking.

To get a tuition break at Resurrection and Immaculate Conception, we've come to tell the priest a story.

—We'll just tell the priest we're a family of good Catholics, Father says.

—But that's a lie.

—Of course it's not, Father says. —It's a healthy lie. Besides, you want to go to the Catholic high school, no?

—But I want to go to public school.

—*Mija*, please, Father says, because we've been over this a hundred times. —Your mother, he adds and sighs.

While we wait for *el padrecito,* Father gets up and inspects the couch cushions.

—Dirt! he mutters. —Like with their feet!

I wish Father hadn't insisted on coming straight from the shop. He's as nubby as a towel. Even his mustache has lint. When he sits back down, I pick the bits of string and tufts of cotton off of him. Father mumbling to himself, making mental calculations. I know what he's thinking. How long it will take to strip these chairs, redo the varnished legs, tie taut the cotton webbing, retie the coils, redo the whole room in a nice bright fabric, not these ugly scratchy browns that Catholic rectories are fond of. But before Father can come up with an estimate, Father Ginter is here, a man with a big bulldog of a face, like a gangster, though his voice is surprisingly high and kind.

—I have seven sons, Father says.

The story begins as it always does, but I never know how it will end.

—Seven sons! My, you must be proud.

Father means children, not simply boys, but I don't think Father Ginter understands.

—I am a good Catholic.

Not true. Father never goes to church,

—My sons . . . here Father pauses for effect, —all, all go to church. Every Sunday. That is how it is in my country.

Father always lets us sleep in on Sunday mornings except the Sundays we go to the flea market. Then we *have* to get up early.

Father Ginter listens, nodding and murmuring praises to Father for being such a devout man.

—Seven sons! Don't you worry, Mr. Reyes. We'll see what we can do.

—Please, it is the Church's duty to help us, no? We are very Catholic in my country, understand? You know la Virgen de Guadalupe Church? There I was baptized. My daughter, look at her, always she is talking of following the road of the nuns.

—Is that right?

—Yes-yes, yes-yes, yes-yes, yes. Everything nice and clean, she likes. Like nuns.

—God finds a way of providing for all, doesn't he? The Lord won't allow your children to go without a Catholic education.

—If God wills it, my children, they will have a better life than their poor papa.

Here Father hangs his head down gently to one side like la Virgen de Guadalupe.

—Have faith, Mister Reyes. We'll see what we can do. How old did you say you were, little lady?

—Fourteen, I say.

—You don't say. I would have guessed older. Just goes to show. Don't you worry. We'll find something for you, missy.

At home, all through dinner, Father brags, —You see, you just have to haggle.

A few days later Father Ginter has found jobs for the boys working after school at a garden nursery. A month goes by, and then halfway into October, Father Ginter sends a note asking me to stop by. What a surprise when he says, —Young lady, how would you like a job as the house-keeper's assistant?

My heart freezes. I'm no good at anything that has to do with house-work. At least that's what Mother says. But this isn't a story you can tell a priest, and I only nod my head and smile.

I have to report to a Tracy, a high school grad who's supposed to train me before she goes away for college. She looks like a Tracy, like the perky, freckle-faced girls on the pages of *Seventeen,* everything, hair, nose, smile, all in a cute little flip. Tracy hands me one of her old uniforms, a fit-ted seersucker dress, the kind beauticians or women in bakeries wear. I don't know how I'm supposed to fit into this doll's dress.

—Maybe my mother can let it out, I say.

Tracy walks me through the house, introducing me to the other priests who live here. This is Father So-and-so, and this is Father This-and-That, who reach out and shake my hand hard and call me by my first name like if I was a man. How rude, like barbarians, but they don't know any better.

In the laundry room, Tracy shows me my duties. —You just have to check and see if there's anything to wash. Separate the colors, and set the machine like so. Then here's the iron. I know this is going to make you laugh, but Father G. likes his boxers starched.

It doesn't make me laugh. I keep worrying if I'll burn anything like I do at home.

—Then you do this, then that . . . On and on she goes, naming things I have to do that I've never done before or never done well.

Finally she leads me to the kitchen and introduces me to the woman who answered the door the day Father and I first called, Mrs. Sikorski, thin and gnarled and knotted as a tree in winter snow. Mrs. Sikorski's kitchen is super clean compared to Mother's. Everything is neat and in order, even when she's cooking. Nothing boiling over and spilling. No matches to light the range, it's electric and quiet. No dried egg yolk on the side of the stove. No smell of fried tortillas. No spattered grease. Everything as spotless as the model kitchens in the appliance section of the Sears. Mrs. Sikorski puts everything away after she uses it. Every salt shaker, every can opener, every glass washed and wiped dry, as soon as possible.

I feel like the girl in the Rumpelstiltskin fairy tale whose father bragged she could spin straw into gold. And now here I am locked in the king's house being asked to spin, and I don't know how, and I feel like crying, but if I cry, it will only make things worse and not better. Like peeing, you can't just cry a little and have no one notice.

When finally I'm allowed to leave and open the front door, the night wind feels good on my face. I sprint down the steps two at a time. The sky already darkening even though it's only seven-thirty. Dark the way dark comes down early in the fall.

I take a bus downtown and have to transfer to another bus. It's night by the time I get to our neighborhood. I run quickly down the street and not on the sidewalk when I turn onto our block. The huddled houses and the dark scare me. Run down the center of the street, not near the parked cars, like I do in Chicago, so there's time to escape in case I have to.

I meant to tell Father Ginter how I never walk home in the dark without a brother. How I'm not allowed to. How I'm used to having someone come for me. How it isn't done, but I didn't know how to tell him this, so I just run. The fear still in my throat and in my chest when I get home. The fear from all afternoon. The glass on the front windows filled with the tears of food cooking. *Albóndigas* and flour *tortillas* when I step in the door, and that smell, it makes me feel like crying. Except I don't cry, I don't say anything but shrug when my mother asks, —Well?

—I'm not going back there.

—Why not?

—Because I'm not.

—Did somebody do something to you?

I shake my head no.

—Well, you don't have to if you don't want to, you know.

—But what about my tuition?

—Well, we'll just have to find a way, that's all.

But what will I tell Father Ginter?

—Pops will think of something when he gets home.

He does.

—Don't worry, Lalita. We'll tell *el padrecito* that I don't permit you to return. It's too dark outside when you come home. How does he expect a young lady to be walking alone after dark? Doesn't he realize we are Mexican? You tell him I refuse to allow you that maid's job. You don't ever have to go back there.

But I do have to go back there, because it's me who has to explain to Father Ginter, to Mrs. Sikorski why I can't work in the rectory as the kitchen assistant. How my mother says I'm no good for anything in the kitchen unless it's burning rice. How I can't even iron my own clothes without scorching them. How I need strict supervision anytime I sew anything. Did I tell you I once sewed my shirt to my pants leg when I was trying to sew a button? I'm not meant for the kitchen even though I'm an only daughter.

When I do the household chores at home it's things I can do—clean the bathrooms, make beds, wash dishes, scrub pots and pans, mop the floors with pine disinfectant, clean out the refrigerator and pantry. But I don't know how to set a table for *güeros*. I don't know how to iron *güero* boxer shorts. My father and brothers wear briefs. I don't know how to cook *güero* food, or how to work in a kitchen where you put everything away the second after you use it. I try to remember all of this when I make my way to the rectory after school the next day, feeling sick, feeling terrible about telling a lie to a priest, even if it *is* a healthy lie.

It's Mrs. Sikorski who answers the door, who listens to me telling her over the threshold why I can't come back. —Because my father won't let me it's too dark when I come home he says he doesn't want me coming home after dark because he won't allow it because I'm a Mexican daughter yes that's how it is. Sorry. Thank you very much. I am. Sorry. Heartily.

Mrs. Sikorski says she understands. I don't know how it is she understands when even I don't understand. When the door closes with a sigh that smells like the house of *güeros,* the smell of potatoes, I realize I won't have to ring the doorbell with the PEACE-BE-WITH-YOU shaped like a fish again, and I skip down the stone steps, running, almost flying.

In my ears, that saying I've heard Father say so many times I don't hear it. God gives almonds to those without teeth.

64

Sister Oh

—Should one be a virgin when one marries?
            Who's asking is a Sister Odilia. Eyes like a mag-
num. Steely blue. Shark bullet blue. Serious, let's-get-down-to-business,
obsessed-with-sex Oh-dilia. Odilia. Oh. Say oh. Thumb and point finger
curled into a circle, her mouth inside that roundness and . . . —Say Oh.
Oh-DEE-lee-ah. That's right.

The school year begins with mass assembled in the gym so that the
entire student body can join in. The Goody Two-shoes strumming on
their hootenanny guitars. It's "Bridge Over Troubled Water," or songs
from *Godspell*, or *Jesus Christ Superstar*, or if we're lucky, that song
"Suzanne." When they get to the nasty part, well, all of us up in the
bleachers just about piss in our pants.

After mass they break us into "rap groups" made up with students
from every level. No guys from next door invited. Pretty boring if you
ask me, until Sister Oh revs up with her sex survey questionnaire.

—Should one be a virgin when one marries? What about one's partner? Do you expect your husband to be a virgin on your wedding night?

Viva Ozuna rolls her eyes and hisses, —Same stupid-ass questions.
Only thing that changes is your mind depending when they ask. Fresh-
men: "Definitely a virgin. No way would my husband want me if I
wasn't. And I don't want him to have fooled around either. Yuck. Who
wants somebody's leftovers!!!" Sophomore: "I think I should be a virgin
I think. But maybe he doesn't have to be. I mean somebody has to
know what they're doing." Junior: "I'm not sure." Senior: "Who the
fuck cares?"

Bozena Drzemala raises a hand. —On my wedding night I'll just let nature take its course.

—Everyone knows she's never been a virgin in her entire life! Viva adds for the information of anyone seated around us, followed by a lot of snickering.

Xiomara Tafoya, a collar of fat hickeys around her neck, "I call them love bites," pretty eyes and fuzzy mustache: —It's not something a lady discusses.

Wilneesa Watkins, two years younger than us because she was double promoted: —Y'all make me sick.

Almost an hour of interrogation. Sister Odilia is worse than the FBI. If she calls on me I haven't a clue what I'll say. Pretend like I'm a *puta* or pretend I'm la Virgen de Guadalupe. Which is worse? Either way, everybody's sure to laugh.

I decide to say I haven't decided, which isn't a lie.

—It's important you not go too far in teasing a young man, Sister Oh is saying. —For a man to stop when he's already . . . impassioned . . . is very difficult. It's different for women. That's why it's up to you as young women to make sure you don't venture too far. It's enormously difficult for a man to stop once he's started. It takes an awful, awful, awful lot of control. Why, it's even painful for him.

And here she winces as if she's caught a finger in a car door.

I'm a virgin. I'm fourteen years old. I've never kissed a boy, and nobody's kissed me. But one thing I know for sure—Sister Odilia doesn't know shit.

65

Body Like a Raisinette

—Hey, Wilneesa. You look great! You look like you finally had an orgasm!

No other student at Immaculate Conception dares to talk like this but Viva Ozuna, a shorty in wobbly platform shoes. She's the only senior in our freshman algebra class because she has to make up the course she failed in her first year. —Because that fucking nun hated my fucking guts, she says. Now there's a new algebra teacher, Mr. Zoran Darko, one of the first lay teachers hired at Immaculate Conception and a fool for Viva's flirting. She calls him Zorro, and he lets her! Mr. Darko is nothing but a stocky boxer in need of a shave. A real loser. Viva flirts just for the hell of flirting, I guess.

During class, Viva passes me notes with all the words written in small letters like e. e. cummings and with little "o"s dotting the "i"s. *do you mind sharing the answers with me? i'll owe you a favor big time. please.*

She has the walleyed *chichis* of a chihuahua, struts shamelessly about the locker room half naked, like a white girl. —Cause I'm half white, Viva says laughing. —The top half, can't you tell?

When classes let out, Viva knots her uniform blouse at the midriff and rolls her skirt up even higher, her ass cleaved in two like a plum. She's swaybacked, so her butt sticks out even more, a pouty, child's body like a pinto bean or a raisinette.

—I saw Janis Joplin in concert last year at the HemisFair, Viva says, flicking her hair off her shoulders. —Got two free tickets from Radio KONO. I'm going to be a songwriter. Got notebooks and notebooks of songs. Soon as I turn eighteen, I'm out of here. Moving to San Francisco.

—Why don't you just move to Austin? I say. —It's cheaper.

—Shit, you can't get famous in Texas. Not until you leave. Don't you know nothing?

Viva has the kind of thin hair that lies flat on her scalp, like if she just climbed out of a swimming pool. Still, she's real pretty, except she tweezes her eyebrows into mean arches like the movie stars in the black-and-white movies. I know; I watch her do her makeup all the time. In algebra, in study hall, the bathroom, at the cafeteria table, wherever. It's a ritual for her. Layers and layers of mascara till her eyelashes are furry. Gobs of lip gloss. Sparkle blush. Eye shadow. Foundation and powder. The works. Even in the daytime. She wants to be a makeup artist, she says. —I thought you said you were going to be a songwriter? —I could be both, why not? She thinks she's going to do a makeover on me, but she's not touching my face, that's for sure! No way!

I meet Viva at our after-school job, straightening up the rows of desks in the study hall. This is the job I land after the housekeeper's gig doesn't work out. A bunch of girls work at our school, some in the cafeteria, some after school like me. Thank God nobody sees me skulking in here after class. No one knows I'm one of the poor girls except for the other poor girls, like Viva.

The first time I see her, Viva Ozuna is holding court seated halfway out the study hall window, smoking a cherry-flavored cigar, blowing the smoke outside, all the while chatting up a storm about her favorite subject. Sex.

—He's this wide, Viva says making a fist. —Mexi-size, and he ain't even Mexican.

—But I thought it was length that was important, I say.

—You stupid virgin! Somebody just made that up so as not to hurt her boyfriend's feelings. Listen, you can't feel nothing unless a man's thing is as wide as a baby's head. Push or pull, it's the width that's gonna make you howl. Width, honey, remember.

I wonder about her name, and one day when I get to know her better, ask her.

—How come your parents named you Viva? Did they want you to live long, or because of a paper towel, or what?

—Stupid! My name is Viviana. And they named that friggin' paper towel after me! Honest to God, you don't know shit.

It's true. I don't know a thing. I mean, compared to Viva. At least until we talk about Mexico.

—I wouldn't know, I've never been there, Viva says.

—No way! You've *never* been to Mexico?

—Only to Nuevo Laredo. My family's from here. Since before.

—Since before what?

—Since before this was Texas. We're been here seven generations.

I can't even imagine staying in one place for seven years.

I like Viva. She spits cuss words out like they're watermelon seeds and knows where the best thrift stores are. We buy old painted Mexican skirts. The cotton ones and the velvet sequin ones with scenes of Taxco or Aztec gods. The longer ones are mine, because my legs are too thick. The little girl skirts Viva claims, the shorter the better she says. If we're lucky we hit Thrift Town on the south side and hunt around for vintage cowboy boots. I found a pair of black Noconas, the pointy ones with the slant heels, for only six dollars! And Viva has a pair of Acmes and a real cute shorty Dale Evans pair. We make Father sew us halter tops out of bandanas and vintage tablecloths—sexy! At least we think so. Father complains we look like ranch people, but what does he know about fashion?

To pay me back for helping her pass the last algebra exam, Viva invites me to her house for dinner. Everything in her house looks like it's been around forever, including her parents. The smell of things soft and worn and faded. Every chipped bowl, nicked tabletop, bent fork, scuffed rug, nubby bedspread, saggy couch, dusty window fan, polka-dotted kitchen curtain remembers, and in remembering has a place here, in this house, home. The smell is everywhere, hallway, closets, towels, doilies, even Viva. Like the smell of boiled hot dogs.

At first I find myself breathing out of my mouth when I'm there, but now I'm so used to it I don't even smell it anymore unless I've been away for a while. People's houses are like that. Nobody who's a member of the family can smell it, name it, or recognize it, unless they've been gone a long, long time. Then when they come back, a whiff of it just about makes them cry.

After all the apartments and kitchens we've inherited, I've become an expert at detecting the smell of previous tenants. Usually I associate a family with a single food item they left behind. A gallon of apple vinegar. A bottle of mouthwash-green ice cream topping. A giant restaurant-size can of sauerkraut. Because we don't know what to do with these things, they stay in our pantry for years until somebody's brave enough to toss them out.

Viva's mom had a stroke a few years ago. She's all there, she just can't walk around real good. Sometimes she gets stuck on one thought, like a record with a scratch in it, and says the same thing over and over. That's why her dad cooks and everything. The mother just sits on the same kitchen chair and touches things with the one arm that still works. And she talks funny, like if her tongue is too fat for her mouth. But she's real nice to me. Says hi and tries to get up and looks at me kindly with those sad, watery eyes of hers.

Viva's got a grouchy older brother who was married once and maybe still is. He left his wife and came back home, and nobody knows when he's leaving, except they wish he'd do it soon. He makes life hell for everyone, yelling and screaming. That's why no one complains when he's out. Where? Who cares.

How they talk to each other in Viva's house is like this.

Viva's mom reaches for an apple on the kitchen table. —Ha! How is it a tree can hold such heavy fruit?

—Viviana, you want me to heat the *tortillas* for lunch?

—It's okay, Daddy. I'll do it.

—How's about the *tortillas*, *mija*. Want me to heat them now?

—No, Daddy, it's okay, let me.

—Ha! How is it a tree can hold such heavy fruit?

—How's about I heat them now, Viviana?

—Don't bother yourself, I'm going to get to it in a little bit.

—Ha! How is it a tree can hold . . .

—Want me to get you another kitchen towel? How's about this towel?

—No, thanks, Daddy, this one is fine. It's clean.

—Ha! How is it a tree can . . .

—But that towel's got holes. How's about I get you another one? Want this one, Viviana, or that one?

—Don't worry, Dad. This one's fine.

—Ha! How is it a tree can hold . . .

—You want me to do that for you, Viviana?

By about this time, I just want to yell, —Gimme that! I'll do it!

They make me so dizzy, I just have to hold on to the walls. In our house Mother ends every sentence with "quick." —Pass me that knife, quick!

Viva says we can move to San Francisco together and be roommates.

How do you like that? And we can both write songs together and become famous and everything. It makes me laugh to think about us writing songs together like Lennon-McCartney. Ozuna-Reyes, I say to myself, and it sounds cool. Except all the songs Viva writes are full of cuss words, and all the ones I write are full of sad shit. Who'd want to buy that?

One day when we're walking home from school, a red Corvette convertible starts following us. It scares me, but Viva acts like this happens to her all the time, and it probably does.

—You girls need a lift?

It's Darko. Viva hangs on the door and talks for the longest time, and finally makes it understood, no, not this time.

They have a strange way of talking to each other, those two. A bunch of put-downs, and how it ends is with Darko saying something, I don't even remember what, before he drives away. Something stupid really, like, —You'll be sorry, you're losing quite an opportunity.

Instead of just laughing, Viva shouts, —Fuck you, Zorro, as he roars away. Then she adds for good measure, —Your mother's a man!

Nobody but Us Chickens

—*El cuarenta-y-uno*, Father shouts from his bedroom at one end of the house.

—*No, el ocho*, the Grandmother counters from her room off the kitchen.

—Forty-one, Father keeps insisting.

Mother spent the day covering her rosebushes with plastic garbage bags and quilted moving blankets because of the freeze, and now that it's nighttime, we have to leave every faucet in the house dripping so the pipes won't burst. The kitchen sink, the bathroom sinks and tubs and showers, the ones in the little apartment in back, even the spigots outside. All that trickling and gurgling and *drip-drip-dripping* just makes me want to pee.

A norther has blown in. *Un norte*, which just makes me think of a tall Mexican in pointy boots and a cowboy hat, people like Mother's family. But a norther here in Texas is a mean wind from up north. From Chicago. And in Chicago it means a wind from across Canada. And up in Canada it's the North Pole wind, and who knows what people up in the North Pole call this. Probably summer.

Ito called from Chicago and said that except for the below-zero temperature, they were all fine and managing without us, and that we should count our blessings to be living in Texas right now. True, but we didn't expect temperatures in the twenties to feel so cold *inside* the house.

—Shouldn't be freezing in San Antonio in winter, Mother says, bringing in her potted aloes and *plonking* them on the kitchen counter. She has to climb over Wilson, who is curled up in front of the stove.

—*¡Quítate, animal bruto!* Like all people from the country, the Reynas believe animals belong outside. But because of the drop in temperature tonight, Wilson has visitor's privileges. When we negotiated for Wilson to come to Texas, I'd promised Mother he'd be no trouble. Now there's newspapers and Pine-Sol all over the kitchen floor because of Wilson and his no trouble.

—It's not normal for it to freeze in Texas, Mother goes on. —If you ask me, must be more of that nuclear monkey business. That's what causes the planet to act weird. It's those secret underground tests the FBI are doing in West Texas and New Mexico and Arizona. I heard about it on public TV. Why the hell did we pick up and leave Chicago if it was going to be just as cold here? Yuck, it feels colder. At least up north the houses are insulated. I knew moving to Texas was a bad idea. You hear me, Ino? I'm talking to you.

She hollers this toward the front of the house where Father is lying in bed watching TV.

—*El cuarenta-y-uno,* Father shouts to his mother, to our mother, to anyone who will listen. This means the Grandmother should punch the remote on her bedroom portable to channel 41, and Mother should turn the dial to 41 on her kitchen TV. —Hurry, Father adds urgently. —María Victoria* is about to appear.

—I don't care about that crap, Mother growls, but only loud enough for me to hear. —No intelligent life around here except my plants.

I've pushed two chairs next to the space heater in the dining room, and this is where I'm trying to read a book on Cleopatra. I've got no privacy to hear my own thoughts in this stupid house, but I can hear everyone else's. Voices echo because the house is still only half furnished, even though Father promised to make us all new furniture as soon as we got here, but that was back in August.

My Cleopatra book is a fat one, which is all I ask from a book these days. A cheap ticket out of here. Biographies are best, the thicker the better. Joan of Arc. Jean Harlow. Marie Antoinette. Their lives like the white crosses on the side of the road. Watch out! Don't go there! You'll be sorry!

Mother marches through on her way to her bedroom, but she doesn't yell, —You're going to go blind, or, —Get away from that heater, you'll get an early arthritis. She doesn't say anything. She just looks at me and shakes her head. She's still mad about the tampons.

—Don't you know tampons are for floozies? Mother had said when she found them in the bathroom, and then she got even angrier because I didn't hide them well enough, but left them in the cupboard under the sink "advertising for all the world" instead of stuffing them in the bathroom closet behind the towels where she'd taught me to bury the purple box of Kotex. —Don't you know nice girls don't wear tampons till they're married? And maybe not even then. Look at me, I wear Kotex.

—Ma, I told you and I told you. I'm sick of wearing those thick *tamales*. And anyway I'm in high school now. Lots of the girls wear tampons.

—I don't care what other girls do, I'm talking about *you*! We don't send you to private school so you can learn those "filthy ways."

Only she uses the Spanish word, which is more like "pig ways," and worse.

—*El cuarenta-y-uno*, the Grandmother shrieks from her room. —There's a black-and-white Libertad Lamarque[†] film. *Se ve que está buena*.

—That's what I've been trying to tell you, Father shouts from the other end of the house.

Every night it's like this. The TV's always hot, the radio with its aluminum-foil, coat-hanger antenna jabbering on top of the refrigerator next to the slouched plastic bag of sliced bread, my brothers stomping up and down the stairs that had a carpet when we moved in, till Mother got the bright idea to toss it because—It smells like a wet dog. Father shouting to his mother to watch what he's watching on TV. They never think of getting up and watching TV together. Maybe because the boys always hog up the big TV in the living room, or maybe because they just like to watch TV in bed. There isn't any room for Father to watch TV in the Grandmother's little bed, and Father would never dare to ask her to his room without Mother starting up.

Father promised me the Grandmother's apartment would be ready soon, and I'd have my own room finally. In the meantime I'm stuck next to the stairs where my brothers thump up and down like a football team in training. And they never talk in a normal voice, they're always yelling.

—We're not yelling, this is how we talk, Lolo says, yelling.

The boys thunder up the stairs to their room, making sure their footfalls are even louder.

—Yeah, and this isn't a library, Memo booms. —If you don't like it, move.

—I wish I could . . . so I could get away from *you*. But by the time I think to add the second part, he's already galloped upstairs, two steps at a time, and doesn't hear me.

I have to wait till everyone is in bed to get any privacy around here. I can hear Father's snoring, Mother's whistled breathing, the sighing and gulping and wheezing coming from the boys upstairs. The Grandmother sleeping with her mouth open, hogging the air like a drain swallowing water, then waking herself up and rolling over with a groan. The house with all its faucets gargling.

I pull down my blankets and sheets from the closet and make my bed on the living room couch. Bury myself under three blankets tonight because of the freeze—a fake-fur leopard blanket Father's seamstresses gave him as a good-bye present, an itchy Mexican wool blanket that weighs a ton and smells like mothballs, and a nubby blue blanket with satin trim that we've had since we were babies. Then I turn off the light.

Somewhere in the middle of all the bubbling and gurgling water, in the middle of the coldest night of the San Antonio winter, the Grandmother gets sick. I mean really. When she doesn't wake up the next morning, Father says she's probably tired, *pobrecita*, and we have to tiptoe around the kitchen till noon. After the breakfast dishes have been washed, Father starts to worry, and finally, he thinks to knock.

—¿Mamá?

We wait, but there's no answer.

Father rattles the doorknob, but the door's locked. It's not one of those hollow doors, but a real door, an old one with four panels, solid, part of the original house, or from some other old house. Father sends Toto around the house to look in the window, and he reports the Grandmother is slumped in her bed. There's some argument about knocking out the window as opposed to knocking down the door, but by then somebody has had the good sense to call the fire department.

They're big guys, these firemen. They come into our house and the house becomes small, their tallness grazing the ceiling, their elbows poking out from windows. They come in with their big voices as if no one is sick and this is just another fire drill, as if it's any other winter morning. The tree by the curb with its tiny golden leaves like melon seeds. This they bring in with them, because firemen never wipe their shoes.

I look around ashamed. The sheets on the couch still warm, my bedding a crumpled mess because I didn't have time to clear it. The bathroom door open, a towel draped sloppily over the shower rod, a T-shirt bunched on the floor.

Crack! The door opens with a crowbar and a good hard shove, and then it's just bodies hovering over her.

Did she take her pills for her high blood pressure? Did she remember to order her medicine? Was anyone watching her?

But as the Mexicans would say, *sólo Dios sabe*. They wheel the Grandmother out on a gurney, but the Grandmother can't answer. She can't say a word, except to stick the tip of her tongue out between her thin yellow beak and give a weak sputter.

Maria Victoria, a Mexican entertainer, was famous in the fifties and sixties for draping herself on a piano and wearing skintight dresses that gathered at the knees and flowed out into a fishtail skirt, which made her look like a magnificent mermaid. Her voice was soft and sexy and not especially strong, but her outfits and her body were unforgettably campy. In a time of blondes, she was dark; black-black hair and the voluptuous body of a Mexican goddess, and this to me makes her wonderful.

†*Libertad Lamarque was an Argentine singer and film star with a voice like a silver knife with a mother-of-pearl handle. Supposedly she was Perón's lover, and for this they say Eva had her ousted from the country. Libertad settled in Mexico, where she had a long and flourishing career. She died in 2001, working till the last on a Mexican telenovela, una señora grande y una gran señora, as beautiful and elegant in her old age as ever, perhaps more beautiful.*

67.

The Vogue

Not class like Frost Brothers, but definitely not cheese like the Kress. —Verrry rrritzy, verrry fancy, verrry Vogue, Viva says in a snooty fake accent she makes up from I don't know where. —Formals, shoes, gloves, hats, hose. Whenever you shop for a special occasion, head over to the Vogue, corner of Houston and Navarro Streets, downtown San Antonio, Viva says breathlessly as she swirls through the doors like a TV commercial.

—We're shopping for the prom, Viva says to the saleswomen trailing us. Not true, but that's how we get to play dress-up for an hour, trying on beaded gowns we can't afford. Viva pulls a purple crocheted number over her head and shimmies until it falls into place, the pearl spangles sparkling when she moves, the neckline plunging like an Acapulco cliff diver.

—Oh, my God, Viva, you look just like Cher!

The Vogue saleswomen have to wear prissy name tags that say "Miss" in front of their first names, even if they're a hundred years old! Miss Sharon, Miss Marcy, Miss Rose.

Viva asks me, —And when you're on your period, do you get real *cacosa?*

—Shit, yes!

—Ha! That's a good one. Me too.

Miss Rose hovering about, knocking on the dressing room door too sharply, and asking a hundred times, —Everything all right, honey?

—Gawd! Can't we have a little privacy here? Viva says, squeezing her *chichis* into a serve-'em-on-a-platter corset gown.

The Vogue is Viva's choice. Mine, the Woolworth's across from the Alamo because of the lunch counter that loops in and out like a snake. I like sitting next to the toothless *viejitos* enjoying their grilled tuna triangles and slurping chicken noodle soup. I could sit at that counter for hours, ordering Cokes and fries, a caramel sundae, a banana split. Or wander the aisles filling a collapsible basket with glitter nail polish, little jars of fruit-flavored lip gloss, neon felt-tip pens, take the escalator to the basement to check out the parakeets and canaries, poke around Hardware looking for cool stuff, or dig through the bargain bins for marked-down treasures.

Viva says who would ever want to shop at the Woolworth's when there's the Kress? She has a way of finding jewels even there. Like maybe picking up thick fluorescent yarn for our hair over in Knitting. Or a little girl's purse I wouldn't ever notice in a thousand years. Or the funkiest old ladies' sandals that turn sexy when she wears them.

But it's over at the Vogue that Viva's happiest. I can't see the point in spending so much time in a store that sells nothing for less than five dollars. —But who cares, says Viva. —Right? Who cares.

We try on every formal dress in the store till I complain I'm hungry. No use. Viva pauses in Jewelry and tries on a pair of gold hoop earrings almost bigger than her head.

—Gold hoops look good on us, Viva says. She means Mexicans, and who am I to argue with the fashion expert. We do look good. —Never sleep with your gold hoops, though, Viva adds. —Last time I did that I woke up and they weren't hoops anymore, but something shaped like peanuts. I'm going to write a list of twenty things you should never do, *nunca*, or you'll be sorry, and on the top of that list will be: Never, never, never sleep with your gold hoop earrings. I'm telling you.

Number two. Never date anyone prettier than yourself, Viva says, trying on a rhinestone tiara. —Believe me, I know.

She still has to pester saleswomen to help her get her hands on a felt fedora, fishnet pantyhose, pearl hair snoods, strapless bras. I'm slumped on a bench over by the elevator when she finally reappears, sighing loudly and snapping, —Number three. Never shop for more than an hour in platform shoes. My feet feel like zombies, and this place bores me to tears. Let's cut out.

—I was hoping we could stop at the Woolworth's for a chili dog, I say. —But it's late. My ma will be pissed.

—Quit already. We'll tell her . . . we were at my house bathing my mother.

Viva is braying over the genius of the story we're going to tell, exaggerating worse than ever, yakking a mile a minute when we push open the heavy glass doors of the Vogue and step out onto the busy foot traffic of Houston Street.

And then the rest, I don't remember exactly. Some big clown in a dark suit behind us barking something, a dark shadow out of the corner of my eye, and Viva's yowl when one grabs her by the shoulder and the little one hustles me by the elbow, escorting us real quick back inside the Vogue while a bunch of shoppers stare at us, and Viva starts cussing, and me mad as hell saying, —Take your hands off her! It happens so fast I really don't know what's happening at first. Like being shaken awake from a nightmare, only the nightmare is on the wrong side.

The two guys in suits say we've stolen something. I mean, how do you like that? 'Cause we're teenagers, 'cause we're brown, 'cause we're not rich enough, right? Pisses me off. I'm thinking this as they shove us downstairs to the basement and trot us down to their offices, where there are mirrors and cameras and everything. Who the hell do they think they are? We haven't done a damn thing. Jesus Christ, lay off already, will you!

Viva is looking really scared, pathetic even, making me feel sick. I would say something to her if they'd leave us alone, but they don't let us out of their sight, not for a minute.

—Take everything out of your bags and pockets.

Viva plucks things out of her purse like she's got all the time in the world. Not me; I dump my army backpack right on the cop's desk so that all my books and papers spill out. I'm so mad I can hardly look anybody in the eye. Then I empty my pockets. I wish I had something really badass to toss on the desk, like a knife or something, but all I've got is two wads of dirty Kleenex, and my bus pass, which I flick down with as much hate as I can gather, like Billy Jack in that movie.

I wonder if they'll force us to undress, and the thought of having to undress in front of these old farts makes me pissed.

But I don't finish the thought because of what Viva tugs out of one of her pockets. A pair of gold lamé gloves, the kind that go up to your armpits, the price tag still spinning from a cotton string.

Swear to God, that's when I get really scared. Then Viva does something that's pure genius.

She starts crying.

I've never seen Viva cry, ever. Seeing her cry scares the hell out of me at first. I'm thinking maybe we should call a lawyer. There must be somebody we could call, only I can't think of anybody's name except Ralph Nader, and what good is that?

Viva begs with real tears for the store cops not to call our parents. That she's already on probation with her dad, who is Mexican Methodist and the worst, and if he finds out about this, she won't get to go to her own prom. And how she had to work after school to buy her dress, and how she only needed the gloves because she was short on cash, and she couldn't ask her dad because he didn't want her to work anyway, and go ahead, call. Her mom's dead, died from leukemia last winter, a slow, horrible death. And I don't know where she gets the nerve to make up such a bunch of baloney, but she does it, all the while sniffling and hiccuping like if every word is true. Damn, she's so good, she almost has me crying.

I don't know how, but they let us go, toss us out of there like trash bags, and we don't ask questions.

—And don't come back here.

—Don't worry, we won't.

We bust out of the double doors of the Vogue on the Navarro Street side. I mean bust out, like the Devil's on our ass. The fresh air makes me realize how hot my face is. I feel dizzy and notice this weird smell to my skin, like chlorine. I'm so relieved, I just want to break into a run, but Viva is hanging on my arm and dawdling.

—Oh, my God, Lala. You better not tell anyone. Swear to God. You promise? Promise you won't say nothing to nobody. You gotta promise.

—I promise, I say.

One minute she's scared, and the next minute I look and she's laughing with her head thrown back like a horse.

—What? I ask. —What is it? Tell me already, will you?

—Number four, never . . . , Viva begins but stops there. She's laughing so much she can't even talk.

—What? You better tell me, girl!

She pulls out of her blouse a cheap memo pad she lifted from the detective's desk.

—Shit, Viva, honest to God, you scare me.

Viva just laughs. She laughs so hard, she makes me laugh. Then I have her laughing too. We have to hold on to the building. We laugh till we're doubled over, our stomachs hurting. When we think it's finally winding down, the laughing rolls back in all over again even stronger. Viva's braying has me snorting like a pig. Till the knees give out. Till Viva has to genuflect right then and there on the sidewalk, on busy Navarro Street, I'm not kidding, and hold it in, pivoting on one foot. She's laughing so hard she can hardly talk.

Then Viva rises to her feet like an actress about to deliver her lines. For a fraction of a moment, like the eye of a camera, I catch a Viva I've never seen before, a sadness she's carried around inside her all this time, years and years and years, since she was a little kid, its silver shimmering, every bad thing that ever happened to her I see in her face, but only for a slippery second, and then it's gone. —Number four, Viva says, dead serious. —Never. Ever get arrested when . . . when you've really gotta piss.

And then it's me dropping down to the sidewalk, and Viva tottering beside me, laughing and laughing, the thin bone of an ankle wedged in our you-know-what holding back a flood, our bodies shaking, and the citizens of San Antonio walking by and thinking—*What the hell?*—and probably thinking we're crazy, and maybe we are. But who cares, right? I mean, who the hell cares?

68

My Cross

When the Grandmother becomes sick, her kids forget she's their mother, and how can you blame them, since she always forgot they were her kids. There's no talking to Aunty Light-Skin. Anytime Father phones her, there's a lot of shouting going on. —Sister, be reasonable, he begs, but the last time he called she snapped back, —God is just, and hung up. The uncles in Chicago also refuse to come, still angry about the money the Grandmother had lavished on her firstborn.

—It's disgraceful, Father says shaking his head. —I can't believe this is my family.

Father has to convince Mother that the Grandmother had been kind to us by paying for the down payment on our house here in Texas, and that there's an inheritance for all her children to think about. I guess that's how he does it, because Mother finally accepts our Grandmother back into our home even though the Grandmother's face is half frozen into a silly grin and no language left to her. She drools. One eye is tilted, looking far off and glazed, like if she's already watching Death coming for her.

Like Jesus hauling his own instrument of torture, Mother feels she's carrying the burden of her death. She takes to calling the Grandmother by a nickname, and why not, she thinks. She'd never called her by a name. A name is something one confers on a human. Mother doesn't consider our grandmother human. This must've been awkward when she was just married. She didn't dare call her "Mother." Madre. Mamá. She wouldn't have said this. How? She couldn't call her Señora Reyes. —I'm not her servant! She did not call her. Ever.

She said "your mother," or "your grandmother," or "your wife" when our Little Grandfather was still alive. But to her face she says nothing. She calls the way an animal calls, by eyesight, by recognition. She couldn't call her when she was in another room. She had to look for her, make eye contact, say, —The phone, it's for you. Or, —Your son wants to know if you will make *mole* for him. Or, —We're missing one yellow sock and a washcloth.

And now that the mother of her husband has suffered a stroke, she finally dares to address her the way she feels fit. She calls her *"tú,"* the familiar "you." Not *"usted,"* which is like bowing. *"Tú."* —Hey, you, she says in Spanish. —What do you mean by leaving me such a pig mess to pick up after? Pig mess, *cochinada,* that's what she says! When Mother is especially disgusted, she calls her "my cross," *"mi cruz."*

—Well, my cross, what work did you invent for me today? All this when Father isn't home.

The Grandmother *is* a lot of *lata.* Mother had been told the Grandmother would be going soon, but the body takes its time dying. It starts rotting from the inside out, like a tree filled with worms. A horrible smell like a dead rat stuck in the wall. —What? Are you still alive? Jeez! Mother says every morning when she has to check on the Grandmother.

What a business it is to die. You think it'll be like in the movies, but it's not like that at all. There's the horror of the body giving up, just giving up, and the nuisance of that collapse, gradual and steady. I'd promised Mother I'd help as much as I could, but the truth is I don't have the courage to look when I'm supposed to look. It's Mother who does all the filthy work, the heavy work, the lifting and changing and swabbing and feeding, as if somehow life has given them each other as a punishment of sorts.

One day, Mother scoops up the Grandmother from her bed. She's as light as an armload of bare branches, all wintered and crazy. She's no trouble at all to carry upstairs and then over to the window. The wide sky. Too many eaves and gutters, and that damn pecan tree. Mother carries the Grandmother over to the landing at the top of the stairs instead and pauses. *I was carrying her downstairs after giving her a bath . . .*

If the Grandmother's face had said nothing, maybe this story would be another story. But at that moment, the Grandmother's left eye decides to speak, and it lets go a little water. Sadness? Dust? Who can say? It's enough to bring Mother back her humanity. She carries the Grandmother back to her room and tucks her in bed under the pictures of la Virgen de Guadalupe and Raquel Welch.

69

Zorro Strikes Again

—Sweetie pie, Viva says, kissing the air next to my cheek and hobbling over on denim platforms. Her hippie scent of patchouli mixing with the smell of fried food, overpowering the entire cafeteria. Her skirt rolled up so many times, she has to shimmy into the seat across from me. Viva mouths a loud hi to a huddle of seniors across the room, leans forward and drapes herself halfway across the lunch table to tell me whatever it is she has to tell me.

Then she delivers her bomb. —Lala, you've got to promise me you won't tell a soul what I'm going to tell you. A soul. Promise, okay? You're gonna flip.

Viva swallows a big gulp of air, and then adds, —Guess!

And then when I shrug and surrender, —No, I really can't guess. Honest. I can't. Cripes. Come on, are you going to tell me or what?

—You'll never guess what Zorro said to me. Never in a million years. Oh, it's too good, it's killer. Promise you won't say nothing.

—Okay already, I promise.

She scrunches her shoulders up and announces, with her little eyebrows rising like hats tossed in the air, —We're engaged!

Honest to God, it's like she hits me upside my head with a sock filled with rocks. —But what about San Francisco? I thought you said we were going to San Francisco.

—We can still go to San Francisco. You, me, and Zorro. Are you going to finish those french fries?

—What about freedom's just another word for nothing left to lose? I mean, what happened to our plans?

—Shit, don't freak on me. I said I'm engaged, I didn't say I was dying. We're still going. We can still become a famous songwriting team. Writers have lives, you know.

I can't believe it's Viva talking. The thought of Mister Darko coming with us anywhere, even to the Woolworth's, just about makes me want to cry.

—I don't feel too good, I say.

—Hey! Don't be mad. Come on, I thought you'd be happy for me.

—Will you just grow up? Don't you realize Darko's an old man? He's a creep. He's ancient. He's thirty years old, he's got crease marks on his face like origami. And, by the way, in case you're forgetting, you're old enough to get him in jail.

—Now you sound like an old person yourself. I'm mature for my age. Zorro says so. I'm what they call precocious. I've always been mature for my age. And anyway why are we even talking like this? It's not like we're getting married soon, we're engaged, get it? Engaged. Like we can wait till I graduate, till I'm eighteen, and then I don't have to get anybody's permission.

—But you said we were going to San Francisco as soon as we both finished school, and I won't finish for three more years even.

—La, don't you get whiny on me. Sad is one thing, whiny I can't stand.

The future Mrs. Zoran Darko dumps the contents of her purse on the table and starts to reapply her makeup. She dips a pinky into a lip gloss jar and comes out with a nasty heap of sparkling grease the color of mashed raspberries and glitter, which she dabs carefully on her lips, all the while watching herself in a compact mirror, until her mouth looks like a jelly donut. Then she wipes her pinky on the bottom of the cafeteria table, chattering and chirping like the little parakeets we see in the basement of the Woolworth's.

—You break my heart, Viva says, working on her purple eye shadow. —You should see yourself. You look like those big teddy bears they give away at the carnivals. Listen, sweets, it's simple. You're the author of the *telenovela* of your life. You want a comedy or a tragedy? If the episode's a tearjerker, you can hang yourself or hang in there. Choose. I believe in destiny as much as you do, but sometimes you've gotta help your destiny along. Hey, mamas, it's not the end of the world. You're still my best friend, right? Right? Come on, Lala, you gotta say yes. I need you as my maid of honor. I'm already designing the coolest dresses we're going to wear.

Viva's mouth opening and closing, her plucked eyebrows rising and falling. On and on like this forever. Same as always. She talking, me saying nothing. On and on and on.

70.

Becoming Invisible

When she was a child and her father remarried. That was the first time. And then again when she was lost among Aunty Fina's tribe, lost to everyone but Uncle Pio's unwelcome attention. Before Narciso noticed her and rescued her from that madhouse.

The Grandmother only became visible when her body changed and garnered the trophy of men's attentions. But then she had lost their attentions as her body shifted and slouched into disrepair after the birth of each child. And then when she no longer was vain and cared about taking care of herself, she began to disappear. Men no longer looked at her, society no longer gave her much importance after her role of mothering was over.

In her forties she was most acutely aware of this shift of herself and of her place in society, and it had made her difficult and quarrelsome, subject to sadnesses that seized her suddenly, and just as suddenly disappeared. Eventually she grew used to being ignored, being not seen, not looked at, not raising men's heads or having their eyes graze her as they had once, and there was some relief to that, some calmness, as if a knife had been put away.

Now that she was ill, with her breathing heavy, and her consciousness rising and falling, she became aware of that familiar feeling of shedding her body once again. It both delighted and frightened her.

She was turning invisible. She was turning invisible. What she had feared her whole life. The body led her, a wide rowboat without oars or a rudder, drifting. Giddy, she didn't need to do a thing, simply be. Like floating in a lagoon of warm water.

Once when her children were little, she had felt like this on a beach in the Yucatán. It was one of the few times Narciso took his family on vacation. After a long hot car trip from Mérida, they had stopped for a rest at a small lagoon, gulf water as clear as the air. Narciso and the children had wandered off in search of soft drinks and food, leaving her in peace finally.

At the shallow lip, Soledad had lain down on the rippled sand. The sand soft beneath her back, the ocean lap-lapping, the sky serenely cool through the palm fronds, and the light on that blue green surface dappled and happily laughing. Soledad fell asleep for a little, the water licking her earlobes, saying things she didn't need to understand. A peace and joy she would remember forever after whenever she needed to feel safe.

That's what she felt now as she was dying and her life was letting her go. A saltwater warmth of well-being. The water lifting her and her self floating out from her life. A dissolving and a becoming all at once. It filled her with such emotion, she stopped thrashing about and let herself float out of her body, out of that anchor her life, let herself become nothing, let herself become everything little and large, great and small, important and unassuming. Puddle of rain and the feather that fell shattering the sky inside it, votive candles flickering through blue cobalt glass, the opening notes of that waltz without a name, the steam from a clay bowl of rice in bean broth, and the steam from a fresh clod of horse dung. Everything, everything. Wise, delicate, simple, obscure. And it was good and joyous and blessed.

71.

The Great Divide

or This Side and That

The night the Awful Grandmother dies, Mother orders us to open all the windows of the house. All of them. Even though it's January. Even though it's the middle of the night. Even though the Grandmother dies in the hospital and not the kitchen bedroom. Because the moment the Awful Grandmother closes her eyes and lets out her last hiccuped sigh, it's as if skinny Death with her dog haunches scampers along the railroad tracks where Madero arrived and organized his Mexican revolution, sweeps herself over the downtown parking lots, across the homes of the south side of San Antonio to our house on El Dorado Street, because Mother says, —I can't sleep, it stinks in here like rotten *barbacoa*.

I can't smell it, but do what I'm told, open the windows just the same. *Barbacoa* reminds me too much of that one Sunday I bit into a *taco* and found a piece with hairs on it. What part of the cow head did I get? The ear? The nostril? An eyelash? What disgusted me most was the not knowing.

And then I start to think about all these things I shouldn't think about. The fatty piece of *barbacoa*. An eyelash. Hair in a man's ears just like the hair in a man's nose. The hairy legs of flies. The spiral of sticky flypaper dangling above the meat counter at Taquería la Milagrosa on South Halsted Street droning, droning, droning that death song—instead of the things I should think about—love and heartily sorry, but I don't feel anything for my grandmother, who at this very moment is no doubt fluttering above our heads searching for her route out of this world of pain and rotten stink.

Barbacoa taquitos. Sawdust on the floor to soak up the blood. When I was born Mother said she needed two things after getting out of the hospital, —Please, a pork chop sandwich from Jim's Original Hot Dogs on Maxwell Street, and a *barbacoa taquito* just down the street at La Milagrosa. And me just born wrapped in my new flannel blanket, hair wet as a calf, face still long from coming through the birth chute, and my mother standing there on Halsted and Maxwell with her pork chop sandwich, and men with gold teeth hawking watches, and the balloon man with his prophylactic-shaped ugly balloons, and right across the street that man Harold my father always fights with every time he buys shoes, and La Milagrosa filled with mice. Don't look!

This is what I'm thinking instead of the prayer I'm trying to compose, because I can't think of anything to say for my grandmother who is simply my father's mother and nothing to me. The more I try not to think of *barbacoa*, the more it comes up like the smell Mother claims, like those bulls' heads and hooves in the Mexico City meat market, an eye sticky with flies, how when someone says, —Don't look—that's exactly what you do.

72.

Mexican on Both Sides

or Metiche, Mirona, Mitotera, Hocicona—
en Otras Palabras, Cuentista—Busybody, Ogler,
Liar/Gossip/Troublemaker, Big-Mouth—
in Other Words, Storyteller

You could be royalty and be poor. You could not have money for nice clothes and still be better than the rat-faced girls with rotten teeth who spit bad words at you. *Bolilla. Perra. Puta.* You could be under a spell. Things could go from worse to worst. Stuff like that happens in *telenovelas* all the time. Right before the happy ending, the cliff-hanger where the heroine has to just hold on because everything's against her. That's what I tell myself to keep going. That's what I've got to believe, because to not believe just depresses the hell out of me.

—We'll need to tighten our belt at least a year, Mother says. —Just till we get back on our feet.

All our money went getting us to Texas, buying the house on El Dorado Street, starting the shop on Nogalitos Street. And then the Grandmother dying, and her hospital bills that swallowed up all her money, and the funeral and burial in Mexico City, well, it's a hard spell, that's all.

Just for a spell. Or just a spell. A spell somebody wicked cast. A somebody like the Grandmother. I don't say it out loud, but it's what I'm thinking. She's the reason we're stuck here.

At the first of the month, Father's forced to tell Mars another story as to why the shop rent is late again. To try to get more business, Father even goes so far as to change the name of his shop. Across the window in big red and gold letters, KING UPHOLSTERY with that same old funky crown perched sassy on the "K."

—Father, don't you like "Tapicería Reyes" anymore?

—*Los güeros,* Father says and sighs. —"King" makes them think of King Ranch. This way they think Mr. King is the boss, and I just work for him.

Belt-tightening. That's how it is I get my wish and am transferred from Immaculate Conception to Davy Crockett, the public school across the freeway.

But Crockett's a vocational high school. That means there's nothing here for me. I don't want to wind up being a farmer or a beautician. I want to take classes like anthropology and drama. I want to travel someday. Be in a movie, or even better, make a movie. I want to do something interesting, I don't know what yet, but you can bet it's not something they offer at a vocational. I'm going to live in San Francisco in an attic apartment with bead curtains. I'm going to design houses, or teach blind kids to read, or study dolphins, or discover something. Something useful.

Davy Crock-of-shit Vocational. Home of the Future Farmers of America. Livestock shows. Rodeos. Majorettes twirling batons. Home Ec. Machine Shop. The Davy Crockett marching band with cheerleaders in raccoon hats and fringed booties. Creeps in nerdy glasses and crew cuts. Girls still wearing their hair poufed into a Patty Duke bubble. Super-straight. Like they escaped from the fifties, I'm not kidding.

Viva says I shouldn't complain. —At least you ain't got nuns on your ass. And think of it this way, La. You get to go to school with guys.

What I don't tell her is that the guys at my new school act like it's me that's the freak. They talk to each other like this:

—Man, you're fatter than shit!

—The good life.

—Damn right.

And this is how they talk to me:

—Hey, hippie girl, you Mexican? On both sides?

—Front and back, I say.

—You sure don't look Mexican.

A part of me wants to kick their ass. A part of me feels sorry for their stupid ignorant selves. But if you've never been farther south than Nuevo

Laredo, how the hell would you know what Mexicans are supposed to look like, right?

There are the green-eyed Mexicans. The rich blond Mexicans. The Mexicans with the faces of Arab sheiks. The Jewish Mexicans. The big-footed-as-a-German Mexicans. The leftover-French Mexicans. The *chaparrito* compact Mexicans. The Tarahumara tall-as-desert-saguaro Mexicans. The Mediterranean Mexicans. The Mexicans with Tunisian eyebrows. The *negrito* Mexicans of the double coasts. The Chinese Mexicans. The curly-haired, freckled-faced, red-headed Mexicans. The jaguar-lipped Mexicans. The wide-as-a-Tula-tree Zapotec Mexicans. The Lebanese Mexicans. Look, I don't know what you're talking about when you say I don't look Mexican. I *am* Mexican. Even though I was born on the U.S. side of the border.

I tell them a story.

—I come from a long line of royalty. On both sides. The Reyes have blue blood going back to Nefertiti, the Andalusian gypsies, the dancing-for-their-dowry tribes in the deserts of North Africa. And that's not even mentioning my mother's family, the Reynas, from Monte Albán, Tenochtitlán, Uxmal, Chichén, Tzin Tzun Tzán. I could go on and on.

—You're just like your father, Mother says. —A born liar. Nothing but a bunch of liars, from his mother all the way back to the great-grand-something-or-other who said he was descended from the king of Spain. Look, the Reyes are nothing but *mitoteros*, and if they say they're not, they're lying. If you ask me, all people from Mexico City are liars. They can't help it. That's just how the *chilangos* are. Kiss you on each cheek when they meet you like they knew you their whole life. And they just met you! Makes me sick. *¡Chilangos, metiches, mirones!* God, if there's anything I can't stand, it's *chilangos*. And the *familia* Reyes. And Mexicans.

How can I explain? Talk is all I've got going for me.

I'm going to try to tell the truth here, though Mother says I'm just like Father. There are at least seven evil enemies at Davy Crockett who'd like nothing better than to slap the crap out of me. Cookie Cantú, who thinks she's a big shit because she works in the office as an attendance aide. Norma Estrada. Suzy Pacheco. Alba Treviño. Elvia Ochoa. Rose Falcón. And Debra Carvajal. They've got it in for me after a history class where I made the mistake of telling the story of my great-grandfather Eleuterio Reyes from Seville.

Is hell San Antonio? Is hell the *urraca* birds, grackles, sounding off like clowns? Sad, strange yelling. Sky so blue it hurts. Heat making white people a goofy pink, and brown people shiny.

Is hell Cookie Cantú and her yappy *perras* talking shit like, —Brown power! Making fists and chanting, —*Viva la raza.* Or, —I'm Chicana and proud, wha'chu wanna do about it, *pendeja?*

Give me a break already.

When they catch me alone, —Bitch! Pretending like you're Spanish and shit.

Then they just let air out from their teeth like a tire with a slow leak.

I don't say a damn thing, but that's enough for those girls to hate my guts.

Pisses me off. What can you say when you know who you are?

They call me *bolilla* when they cross my path, or worse, *gabacha.* Who wants to be called a white girl? I mean, not even white girls want to be called white girls. Words I can ignore. It's the *chingazos* that do the damage.

Father promised us all new stuff when we moved to Texas, but our house would be as empty as a ransacked tomb if it wasn't for Mother. Almost everything we have is loot we found at yard sales, flea markets, and at the secondhand shops.

—You'll see, when the seat's reupholstered it'll look just like the chairs your father made for his Winnetka ladies.

In Chicago, Mother and I would walk for blocks over to the Salvation Army for treasures, sometimes as far as the Goodwill. We had to pass the Cook County hospital, where the patients looked like their faces were sliced in a knife fight, crooked black stitches like the twine Father uses when he is basting something. Even Father sewing with his feet could do a better job than those doctors. Terrible as Frankenstein, the county hospital patients were something awful to look at. But we *had* to. It was the shortest route to Goodwill.

In San Antonio, almost as soon as we get here, Mother scouts out the thrift stores, yard sales, and rummage sales. There's a giant Goodwill a few miles north from Father's shop, and we take to walking there in the sun with our umbrellas, like the natives. If we're lucky, it's overcast and we can forget the umbrellas. —Beautiful day, no? This is the only place I've ever lived where a cloudy sky means a beautiful day.

The smell of old men and shirts ironed too long is what probably makes people not want to buy used, is what probably makes Father pissed when he finds out we've been to *la usada* on the sneakity-sneak. Father would rather die than own anything that belonged to someone else. We don't tell him that half the things in our house are from the secondhand stores. Better he doesn't know. Why start trouble? So as not to upset him, we make up stories, healthy lies about where a certain table or a chair came from. A hand-me-down we found stored in the back shed. A gift from our neighbor's cousin. Or, if we're desperate, —You gave it to us, remember?

At the big Salvation Army on South Flores Street, between a bin of bunched brassieres and saggy slips with the elastic gone *guango*, Mother has me guarding a lazy Susan table while she sizes up a box full of china, turning dishes upside down to see if there are any stamped "France" or "England." Mother's an expert at sorting out the jewels from the junk. I'm thinking what story we can tell Father about a Duncan Phyfe chair I've got my eye on when a voice startles me: —*Pura plática*. You're nothing but a *mitotera*. You act like you're better than us, but look at you, Miss Full-of-Shit. Shopping at *la segunda*.

It's her. Cookie Cantú wearing a smock apron with a Salvation Army name tag. I walk away like she doesn't mean a thing to me.

Cripes! Why the hell did we have to come to *this* Salvation Army? *This* one. Of all the stinky, half-ass hellholes, we have to pick the very one where Cookie Cantú works. Like if it's not bad enough we've got to skulk around, now everybody has to know we buy used stuff.

Like I care? It's just I don't want to go around announcing it to everybody so that everyone looks at me like I've got *piojos* or something. Like if life isn't hard enough already being new and not even coming from Texas and shit. Damn! I want to go home right then and there, but Mother yells at me, loud and in front of everybody, because I've forgotten about the lazy Susan.

On the walk home, I get to carry the lazy Susan while Mother complains about my bad attitude. I can't bring myself to tell her what's wrong. I know she'll just laugh at me like she always does. Shit, I can imagine Cookie Cantú mouthing off how she saw me buying secondhand stuff. Maybe she'll feel sorry for me. That's all I need is somebody like her looking at me with pity.

Just when I can go to sleep again without thinking about Cookie Cantú, Cookie Cantú pops up in my life again to terrorize me. It happens on my way home from school. Under the freeway, they're waiting for me, on both sides of the sidewalk and some even down in the cement drain ditch. Circling like *zopilotes*, the ugly vultures we'd see on our trips down to Mexico.

Cookie Cantú and her friends. They start throwing words and end up throwing rocks at me.

—What you looking at, *bolilla*? Think you're so smart because you talk like a white girl. *Huerca babosa*. You think you're better than us, right? *Pinche* princess, you're nothing but *basura*. See who'll come and help you now.

Somebody hits me upside my head with her purse, and the blow leaves my ear ringing. I can feel the heat rise on the side of my face, but before I can even raise my hand, somebody else kicks me in the kidneys, and then they all just descend, all claws and black feathers. I try to shove them off my hair, and twist out of their grip, and when I realize how useless that is, I just take off running, first back toward the school, then along the access road north, thinking I can cross over on the next overpass. But before I even get there, I can see some girls waiting there for me too. At least I think they're waiting for me. It's too risky to find out.

There's no choice but to scramble over the chain-link fence and make a run for it through the interstate. It's not rush hour yet, but the traffic is already heavy in both directions. I can feel the whoosh of wind as the trucks roar past me. When the traffic lets up, I run. A pickup honks and changes lanes to avoid me, I don't care, I don't care. *Que me lleven de corbata*. Take me, dangle me from the bumper. I don't care, I never belonged here. I don't know where I belong anymore. And the sting from the beating like nothing compared to how much I hurt inside.

I run across the interstate like my hair's on fire, my scarf loose and one shoelace undone. I don't know how, but I make it to the middle strip where the guardrails divide the traffic headed downtown from the cars aimed toward the border. My heart a rabbit, the air in my lungs burning. To climb over the guardrail I have to steady myself with a post to get any footing. Just when I straddle the top, a big semi whooshes past *tooting* its horn.

—Asshole! I scream at the top of my lungs, but out here, with all the cars rushing about, the word flutters away like paper. I *plunk* myself down on the guardrail, and then I just bust up like a little kid, puking up tears, my chest heaving and heaving them up. All about me the highway roars wildly, little bits of gravel striking me now and then.

I'm too scared to run across the three lanes of traffic headed south and too scared to stay put. I don't know what to do, the fear freezing me.

—Celaya. Something says my name in a hard whisper. —Celaya. The voice is so sharp and clear and close to my ear, it hisses and sizzles and makes me jump. Celaya.

Then I just take off on automatic, running and running, leaping off the guardrail and sprinting across the three lanes so fast, I don't stop till I'm over by the grassy hill beyond the exit ramp. I fumble over the chain-link fence and heave up some burning phlegm. My body cold and hot all at the same time, my lungs hurting when I breathe.

Celaya. Somebody or something said my name. Not "Lala," not "La." My real name. *Who the hell was that,* I think to myself. *Who was that?*

When I cross over to the residential streets, my legs are trembling. *Una viejita* busy watering her porch plants looks up at me from her yard, a fat little bug-eyed dog wearing a Big Bird T-shirt *yap-yapping* at me from her side of the fence.

—Shame on you, Maggie, Maggie's owner scolds. But Maggie just keeps barking till I'm out of sight.

I drag myself home shivering and sweating, words and feelings thrashing inside my chest like big black bats trapped inside my bones.

When I get home, I lock myself in the bathroom, undress, and assess the damage, examining all the parts of myself that are bruised, or skinned, or throbbing.

Celaya. I'm still myself. Still Celaya. Still alive. Sentenced to my life for however long God feels like laughing.

73

Saint Anthony

Father's hands are numb from working on a set of lounge chairs for the Saint Anthony Hotel. Leather is rough on the hands. His hands calloused from tugging the twine hard and taut. After six days, he comes home and can't untie his own shoes, his hands swell as fat as a mattress of needles. It's a good job, one he can't afford to pass up. We need the money, and landing the hotel account is something Father is proud of.

But now his hands are as big as Popeye's. He's so tired he eats his dinner on a TV tray in the living room. —Please, a bucket of hot water for my feet and another one for my hands. Mother brings him two plastic buckets, one for each foot, and two dish tubs for his hands. Then Father just lies there splayed in his La-Z-Boy. Mother feeds him *albóndigas,* Mexican meatballs, with fresh flour *tortillas,* because that's what Father loves best. She feeds him herself, as if she is feeding a baby.

—Your father works hard, she says.

74.

Everything a Niña Could Want

—¿*S*ola? But why would you ever want to be alone? You have everything a *niña* could want here. Why would you leave all this?

Father waves a butter knife in the air, pointing around the kitchen. The window fan is stirring up the impossibly hot air from outside and pushing it inside. The kitchen table is full of bread crumbs and greasy with butter. Father is finishing his breakfast toast and a three-minute egg.

I rinse another glass under the faucet and wash another dish without turning around to look at the splendors Father is pointing out to me. A refrigerator sticky with handprints nagging to be washed, a loaf of bread perched on top alongside the radio with the aluminum foil antenna and some cooking pots fuzzy with dust. Cheap kitchen cabinets with the varnish wearing thin. A creaky wooden floor bald in places, crying out for stripping and revarnishing. A set of kitchen chairs Mother found at the Salvation Army, don't tell Father, with the seats all redone in what my brothers get a kick out of calling "*Nalga*-hide." And the yard-sale kitchen table. Everything Father points to means work for me. Already the house feels too small, like Alice after she ate the "Eat Me" cookie.

—It's just that I want to be on my own someday.

—But that's not for girls like you. Good girls don't leave their father's house until they marry, and not before. Why would you ever want to live by yourself? Or is it . . . you want to *do* something that you can't do here?

—I just thought maybe I would want to try stuff. Like teach people how to read, or rescue animals, or study Egyptian history at a university.

I don't know. Just stuff like . . . like you see people doing in the movies. I want a life like . . .

—Girls who are not Mexican?

—Like other human beings. It's that I'd like to try to live alone someday.

—¿*Sola?* How? Why? Why would a young lady want to be alone? No, *mija,* you are too naive to know what you are asking for.

—But all my friends say . . .

—Oh, so your friends are more important than your father? You love them more than me? Always remember, Lala, the family comes first—*la familia.* Your friends aren't going to be there when you're in trouble. Your friends don't think of you first. Only your family is going to love you when you're in trouble, *mija.* Who are you going to call? The man across the street? No, no. *La familia,* Lala. Remember. The Devil knows . . .

—More from experience than from being the Devil. I know, I know.

—If you leave your father's house without a husband you are worse than a dog. You aren't my daughter. You aren't a Reyes. You hurt me just talking like this. If you leave alone you leave like, and forgive me for saying this but it's true, *como una prostituta.* Is that what you want the world to think? *Como una perra,* like a dog. *Una perdida.* How will you live without your father and brothers to protect you? One must strive to be honorable. You don't know what you're asking for. You're just like your mother. The same. Headstrong. Stubborn. No, Lala, don't you ever mention this again.

When I breathe, my heart hurts. *Prostituta. Puta. Perra. Perdida. Papá.*

75

The Rapture

You're supposed to love your mother. You're supposed to think good thoughts, hold holy her memory, call out to her when you're in danger, bid her come bless you. But I never think of Mother without dodging to get out of her way, the whoosh of her hand quicker than the enemy's machete, the pinch of her thumb and index finger meaner than a carnival *guacamaya*.

It's Toto's fault. On the first warm day of the season, when the sky is blue again and the wind so mild we can shut the space heaters off and open the windows, he comes home pleased with himself for finally coming up with something original. —Guess what! I've enlisted.

Can you beat that? Mother's Toto has turned conservative on us. They take him in June, the week after he graduates from Resurrection. And Mother's been a terror ever since. Forget about running to Mexico, Toto won't hear it. Toto says he's cut out for the military. —I've never met anyone as pigheaded as you, Mother screams, disgusted, not realizing where he gets it from. What can you say to Toto after all and everything? He's eighteen. He's made up his mind already. He doesn't want to be a mama's boy forever.

I don't blame him. Viva's right, sometimes you've got to help your destiny along. Even if it calls for drastic measures. Father says the army will do Toto good, make a man out of him and all that shit. But what's available to make a woman a woman?

If I could, I'd join up with something, too. Except I don't know who would have me. I'm too young to belong to anything except the 4-H Club, and forget about that.

Look, I don't mean to spook anybody, and you can believe whatever you want to believe, but I swear this is true. Every time I so much as step in the Grandmother's bedroom off the kitchen, the smell of fried meat just about knocks me out. Mother says I'm imagining it, and the boys say I'm just telling stories.

That's why I go back to sleeping on the living room couch, and how it is Toto nabs the room as his. Lolo warns me it's his after Toto moves out this summer, and I tell him no problem, he can have it.

I don't care. I don't care about anything anymore. I don't go to the thrift stores with Viva or Mother, and I don't hang around downtown after school. Viva makes me sick. And Mother. Mother's never been on my side about anything.

I can't explain it except to say they don't even know who the hell I am. This is what hurts me the most. Viva too wrapped up in Zorro, and Mother too wrapped up in Toto. I don't mean to come off sounding like Eeyore, but it's the truth. Father would like to think me and Mother are friends, but what kind of friend can't hear you when you're talking to her? I'm tired, that's all.

I blame Mother with her crazy projects. Mother who insists we fix the back apartment and get it rented, but who's going to fix it? Father's in his shop, the boys busy with their after-school jobs. That leaves me and Mother battling dust and decay. The house, like a big bully taking our puny blows, watching and laughing at us.

I can't live like this is all I'm saying.

When I don't expect it. When I'm alone. When I don't want it to. The Grandmother comes and gets me. When I shut my eyes. A furious heat behind the sockets, deep inside my head, from somewhere I can't even pinpoint. Like light, or a dance, or a tattoo needle, because there's no name for what I'm naming. And it's like a doorbell or a fire alarm without a sound. It comes, and if I will it not to, it rolls in even stronger like a wave.

I know when I open my eyes, she'll be there. As real as when she was alive, or, if you can imagine this, even more alive now that she's dead. Her. The Grandmother. With her stink of meat frying.

The first time I realized it was that day I ran across the interstate, and since then the Awful Grandmother just keeps appearing. She drops cleanser in the tub from behind the plastic shower curtain when I'm peeing. She clears her throat and coughs when I swear. Her *chanclitas flip-flop* behind me from room to room. Leave me the hell alone!

Mother says that when her mother was alive, she used to tell a story about the day all the pots in the kitchen sang. Every pot and pan, glass and dish crashed and banged and rattled one morning. This was when all the kids were at school and her husband at work, and she was home alone in bed with the baby. What was she to think? A thief in the house? And if so, what could she do? After what seemed like forever the crashing stopped as sudden as it had started. When she was brave enough to get out of bed, she and the baby finally peeked into the kitchen, expecting to find a mess. But look—everything was in its place. The glasses and cups on their shelf, every skillet and pot hanging still from its nail. She looked about— nothing. She checked the doors and windows—locked. Then she remembered the recent death of her brother. Is that you, Serapio? Do you want me to pray for you? Because over there they believe if somebody dies but hasn't settled his business on Earth, their spirit hangs around tied to the world of the living, rattling dishes or leaving a door open just to tell you they've been there.

That's why I think the Awful Grandmother, who couldn't let go of everyone else's life when she was living, can't let go of this life now that she's dead. But what does she have to do with me?

—*Vieja metiche,* I hear myself muttering like my mother. —*¡Vieja metiche!* I shout good and loud sometimes. I don't care who hears me.

It was bad enough when she was alive. But now that she's dead, the Awful Grandmother is everywhere. She watches me pee, touch myself, scratch my butt, spit, say her name in vain, watched me with my scarf come loose and one shoe untied running across Interstate 35. My clothes fluttering in the wind. And I should've kept running. I should've let a fender take me. *¡Te llevo de corbata!* Take me already!

At meals, I space out, staring at the Mexican calendar that's been hanging on the kitchen door since 1965. A *charro* carrying off his true love, a woman as limp as if she's sleeping, a sky-blue *rebozo* draped around her shoulders, the *charro* wearing a beautiful woolen red *sarape,* the horse golden, the light glowing from behind his *sombrero* as if he's a holy man. If you look close, you can see the silver trim on his trousers, hear the creak of the tooled-leather saddle. The night sky cold and clear. Behind them a dark town they're running away from, maybe. The moment before a kiss or just after, his face hovering above hers. *El rapto.* The Rapture. And for a moment, I'm carried out of here on the back of that horse, in the arms of that *charro.*

Until somebody yells, —Pass me the *tortillas*—and snaps me back to reality.

To wake up sad and go to sleep sad. Sleep a place they can't find you. A place you can go to be alone. What? Why would you want to be alone? Asleep and dreaming or daydreaming. It's a way of being with yourself, of privacy in a house that doesn't want you to be private, a world where no one wants to be alone and no one could understand *why* you would *want* to be alone. What are you doing? That's enough sleep. Get out of there. Get up now. People drag you like a drowned body dragged water-sodden from a river. Force you to talk when you don't feel like it. Poke under the bed with a broom till they scuttle you out of there.

—What's wrong with you? Mother asks.

—I'm depressed.

—Depressed? You're nuts! Look at me, I had seven kids, and I'm not depressed. What the hell have you got to be depressed about?

—Since when do you care? I say to Mother. —All you ever worry about is your boys.

And for the first time I think Mother is about to slap me. But instead she starts yelling. —You spoiled brat, selfish, smart-mouthy, smart-alecky, smart-ass, I'll teach you. There are tears in her eyes that she won't let out of her eyes. She can't. She doesn't know how to cry.

It's me who winds up crying and running out, the screen door banging like a gun behind me.

—Come back here, crybaby, Mother shouts good and loud. —Where you going? I said come back here, *huerca*. I'm talking to you! When I catch you I'm going to give you two good conks on your head with my *chancla*. You hear me! Do you hear! Then you'll know what depressed means.

76

Parece Mentira

If I had to pick the last person on the planet I'd ever fall in love with, Ernie Calderón, it would be you. The goofiest. Honest to God. Completely out of it. Look at you. You dress like you're still in the sixth grade. Striped polo shirts and white jeans—and not even bells! Sneakers instead of boots. Hair as short as if you're in the military. Not a trace of a beard or mustache, not even a little bit of sideburns. And where did you get those funky black glasses? At least get wire-frames. To top it off, you're too short for me. You look ridiculous. How did I ever wind up with somebody like you?

Father likes you, though. He would. You're the type fathers like. Safe. That's what you are. The kind who goes to confession every Saturday and to mass every Sunday. —*Un* good boy. That's what Father says when Toto brings you home from school one day and announces, —This is Ernie. Because you look like what you are, Ernie. A good Catholic Mexican Texican boy.

Somebody comes up with the idea of starting a band, and then there's no avoiding you. You and Toto screeching away on electric guitars, Lolo with his god-awful trumpet, and Memo banging on paint cans pretending he's a drummer. Bits and pieces of Santana, Chicago, Grand Funk Railroad, because you haven't learned to play a whole song yet. Thank God Mother makes you practice out in the garage apartment, but even if you were over at Father's shop on Nogalitos Street, I bet we could still hear your sad, slow-motion version of "25 or 6 to 4."

That's how it is you start coming around. First for the jam sessions, and then because of the after-school business my brothers and you start, doing yard work, mowing lawns, hauling and cleaning trash.

Ernie.

Honest to God, at first I don't even notice you. Who would notice you? And then the next thing you know, you're very beautiful. Or very ugly.

Depending. But isn't it always like that with love?

Before love. And during. During changes you. I don't know how it is after. I've never really been in love with anyone before except for Lou Rocco in the fourth grade and Paul McCartney, but they don't count. That wasn't love, was it?

Ernie.

It's the time of the meteorite showers. You drive over in your funky white truck, the one you and the boys use for the lawn-mowing business, a big clunky pickup full of dents and rust and dirt. I've never seen a falling star.

—What, never?

—Never.

—Not even in Mexico?

—Nope.

—So come with us.

Because it's you, and my brother Toto, and me, Father lets me go, can you believe it? But Toto wants to meet friends downtown and play foosball first. And then it winds up we drop him off and promise to come back for him later. That's how it is we drive up north to the Hill Country, you and me, Ernie.

Ernie.

You're nothing but a big baby. A big *chillón*. Worse than a girl. Any little thing and your feelings get hurt. How I know is this.

On the night of the falling stars, we don't see any stars. Not a goddamn one. It's too cloudy. We sit outside in the bed of the pickup, and you ask, —Want to hear a song I wrote? And before I can answer, you leap out, haul out your guitar from the cab of the truck, and start playing.

Not bad. Until you open your big mouth and start singing. Way off-key. I mean way off. *Perdido estoy. Yo siento el Destino llevándome a tu amor, tu amor, tu amor.*

At first I think you're kidding, and I start to laugh. Until you put your guitar back in its case, snap it shut, and won't look me in the eye. A terrible silence. The sound of the wind, the sharp scent of cedar. In the darkness, your eyes glinting.

What a girl you are, but I don't say this. How can I? You aren't at all like my brothers, are you? You're not like anybody I've met. Except for me. Swear to God. Swear to God, Ernie, and I think to myself, I promise I'll never make you cry again. And I won't let anyone else make you cry either. This is what I'm thinking.

—So what's your real name? I ask.

—What?

—What do they call you?

—Ernie.

—No, I mean, haven't you got a nickname or something? What do they call you at home?

—Ernie, you say again, and this time you give a little tee-hee like a comic-strip cartoon.

Ernie! I let go a sigh. It lacks dignity, respect, mystery, poetry, all the ingredients necessary to fall in love. Only how can I tell you that?

—I'll call you Ernesto.

And that's what I call you. Since the night of the falling stars when we didn't see any falling stars. Ernesto, then and since.

77

On the Verge of Laughable

*J*ust like that picture on the Mexican calendar, *El rapto*, Ernesto arrives in my life to rescue me. His white pickup waiting at the school curb every day at three, saving me from Cookie Cantú and her *desesperadas*. I've always been a daydreamer, but all I need is for Ernesto to look at me and remind me I'm not a ball of light, a dust mote spiraling in a sunbeam.

He's a porcelain salt shaker, my Ernesto. *Muy delicado* is how they would describe him in Spanish, *muy fino*, as if he was a cigar. With a face and hands that sweat a lot, and a slight hunch to his thin shoulders as if his body is saying, —Don't hit me.

Up until Ernesto, Father gave any boy who came near me that eye of the rooster he's famous for, a sideways once-over as if he'd suddenly had a seizure and can't look at you face-to-face. But with Ernesto, well, I guess he's just satisfied he's Mexican.

I believe in la Divina Providencia. The Calderón family is from Monterrey, Mexico, and they travel back and forth from Texas to Nuevo León all the time. When Ernesto saw me put sour cream on my enchiladas and didn't say, —Yech—like the other kids from San Antonio, I just knew. I don't have to explain everything, about the different foods we eat depending on the different regions our families come from—the desert north of Mexico with their flour *tortillas*, the Yucatán south with their fried bananas and black beans. The pink-skinned beans and the black-skinned beans, the pink-skinned Mexicans and the black-skinned Mexicans, and all the Mexican shades in between. Ernesto doesn't have to ask me if I'm Mexican. He knows.

Okay already. Just the sight of me and Ernesto together makes people laugh. Because he's so Catholic, my brothers call him "the altar boy" behind his back, and me "Lala, the lady wrestler" to my face, but it only makes me want to protect Ernesto even more from the cruelty of the world. Me, I'm used to it, but *pobre* Ernesto with his heart like a soft-boiled egg, he hasn't a clue.

To tell the truth, Ernesto Calderón is corny. Not quite funny, but funny himself. On the verge of laughable. Know what I mean? His jokes always a little off.

—So the teacher asks Juanito to use the words "liver" and "cheese" in a single sentence.

And Juanito says, "Liver alone, cheese mine."

Lo más triste is Ernesto at parties. He does card tricks and bad impersonations—an Irish brogue, an Italian tourist, a Hindu holy man. Pathetic. And the saddest thing is he thinks he's pretty good. Poor thing.

He has a sexy voice, Ernesto does. A velvety velour to it, like the Prince Popo paintings painted on black velvet you find at the flea markets. As regal as a drum. But the worst laugh on Earth, I'm not kidding. Goofy as a hyena. The kind that makes people in a restaurant look up from their plates and ask, —My God, what's that?

And when he laughs he throws his head back like a cartoon hippopotamus, tonsils showing and the bottom of his molars exposed. I can see all his dental work, but what surprises me is that he has extra teeth alongside his molars, a whole extra set like a monster or something, only it's not a detail you can point out. —Hey, you've got extra teeth, huh? Especially with his being so sensitive, so I don't say anything.

Ernesto takes me to see *The Good, the Bad, and the Ugly,* but believe it or not, when we get to the theater we find it's paired with a funky Elvis-in-concert movie. Of course, it's the Elvis film that's first and lasts forever. Neither Ernesto nor me can stand Elvis, but what are we going to do? We got here early. I tell him about how my cousin is named after Elvis and how my grandmother had a fit every time she heard his name, because of what Elvis said about Mexicans.

—No lie?

—Swear to God. Ask my brothers if you don't believe me.

Somebody in the back blows their nose like a bugle playing reveille. Christ Almighty! I look over my shoulder, and way off in the last row I see an old lady dabbing her face with a handkerchief.

Then Ernesto does something that makes me forget everybody else in the theater. He makes a little circle on my hand with one finger, a spiral round and round with spit. I have to shut my eyes, it makes the skin tingle, all the hair on my body stands up. Until a *viejita* down the row from us starts hacking a throatful of phlegm, a nasty business that's a real mood breaker.

Ernesto keeps playing with my hand, moving up my wrist, oblivious to everything but me, only I can't keep from peering over at the hacker— an old fart who looks just like my grandmother—till Ernesto takes my face in his hands and gives me a kiss that tastes like popcorn and pot. Honest, he takes me so off guard, I almost ignore the coughing coming from the row behind us.

Somebody must be unwrapping a *taco* or *torta*, because the place smells like fried meat. That's when I jerk my eyes open and see her. Her with her stink of *barbacoa*! The Awful Grandmother sitting right behind me watching me being kissed by Ernesto Calderón!

—Oh, my God, I say, pushing Ernesto off of me. I grab my purse and bolt toward the exit doors like if the place is on fire.

Ernesto catches up with me in the lobby by the hot dogs, but the smell of meat makes me feel like gagging.

—Ernesto, just take me home, okay? Please. I think I'm sick.

—What about *The Good, the Bad, and the Ugly*?

—I've already seen the bad and the ugly. The good can wait.

I don't tell Ernesto about the Grandmother. Later, when we're in the truck and I'm feeling better, I begin to think maybe it was just someone who *looked* like my grandmother. It just spooked me, that's all. That's how it is after Ernesto blasts me back to the real world with a cheeseburger and fries at Earl Abel's and a bad joke about Elvis Presley.

The worst thing about Ernesto is he does crazy things that are idiotic or cocky, like wearing a Levi's jacket with a marijuana plant painted on the back in Magic Marker. I mean, why do that? Might as well wear a sign that says to the cops, BUST MY ASS.

Shameless people like Ernesto amaze me. I wonder if this overconfidence comes from his being the man of the family. His father died a long time ago, and it's always been just him and his mom and sisters. Maybe his mother and sisters did the reverse of what my brothers did to me. Laughed at every joke, encouraged him to sing out loud as a child, applauded too much his performances at birthday parties, and brainwashed him by saying over and over, —Oh, Ernie, you kill me.

But I love him, corny jokes and everything. The truth, I love Ernesto because he's a goofus. Because he reminds me of my six brothers. Because he isn't anything like my six brothers. Because of his stupid sixth-grade humor, his boring card tricks, bad singing, and terrible posture. Weak chin, horrible laugh, skinny arms, and all. So Ernesto Calderón's not cool and handsome. So what? Don't matter. He's cool and handsome. . . .

. . . To me.

78

Someday My Prince Popocatépetl Will Come

—Marry someone who adores you, Mother said once. —Listen, you want a good life, make sure you're adored. Adored, you hear me? Lala, I'm talking to you. Everything else is crap, she said, ransacking the trash for the missing basket from her electric percolator. —Now where the hell did that coffee thingamajig go?

Maybe I'd met that someone who adored me. Could it be Ernesto Calderón was him? I'd had a dream about Ernesto even before I met Ernesto, and when he did appear, it was like I was trying to remember someone I already knew, someone I'd always known, even when I was floating around the Milky Way as milky dust.

Because of Father, I'm used to being adored. If somebody loves me they've got to say corny Mexican things to me, or I can't take them seriously. It makes me dizzy to hear Ernesto tell me, —Baby, if I die who will kiss you? You're my life, my eyes, my soul. I want to swallow you, masticate you, digest you, shit you.

Is that heavy or what?

So when Ernesto comes around on the very morning Mother's lecturing me on marriage, I don't know what to think. After all, maybe Ernesto Calderón is my *destino*.

—Listen up, Ernesto. You've *got* to ask my parents for their permission.

—For what?

—To marry me, silly, what else?

—Very nice. You've got it all figured out, haven't you?

I shrug, pleased with myself.

—Only you forgot one thing, Ernesto says. —You didn't ask me!

—Not with words exactly. With my body and soul.

—But don't you think we're too young to get married?

—We can be engaged till we're old enough. Lots of people do that.

—Look, don't even. I'm going to get in trouble, Ernesto says. —Forget about it.

—Don't you want to make *us* all right in the sight of God? You're the one always complaining I give you religious conflicts.

—God I can handle. It's my ma I worry about.

—Well, don't you want to?

Ernesto chews on the chain of his Virgen de Guadalupe *medalla* and looks at his sneakers. Then I hear him say, —Okay, I guess.

My heart winces, as if I'd let go a well rope, the bucket singing to the bottom. Too late. Ernesto is already on the other side of the screen door, saying hello to Mother, who's ignoring him.

I don't know why, but Mother has to choose today to experiment in the kitchen. The hottest month of the year, on the hottest dog day. Mother isn't a cook. She hardly ever cooks anything but stock Mexican ranch food—*fideo* soup, rice and beans, *carne guisada* stew, flour *tortillas*. But once in a while she gets these crazy ideas to create something new, and today is one of those onces.

When Father's truck crunches in the driveway, the house is hotter than ever, even with all the fans going. Mother's project is a foreign recipe she clipped from the pages of the *San Antonio Express-News*—chicken-fried steak—*güero* food. She spent the day preparing exotic items we could just as easily have ordered at the Luby's cafeteria—green beans with almonds, broccoli casserole, candied yams, pecan pie—but Mother swears, —Nothing beats homemade. And now here's Father blowing in like a northern wind across the plains states, swirling everything in his path.

—*¡Vieja!* My papers! Father says shouting. —Zoila, Lala, Memo, Lolo, everybody, quick! *¡Mis papeles!*

—What's happened?

—*¡La Migra!* Father says, meaning the Immigration. —They came to the shop today, and what do you think? Somebody told them I hire *ile-*

gales. Now they want proof *I'm* a citizen. Zoila, where are my discharge papers? Help me look for my papers!

When the Grandmother died, her photo and the framed Virgen de Guadalupe were moved to the living room next to the dual portrait of Presidents LBJ and Kennedy. That's when we had to stop watching television.

—To honor my mother, *vamos a guardar luto.* No television, no radio, Father had ordered. —We are in mourning.

Then he went into every room and drew all the curtains. He also covered the mirrors because that's the custom on the other side, but when we asked him why, he simply said, —Because it's proper. Maybe we weren't supposed to be thinking about how we look, or maybe he meant to keep Death from looking at us.

We lived without the jabbering of the television and radio for a while, like the house needed time to think, to remember, to think. When we talked we even lowered our voices like if we were in church. But we weren't in church. We were in *luto.*

The mirrors stayed covered for only a few days, but the curtains have been drawn tight ever since. Father's already ripping them open and filling the house with the steel-white Texas light of August. Dust swirls in the air.

—*Buenas tardes, señor.*

—Ernesto! Be of some use and help me look for my shoe box.

Father unlocks the walnut-wood armoire, dumping the contents of the drawers on the bed.

—They're coming back for me after lunch, he goes on. —Mother of the sky, help me!

Ernesto whispers to me, —Why's he looking for a shoe box?

—That's where he keeps all our important papers and stuff. Before Father inherited the walnut-wood armoire, he stashed everything in his underwear drawer. Now he stores them in a shoe box from one of his wing tips. But since we moved, well, who knows where the hell it is?

—But why would someone report you to la Migra, *señor?*

—The envy. People yellow from jealousy. How do I know, Ernesto? This is no time for talk, help me!

—Did you tell them you served in the U.S. Army, Father?

—I told, I told.

Then I imagine Father talking to the INS officers. Father's English has never been good. When he's nervous it comes out folded and creased, worse than in those old books he'd sent away for when he first came to this country and worked for Mister Dick. *How you say?*

—I told about Inchon; Pung-Pion; Fort Bragg; New Cumberland, Pennsylvania; Fort Ord; SS *Haverford Victory;* Peggy Lee, get out of here give me some money too. I even told a story.

—A story?

—How on our first trip to Tokyo we had to turn back to the Honolulu hospital when those *güeros* broke their arms and legs. You know how they like to sunbathe. They lay out on the deck, but then, what do you think? Out of nowhere the sea turned wild on us. I swear to you. A big wave came and rocked the boat like a hammock. A whole shipload of soldiers tumbled off the deck and wound up with broken arms and legs, and because of this we had to turn back. Ha, ha! What do you think la Migra said then? "We don't need stories, we need papers." Can you believe it! We don't need stories, we need papers! They even asked about your brothers, Lala. Thanks to God they were born on this side.

We turn the house upside down, but we can't find Father's shoe box. All the while Ernesto is pecking at Father, trying to find a way in to talk about him and me, but Father keeps saying, —Later, later. Father's desperate. We find drawers stuffed with old bills, letters, class photos, drapery rings, homemade birthday cards, food coupons, rubber bands, Wilson's rabies tags, but no shoe box. Father always prides himself on being organized. In his shop, every tool, every bolt of fabric, every box of tacks is in place, a scrap swept away before it hits the floor. It drives everyone nuts. But at home, Mother's chaos rules.

—All I ask for is *one* drawer for myself, is that too much? *One* little drawer and everyone sticks their hands in here. Zoila, how many times have I told you, don't touch my things!!!

—I'm not the only one who lives here, Mother wails. —Always, always blaming me, I'm sick and tired . . .

—Sick and tired, Father parrots in English. —Sick and tired . . . disgusted!

Everything has happened so fast after the Little Grandfather's death, after the Grandmother's stroke, after packing up and leaving one city for another, and then another, burying the Grandmother, giving away her things, the quarrels, the arguments, the not speaking, the shouting, and slowly life settling down for us to begin all over again. And now this.

—My things, my things, Father says, pulling his hair and jumping up and down like a kid having a tantrum. —They're coming back after lunch!!! And he whips back the drapes in each room, opens closets and dresser drawers, pokes under the bed.

—You're nuts, Mother says. —You act like they're going to deport you. I'll call the INS and see what's what.

Mother gets on the phone, and starts talking her English English, the English she speaks with *los güeros,* nasally and whiny with the syllables stretched out long like wet laundry on the clothesline. —*Uh. huh. Yesssss. Mmm-hhhhmm. That's right.* But after a while she hangs up because they put her on hold for too long.

—Now? Ernesto asks, meaning, Should I ask him now?

—No, Ernesto, wait!

Lolo and Memo have their lawn-mowing business to worry about. With the heat, they only do hard work in the early morning or after dusk. They save the hottest part of the day for the public pool. Only Lolo is home when Father appears, and when the shoe box doesn't turn up right away, he starts worrying he'll miss his appointment at the pool.

—So your friends are more important than your father? Father says. —This is an emergency. Lolo and Ernesto, please—go look for Memo. Bring him home now!

That's how it was we're all home when the shoe box turns up.

—Here it is, Mother says, disgusted.

—But where was it?

—In the *ropero,* she says. —The walnut-wood armoire.

—But who put it there? I looked in there.

—Your mother. How do I know? It was there.

Ernesto is plucking my elbow and twitching his eyebrows. —Not now, Ernesto, I whisper.

It isn't enough, though, that the box is found. We all have to climb in the van and accompany Father to his workshop on Nogalitos Street, even Ernesto. —Five minutes, Father says. —I promise. But after what seems like forever, when it seems Father has hauled us all to witness nothing, the INS drive up in those famous green vans. There are two officers, and what's really sad is one of them is Mexican.

—Now you see, I no lie, Father says, waving his papers. One dated the 23rd of November, 1949, said he was honorably discharged from the Armed Forces, and the other says:

> *Private Inocencio Reyes ASN 33984365 has successfully completed the Special Training Course conducted by this Unit and is graduated this twenty-first day of June 1945 at New Cumberland.*

But the one Father is proudest of is signed by the president.
—This one, Lala, you read to everybody, Father says.
—Do I *have* to?
—Read! Father orders.

REYES CASTILLO, INOCENCIO

To you who answered the call of your country and served in its Armed Forces to bring about the total defeat of the enemy, I extend the heartfelt thanks of a grateful Nation. As one of the Nation's finest, you undertook the most severe task one can be called upon to perform. Because you demonstrated the fortitude, resourcefulness and calm judgment necessary to carry out that task, we now look to you for leadership and example in further exalting our country in peace.

/signed/ Harry Truman
The White House

The INS officers simply shrug and mumble, —Sorry. But sometimes it's too late for I'm sorry. Father is shaking. Instead of —No problem, my friend which is Father's usual reply to anyone who apologizes, Father runs after them as they're getting in their van and spits, —You . . . *changos*. For you I serving this country. For what, eh? Son of a mother!

And because he can't summon the words for what he really wants to say, he says, —Get outta here . . . Make me *sick*! Then he turns around and comes back in the shop, pretending he's looking for something in the stack of fabric bolts.

We drive back home in silence, the *chicharras* droning in the pecan trees, the heat a wavy haze that rises from the asphalt like a mirage. Father looks straight ahead like a man cut out of cardboard.

When we pull up the driveway, I send Ernesto home and tell him to forget about it, forget about everything. —Tomorrow, maybe? Should I come back and ask him tomorrow?

—Just will you quit it already, Ernesto, I hiss. —Leave me alone!

Even before we open the door, there's a terrible smell from the kitchen, worse than beans burning—Mother's home-cooked dinner! Mother has a fit. —All that work, for what? For your shit! I've had it!

It's the closest Mother's ever come to breaking down and crying, except Mother's too proud to cry. She tears off one shoe and throws it against the living room wall on top of the television set before locking herself in the bedroom. I think Mother was aiming at the Grandmother's portrait, or maybe the ones on either side, la Virgen de Guadalupe or the one of LBJ/Kennedy, I'm not sure. But the shoe strikes the wall, leaving a big black scuff mark like a comet and an indentation we have to plaster with spackle and paint over when we move.

Father scratches his head with both hands and stands in the living room blinking. The house a mess. Drawers open, couch cushions on the floor, dinner burnt and stinking, Mother locked in the bedroom. And here's Father with his shoe box, a few papers, his wooden domino box stuffed with my childhood braids, the Grandmother's toffee-striped *caramelo rebozo*, which he wraps around himself like a flag.

—Sick and tired, he says, slumping into his orange La-Z-Boy. For a long time he just sits there guarding that box of junk like the emperor Moctezuma's jewels. —My things, he keeps muttering. —You understand, don't you, Lala? Your mother . . . You *see*? You *see* what happens?

It's like when I was little. —Who do you love more, your mother or your father? I know better than to say anything.

Almost immediately after, somebody takes down the double portrait of LBJ/Kennedy. And just as soon as the *susto* is over, Father is on the telephone to anyone and everyone who will listen. Monterrey. Chicago. Philadelphia. Mexico City.

—Sister, I'm not lying to you. So there I was, it was my word against the government's . . . You don't have to believe me, brother, but this happened . . . What a barbarity! *Compadre,* who would believe this could happen to me, a veteran . . . It's an ugly story, Cuco . . . But to finish telling you the story, cousin . . . And there you have it.

And there it is.

79

Halfway Between Here and There, in the Middle of Nowhere

Father comes home with the news, and the words cause my heart to freeze. —We're going home.

Father had a big fight with Marcelino Ordóñez of Mars Tacos To Went that ended with Father cursing his old friend Mars of long ago, cursing all Chicanos for acting like Chicanos and giving Mexico a bad name, cursing the borrowed fifty dollars, the Second World War, the savage border, this rinky-dink stinky *calcetín* of a Texas town, then heaving into a flash flood of tears at the memory of his mother.

—I curse you and the mother who bore you, Father said. Well, not exactly. What he really said was a little stronger, but, since he *is* my father, I can't repeat it without some disrespect.

I curse you and the mother who bore you. At the word "mother," Father remembers the wheeze in his heart. —¡*Ay! madrecita*, if you'd lived to be a thousand years, it would not be enough! And it's as if at that very moment his mother is putting a pin through his heart to see if he's still alive, as if his mother is holding him again in her soft, fleshy arms. Mother with her smell of food fried in lard, and that smell the smell of home and comfort and safety.

Mars raised the rent on Father's shop again.

—I'm losing money. Building needs repairs. See that crack? Whole damn foundation's about to buckle, I kid you not. And the roof is leaking. And taxes. What else can I do? Ain't rich, you know.

Father picks on a tack on the bottom of his shoe. A whole lot of nothing, Father thinks, to explain who knows what.

—You it was who called la Migra!

—What'chu talking about, man?

—You it was. You called la Migra. Explain. How is it the Immigration only came to my shop that day, and not yours, eh?

—Man, *estás zafado*. You shitty *chilangos* always think you know everything!

—*Baboso*. Can't even speak your mother tongue!

—I can speak my mother tongue all right, but you can bet it ain't Spanish.

The words turn from bad to ugly to worse until how it ends is this.

Father has to move.

We pack up the compressor, the sawhorses, the pegboard of hammers and scissors and tack strippers and clamps, the rolls of cotton batting and bolts of fabric, the webbing, coil springs, Italian twine, yardsticks, chalk, staples, and tacks, disassemble the homemade cutting tables and shelves, the slouched books of fabric samples in ring binders, the prize Singer one-eleven W fifty-five.

When the shop is almost empty, Father tugs at his mustache and looks out at the street, past the red and yellow letters of KING UPHOLSTERY, to something beyond that we can't see.

—*Estoy cansado*. Sick and tired, Father mutters in his funny English. —Make me sick.

Nogalitos. Old Highway 90. Father remembers too clearly the route south, and it's like a tide that tugs and pulls him when the dust rises and the cedar pollen makes him sneeze and regret he moved us all to San Antonio, a town halfway between here and there, in the middle of nowhere.

That terrible ache and nostalgia for home when home is gone, and this isn't it. And the sun so white like an onion. And who the hell thought of placing a city here with no large body of water anyway! In less than three hours we could be at the border, but where's the border to the past, I ask you, where?

—Home. I want to go home already, Father says.

—Home? Where's that? North? South? Mexico? San Antonio? Chicago? Where, Father?

—All I want is my kids, Father says. —That's the only country I need.

There is only one bed in the entire Hotel Majestic that isn't a single. Can you believe it? *Una cama matrimonial* is what Ernesto asks for, and *una cama matrimonial* is all there is, literally. The Hotel Majestic makes its money on Mexico City tourists, not honeymooners. Lucky for us, that one bed is ours. Room 606, a corner room on Madero and the main plaza—el Zócalo, a little noisy, the desk clerk warns, because of the rooftop cafe, will we mind? We won't.

Ernesto's Monterrey cousin gets us the room. He's a travel agent and has connections with the "O-tel Ma-yes-tic." That's how we get a cheap deal for the week, and the no-questions-asked about my lack of a visa. Papers? Andrew Jackson's face on a twenty.

Room 606. The most beautiful room in the world! Our *cama matrimonial* crowned with an iron headboard as elegant as a Picasso. Candelabra sconces on either side too. A little plaster angel on one wall. And tall French windows wearing a crooked pair of nubby curtains, and white sheers that look great when the wind blows through them. Because of Mexican Independence Day, buildings are draped with strings of colored lights, and strands of the green, white, and red climb like a spiderweb along the whole facade of the Hotel Majestic, including room 606.

Perfect. I try to memorize everything so I'll never forget it the rest of my life. And to top it all off, there's a huge mirror on one wall, so big you wonder how the workmen ever got it upstairs without laughing. As soon as the bellhop disappears, Ernesto and I jump on the bed like little kids, leap at each other, happy as dolphins.

The ceiling with its scrolled molding like frozen cream pies.

—Did I ever tell you, Ernesto, how we always had to share food?

When you have nine people in a family, you can never buy luxury food like Lucky Charms cereal. You get cornflakes. Like that. You could never get anything just for yourself. But once in a while, if Father went shopping with us for groceries, he'd buy something deluxe, like a Morton frozen pie. Except after we divided it among so many people, we only got a tiny sliver, a piece from four to five o'clock, hardly enough to satisfy you. Once I saved up my money and bought a whole pie, just for me. Strawberry, I remember it was. I ate a wedge as wide as twelve o'clock to seven. Then I was satisfied, and only then did I offer any to my brothers. That's how I feel here in this room. Like I got the whole pie.

Viva's right, about destiny I mean. About helping it along sometimes. I feel like I'm in a movie, my arm against the pillow, Ernesto's shoulder against the sheets. Me living my life, and me watching me live my life. Like some great movie. Better than a cheesy movie, because I'm in it.

It's wonderful to lie on a bed after sleeping on a bus for two days. I unpack the *caramelo rebozo* and drape Ernesto in it. When I rummaged the walnut-wood armoire for my birth certificate just before leaving, I grabbed the Grandmother's *rebozo* on an impulse. "Good lucky." Ernesto looks beautiful in it, I'm not kidding. That boy body of his, hairless and smooth, the candy stripes against his skin. A real sin men don't wear *rebozos.*

Ernesto pulls me toward him, but I push him away, so I can look at him a little longer. Whenever Father eats anything especially delicious, he always force-feeds me a bit. —*Prueba,* try it, he says, holding something so close to my face I can't see it. Ernesto's like that, pushing himself so close to me, I can't stand it. And I almost wish he'd shut his eyes so I could watch him without having him watch me.

—Lalita, he says, calling me by my baby name. —Lalita.

All the parts of me coming back from someplace before I was born, and me little and safe in the warmth of that name, well loved, myself again. The syllables making me arch and stretch like a cat, roll over with my belly showing, preen. And laugh out loud.

—Once I'm pregnant, then they'll *have* to give us their blessing, your ma and my father, I mean. Then they won't be able to say anything, and we can get married.

—Will you forget about them for now, Ernesto says, gathering my face in both hands as if I'm water.

We're thirsty, thirsty. We're salt water and sweet. And the bitter and the sad mixes with the *dulce*. It's as if we're rivers and oceans emptying and filling and swelling and drowning one another. It's frightening and wonderful all at once. For once, I feel as if there's not enough of me, as if I'm too small to contain all the happiness inside me.

We fall asleep to the noise of el Zócalo, the rush of traffic. The green, white, and red lights draped across our window blink on and off, casting shadows in the room. When we wake, our room is dark, the bulbs have quit their flickering. Trash tumbles across the empty square. Here and there a few stragglers wander home. Ernesto comes up from behind and presses himself against me, me and him leaning out on the balcony taking in the Mexico City night.

A huge Aztec moon rises above the Presidential Palace.

—Man, Lala, just think! Everything happened in this square. The Ten Tragic Days, the Night of Sorrows, the hangings, shootings, the pyramids and temples, the stones taken apart to build the mansions of the *conquistadores*. It all happened right here. In this Zócalo. And here we are.

But I'm thinking of the women, the ones who had no choice but to jump from these bell towers not so long ago, so many they had to stop letting visitors go up there. Maybe they'd run off or been run off. Who knows? Women whose lives were so lousy, jumping from a tower sounded good. And here I am leaning on an iron balustrade at the holy center of the universe, a boy with his hands under my skirt, and me with no intention of leaping for nothing or nobody.

Some old guy in a fedora cuts a diagonal across the plaza, and just when he gets to the the circle of light of a fluted lamppost beneath our window, just stands there and looks up, as if he can see us on the sixth floor of the Majestic leaning out the balcony of room 606. He's a thin man wearing clothes from the time of before, wide tie, big-shouldered, double-breasted suit like an old gangster movie. He bends down to tie his shoe but doesn't take his eyes off me. He looks like my father. He looks as if he's pissed. As if he knows. But he can't really see what we're doing, can he?

And just when I'm beginning to worry, the bell towers begin to clang. Midnight. The witch's hour. That man down there just looking up at me, lighting a cigarette, taking his time standing there, and I want to push Ernesto away, and I want Ernesto to stay, and the bell towers of the church clanging and clanging in alarm, in protest, holding in a howl that could shake all the bats from el Zócalo. That dizzy joy, so when the moment rises and shivers and passes, and the church quits its riot, there's only me laughing my witch's laugh.

The man down there is gone. Like if he'd never been there.

*A*t 6 A.M. the reveille and drum from the soldiers in el Zócalo raising the Mexican flag.

Ernesto and I tumble and toss and bury ourselves under blanket and pillows till they quit, an unbearably long time it seems. In my half sleep, I hear the ticking motor of a van and think it's Father. Then I remember where I am. Father's miles from me.

We fall into a delicious half-sleep just as the city is waking, revving up to go, and the main heart of the revving is right here at the center of the universe . . .

El Zócalo. The Mexico City Monte Carlo Grand Prix. *Vroom-vroom.* Cars howl, VW taxis the color of M&M's *putt-putt*, a police siren yowls, brakes squeal, motors grunt, a stalled engine whinnies but won't turn, the first few notes of "La Cucaracha" play on a fancy car horn, motorbikes bleat, horns *toot-toot* an impatient trumpet tap, motors flubber, blurt, fart, hiccup, belch, rumble in the screech of a left-hand turn, a heat rises, the light in the room bright even with the curtains closed, a truck gurgles, growls, an endless roar of engines heaving and pulling in a great wave like the ocean, a coughing, sputtering, gargling of motors and wheels, while a hubcap pops and flips and rattles to a stop like a drum finale.

Then the bells of *la catedral* begin to clang, all twelve of them, one at a time, like a woman banging on the bars of her cell demanding to be let out.

Above us, the horrible grating of iron chairs being dragged across tiles, the restaurant opening for breakfast. There's so much racket reaching room 606 it's laughable. Just when I fall back to a lukewarm sleep, I dream this dream. Ernesto kissing the instep of my foot. When the door clicks shut, I wake up, and I'm alone.

On the bedside table, a gardenia in a toothbrush glass; a half-smoked Cuban cigar; five snuffed votive candles to la Virgen de la Macarena, the Virgin of the matadors; and a plate with half a cantaloupe rind. When I get up to pee, I find a note written on the mirror with soap—WENT TO MASS.

I go back to bed. On the opposite wall, the little plaster angel frowns at me. It looks like the little angel under la Virgen de Guadalupe. In fact, it *is* the same angel.

The plaster angel starts it:

—Your grandmother's *rebozo*. And with the Church as witness. And that man who could've been your father watching. You should be ashamed.

—I *should* be ashamed . . . How come I'm not?

—*Válgame, San Rafael,* says the little angel. Then he begins with his you-oughts and you-shoulds, and that's when I get really mad.

—Shut up! But when he won't, I throw my sandal at him. That makes him quit, and I feel better.

—Pain in the ass, I say, opening the French windows. The morning breeze plumps open the white sheer curtains, the heat and the noise of el Zócalo comes in even stronger. The light powdery like silver dust. There are no volcanoes in sight under all the smog, only the merciless Mexico City light.

I watch the world below going about its business, crisscrossing, a speaker blasting a fuzzy version of "Waltz of the Flowers," brilliant masons lining up for work, beggars begging, women selling pink meringue cakes, vendors of cream of abalone, emery board sellers, students, clerical workers. Everything has always been here, will always be here. Millions of citizens. Some short and stocky, some lean and tall, some charming, some cruel, some horrid, some terrible, some a pain beyond belief, but all of them to me beautiful. In fact, the most beautiful in the world.

I think about walking over to La Villa, just to see what my grandmother's house looks like, just to walk around the neighborhood, but I can't move. I write in my journal. I lounge around wearing Ernesto's T-shirt and tell the housekeeping maid to go away. I order breakfast *flautas* and eat these in bed with the wind blowing the white sheers in and out, puffing them up, whipping them out, a mouth exhaling, inhaling.

Every once in a while I stand at the balcony and take it all in. I'm so happy I feel like shouting, but what would I say? There aren't enough words for what I'm feeling. I consider writing a song and fill eleven pages in my journal with babbling, a tiny knot of handwriting so tangled and tight it looks like crocheting. Maybe hours go by, maybe minutes, I don't know or care.

When I hear the key scratching at the lock, my heart spirals. I swallow Ernesto with my arms and my legs and my mouth. I want to dissolve him inside me again. I want to be him and for him to be me. I want to empty myself and fill myself with him.

—No, don't. Don't, don't, don't . . . Ernesto says, pulling me off him by the wrists. Don't, he keeps saying over and over.

His mouth shaking. A little tree before rain.

—What's the matter? Hey, don't, Ernesto, please. Don't cry.

But it's hopeless to talk him out of it. His face crumples, and he hiccups into a long uncomfortable seizure. I don't know what to do. It's like he robs the tears from me. And now I have to fish a crumpled Kleenex from the bedside table and hand it to him.

—Here, I say. —It's not too dirty. He bugles away.

Too late. No use getting words out of this one. I watch and wait and wonder.

Then he tells me a story so unbelievable you'd think I made it up.

—Lala, you and I, we can't . . . Ernesto says between sniffles. —I can't marry you.

My mouth crimps like if he'd hit me with a stick. —What are you talking about? I try to sound tough, but it comes out thin and squeaky. I look at him carefully, like if I'd never seen him before, and in a way, I haven't. He's radiant, glowing, like if he's emitting light. I try to sit close to him, on top of him even, but he's the one pushing me away this time.

—Now just let me talk, Ernesto says seriously, without looking me in the eye, almost as if he can't look me in the eye. He moves to a chair opposite the corner of the bed, like a lawyer about to deliver bad news. —I went to mass across the street, and before mass they were hearing confession. And then the next thing I know I'm talking to this priest. About how we came to be here, me and you. And how my mother doesn't know where I am right now. And he got me thinking.

Ernesto pauses here like he's having a hard time putting his thoughts into words. Then he just delivers his blow: —So we're a sin, Lala. You and me. We can't just run off and then expect to marry and make it all better. Sex is for procreation only. The Church says so. And we're not married yet. And the fact is, I can't marry you; you're not even Catholic.

—It's your ma, right? Your ma's behind all this. Your ma and that twisted religion that thinks everything's evil.

—Don't make fun of my faith, Ernesto says, getting mad. —Anyway, Ernesto continues, pulling himself together and looking at his hands, —the *padrecito* made me realize . . . understand stuff.

—Like what kind of stuff? I say, trying not to flinch, because by now I can feel my face getting hot.

—Stuff I'd been feeling. Been mixed up about, only I didn't want to scare you, Lala. And what he made me see is this. My mother is like la Virgen de Guadalupe, and I'm her only son, and now I've hurt her. I just understood everything. Then when I asked for forgiveness, it's like I've become myself again. I decided to maybe think about religion first. Practice celibacy maybe.

—Like become a priest?

—Well, no, yes, maybe. I don't know. But at least for now. I made a vow to quit putting unholy things inside me, like pot and shit.

—Or putting yourself into unholy things, like me, right?

Ernesto shakes his head. —You just don't get it, Lala. You just don't want to get it, is all.

—Oh, I get it, all right. You just had to get God's permission to get you off the hook. You're scared. You're too chickenshit to think for yourself and become a man. So you have to ask the Church to tell you what's right and wrong. You can't brave listening to your own heart. That would cost you too much. After all, we wouldn't want to upset your mother.

—That's what I mean, Ernesto says angrily. —We don't have the same spiritual values. How can we get married if we don't even believe in the same things? Don't you see? It's just a disaster waiting to happen, Lala. Look, I still care about you . . .

—Care! I thought it was love a few hours ago.

—Okay, I still love you. Look, this room's already paid for till the end of the week. We can, I can still stay here with you, if you want me to. Do you want to? As friends?

—Friends? What's that?

He holds me in a strange awkward way, without our pelvis touching. I feel like laughing except I feel like crying. And I do cry, all day and all night, a hot oozing, like a wound that's draining. Ernesto wakes up every now and then and hugs me and cries too. We sleep twisting and turning all night, like a bad mattress commercial, and that God that I saw when he touched me flies out of the room, and the little angel on top of the bed seems to smirk and is full of it.

It's only later, weeks, I'll realize those tears, they're the only honest thing he ever said to me.

By the next morning, Ernesto is gone, leaving enough money for food for a few days and a bus ticket back to San Antonio, asking me to take care of myself, making me feel terrible about having begged him to "steal" me, because, after all, this was my great idea.

I'm as evil as Eve. I feel sick and room 606 looks small and grimy, closing in on me. When I get up to pee, I realize my period has begun, and it's as if my whole body has been holding its breath, and now it can finally release everything I've been holding inside. I gotta get out of here, I think.

I get dressed, tie the Grandmother's *caramelo rebozo* on my head like a gypsy, and start sucking the fringe. It has a familiar sweet taste to it, like carrots, like *camote,* that calms me. I wander downstairs and out into the downtown streets of the capital, walking this way and that, till I wind up in the direction of La Villa. I don't stop until I find myself in front of the house on Destiny Street. But everything's changed. They've painted it an ugly brown color like *caca,* which only makes me feel worse.

The house on Destiny Street is ugly. A chubby woman walks hurriedly out the gate clutching a plastic shopping bag, but she doesn't pay any attention to me. Those rooms we slept in, the patio where we played with la Candelaria, the street of our remembrances gone.

I walk over to the *basílica.* The streets turned into trashy aisles of glow-in-the-dark Guadalupes, Juan Diego paperweights, Blessed Virgin pins, scapulars, bumper stickers, key chains, plastic pyramids. The old cathedral collapsing under its own weight, the air ruined, filthy, corncobs rotting in the curb, the neighborhood pocked, overpopulated, and boiling in its own stew of juices, corner men hissing *psst, psst* at me, flies resting on the custard gelatins rubbing their furry forelegs together like I-can't-wait.

The old church is closed. They've built an ugly new building with a moving escalator in front of Juan Diego's *tilma.* Poor Virgen de Guadalupe. Hundreds of people ride the moving conveyor belt of humanity. The most wretched of the earth, and me among them, wearing my grandmother's *rebozo* knotted on my head like a pirate, like someone from the cast of *Hair.*

I didn't expect *this.* I mean the faith. I mixed up the Pope with *this,* with all *this, this* light, *this* energy, *this* love. The religion part can go out

the window. But I didn't realize about the strength and power of *la fe*.
What a goof I've been!

A wisp of a woman sweeping herself feverishly with a candle. A
mother still in her apron blessing herself and blessing her daughters. A
ragged *viejita* who walked here on her knees. Grown men crying, machos
with their lips mumbling prayers, people with so much need. Help me,
help me!

Everybody needs a lot. The whole world needs a lot. Everyone, the
women frying lunch putting warm coins in your hand. The market sellers
asking, —What else? The taxi drivers racing to make the light. The baby
purring on a mother's fat shoulder. Welders, firemen, grandmothers,
bank tellers, shoeshine boys, and diplomats. Everybody, every single one
needs a lot. The planet swings on its axis, a drunk trying to do a pirouette.
Me, me, me! Every fist with an empty glass in the air. The earth throbbing
like a field ready to burst into dandelion.

I look up, and la Virgen looks down at me, and, honest to God, this
sounds like a lie, but it's true. The universe a cloth, and all humanity
interwoven. Each and every person connected to me, and me connected
to them, like the strands of a *rebozo*. Pull one string and the whole thing
comes undone. Each person who comes into my life affecting the pattern,
and me affecting theirs.

I walk back to the hotel. I walk past pilgrims who have walked here
all the way from their villages, past dancers performing with rattles on
their ankles and great plumed headdresses, past vendors hawking candles
and night-light Lupes. I walk through the Alameda, green oasis, and sit
down on an iron bench. A man carrying a pyramid of cotton candy floats
by as ethereal as angels. A pushcart full of sweet corn rolls past and makes
my stomach grumble. A girl and her young lover neck hungrily across
from me. They remind me of me and Ernesto. Seeing them so happy only
breaks my heart.

And then what happened? I hear my mother asking me. And then I felt
as if I'd swallowed a spoon, like something had lodged itself in my throat,
and every time I swallowed, it hurt.

Me duele, I say softly to myself, I hurt. But sometimes that's the only
way you know you're alive. It's just like Aunty Light-Skin said. I feel like
I'm soaked in sadness. Anyone comes near me, or just brushes me with
their eyes, I know I'll just fall apart. Like a book left in the rain.

I get back to room 606 at the Hotel Majestic just as the sun is slanting, sending deep shadows along the downtown buildings, making the buildings along the other side of the hotel, the Presidential Palace and *calle de la* Moneda, glow like the paintings you see of Venice. But I'm too tired to appreciate the light.

I throw myself on the bed and fall asleep immediately. I sleep like I've been swept away by rain and river. And just before waking, I dream this dream. The night sky of Tepeyac when the dark is fresh. And in that violet ink, I see the stars tumble and nudge and somersault until they assemble themselves into the shape of a woman, into the shape of the Virgin. La Virgen de Guadalupe made up of stars! My heart floods with joy. When I wake up, the pillow is damp, and the sea is trickling out from my eyes.

Always remember, Lala, the family comes first—la familia. *Your friends aren't going to be there when you're in trouble. Your friends don't think of you first. Only your family is going to love you when you're in trouble*, mija. *Who are you going to call? . . . La familia*, Lala. *Remember.*

The twinkling lights strung outside the balcony are lit. In that carnival of darkness and light, I fumble for the phone and hear my voice ask for a long distance line, please, *por cobrar.*

—Do you accept?

—Yes, yes! I hear Father's voice say desperately. —Lala! Lalita? *Mija*, where are you, *mi vida*?

My mouth opens as wide as a fatal wound, and I hear myself howl, —Papá, I want to come home!

81.

My Disgrace

*I*n the lobby of the Hotel Majestic, I wait with my bags ready for Señor Juchi, Father's *compadre*, the one I used to call Coochi when I was little. Every now and then, I peer out on Madero Street, expecting a car to stop at any moment for me. But when Señor Juchi finally appears, it's from the direction of el Zócalo, and on foot, with a woman he introduces as his *señora*.

Father sent them. Until Father can get here himself, I'm to stay with Señor Juchi and his wife at their apartment in Barranca del Muerto. It's a short metro ride from el Zócalo with only one change of trains. I've never met *la señora* till now. I like her. I like her way of calling me *mija* and walking alongside me arm in arm, the way women do here when they walk together, with a lot of affection and protection radiating from them like the sun.

Señor Juchi and his wife pretend not to stare at me on the subway ride to their place, but I can feel their eyes on me. Their faces filled with worry and something else, which I can only call heartsickness. A look of absolute pity mixed with shame. I ought to know. I feel it too, but not for myself. They act like I've been in the clutches of Jack the Ripper and not someone I love. And how can I tell them any different? People only believe what they want to believe sometimes, no matter what story you're ready to tell them.

Señor Juchi is all talk, just the way I remember him, with those green eyes of his staring holes into your soul. He acts like he's a cop or something. That this, and that, and this. —When we call the authorities . . . *ese muchacho* can't get away . . . and do you know where he might be hiding?

Christ Almighty! Maybe he thinks it's for my own good that he should tell me how evil Ernesto is. How he's going to split him open with a Collins machete and beat him till he's *chicle,* or whatever else they do with men who run off and don't fulfill their obligations. It's such a corny old plot, isn't it? I don't know whether to laugh or cry.

That's a lie. Just as soon I get to their apartment and am installed in their guest room, I do know. I throw myself on the narrow twin bed and begin. Father's friends must think I'm crying because of *mi desgracia,* but it's not that at all. How can I explain, and even if I did, they don't want to hear it.

And it's like Aunty's dream about the handkerchiefs. I have a lot of tears to spend, lots and lots. I cry for hours, even in front of Señor Juchi and his wife, who are like strangers to me. I can't help it. I can't stop. Even when *la señora* knocks on the door and brings me a cup of chamomile tea, that Mexican antidote to everything. I slurp it up between sobs, lie down still hiccuping on the little twin bed in the room that was once her son's and, now that he's married, is *la señora's* sewing room, a room all done up in white now, like if it was waiting for me. And I'm thinking how when I was little Señor Juchi promised me a room of my own, a girl's room just like this one. Isn't it funny? That's what I'm thinking when they finally shut the door, and I'm lying there in the darkness on the narrow bed with the slippery chiffon bedspread, white as a wedding gown.

I know they're talking about me on the other side of the wall. I know they're *tsking-tsking,* and thinking all kinds of things, wondering how I could do such a thing to a nice guy like my father, and how it's things just like this that happen to girls over there on the other side, and how glad they are they have no daughters where you have to worry about someone filling up their head with so much nonsense that they don't believe the ones who really love them but are willing to throw themselves in front of the first one who so much as tosses them a pretty word.

Oh, I can't explain. I can't in a million years tell them. I can't tell anyone. A huge sadness rises up in the chest, heaves like an Acapulco wave, and takes me with it. I put my hand on my belly bubbling and gurgling with my period. How can I tell Señor Juchi and his sweet wife that I don't want to talk about *ese muchacho,* that it doesn't do a bit of good to try to close the door and talk to me *a solas,* woman to woman, that I don't need to see a doctor, thank you, that I'm bleeding down there, and it would only embarrass me to have them examine me, no, thank you, I'm all right, honest I am, please.

Instead, I ask to be taken to La Villa, to the *basílica*. I ask, but *la señora's* sworn to my father not to let me out of her sight, and she's so kind, I can't argue. Father and Memo are on their way here, they tell me. They've been driving all night and should arrive pretty soon, if I know Memo. I'm relieved it's Memo and not Rafa who's coming for me. Memo I can handle. It's Father I worry about.

I feel so alone-alone.

In first grade I remember feeling like this; so miserable, all I ever drew was pictures of my family. Every day the same thing. I began at the left and ended at the right, like writing my name—family portraits on sheets of thick cream-colored paper the teacher called "manila," which I heard as "vanilla," maybe because they were the same color as ice cream.

First I drew me. Then I drew Memo, a step taller. Next to Memo, I drew a larger Lolo. Then Toto. Tikis. Ito. Rafa. Mother. And at the tallest end I drew Father with a cigarette beneath a thin mustache like Pedro Infante.

I could never draw myself without drawing the others. Lala, Memo, Lolo, Toto, Tikis, Ito, Rafa, Mama, Papá. Father's name in Spanish with the accent on the end. Papá. The End. *Tan tán*. Like the notes at the end of a Mexican song that tell you to applaud.

I'd never been alone in my life before first grade. I'd never been in a room where I couldn't see one of the brothers or my mother or father. Not even for a borrowed night. My family followed me like a kite tail, and I followed them. I'd never been without them until the day I begin school.

I remember I cry all day. And the next day, and the next. On the walk to school I drop my cigar box of crayons on purpose, or walk so slowly we get there after the doors are already locked.

Ito complains. —If I come late one more time teacher says you have to come to school, Ma.

Father solves everything. —*I'll* walk her to school. She's your *only* sister, he says, scolding the boys, especially Ito. —Don't you know it's a pleasure to walk your sister to school? But this just makes them groan.

—Don't tell anyone but you're my favorite, Father says, winking, though it's no secret.

On the walk to school, I show Father the Chinese laundry on the corner where my friend Sam works. —Father, did you ever go to China?

I make Father look at a house that has gold stars painted on the inside of a blue porch roof. —Who put that there?

I point out the mean dog and the meaner crossing guard lady. It's wonderful talking and not talking with Father next to me. I almost forget to feel sad until we get to the school door, then I make him promise not to leave me yet. —I don't like it here. Please don't leave me here, please don't leave me.

Father takes me home.

Mother's furious. —Take her back!

—But she doesn't *want* to go.

—I don't care! She *has* to go! Take her back!

This time we ride in the car. Father has to go to work, and he's already late. I must be crying, because Father is saying, —Don't cry anymore, don't cry anymore—over and over, gently and very quietly like he's the one crying.

When we get to my classroom, I remember Father standing in the doorway a long time, even after the door is closed. Inside the narrow door window, his long, thin face with the eyes like little houses.

I fall asleep with all my clothes on, on top of the chiffon bedspread, without bothering to get under the covers, and wake up with my head hurting, my mouth dry. Fumble to the bathroom, flick on the lights, and it's her! The Grandmother's face in mine. Hers. Mine. Father's. It scares the hell out of me, but it's only me. Amazing the way I look different now, like if my grandmother is starting to peer out at me from my skin.

—What you looking at? I say in my toughest voice. But she hasn't appeared to me since I crossed the border. I suppose she'll arrive with Father. And she'll let me have it. *Foolish girl! Your father loves you, and you chose to leave! I would never abandon someone who loves me. Why, in my day, my own father abandoned me, and I never forgot or forgave him. And here you are, ungrateful little fool.*

I go over what I'm going to say:

It's that I thought, we thought we'd get everybody's permission for us to marry. We thought this way we wouldn't be refused.

I can't tell Father it was all my idea, that I made Ernesto "steal" me, can I? That's not the kind of story you can tell your father. I don't want to hurt him even more, so I won't say anything I've decided. I won't cry like a girl either.

But when Father and Memo arrive, my heart hurts. Memo marches into the room first, shaking his head like I'm an idiot. I'm sure Father has made him swear not to say anything to upset me, because all he does is give me that look and shake his head, like I'm too stupid to even talk to. Then, before Father steps in, he adds, —Man, Lala.

—*Mija,* Father says when he sees me, and breaks into tears. He's shivering and heaving like if I'd died and came back from the dead. To see Father so overwhelmed is too much for me, and everything I told myself I wouldn't do when Father got here flies out the window.

Once Mother and Father had a big fight over something, and Mother was so pissed she threw Father out. He didn't come back home that night to sleep. Nor the next night, nor the next. He was gone four long days. Finally our cousin Byron told us Father was sleeping in the shop on a striped sectional. When Mother finally let Father come home, Father was changed. He ate his dinner on the TV tray on his orange Naugahyde La-Z-Boy with the TV tuned to the Spanish-speaking news, same as always, his feet soaking in a pink plastic washtub. But he looked different. Tired. Smaller. His face gray, with a lint-covered beard and his hair a mess. He looked *acabado,* finished. When he was through eating, he made a little room for me on the arm of his chair, hugged me hard, and whispered in my ear, —Who do you love more, your mother or your father? That was the one time I said, —*Tú,* Papá. You.

And now looking at Father so broken, so *acabado,* I want to tell him the same healthy lie.

Father holds me in his arms and sobs on my shoulder. —I can't, Father hiccups. —I can't. Even take care of you. It's all. My fault. I'm. To blame. For this. Disgrace.

I had thought Father had come to comfort me. But it's me who has to hold him up, who has to say, *I'm sorry. I love you, Father. Please don't cry, I didn't mean to hurt you.* But I can't say stuff like that. I don't say a word. My mouth opens and closes and the only thing that comes out is a thin, slippery howl, like raw silk unspooling from my belly. The body speaking the language it spoke before language. More honest and true.

82

The King of Plastic Covers

Sit beside the breakfast table
Think about your troubles
Pour yourself a cup of tea
And think about the bubbles

You can take your teardrops
And drop them in a teacup
Take them down to the riverside
And throw them over the side
To be swept up by a current
And taken to the ocean
To be eaten by some fishes
Who were eaten by some fishes
And swallowed by a whale
Who grew so old
He decomposed

He died and left his body
To the bottom of the ocean
Now everybody knows
That when a body decomposes
The basic elements
Are given back to the ocean

And the sea does what it oughta
And soon there's salty water

(that's not too good for drinking)
'cause it tastes just like a teardrop
(so they run it through a filter)
And it comes out from a faucet
(and is poured into a teapot)
Which is just about to bubble
Now think about your troubles

—"Think About Your Troubles," by Harry Nilsson, from The Point!

ig changes. Tapicería Tres Reyes is prospering under Uncle Baby and Uncle Fat-Face's direction. Father can't believe it. Father is invited to come back into the business. After all, he's family. But on the condition that he leave the managing to Fat-Face.

Uncle has redesigned the whole operation. He found an old taffy-apple factory on Fullerton Avenue, and now they take in mass volume restaurants, hotels, funeral parlors. Tapicería Tres Reyes is one of the main sponsors on José Chapa's morning radio show. Kennilworth, Winnetka, Wilmette have given way to work from Pilsen, Little Village, Humboldt Park, Logan Square, and Lakeview. The Brothers Reyes have their pictures taken with crowns and kingly gowns, and really it would all be great if Father didn't look so tragic. He wears the face of a King Lear instead of a King Melchor.

Who knows why, but eventually only Father's picture is featured in the advertisements. In both the pages of El Informador and La Raza newspapers, as well as on commercials on Channel 26, Father appears wearing an oversized crown beneath the caption—"Inocencio Reyes, El Rey de Plastic Covers."

Father's not happy. He doesn't want to be known as "The King of Plastic Covers," but that's what he is. How can he complain when they're overwhelmed with customers? But it's the kind of customer that wants his chrome kitchen chairs reupholstered or his car seats redone in tiger stripes. Father has to hire americanos, and slowly los polacos, los alemanes, even los mexicanos, give way to 'Mericans with their impatient trigger fingers on the staple gun. They're a younger generation of upholsterers who don't know how to hold a hammer and have never tasted a tack. In less than an hour they knock out huge curved couches made of crumpled blue velvet and circular swan beds with red satin headboards.

Father is forced to accept whatever job comes—barstools, booths, waterbeds, truck cabs, even a coffin lining for someone's pet cat. Uncle Fat-Face and Uncle Baby don't mind. They've always been careless about their craft. But Father's a perfectionist. This new prosperity makes him ashamed to call himself an upholsterer and confirms his worst suspicions. The public likes junk.

—But that's what the customers want! To look as if they live in Pancho Villa's villa. Oh, my Got! Father says.

It's true. The poor want to pretend they're kings. They don't like being poor, and if they can fool themselves a little with a bed that looks like the empress Carlota or Elvis slept there, all the better.

The good thing is Father doesn't have to pick up a hammer anymore, and he's a boss now with a whole workshop full of workers, but it makes him grieve to lose the fine antiques he once worked on. He sighs for the lost coins and cuff links, the blue pearls in the loose down cushions of his past.

There's more. Father and Mother are about to become grandparents. We came back to find Rafa hadn't been living with Ito and Tikis after all, but had moved in with his fiancée, Zdenka, a blonde as pale as a magician's rabbit. Their baby is due in a few months, and nobody even leaked a word about it to us, can you believe it? My brothers have always been experts at covering up for each other with healthy lies. They're not like me, determined to bludgeon Father with the truth at any cost.

Ito and Tikis are another story. They've gotten used to living as bachelors and refuse to come back and live under Father's roof. Father has to accept this. —They've become too American, Father says and sighs, —They sleep on the floor with milk crates for furniture. Like hippies! Father blames himself, and says he failed us.

It's too much. —*Ya no puedo,* Father says every evening when he collapses into his Naugahyde La-Z-Boy. —I can't anymore. And something about saying this makes his body believe it. But nobody takes Father seriously, because for the first time in his life, Father's making good money. In the words of Uncle Fat-Face, Tres Reyes is making a killing.

—Father, does that mean you're dealing *drogas* now? I joke.

Father says nothing. Then with a sigh:

—The ones on *drogas* are the customers.

But the biggest change since we've moved back to Chicago is how people act around me. Nobody mentions my "abduction." The more they don't mention it, the more it's obvious. Like the square on the kitchen door where that old Mexican calendar once stood. Somebody tore it down before I got back to Texas. But that rectangle, a paler shade than the rest of the door, just shouts, *What's missing here?*

My brothers. I thought they'd say something like if they ever catch Ernesto they're going to kick his ass. That's what brothers are supposed to say to save the family honor. "Honor." That's the word they're using nowadays to bring home the boys from Vietnam. But they don't say a thing, my brothers. I feel like I'm dragging around a clubfoot. Everybody refuses to look at me, and that just makes it worse.

I don't know anything, but I do know this. I'm not ashamed of my past. It's the story of my life I'm sorry about.

When I got back to San Antonio Viva gave me a good *regañada* for not knowing anything about birth control. —Shit, if you can't control your own body, how can you control your own life? What do you want? To self-destruct or something? She made me march over to Planned Parenthood with her, and I learned more about myself in that one visit than a year with Sister Odilia, that's for sure.

Viva's smart. Broke up with Darko after she started college. She finally figured out she didn't want to *marry* Darko, she wanted to *be* him. Isn't that funny? He's the one who got her thinking about going to school and helped her figure out financial aid. Everybody who comes into your life affecting the pattern. Darko got her unknotted and moving and all. But you sure don't have to marry him as a thank-you, right?

Ernesto got married. Viva said he knocked up some little *católica* who won't even let him smoke pot, can you believe it? Mister Holy Roller. Destiny's like that. Whatever you don't expect, you just better hunker down and duck.

It's just like the story of the volcanoes my Little Grandfather told me when I was a kid. That's just the way Mexicans love. They're not happy till they kill you.

You're the author of the *telenovela* of your life all right. Comedy or tragedy? Choose.

Ernesto. He was my destiny, but not my destination. That's what I'm thinking.

— *L*ate. Every first of the month they give us a story, Mother says. —They never pay the rent on time. Do they think we're made out of money? We've got bills too. They're taking advantage of us, that's what. *Te hablo.* I'm talking to you, Inocencio.

We bought a two-story walkup on Homan near Fullerton. We live on the top floor, and Rafa and Zdenka moved in downstairs. There's a family of *chaparritos* from Michoacán renting the basement. Mother thought it would be great to be a landlady. Until she became a landlady.

Mother has a steak sizzling on one burner, *tortillas* on another, and on another she's reheating *frijoles* for Father's dinner. —All hours, all hours I'm heating and reheating food. I'm going to retire. Then what, eh?

She complains, but food is the only language she's fluent in, the only way she can ask, *Who loves you?*

—*Mija*, please, Father says, snuffing out a cigarette and lighting another. —I suffered a big *coraje* with Fat-Face this morning over a love seat, and now this. I'm tired.

—Well, I'm tired too, Mother continues. —I've had it with those tenants. I tell you, if you don't do something, I will! Do you hear me?

—Don't worry, I'll take care of it, Father says.

And a short time later he comes back, mission accomplished.

—I fixed it.

—You're kidding. Already? How?

—I lowered the rent.

—Holy cripes! Are you crazy? I leave things for you to take care of and now look . . .

—Listen, Zoila, listen to me! Don't you remember when ten dollars meant a lot to us? Don't you? Remember when sometimes we didn't even *have* ten dollars, not even *that* sometimes till the end of the week? That wasn't so long ago, and I don't know about you, but never, *never* will I forget how ashamed I felt having to grovel to that dog Marcelino Ordóñez every first of the month. In English he adds, —Make me sick.

And he does look sick, his face an odd color, like silly putty.

Mother says nothing. I don't know if she's humbled, angry, or what, but something holy descends into the room and blesses her with the wisdom of silence for a little, just this once.

—You, to the kitchen, Mother says to me. —Help me with your

Father's dinner. Then, when he is out of hearing range, she adds, —He works hard.

Mother slices an avocado and chops up some *cilantro*, and has me squeezing limes for Father's limeade.

—You know what your problem is, Mother shouts into the living room. —You can't leave your work at the shop. Stop thinking about your troubles. You and Lala are always going over the past. It's over, it's finished! Don't think about it anymore. Look at me. You don't catch *me* worrying. Are you going to sit at the table, or do you want a tray? Mother shouts, tucking the *tortillas* into a clean dishcloth.

No answer.

—Inocencio, I'm talking to you, Mother continues.

Again, no answer.

—*Te hablo, te hablo.*

But Father doesn't answer.

A Scene in a Hospital That Resembles a Telenovela When in Actuality It's the Telenovelas That Resemble This Scene*

When I was little, there were things I couldn't think about without getting a headache. One: the infinity of numbers. Two: the infinity of the sky. Three: the infinity of God. Four: the finiteness of Mother and Father.

I've gotten over numbers one to three, but number four, well, no matter if you have a couple of lifetimes to get used to it, I don't think anybody is ever ready for their mother or father to die, do you? They could be one hundred and fifty years old, and you'd still yell, ——Hey, wait a minute!—when their time came. That's what I think.

In a way, you're waiting your whole life. Like a guillotine. You don't have to look up to know it's there. Somehow you think you're going to be courageous when the hour arrives, but I felt as if my bones had been drawn from me. The shock of seeing Father strapped in a hospital bed, anchored by machines and tubes, and Father not being able to talk, his body bubbling over in rage and fear and pain. I couldn't hold myself up. Like those mummies in the basement of the Field Museum; they pulled their innards out through the nostrils and stuffed them with cloves. That's how I felt when I watched Father, nurses hustling around him and hustling us out. I couldn't hold myself up.

Father's been moved to Intensive Care. He's only allowed visitors one at a time, and right now Mother is in there.

I'm scared.

I plant myself on a vinyl couch in the waiting area, but the room is full of little kids pretending to do their homework while watching *The Newlywed Game,* laughing too loudly and spitting sunflower seed shells at each other. I want to listen to anything but their racket and that stupid TV show. I keep trying to pray, but the words to the Hail Mary get tangled inside my head, like when you crochet and miss a stitch and have to unravel what you just did. It's been such a long time since I prayed. I wander out to the hall and find a row of plastic stack chairs, and this is where I arrange myself with my eyes shut so I can concentrate on praying.

—He wants to see you, Mother says, plopping herself in the plastic chair next to me. I must've been asleep, because the sound of her voice makes me jump. Then I don't have an excuse, I *have* to go in there.

—Lala.

Mother calls me back, patting the plastic chair next to her, motioning for me to sit down again.

—Lala, listen to me. She takes a deep breath. I know you think your father's perfect . . . Don't roll your eyes, smart aleck. You don't even know what I'm going to say. Listen. You think he's perfect, but you don't know him like I know him.

—I've known him my whole life!

—What's your life? You've only been on the planet fifteen years! What the hell does a *huerca* like you know?

—I know lots of things.

—Just enough to get you into trouble.

She means Ernesto. The fact that she's right only makes me more pissed.

—Lala, I'm talking to you. I was waiting to tell you this for when you were older, but with your father this sick, he might . . . Well, I just think it's time.

A pain flutters through my chest like a fish darting through a current of cold water, and I hear a voice inside my head say, *Pay attention! Listen. Even if it hurts.* Especially *if it hurts.*

—Your father, Mother says. —Before me and him got married . . . he already had a kid. Out of wedlock I mean. I didn't know about this before I married him, and even after, nobody told me nothing. For the longest.

His family kept it quiet. I didn't find out till after I had all you kids. Remember that trip we took to Acapulco? That's when I found out. I don't know if you remember this or not, but there was a *criada* who went with us. I can't think of her name. Her. That girl was your father's first kid. Your grandma was the big-mouth. She acted like I knew all along, but she was just taking her time, a fat spider waiting in her web. That was her, your grandmother, nothing but a troublemaker. If there was a way for her to tie knots in other people's lives, believe me, she'd find it.

She was shameless. For crying out loud, she had both the mother and daughter working for her right under her own roof. Even when we were there visiting! If that don't beat all! That's what kills me when I think about it. Right under my own nose she did this. I mean what kind of woman . . . ? And how the hell do you think *I* felt? No respect for me, his wife. What kind of lowlife? And los Reyes always pretending to be better than my family. We were poor, but we didn't do any filthy things like that, that's for sure. Christ! I feel like slapping the crap out of somebody even now.

Look, I didn't want you to find out from somebody mean and be surprised and hurt like I was, Lala. I just thought you should know, that's all.

I think about Candelaria bobbing in the sea at Acapulco. The sun sparkling in little gold flecks all around her. Her face squinting that squint that I make, that Father makes. Her face suddenly Father's face.

And I think about Candelaria's mother, the washerwoman I remember as being so old and ugly. Was Father in love and did love make her beautiful once? Or was he just a *chamaco* driven by hungers that have nothing to do with love? Did he ever lie awake nights and wonder about her? Did he ever worry what happened to his first daughter? Does it hurt to think about them? Is that why he's been so good to us? Father's always been such a sucker when it comes to kids.

—Poor Papa.

—That's *it*? Poor Papa? What about me! *I'm* the one that got treated like dirt. And he's never even said I'm sorry or anything. All these years. That's the worst of it. Your father . . .

—Ma, he's sick! Give him a break!

—Okay, so he's sick. It still don't make it right . . . Well, you going to go in and see him or what?

—You drop a bomb like this, and then you want me to go in there? Can't I just think for a minute?

—I ain't got all day. Hospitals make me sick. I need to get home. It's getting dark already.

—So go, go. The boys will be here soon. I'll get a ride home with somebody.

*F*ather has his eyes shut. He doesn't even know I'm here. A machine monitoring something inside him makes mountain ranges of "v"s across a screen. That nervous needle jumping up and down and bleeping now and then, and my father's heart not too good, and how I wish I could trade hearts, give him mine because it's too terrible to see Father like this, hooked up to tubes and plastic bags and machines, his body ragged and tired and broken, *acabado,* I think.

I pull a chair up next to his bed, and lay my head down on the sheets. Sometimes fluorescent lights seem almost peaceful, the roar of air conditioner and the soft beeping of some equipment doing its job. Sometimes the phones purr when they ring. Powder-blue uniforms march about silently in thick rubber shoes on blue tiled floors. The fluorescent lights, white cork ceilings, white sheets and white flannel blankets, and snowflake hospital gowns, the polished sheen of serious chrome and steel. Everyone laboring so quietly at times. And sometimes, but only sometimes, a voice, a laugh, a louder-than-life noise startles you from your hum of sleep.

The room floods with the stink of fried meat. Perched on the headboard, it's her! The Awful Grandmother. At the sight of me she clambers down and wraps herself around him.

—You've had him long enough. Now it's my turn, she hisses.

—No! Not yet, I say, anchoring Father by the ankles. —Let go of him, you greedy *perra.*

—You can't talk that way to me. I'm your grandmother.

—You're still a greedy bitch. Same as always. Nothing but a *metiche, mirona,* and *mitotera.* A busybody, an ogler, a taleteller. *Una hocicona.*

—Well, that's fine, because I'm you.

Then she laughs a terrible laugh like a knife slicing my cheek. This takes me by surprise, and I let go of my grip.

And I know I exaggerate a lot, but this is the truth. Father's face is no longer his face. His skin turns into the skin of a plucked chicken, wattled and fatty and yellow. And his eyes suddenly open, mean and beady, sweeping across the room from floor to ceiling like searchlights, like bells. It's the Awful Grandmother.

A little cry wants to come out of my mouth, but I'm too scared to cry. That awful face on top of the face I love. I don't know what to do. Father shuts his eyes again, and for a wisp of a moment all the life is drawn out of him, his body turns the color of wet sand. Very quickly. All of this happening in seconds before my eyes. The Awful Grandmother holds him to her breast, sighs, —*Mijo.*

—Live, live, I say to Father.

—He's tired of living, the Awful Grandmother snaps.

—Who are you to say? He needs us. We need him. We can't . . . I can't . . . live without him.

—And do you think I can live without him?

—But you're not living, you're dead.

—That's right, he's killing me. I'm all alone here!

—Alone? Aren't you . . . on the other side?

The Grandmother's face crumples and her mouth opens wide. —Well, it's that I'm halfway between here and there. I'm in the middle of nowhere! *Soy una ánima sola.*

Then she starts to howl and lets go of Father, and Father's color is his own again. And for the first time in my life, I feel sorry for the Grandmother. Her cries are like the yelping of a dog hit by a car, a terrible, ancient sadness, from below the belly. I've heard that cry before. I cried like that too, when the ambulance came for Father. A cry like a hiccup, over and over, and you can't do a thing about it.

—Grandmother?

I want to touch the Grandmother's shoulder, but don't know how. I never hugged her when she was alive, and it's too late to start now. —Grandmother, why do you keep haunting me?

—Me? Haunting you? It's *you,* Celaya, who's haunting *me.* I can't bear it. Why do you insist on repeating my life? Is that what you want? To live as I did? There's no sin in falling in love with your heart and with your body, but wait till you're old enough to love yourself first. How do you know what love is? You're still just a child.

—But I saw God when we made love.

—Of course you did. You think that's a miracle? Smell a flower and you'll see God too. God's everywhere. And yes, he's in the act of love too. And so? That boy's not the only one who can love you like that. There'll be others, there ought to be others, you *must* have others. *Ay*, Celaya, don't wind up like me, settling with the first man who paid me a compliment. You're not even a whole person yet, you're still growing into who you are. Why, all your life you'll be growing into who you are. That's the trouble. God gives us the urge for love when we're still children, but the age of reason doesn't arrive till we're well into our forties. You don't want somebody who doesn't know his own heart, do you? Look, he's a little boy, and you're a little girl. You'll find someone who's brave enough to love you. Some day. One day. Not today.

—Father says, "You'll never find anyone who loves you as much as your *papá*."

That's because he's jealous. Listen to me, jealousy is a terrible thing. Look where it got me. *Ay*, Celaya, no wonder I'm here, neither alive nor dead.

The Grandmother arranges herself on Father's pillow like a big, sad vulture, a pitiful thing to look at, sniffling and crying.

—Grandmother, that day on the boat in Acapulco, you told my mother about Candelaria, didn't you? That Father was also Candelaria's father, am I right? Why did you do that? Why? She didn't have to know, my mother. Why hurt her?

—It was because of love.

—Love!

—Yes, go ahead, make fun of a miserable like me. I told because of love, believe it or not. I wanted your father for my own. I didn't want to share him anymore. I told because your mother makes me sick with her smart remarks. I told because your mother hated me so, she hates me still. That's why I'm stuck here. I need everyone I hurt to forgive me. You'll tell them for me, won't you, Celaya? You need to tell them for me, I'm sorry Celaya. You're good with talk. Tell them, please, Celaya. Make them understand me. I'm not bad. I'm so frightened. I never wanted to be alone, and now look where I am.

—And why hasn't Father told me about Cande?

There are some stories a parent can't tell his child.

—But I thought Father was *un caballero*.

—He is. He's a gentleman. *Feo, fuerte, y formal*. That's your father.

Can't you see it's mortified him his entire life? That's why he tries so hard to be a good father with you all. To make up for it. He tries, Celaya. I hear him thinking late at night. I hear his thoughts.

Look, I didn't mean to hurt anyone, Celaya, I swear to you. But then I didn't understand how your father loved me. And I was so afraid. He came to visit less and less, and he had all you children to love. And I'd already lost Narciso years ago, and before that my own mother and father.

—But you have other kids, Grandmother.

—They don't understand me or love me the way Inocencio loves me. So completely you think you'll die when you lose that love, you think no one will ever love you like that again. Celaya, it's so lonely being like this, neither dead nor alive, but somewhere halfway, like an elevator between floors. You have no idea. What a barbarity! I'm in the middle of nowhere. I can't cross over to the other side till I'm forgiven. And who will forgive me with all the knots I've made out of my tangled life? Help me, Celaya, you'll help me cross over, won't you?

—Like a *coyote* who smuggles you over the border?

—Well . . . in a manner of speaking, I suppose.

—Can't you get somebody else to carry you across?

—But who? You're the only one who can see me. Oh, it's terrible being a woman. The world doesn't pay attention to you until you grow *tetas,* and then once they dry up, you turn invisible again. You're the only one who can help me, Celaya. You've got to help me. After all, I'm your grandmother. You owe it to me.

—And what do you owe me?

—What is it you want?!!!

I flick my chin toward the man sleeping between us. —Him.

The Grandmother cradles Father in her arms as if she has no intention . . . Then she looks up at me, with those eyes that are my eyes, and sighs, —For now. Not for always, but for a little while longer.

I feel a great relief, like if I'd forgotten how to breathe until now.

—You'll tell my story, won't you, Celaya? So that I'll be understood? So that I'll be forgiven?

—Tell, I'm listening.

—Now? Here? Well. All right, then. If you insist. Well, where do I begin?

—Where does the story begin?

—In my day, the storytellers always began a story with "So here my history begins for your good understanding and my poor telling . . ."

And so the Grandmother began: —Once, in the land of *los nopales*, before all the dogs were named after Woodrow Wilson . . .

A famous chronicler of Mexico City stated Mexicans have modeled their storytelling after the melodrama of a TV soap opera, but I would argue that the telenovela *has emulated Mexican life. Only societies that have undergone the tragedy of a revolution and a near century of inept political leadership could love with such passion the* telenovela, *storytelling at its very best since it has the power of a true Scheherazade—it keeps you coming back for more. In my opinion, it's not the storytelling in* telenovelas *that's so bad, but the insufferable acting.*

The Mexicans and Russians love telenovelas *with a passion, perhaps because their twin histories confirm la Divina Providencia the greatest* telenovela *screenwriter of all, with more plot twists and somersaults than anyone would ever think believable. However, if our lives were actually recorded as* telenovelas, *the stories would appear so ridiculous, so naively unbelievable, so preposterous, ill-conceived, and ludicrous that only the elderly, who have witnessed a lifetime of astonishments, would ever accept it as true.*

84

No Worth the Money, but They Help a Lot

*I*t's just as the Grandmother promised. Father is getting better, doing amazingly well, in fact, astonishing us all, though he complains too much, especially about the food. Mother brings Father his favorite—confetti Jell-O. He's eating this straight from the deli container with a plastic spoon. Now that he's out of Intensive Care, he has a television, and this is what he's watching. I know Death can't come and take him now that he's laughing at Cantinflas.

We sit around watching Cantinflas like he's God, and in a way, he is.

—How you doing, Mr. Reyes? At long last, Father's doctor arrives.

—Fine, thank you, doctor.

—No, not fine, Mother says. —All you do is complain, and now here's your chance to complain—so complain!

Filipino nurses pop in nonstop and joke with Father.

—Papacito, how are you today?

—*Mabuti*, Father says, surprising us with his Tagalog. —*Me siento mabuti*.

My brothers are arguing about whose fault it is a chaise lounge hasn't been delivered on time. Stop it! Here's Father sick and they're wasting oxygen over nothing. I try to think of something to change the subject so that Father won't get upset too.

—Father, can you remember your first memory? What's the oldest memory you can remember? The oldest, earliest thing you can think of.

Father pauses between spoonfuls of the confetti Jell-O and thinks. —Two men shot by the firing squad. This from the time when we lived in a house next to the army barracks. I used to wake up with the bugler. I remember once waking up one morning and standing on the bed, your grandmother still asleep with baby Fat-Face, the others weren't born yet. It was just me. I looked out the window looking for the bugler, and there he was, same as always, but what do you think? This morning they have two *pobres* with their eyes covered and their backs to the wall. And then I hear the guns go off, *boom!* And the two fall to the ground. Just like in the movies. *Boom* and they're dust. It gave me a fright I never forgot. I woke your grandmother with my crying. That's what I remember.

—Was this during the Cristeros uprisings?

—I don't know. I just know what I saw.

—How come you never told any of us this before?

— Nobody asked.

His life, mine, theirs, each, oh. And here is Father, a little leaf. Dry and light as snow. The wind could take him. THANK YOU, CALL AGAIN. I'd better ask now.

—And what is it . . . I mean, what would you say is the most important thing you've learned from all your years being alive? What has life taught you, Father?

—*¿La vida?*

—Yes.

He licks his plastic spoon and stares at the wall. A long silence.

—*El dinero no vale pero ayuda mucho.* No worth the money, but they help a lot.

—Money's worthless, but valuable?

He nods and goes back to his Jell-O.

I sigh.

—Father, did you know that the Carnicería Xalapa on the corner is expanding. They bought the whole block and are going to open a super-*supermercado.*

—*Drogas.* That's what they're really selling. No wonder I can't make a go of it. I'm too honest.

—Tell Father the good news. Go on, tell him.

—Father, when you were sick we had a family meeting, Rafa says. —And we've decided to go into business together, to use what we've learned in school and pool our resources, help you with your business. You have all the contacts and expertise, and Ito and I both have business training. Tikis can help if he wants when he finishes school. And the younger boys are already working with you summers. So we decided we should start our own business, and not have you working with Tres Reyes anymore. It's bad for your health. You should have your own shop, with your sons, and hire real upholsterers, the kind who know how to work with a hammer.

—Custom, quality work, Father says, excited. —Maybe Toto will want to join when he gets back from the army, no? And what about your sister? She can be the receptionist. Right, Lalita? You like to sit at a desk and read, don't you?

For once I have the good sense not to say anything.

—And guess what else, Father? We got the truck painted up with the new name, Inocencio Reyes and Sons. Quality upholstery. Over forty years experience. It looks real nice.

—Wow! Has it really been forty years already, Father?

—Well, yes, but no. More or less, Father says. —It's what the customer wants to hear.

Father's tired. Mother makes us all kiss him good-bye, and we walk out to the parking lot where the shop van is waiting, the new business name painted on both sides and on the back door. INOCENCIO REYES AND SONS, QUALITY UPHOLSTERY, OVER FORTY YEARS EXPERIENCE.

Rafa's right. It looks real nice.

85

Mi Aniversario

—*Cinco mil bolos*, brother.

Father is busy on the phone. Calling Baby, calling Fat-Face. Dialing caterers and musicians. Looking up rental halls. —*Mi aniversario*, he keeps saying. His thirtieth wedding anniversary, although we know Father and Mother haven't been married thirty years. It's more like twenty-something, but Father's afraid he won't live that long.

—*Ya me voy*. I'll be going soon.

—Where you going?

Father's making his phone calls sitting propped up in bed on a mound of flowered pillows. He's stretched out on top of the covers in a faded pair of flannel pajama bottoms, his legs crossed at the thin white ankles. He's wearing a T-shirt so old the neck is stretched *guango*, making him look skinnier than ever, his neck beginning to sag like the wattle of a turkey, the crispy chest hairs sprouting white here and there. He could use a shave and a haircut, and his bare feet with the long curved toenails look like Godzilla's.

—How much?!!! Father shouts into the receiver. —But I have seven sons!!! Think! Seven!!!

Above the bed, la Virgen de Guadalupe keeps watch over Father from her gold frame, and beside her, in a plastic frame behind cracked glass, the black-and-white family portrait of our trip to Acapulco when we were little. The room is dark except for the blue light thrown from the television and the dim yellow light of a bedside lamp. Everything is in disorder. There are clothes, clean and dirty, cluttered here and there, the clean stacked in folded piles waiting to be put away, the dirty draped lazily on doorknobs and bedposts awaiting collection. On the floor a balled sock sits next to a mountain of magazines—Mexican comic books, *¡Alarma!* tucked modestly in paper bags because Mother can't stand the gory covers, *ESTO* sports newspapers, the glossy photo of a thick-thighed Mexican starlet on the back cover of a respectable news journal. Balls of crumpled Kleenex roam the hills and valleys of the blankets like stray sheep.

—Yes, my friend. Thirty years thanks to God! Father continues bragging to some stranger on the other end of the line.

Except for the bottles and vials of medicine on the bedside table, you'd never guess Father's been sick. There's Father's last snack, a banana peel and an empty glass coated with milk. And, always within reach, "my toy," Father's remote control device for the TV.

—Hi, *mija*, Father says in his baby voice when he hangs up. —How's my pretty girl? How's my little queen? How's my *niña bonita?* Who loves you more than anyone in the world, my heaven?

—You do, I say, sighing and leaning over to kiss his grizzled cheek. He smells like a jar of vitamins. Thank God the stink of death is gone.

—Only one kiss? But you owe me more than one kiss. You owe me so many kisses. How many kisses do you calculate you owe me by now?

—For crying out loud . . .

—See how you are. How mean you are to your papa. You're stingy with your kisses. Poor papa. When he's in heaven then you'll think of him. And then you'll realize how much your papa loved you. Remember, no one loves you like your papa. You'll never find anyone on this earth, no one, no one, no one who loves you like your papa. Ever. Who do you love more . . . your mama or me?

—¡Papá!

—Just joking, *mija*. Don't get mad . . . Lalita, Father adds, whispering, —do you think you could buy your poor papa some cigarettes?

Mother marches into the room with another stack of clean clothes.

—No cigarettes. Ever! Doctor's orders, Mother says. —Christ Almighty, this room stinks. Get in that tub, old man.

—No, I don't want to, Father says in the voice of a child. —Leave me in peace. I'm here nice and comfortable watching TV, not bothering anyone.

—Listen to me, I'm talking to you. I said I'm talking to you!

—*Ay caray,* I'm trying to watch television. *Mija*, please, Father says, suddenly interested in the show he was ignoring.

—I said get in that tub. I can't believe how stinky you've become in your old age. Honest to God, if your mother could see you now. Lala, you won't believe it, but when I met your father he used to dress like *un fanfarrón*. Now look at him. How many days are you going to wear that T-shirt? This room smells like a cemetery. Do you hear me? When I finish mopping the kitchen you better be in that tub.

Father stares mutely at the television, only coming to life once Mother marches to the kitchen.

—Lala, he says, winking, —guess what I've gone and done?

—I don't even want to try to imagine.

—I hired the *mariachis*. And I'm getting price quotes from bands that specialize in music from my time. For my party.

Mother yells from the kitchen, —I already told you, I'm not going!

—*Tu mamá*, Father says, shaking his head. —She has the ears of a bat. But guess what else? he says, lowering his voice. —I already found a photographer, and a really good price for the gold-lettered invitations. And I called a place that will give us a group discount on the tuxedos.

—Tuxedos? Do you think the boys will go for that? They don't even like to wear ties.

—Of course they will. And you and your mother are going to wear formals. *Ay*, Lala, it's like the party I always dreamed for your *quince* that I was never able to give you. We're going to have a wonderful time.

Again from the kitchen, —I already told you, I'm not going, do you hear me?

Father goes on talking about *"mi aniversario"* as if Mother has nothing to do with it. How he wants to look for a tuxedo with tails and maybe even a top hat, because he remembers a friend from before the war who had one just like it. It's as if Mother's complaints only make Father more determined. He's already phoned all his friends. El Reloj, el King Kong, el Indio, el Pelón, Cuco, el Capitán, el Juchiteco. All the friends Mother says are just like him.

—Nothing but a big bunch of show-offs, Mother says to me while cooking Father's favorite rice pudding. —Your father, I can't stand him. His head is so fat he can kiss his behind. He makes me sick!

—Well, then, why don't you divorce him?

—It's too late. He needs me.

It's too late. She means, I need him, but she can't say that, can she? No, never. It's too late, I love you already.

—*¡Mija!* Father shouts from the bedroom.

—*¿Mande?* I say, running to his room like a subject being summoned by his pasha.

—No, not you, Father says. —I meant your mother. Then he starts shouting again, —Zoila, Zoila! Come see the star from *Till Death Do Us Part*. She's about to sing.

—I don't care about those stupid *telenovelas*, Mother shouts angrily. —I swear there's no intelligent life around here.

—Zoila, Zoila! Father continues shouting.

—You see? He keeps yelling for rice pudding. A banana. Jell-O with some half-and-half. Pancakes. A cup of Mexican chocolate. That's how it is, all day yelling for me over and over like a man drowning. Drives me nuts, Mother says, but there's something in the way she says it, like she's bragging. —Help me carry your Father's supper over to his room.

By the time we've set up his tray, Father's already punched the mute button on the television remote and is on the phone talking long-distance. I know this because he always shouts when he talks to Mexico.

—Of course, you can stay here, Father is yelling. —Sister, don't insult me, I wouldn't think of it. Yes, and Antonieta Araceli and her family too. You're all welcome.

—Like hell! Mother mutters. —The Hilton this ain't. I'm sick of picking up after people my whole life. I'm retired, you hear me, retired!

Father ignores her until he hangs up. Then he begins . . .

—Zoila, don't mortify me. After all those years we stayed with her in Mexico, how am I going to tell my sister she can't stay here, how?

—I'm sick and tired . . .

—Sick and tired, Father parrots in his gothic English. —Disgusted!

Then Father asks me for one of Mother's nylon stockings. He has a migraine.

Mother gathers up all the dirty clothes in a dirty towel and carries this bundle over to the washer. She slams and opens doors, cranks the button to start it up, and won't look me in the eye.

—Your father, he's terrible, Mother says, close to tears. —I've had it.

When I get back to the bedroom, Father is wearing the nylon stocking tied around his forehead, Apache style, eating his rice pudding in the blue light of the television.

—*Tu mamá*, Father hisses without taking his eyes off the screen. —*Es terrrrrrible.*

The Children and Grandchildren of Zoila and Inocencio Reyes Cordially Invite You to Celebrate Thirty Years of Marriage

Okay, so it's not the Ritz. It's the Postal Workers' Union Hall. So what? We've done the best with what we've got. Crepe paper streamers twisted and gathered at the center of the ceiling, where a huge disco ball does a slow, sexy turn and shatters light into a million pretty splinters over the wooden dance floor.

Somebody found a wire florist arch in a back room, and we tied balloons on it, and this is what you have to pass under as you enter the hall. The place is still as dark as a cave; a varnished, masculine room with wood paneling, like a hunter's lodge or a tavern that reeks of sour beer and cigarettes, but we worked all last night to make it look nice. Plastic champagne cups filled with pillow-shaped mints in pastel colors. Scalloped napkins embossed in gold lettering with "30 Zoila & Inocencio." I wonder if anyone cares that it isn't quite thirty years. But who's counting?

We're decked out in our best. Mother bought a floor-length evening gown, and even the boys agreed to wear tuxes. I found a dress that doesn't make me look too freaky. A vintage shantung silk number that reminds me of that fuchsia dress Mother used to have. It's cocktail length, but I dressed it up with the Grandmother's *caramelo rebozo*. It's okay, it was the Grandmother's idea.

People have come from all directions for the party. From all over Chicago and the northern suburbs, from Wilmette and Winnetka, from as far west as Aurora and as far east as Gary, Indiana, from the cornfields of Joliet, by plane and by car from Mexico, California, Kansas, Philadelphia, Arizona, and Texas. The scattered Reyes and Reynas, and the friends of los Reyes and Reynas, have gathered here tonight to honor Mother and Father, to say, —*¡Caray!* Who would've thought? I didn't think it would last, did you? Or to raise a glass and thank God that Zoila Reyna and Inocencio Reyes are still alive, still on the planet giving trouble, still bothering everyone and still being bothered with the nuisance of living.

— *I*s that what he told you? Picked up off the streets of Memphis and made to enlist? *¡Puro cuento!* He *wanted* to enlist. I know. I was there. He said to my father, "Uncle, drive me to the enlistment center, I want to become a U.S. citizen. I want to become a U.S. citizen."

That's what he said. And it wasn't Memphis either. It was Chicago . . .

— *W*hen I was little I used to dance with your father. I thought he was handsome, handsome, handsome. He looked just like Pedro Infante, only skinny . . .

— *O*ur dog eats them if you put butter on them. If you hold up a *tortilla* and it's not buttered, forget it, he won't even look at it . . .

— *¿Q*ué tienes? ¿Sueño o sleepy?

— *A*nd whose fault is it that wing chair wasn't delivered on time? I suppose now you're going to blame me?

—Can't you stop talking shop now? This is supposed to be a party. Forget about the wing chair.

—Forget? You're the one who promised Mrs. Garza she could have it by today!

*Y*ou believe her? Married, my eye! Look, I hate to talk badly about my sister, but your Aunty Light-Skin can't tell the truth to save her life! And I ought to know, I'm her brother. She wasn't married. She just likes to talk a good story.

*T*hey say he even made a sofa that's in the White House.
—*¡A poco!*
—That's what they say. It seems like a lie, but it's true. The White House. Imagine!

*A*ll he wants is food that's so much *lata* to make. Especially that damn *mancha manteles mole* that really does stain tablecloths and is so much trouble to wash out not even Tide will get it clean.

*Y*ou know what they say. The truth is God's child . . . That's not how it goes. How does it go? Truth is the daughter of God; a lie the Devil's daughter. And I had the truth on my side, yes, I did. You believe me, right?

I was not making *ojitos* at her, I was just being polite.
—Liar! I saw you! You don't think after being married to you for twenty-five years I don't know who I'm married to?
—*¡Ay caray!* Why are you so cruel with me? You love to make me suffer! Why do you mortify me?
—No, you got it wrong, buddy. It's YOU who always mortifies ME!

—Honest to God. When he was young his father shot an elephant, an elephant that had gone crazy on a set they'd been
filming. It was a circus elephant. This is what they say, I don't know, I
didn't see it. And he says that when . . . Ah, no, that's a lie. That's not
what he said.

—A body like María Victoria, remember her?

—And then we would go to Plaza Garibaldi to pick up *gringas,*
order a Carta Blanca, or a Brandy Sagarniac. We'd dance
danzón and boogie-woogie all night at el Salón México.

—His mother was the type who wouldn't sit on a chair without
wiping it first.

—If you really want authentic Yucatecan food while you're in
Mexico City, eat at El Habanero in the *colonia* Nápoles on
Alabama 54, corner of Nebraska.

—Right? You love me the best?

—I read that Buster Keaton filled his swimming pool with champagne. Can you believe it? So that the bubbles would tickle the
soles of his guests' feet. That's what I read in a book in Mexico.

—In my time it was Packards, Lincolns, Cadillacs.

—*Yo nunca quise a mi marido. Mi familia era de mejor categoría,
pero como no tuve recursos . . .*

— I haven't cried so much since I got that five-dollar haircut at the beauty college.

— A whole bag! He ate the whole thing, and you know fluorescent food can't be good for you.

— Have your teeth gotten bigger, or did you lose weight?

— She looks just like her father, don't she? I said when I saw her, there's Inocencio all over again.

— ¿Y tú—quién eres?
   —Soy una niña.

— Remember when Grandfather used to get angry with us for eating our rice and beans mixed together? Remember?
—No, I don't remember.
—Aw, you don't remember anything. How's about when he used to line us up for military inspection. You gotta remember that.
—I don't think so.

— Don't tell anyone, but you're my favorite.

— She's the most beautiful of all us sisters, but she was born a little retarded. That's why our father loved her best. Sometimes she goes into heat and our mother has to throw water on her.

— Pillsbury or Duncan Hines?
   —No le hace. Lo que sea. Whichever one is cheaper. They both taste good.

—¡*Ay, no!* The ones with lace I can't wear. They make my nipples itch.

— *I* know you don't know her, but she's your cousin from your Uncle Nuño. Don't shame me, you're going to go over and say hello.

— *Se llama* Schuler, Mamá. Schu-ler.
  —*¿Como azúcar?*
—*No*, Mamá. Schuler. *No* sugar.

— *Ya nadie hace comida como antes. Nada sabe igual. La comida sabe a nada. Ni tengo ganas de comer a veces, y a veces ni como.*

— *Y*ou can tell from her eyebrows she probably has a lot of hair all over her body.

— *T*his is the family photo from our trip to Acapulco when we were little. But I'm not here, I was off to the side making sand castles, and nobody bothered to call me when the photographer came by. Same as always, they forgot all about me.
—What are you talking about? You weren't making sand castles, Lala. You want the truth? You were mad, and that's why when we called you over, you wouldn't come. That's the *real* reason why you're not in the picture. And I ought to know, I'm the oldest.

— *I* don't argue more! You argue more!
  —*Estás loca. Te gusta mortificarme, ¿verdad? Tú eres la que . . .*
—Liar!!!

inally, late as always, the program starts with Father entering the dance floor in his beautiful black tux with tails, looking like a Fred Astaire, every bit the gentleman. The *mariachis* start up with the bull-fighting song, who the hell knows why. Everyone applauds. Mother enters the ring as brave and full of energy as a little bull. She's spirited from being housebound for weeks taking care of Father. She's nodding and waving in her new empire-waist aqua chiffon gown, waving stiffly like the queen of England. Father is kissing Memo's hand, holding Toto's face to his cheek, kissing each of his sons on his forehead or the top of his head. It's enough to make you cry.

Then the *mariachis* open with a slow song, "Solamente una vez." And Mother and Father are forced to dance. Mother acts stiff at first; that's the first sign to get a few highballs into her, quick, then she'll let loose. Mother and Father dancing like they've danced with each other forever, like only two people who have put up with each other and love each other can.

Finally, the deejay we hired takes over after the *mariachis* leave. He's really great, has all kinds of music, from Pérez Prado to Stevie Wonder. When he plays "Kung Fu Fighting," suddenly all the moms are up and tugging their husbands, who won't join them. It's their little ones who dance with them instead. The babies love it. They're whimpering and whining, asking to be picked up. Brats are kicking the air, giving each other a sharp chop on the neck, or sliding across the dance floor. Little girls, the princesses at least, are dancing with their daddies, and the ones who aren't royalty are dancing with each other. Rafa's *chiquillo* is howling, and he and his wife, Zdenka, keep passing him back and forth to each other until Father volunteers to take him for a walk outside, so that the kid will calm down, but we all know he's sneaking out for a forbidden cigarette snitched from one of his buddies.

After "She Loves You," "The Twist," "These Boots Are Made for Walkin'," "Midnight Train to Georgia," "I Shot the Sheriff," "Crocodile Rock," and "Oye Cómo Va," the deejay settles into some music from Mother and Father's time, finally selecting something sure to get all the generations rising from their seats at the same time—a *cumbia*. Sure enough, everyone gets on the dance floor—kids, newlyweds, old people, even the ones with walkers and wheelchairs, the big and the thin relatives, the sexy aunties who look like inflated sea horses, voluptuous, enormous, exploding from the tops of their dresses, big mermaid hips and big mermaid *chichis,* dresses so tight it's laughable and wonderful. Everyone, but everyone, moving in a lazy counterclockwise circle. The living and the dead. Señor and Señora Juchi who have flown up from Mexico City. Aunty Light-Skin with a toddler in each hand, her two grandsons. Uncle Fat-Face and Aunty Licha, Uncle Baby and Aunty Ninfa, all the cousins and their kids, my six brothers with their partners and little ones. Toto is dancing with his new baby girl, and Mother is cross and angry because he's ignoring her. Father is making Toto's wife laugh. She's Korean American, and he's showing off, singing a song for her in Korean, something he learned when he was in the war.

And I realize with all the noise called "talking" in my house, that talking that is nothing but talking, that is so much a part of my house and my past and myself you can't hear it as several conversations, but as one roar like the roar inside a shell, I realize then that this is my life, with its dragon arabesques of voices and lives intertwined, rushing like a Ganges, irrevocable and wild, carrying away everything in reach, whole villages, pigs, shoes, coffeepots, and that little basket inside the coffeepot that Mother always loses each morning and has to turn the kitchen upside down looking for until someone thinks to look in the garbage. Names, dates, a person, a spoon, the wing tips my father buys at Maxwell Street and before that in Mexico City, the voice that gasped from that hole in the chest of the Little Grandfather, the great-grandfather who stank like a shipyard from dyeing *rebozos* black all day, the car trips to Mexico and Acapulco, *refresco* Lulú soda pop, *taquitos de canasta* hot and sweating from a basket, your name on a grain of rice, *crema de nácar* sold on the street with a vendor doling out free samples like dollops of sour cream, feathered Matachines dancing in front of the cathedral on the Virgin's birthday, a servant girl crying on television because she's lost and doesn't know where in Mexico City she lives, the orange Naugahyde La-Z-Boy. All, all, all of this, and me shutting the noise out with my brain as if it's a film and the sound has gone off, their mouths moving like snails against the glass of an aquarium.

It hits me at once, the terrible truth of it. I am the Awful Grandmother. For love of Father, I'd kill anyone who came near him to hurt him or make him sad. I've turned into her. And I see inside her heart, the Grandmother, who had been betrayed so many times she only loves her son. He loves her. And I love him. I have to find room inside my heart for her as well, because she holds him inside her heart like when she held him inside her womb, the clapper inside a bell. One can't be reached without touching the other. Him inside her, me inside him, like Chinese boxes, like Russian dolls, like an ocean full of waves, like the braided threads of a *rebozo*. *When I die then you'll realize how much I love you.* And we are all, like it or not, one and the same.

There in the crowd, do I imagine or do I really see my sister Candelaria dancing a *cumbia*, like a Mexican Venus arriving on sea foam. And I see the Awful Grandmother marching alongside and winking at me as she passes, and behind her, paying her no mind, the Little Grandfather shuffling with his short quick Pekingese steps. Next, Catita and her daughter without a name *cumbia* past, and Señor Vidaurri lumbering behind them with his big burnt face like "el Sol" in the Mexican Lotería game.

And I see people I've never met before. Great-grandmother Regina lifting her skirts and prancing like a queen, and next to her swaying clumsily like a dancing bear, the Spaniard, Great-grandfather Eleuterio. A huge Aunty Fina swaying gracefully with a little guy in a beautiful *charro* outfit; no doubt her Pío. And that must be the tiny witch woman María Sabina dancing *descalza* in her raggedy *huipil*. And Señor Wences, *muy galán* in his top hat and tails, his fist-puppet, Johnny, singing along in a loud, high voice. The handsome Enrique Aragón with his arrogant film star good looks, enchanted, entranced, walking happily behind Josephine Baker shimmying in a banana skirt. The sweetheart from the hotlands, the one my grandfather loved, in her *iguana* hat, *cumbia*-ing arm in arm with the woman who ran off with her heart, the smoky-voiced singer Pánfila dressed in *campesino* whites. And Fidel Castro strolling like a young boy holding hands with his lost love, the stunning Gladys. And look, it's the barefoot Tongolele doing a Tahitian version of a *cumbia* in a leopard-skin bikini! Isn't she lovely? Everyone, big and little, old and young, dead and living, imagined and real high-stepping past in the big *cumbia* circle of life.

—Lala!

It's Father collapsing into the chair next to me, just sitting there looking at me, shaking his head.

—All these years I've saved this for you, Lala. But I'm getting old. I'll be going soon.

—Where you going? You just got here.

—*Mija*, don't make fun of me.

Father places a wooden box in my hand. It's his lucky dominoes box, a wooden casket with a lid that slides off the top. It's as light as if it holds a dead bird.

—Open it, go on, it's for you.

Inside, wrapped in blue tissue paper, my braids, the ones from Querétaro. They've been woven into a ponytail instead of the two braids the stylist had snipped.

—I sent them to be made into one hairpiece, Father says proudly.

The hair is a strange light brown color my hair isn't now. It's been styled so that it curls into a spiral a bit, or maybe that was once my natural wave, who knows?

—So does this mean I'm an adult now?

—*Siempre serás mi niña*. Father says this with so much *sentimiento*, he's forced to take out his handkerchief and blow his nose. —*Ay*, Lala. Life's never like you plan. I wanted so much for all of you. I wish I could've given you children more.

—No, Father, you've given us a lot.

—I worked hard my whole life, and I've got nothing to show for it. And now look at me. The king of plastic covers.

—No, Father, you've always given us so much. It was just enough, but not too much. You've taught us wonderful things. Necessity. We've had to make do. How could we have learned that valuable lesson? To be generous. To be dependable and be there for each other, because we're *familia*. To take pride in our work. And to work hard. That's what you've taught us. You've been good and kind. You've been a wonderful father, a king. And we're your kingdom—your kids.

—*Mija*, you think you know everything, but I have something to confess to you. I tell you this, because I want you to take care of yourself, Lala. *Cuídate*. We are Reyes, *nosotros no somos perros*.

My heart squeezes. I already know what he's going to tell me. He's going to tell me about my half sister! I can't look him in the eye. I start to fiddle with the fringe of the *caramelo rebozo* looped around my shoulders.

—It's about . . . your grandmother.

—My grandmother!

—When she was very young, just your age in fact, she conceived a child. Me. And she did this from love, before she was married, I mean to say. When my father found out she was expecting, he wanted to run away, but it was your great-grandfather who reminded him we are Reyes, we are not dogs. Think of it. My father was just a *chamaco,* just a boy, but thank God your great-grandfather had the wisdom of years to remind his son of his obligation. And I tell you this so you'll listen to me. I'm older, I've made lots of mistakes, Lala. Don't throw your life away, don't waste even a day. Don't do reckless things that will leave you angry and bitter and sad later when you're old. You don't want to have regrets, do you? The Devil knows more . . .

—From being old than from being the Devil. I know, I know, I've heard it a million times. But . . . is there anything *else* you need to tell me, Father?

—What more is there to say?

I want to ask Father questions about the girl Candelaria, my sister. About his other daughter, the one he made before we were all born, when we were dirt. I want to know about Amparo, about her child. *All my life you've said I was "the only girl," Father. You've scolded my brothers and told them they had to look after me because I was their "only sister." But that's not true, Father. Why would you tell a lie? And was it a healthy lie? And if it wasn't, what was it?*

*Why weren't you a gentleman? I thought we weren't dogs. I thought we were kings and meant to act like kings, Father. And why didn't the Little Grandfather remind you of your responsibility if he was so feo, fuerte, y for-*mal? *Why don't you tell me, Father? I'll understand. Honest to God.* But I don't say a word.

I think crazy things. How maybe I can hire a detective. How maybe I can place an ad in the paper. *In the* colonia *Industrial in 1940-something a girl named Candelaria was born to a washerwoman named Amparo. If you know the whereabouts . . .* How maybe a thousand washerwomen's daughters would appear, a long long line of daughters claiming to be my sister, telling stories more melodramatic than any *telenovela.* The hiccuping tears, the faces of brown women like the faces of the lost servants who appear on television. *If anyone knows where this young girl lives, please come and claim her.* Candelaria hiccuping up tears and crying and crying. And someone leading her to a blind doorway and leaving her there. And when she opens her eyes and realizes it's no game, then what? The girl Candelaria with the dark Andalusian eyebrows of our *sevillano* grandfather, the skin darker and sweeter than anyone's. The girl Candelaria my sister, the oldest, and me the youngest.

You're not supposed to ask about such things. There are stories no one is willing to tell you.

And there are stories you're not willing to tell. Maybe Father has his own questions. Maybe he wants to hear, or doesn't want to hear, about me and Ernesto, but he doesn't ask. We're so Mexican. So much left unsaid.

I'm afraid, but there is nothing I can do but stare it in the eye. I bring the tips of the *caramelo rebozo* up to my lips, and, without even knowing it, I'm chewing on its fringe, its taste of cooked pumpkin familiar and comforting and good, reminding me I'm connected to so many people, so many.

Maybe it's okay I can't say, "I'm sorry, Father," and Father doesn't tell me, "I forgive you." Maybe it doesn't matter Father never told Mother, "*Perdóname,*" and Mother never said, "You're pardoned." Maybe it's all right the Grandmother never apologized to Mother, "I hurt you, please forgive me," and Mother never said, "Hey, forget it, I'm over it." It doesn't matter. Maybe it's my job to separate the strands and knot the words together for everyone who can't say them, and make it all right in the end. This is what I'm thinking.

I wish I could tell Father: "*Te comprendo,*" or, "I love you," which is the same thing. But it's strange to even think of saying this. We never say "I love you" to each other. Like when my brothers hug me, because we hardly ever hug one another, though Father hugs us each a lot. And how as foreign as it is being hugged by my brothers, how familiar it is. Their smell like their pillows. That scent of hair and their maleness, like Father, like his jar of Alberto VO 5 hair pomade, which I have *never* liked, but this time when I hug Father, that smell just about makes me want to cry.

—Imagine the unimaginable, Father says, looking out into the dance floor at the bodies shaking and marching and prancing and strutting in a circus circle. —Imagine the unimaginable. Think of the most unbelievable thing that could happen and, believe me, Destiny will outdo you and come up with something even more unbelievable. Life's like that. My Got! What a *telenovela* our lives are!

It's true. La Divina Providencia is the most imaginative writer. Plotlines convolute and spiral, lives intertwine, coincidences collide, seemingly random happenings are laced with knots, figure eights, and double loops, designs more intricate than the fringe of a silk *rebozo*. No, I couldn't make this up. Nobody could make up our lives.

The *cumbia* ends, and suddenly a waltz starts up, scattering the dancers off the dance floor like a bomb.

—Who asked for a waltz?

—I did, Father says. —*Ven,* you're going to dance with your papa now.

—But I don't know how.

—Don't worry, *mija. Así como sea.*

Father stands up and leads me out to dance like the *caballero* he is. Everybody applauds and gives us the entire dance floor, which really has me sweating, but after a while I forget about everyone, and when I finally get the hang of waltzing, a whole bunch of Father's buddies get up and join us, some of them tugging their wives, and some of them tugging younger members of the family, until the dance floor is filled up again, first with some pretty good dancers, the old-timers, and later with some pretty bad dancers, the younger ones, but nobody cares, everybody having a hell of a time.

—Who's my *niña bonita?*

Father dances like if he's a young man, like if he's the same guy twirling about in the dance halls during the war, I imagine. The one my mother met who was so full of it. His face gone slack and tired, but his hair and mustache still furiously black.

—And what would you say you've learned from your life? What has *la vida* taught you, Father?

—*¿La vida?* . . . To labor honorably.

—That's *it?*

—That's enough for one life . . .

Say what they say, no matter what my father's life, he's lived it as best as he could, has labored honorably. Okay, maybe he made some mistakes. Maybe he's told a few healthy lies during his day. So? Here we are, aren't we? Here we are.

—But Lala, Father whispers in my ear, —these things I've told you tonight, my heaven, I tell them only to you, Father says, adjusting the *caramelo rebozo* on my shoulders properly. —Only you have heard these stories, daughter, understand? *Sólo tú.* Be dignified, Lala. *Digna.* Don't be talking such things like the barbarians, *mi vida.* To mention them makes our family look like *sinvergüenzas,* understand? You don't want people to think we're shameless, do you? Promise your papa you won't talk these things, Lalita. Ever. Promise.

I look into Father's face, that face that is the same face as the Grandmother's, the same face as mine.

—I promise, Father.

Fin

Pilón

Like the Mexican grocer who gives you a pilón, *something extra tossed into your bag as a thank-you for your patronage just as you are leaving, I give you here another story in thanks for having listened to my* cuento . . .

On Cinco de Mayo Street, in front of Café la Blanca, an organ grinder playing "Farolito." Out of a happy grief, people give coins for shaking awake the memory of a father, a beloved, a child whom God ran away with.

And it was as if that music stirred up things in a piece of my heart from a time I couldn't remember. From before. Not exactly a time, a feeling. The way sometimes one remembers a memory with the images blurred and rounded, but has forgotten the one thing that would draw it all into focus. In this case, I'd forgotten a mood. Not a mood—a state of being, to be more precise.

How before my body wasn't my body. I didn't have a body. I was a being as close to a spirit as a spirit. I was a ball of light floating across the planet. I mean the me I was before puberty, that red Rio Bravo you have to carry yourself over.

I don't know how it is with boys. I've never been a boy. But girls somewhere between the ages of, say, eight and puberty, girls forget they have bodies. It's the time she has trouble keeping herself clean, socks always drooping, knees pocked and bloody, hair crooked as a broom. She doesn't look in mirrors. She isn't aware of being watched. Not aware of her body causing men to look at her yet. There isn't the sense of the female body's volatility, its rude weight, the nuisance of dragging it about. There isn't the world to bully you with it, bludgeon you, condemn you to a life sentence of fear. It's the time when you look at a young girl and notice she is at her ugliest, but at the same time, at her happiest. She is a being as close to a spirit as a spirit.

Then that red Rubicon. The never going back there. To that country, I mean.

And I remember along with that feeling fluttering through the notes of "Farolito," so many things, so many, all at once, each distinct and separate, and all running together. The taste of a *caramelo* called Glorias on my tongue. At la Caleta beach, a girl with skin like *cajeta*, like goat-milk candy. The *caramelo* color of your skin after rising out of the Acapulco foam, salt water running down your hair and stinging the eyes, the raw ocean smell, and the ocean running out of your mouth and nose. My mother watering her dahlias with a hose and running a stream of water over her feet as well, Indian feet, thick and square, *como de barro,* like the red clay of Mexican pottery.

And I don't know how it is with anyone else, but for me these things, that song, that time, that place, are all bound together in a country I am homesick for, that doesn't exist anymore. That never existed. A country I invented. Like all emigrants caught between here and there.

CHRONOLOGY

1519   Cortés and Moctezuma meet in Mexico City. Bernal Díaz del Castillo, one of four Spanish eyewitnesses to have left a written account of the conquest, notes in his wonderfully detailed memoirs: Moctezuma "was seated on a low stool, soft and richly worked . . ."

1572   The first published mention of the *rebozo* is made by Fray Diego Durán.

1639   The first deportations. Pilgrims at Plymouth Rock authorize "pauper aliens" removed from their community. Virginia and British Colonies follow their example.

1776   Upholstery business owner Betsy Ross, struggling to make a living, is approached by three wise men to make a flag. The rest of the story, they say, is history. Recent historical research, however, claims this famous anecdote is nothing but story invented by Ross's descendants a hundred years after her death. Which just goes to show the power of a good tale told well.

1798   Alien and Sedition Acts bar entry to "aliens," who jeopardize the peace and security of the nation, as well as making possible their expulsion.

1830–1840s   Catholic, German, and Irish immigrants are attacked. The Know-Nothing "nativist" movement is formed.

1846   U.S. invades Mexico. The Mexican War. Or, the American War of Intervention, depending on your point of view.

1847   The "Boy Heroes" of Mexico City's Chapultepec Castle leap to their death defending this military stronghold, rather than surrender to the incoming U.S. invaders.

1848   Treaty of Guadalupe Hidalgo, the basis for bilingual education and bilingual ballots, is signed, ending the Mexican-American War. In theory, it protected the cultural and property rights of Mexicans choosing to remain and become U.S. citizens.

1860–1870's   New immigrants are attacked, especially the Chinese and the Irish. Most U.S.-citizen Mexicans are stripped of their lands and rights, and some are lynched.

1882   Chinese Exclusion Act suspends Chinese labor immigration and naturalization. Mexican immigrant numbers increase.

1891   Immigration Act. The first comprehensive law for national control of immigration.

1900–1933   An estimated one-eighth of Mexico's population moves north to the U.S.

1907   U.S. economic depression. Teddy Roosevelt's "Gentleman's Agreement" bars entry of Japanese laborers. • Francisco Gabilondo Soler, Cri-Crí, the Singing Cricket, is born in Orizaba, Veracruz; the composer of three hundred children's songs famous throughout Latin America and Europe, especially in the former Yugoslavia.

1909   U.S.–Mexico treaty imports Mexican laborers to California to harvest sugar beets.

1911   Mexican Revolution begins.

1916   General Pershing sent into Mexico to get Pancho Villa.

1917 $130 million later, U.S. troops return from Mexico without Villa. • The U.S. imports Mexican workers again in face of labor shortages caused by their entry into World War I. • Immigration Act further restricts entry of Asians and introduces literacy requirements and an $8 head tax for entry. • German Americans living in the U.S. viewed with suspicion due to World War I. German communities, once separated from each other by religion, unite against anti-German sentiments. German disappears from pulpits and from street signs, as well as from newspapers. American flags are raised overnight on the porches of German American homes, and children are punished by their elders for speaking anything but English.

1920   Mexican Civil War ends. • U.S. Congress proposes a ceiling on the number of Mexican immigrants allowed to enter. • Buster Keaton fills his swimming pool with champagne so that the bubbles will tickle the soles of his guests' feet. • The Charleston is outlawed on the sidewalks of New York.

1921   November 14, a bomb is planted in la Virgen de Guadalupe's *basílica* in Mexico City, but, miraculously, the *tilma* is unscathed. • The U.S. Temporary Quota Act creates the first step toward immigration quotas.

1924   Immigration Act imposes first permanent quota system, biased toward admitting North and Western Europeans, lasting until 1952, establishes the country's only national police force, the U.S. Border Patrol, and provides for deportation of those who become public charges, violate U.S. law, or engage in alleged anarchist or seditionist acts.

1926   José Mojica, the Mexican Valentino, records "Júrame."

1927   Lupe Vélez and Douglas Fairbanks make a film together. • In Belgium, the ex-empress Carlota dies. *Adiós, mi Carlota.*

1928   As a result of the Cristeros uprisings and postrevolutionary Mexico's feuds between Church and state, Mexican president Obregón is assassinated by a Catholic nun and a religious fanatic in La Bombilla Restaurant in Mexico City.

1929   Legislation fixes the quota system, guaranteeing the numerical predominance of white people in the population and making it a crime for a previously deported alien to try to enter the country again. • Stock market crashes.

1930's   "Mexican scare" in early years of Great Depression rounds up and deports hundreds of thousands of Mexicans from the U.S.

1933   Separate immigration and naturalization functions are consolidated in the Labor Department, creating the INS (Immigration and Naturalization Service).

1935   Mexico inaugurates the Pan American Highway on July 1, crossing tropical canyons, valleys, rivers, and mountains.

1940   The brilliant Gabriel Vargas initiates *El Señor Burrón o vida de perro*, precursor to *La familia Burrón* comics. • Frida marries Diego—again! • Tens of thousands of U.S.-citizen Japanese stripped of their properties and thrown into concentration camps. • Tens of thousands of Jewish refugees refused permission to enter the U.S. again. • INS is transferred to the U.S. Department of Justice in response to international tensions and war.

1941   The U.S. enters World War II. Mexican migration to U.S. reinvigorated during the war. • Ensconced in a house called La Escondida, Dolores del Río returns to Mexico because she loves Mexico, she says, but in reality it's because the love of her life, that *gordo* Orson Welles, the only one she really loved because we always love the one who doesn't love us, has dumped her for another Latina—Rita Cansino, or Rita Hayworth, who will dump Orson for the Aga Khan.

1942   *Bracero* program provides 5 million Mexican laborers for U.S. employers during the next two decades. • Mexico joins the Allies in declaring war on the Axis; Mexico's *chiquitos pero picosos* Squadron 201 sent to the Pacific.

1943   Repeal of Chinese Exclusion Act. • The Los Angeles "Zoot Suit Riots," or "Military Riots," depending on your point of view, weeks of U.S. servicemen hunting down and beating up zoot-suit-dressed *pachucos*, make front-page news in newspapers all over the nation. • In Mexico, baby volcano Paricutín is born in Dionisio Pulido's cornfield.

1945   World War II ends. Mexicans earn more Congressional Medals of Honor than any other ethnic group. • María Félix's new film, *La devoradora, The She-Devourer*, just released.

1948   Tongolele erupts in Mexico City.

1949   Economic recession causes massive roundups of undocumented workers. Korean War breaks the recession, but after the war, 1953–1955, another roundup of Mexicans begins anew because of another recession.

1952   Immigration Act. National origins quota is continued, as well as quotas for skilled aliens whose services are needed.

1953   "Professional, longtime Mexican hater" Joseph M. Swing appointed commissioner of the INS. An ex-soldier who was in Pershing's expedition to hunt down Villa in 1916, he requests $10 million to build a 150-mile-long fence along the border to keep out Mexicans. Military sweeps in the mid-1950's subject Mexicans to raids, arrests, and deportation drives.

1957 Earthquake rocks Mexico City.

1963 Elvis has *Fun In Acapulco,* dives off the cliffs of la Quebrada, is chased by Ursula Andress and a Mexican lady-bullfighter, and finishes the film singing "Guadalajara" with a bunch of *mariachis.*

1965 Immigration and Nationality Act Amendments. Repeals national origin quotas. Establishes system for family unification. Sets 20,000 per country limit for Eastern Hemisphere, and a ceiling for Western Hemisphere is set for the first time.

1973 U.S. troops leave Vietnam. Chicano soldiers are the highest per capita of the number receiving medals for bravery in the Vietnam War. They also died in disproportionate numbers.

1976 Immigration and Nationality Act Amendments. Limits the number of legal visas issued to Mexican immigrants each year to 20,000.

1980 Refugee Act. Establishes first permanent procedure for admitting refugees; defined according to international standards.

1985 Major earthquake devastates Mexico City.

1986 Immigration Reform and Control Act. Employers are sanctioned for knowingly hiring illegal aliens. Legalization programs are created; amnesty to foreigners who can prove they have resided in the U.S. continuously since 1982. Border enforcement increases.

1990 Immigration Act increases legal immigration ceilings by 40 percent, establishing, among other things, temporary protection status for those jeopardized by armed conflict or natural disasters in their native land. • Mexican composer Francisco Gabilondo Soler, Cri-Crí, dies on December 4.

1994 Zapata is not dead, but rises up again in Chiapas.

1996 Mandatory detention of everyone seeking asylum in the U.S. without valid documents. More border enforcement. A fourteen-mile triple fence south of San Diego is constructed, and penalties increased for smuggling undocumented workers into the U.S., as well as for using false documentation. • Lola Beltrán, the great singer of Mexican *rancheras,* dies on March 26. Although already a legend in her time, she performed at the Palace of Fine Arts in Mexico City only a few years before her death, and the auditorium was half empty.

1997 The bipartisan Commission on Immigration Reform advisory group, appointed by Congress and the president in 1990, recommends abolishing the INS and parceling its duties out to other federal agencies.

2000 Census reveals Latino and Asian immigrants, their children and grandchildren, are remaking small towns and big cities across the American heartland.

2001 Subcomandante Marcos and the Zapatistas march into Mexico City on behalf of indigenous rights. • Mexican Bracero laborers sue for back pay with-held since the 1940's. • The World Bank estimates 1.3 billion people around the world live on less than one dollar a day, 75 percent of them women. • In the wake of the World Trade Center and Pentagon attacks, the U.S. tightens its borders.

2002   Pope John Paul II canonizes Juan Diego as a saint despite controversy over whether Juan Diego ever existed. Some state that he was simply a story told to the Indians in order to convert them from their devotion to Tonantzín, the Aztec fertility goddess. • María Félix, Mexican movie diva, star of *El rapto* and ex-wife of Agustín "María bonita" Lara, dies at eighty-eight in Mexico City. Her funeral cortege from the Palace of Fine Arts to the Panteón Francés causes pandemonium in the streets.

All over the world, millions leave their homes and cross borders illegally.

¡Ya pa' que te cuento!

ACKNOWLEDGMENTS

Writing this book has been like making a walking pilgrimage to Tepeyac from Chicago. On my knees. Many fed and sheltered me along the way, and to all, I am grateful. A special thank-you to my friends Barbara Renaud González, Josie Méndez-Negrete, Josie Garza, and Ellen Riojas Clark. Bert Snyder, thanks for my daily dose of Vita-Berts. A Vita-Bert a day keeps the writer's block away! To Ito Romo and to Gayle Elliott for driving me along the route my father drove from Chicago to San Antonio, thank you. *Gracias a* Dorothy Allison and Eduardo Galeano for the manna and water of their words. Thanks to the angels who kept my home in order while I was away: Juanita Chávez and Janet Silva, Armando Cortez, Mary Ozuna, Daniel Gamboa, Roger Solís, and Bill Sánchez. Thanks as well to Reza Versace for nurturing body and spirit.

For research assistance I am indebted to several individuals for their *testimonios* and investigations. First, to my father's cousin, *mi querido tío Enrique Arteaga Cisneros, hombre de letras, cuyas páginas me ayudaron para inventar el mundo* "when I was dirt." Mr. Eddie López for sharing his personal papers on World War II, and to his wife, la Sra. María Luisa Camacho de López, for her invaluable knowledge on *rebozos*. Mario and Alejandro Sánchez assisted on library research. The historian Steven Rodríguez reviewed my historical references. I would also like to thank my friends Gregg Barrios and Mary Ozuna for memories of San Antonio in the early 1970's, and thanks too to my sister-in-law Silvia Zamora Cisneros for her Chicago memories. Garrett Mormando, Pancho Velásquez, Marisela Barrera, César Martínez, Franco Mondini, Jasna Karaula, Ito, Barbara, Alejandro, thank you for conversations that allowed me to steal from your past. Liliana, I owe you for the grandfather story. Prayers were provided by spiritual mothers Elsa Calderón y la Sra. Camacho de López. Quality-control proofreaders: Ruth Béhar, Craig Pennel, Liliana Valenzuela, Ito Romo, Norma Elia Cantú, Barbara Renaud González, Gregg Barrios, Macarena Hernández, and Ellen Riojas Clark. Thank you! The patient staff at Mail Boxes Etc. on West Avenue off Blanco in San Antonio, Texas, deserves to be publicly thanked for their excellent care with this manuscript and with me: Felicia, Dorothy, Connie, Jeffrey, and Priscilla. Thanks to María Herrera Sobek for song research.

ACKNOWLEDGMENTS

A writer is only as good as her editors. I am indebted to Dennis Mathis, who pilgrimed alongside me the entire trek. Ito Romo and Alba De León were my *coyotes* across the borderlands, and Liliana Valenzuela was my scout into the interior. Susan Bergholz, the literary agent/guardian angel who never sleeps, read these stories as I slept, and sent them back with comments before I resumed my journey the next morning. Thanks to *la santísima* Robin Desser, my editor at Knopf, whose absolute faith in me kept me hobbling forward.

I thank my family in Chicago for patiently accepting the distance and silence this book required. I wish to thank my spiritual family in San Antonio for the same.

The book's epigraph comes courtesy of Ruth Behar's *Translated Woman: Crossing the Border with Esperanza's Story* (Boston: Beacon Press, 1993), p. 18. I am indebted to the excellent research of Rodolfo Acuña's *Occupied America*, James D. Cockcroft's *Outlaws in the Promised Land*, Carlos Fuentes' *The Buried Mirror*, and Elena Poniatowska's *Todo México*.

Doy gracias a las ánimas solas, those souls in perpetual fire, my fellow writers clanging their chains in support. Denise Chávez, Julia Alvarez, Norma Elia Cantú, Norma Alarcón, Helena Viramontes, Sonia Saldivar-Hull, Tey Diana Rebolledo. *Gracias a todas, todas*.

I would like to give thanks to the John D. and Catherine T. MacArthur Foundation for their assistance, wings that allowed the manuscript to take flight and become the book I saw in my heart.

There are many individuals, many circumstances in my life that helped me to become a writer, but five major elements bear repeating here. My father's opposition to my life as a writer. My mother's support of my choice. The Chicago Public Library. Dennis Mathis, the most wonderful friend and my literary mentor. Susan Bergholz, my agent, who dreamed beyond my dreams and allowed me to earn my keep with my pen. I am indebted to all.

During the decade I was writing *Caramelo*, these lives slipped across the border from this life into the next: Thomasine Cordero Alcalá, Eulalia Cordero Gómez, Efraín Cordero, Joseph Cordero, Dolores Damico Cisneros, James P. Kirby, Gwendolyn Brooks, Carolyn Schaefer, Jeana Campbell, Marsha Gómez, Arturo Patten, Jerry Mathis, Albert Ruíz, Kevin Burkett, Kip, Danny López Lozano, Drew Allen, Paul Hanusch, Emma Tenayuca, Libertad Lamarque, Federico Fellini, Lola Beltrán, Astor Piazzolla, Wenceslao Moreno, Manuela Soliz Sager, José Antonio Burciaga, Ricardo Sánchez, Jim Sagel, Eugene P. Martínez, Hector Manuel Calderón, Jozefina Martinovic Karaula, María Félix, Peggy Lee, and my father, Alfredo Cisneros Del Moral. Countless whose names I do not know, die daily attempting to cross borders across the globe. As I was completing this book, thousands died in the disaster of the 11th of September, 2001. Thousands of deaths led to these deaths, and, I fear, thousands will follow. Each connected each to each. With them die a multitude of stories.

A la Virgen de Guadalupe, a mis antepasados. May these stories honor you all.